KATIE
MACALISTER
MOLLY HARPER
JESSICA SIMS

THE
UNDEAD
IN MY
BED

Pocket Books

New York   London   Toronto   Sydney   New Delhi

Pocket Books
A Division of Simon & Schuster, Inc.
1230 Avenue of the Americas
New York, NY 10020

This book is a work of fiction. Names, characters, places, and incidents either are products of the author's imagination or are used fictitiously. Any resemblance to actual events or locales or persons, living or dead, is entirely coincidental.

Shades of Gray copyright © 2012 by Katie MacAlister
Undead Sublet copyright © 2012 by Molly Harper White
Out with a Fang copyright © 2012 by Jessica Sims

All rights reserved, including the right to reproduce this book or portions thereof in any form whatsoever. For information, address Pocket Books Subsidiary Rights Department, 1230 Avenue of the Americas, New York, NY 10020.

First Pocket Books paperback edition October 2012

POCKET and colophon are registered trademarks of Simon & Schuster, Inc.

For information about special discounts for bulk purchases, please contact Simon & Schuster Special Sales at 1-866-506-1949 or business@simonandschuster.com.

The Simon & Schuster Speakers Bureau can bring authors to your live event. For more information or to book an event, contact the Simon & Schuster Speakers Bureau at 1-866-248-3049 or visit our website at www.simonspeakers.com.

Designed by Jacquelynne Hudson

Manufactured in the United States of America

10 9 8 7 6 5 4 3 2 1

ISBN 978-1-4516-5679-4
ISBN 978-1-4516-5680-0 (ebook)

Contents

Shades of Gray

Katie MacAlister

Chapter One

hat woman is hopelessly inept at trespassing."

The female form clinging to the top of the stone wall attached on either side of the massive wrought-iron walls weaved perilously.

"If she's not careful," I told the cat standing next to me, watching as the female peered down at the shrubs beneath her, "she's going to fall right into that patch of . . . there, you see?"

The trespasser, I was mildly interested to note, wasn't the angular blonde who'd attacked me the day before. This woman was smaller and rounder, pleasantly plump, with a mass of dark red curls pulled back from her face. A few strands had escaped in her efforts to scale the wall, and I wondered if she knew that a clump of leaves was listing to the side, tangled in the depths of her hair.

She must have realized that she had landed in a patch of poison oak, because after a few seconds of muttering to herself, she leaped up shrieking and drew a few quick symbols in the air.

"Did she just ward herself?" I asked the cat.

He sneered.

"That's what I thought." I frowned at the woman as she gathered up the things that had fallen out of her handbag. As she turned, I got a better look at her face. A jolt of electricity tingled up my spine when I realized that she was the nun I'd seen the night before. "What sort of a holy woman knows about wards?"

Johannes did not answer, not that he could—a small blessing for which I'd been thankful over the course of the last three centuries.

"It doesn't matter," I said with grim determination as I strode after the woman when she hurried past me on the pitted gravel drive. "Whatever it is the little nun is doing here, it's going to stop right now."

She didn't hear me until I was about to grab her, and then she barely had time to gasp as she whirled around. I slapped one hand over her mouth, the other on her neck.

Wide gray eyes considered me for three seconds before the lids fluttered closed as she toppled forward. I released my hold on her neck, catching her and swinging her up into my arms. "Now we'll get some answers," I told the unconscious woman as I carried her into the lodge.

She felt warm and soft in my arms, the faint scent of lilacs teasing my nose. I sternly told my libido to stop noticing just how nice a scent that was or that her face was lightly freckled, her skin as smooth as satin, all of which left me with the desire to stroke her soft curves. Her mouth looked as soft as the rest of her, a delicate rose in color, as if she'd been eating strawberries. A sudden rush of blood to my groin had me reminding myself that lusting after a nun was not appropriate, especially one who disregarded newly installed chains and locks and innumerable "No Trespassing" signs scattered around the estate. Still, it took some effort to force my gaze away from the temptation of her sweetly curved lips.

It took ten minutes to round up some twine from the remains of a broken packing box, but after a few minutes, I stepped back and admired my handiwork. The woman was slumped in a chair, her hands bound behind her, a gag around her neck waiting to be pulled forward and put into place in case she started screaming.

Johannes sniffed at her feet and turned away, apparently bored. I wasn't fooled in the least. He always took profound interest in any female.

"Hrn?" The little nun snorted and blinked, squinting at me as I stood before her, my arms crossed. "Fleg?"

"Do you speak English?" I asked, switching to French. "French? German?"

"I'm English," she answered, blinking rapidly as she obviously tried to bring me into focus. "Who are you? Did you . . . ugh, my head . . . knock me out?"

"I applied pressure to your neck, causing you to black out," I said sternly, trying hard not to notice how her breasts swelled when she struggled to bring her arms forward.

"You Vulcan neck-pinched me? Why am I tied up? And did you know you're a Dark One?"

I frowned. "What does a nun know of either Vulcan neck pinches or Dark Ones?"

She stopped trying to free her hands. "I'm not a nun, I'm a Guardian. And a Beloved, so I know a Dark One when I see him. Or her. But mostly, you're hims, not hers, aren't you? Do you have any pain tablets? I had a repulsively annoying headache before you Vulcanized me, and now it's just that much worse."

"No," I answered, increasing the intensity of my frown. The little nun didn't seem to be the least bit intimidated to find herself bound and held prisoner.

"No you don't know you're a Dark One, no you're not mostly males, or no you don't have any pain meds?" Her eyes shimmered with gentle curiosity.

"Of course I know I'm a Dark One," I snapped, annoyed and at the same time strangely pleased that she wasn't afraid of me. "I've been one almost my entire life. You are not a Beloved, however."

"I am," she said, looking down at her feet. "Hullo. Is that your cat?"

"No. Don't talk to him." I scented the air. The lodge, like the Abbey itself, was a damp, mildewed, crumbling relic of grander times. The air was redolent with the smell of molds, wetness, and the leavings of various small animals that had claimed the lodge for their own. Tattered bits of wallpaper moved gently in a draft from a broken window, the walls streaked with equal amounts of grime and quiet despair.

And yet, despite the odors of the decaying building, the scent of sun-warmed lilacs lingered, stirring something deep in my belly.

"If you were a Beloved, I would know," I told her.

"Is something wrong with his mouth?" she asked, making little chirruping noises at Johannes until—as I knew he would—the massive cat leaped onto her knees and purred at her, his eyes half-closed.

"Yes. You are *not* a Beloved."

"I thought so, because most cats don't have one lip pulled up so a fang shows all the time. Was he hurt or something?"

"No, it is simply how he is," I answered, wanting to simultaneously shake her and kiss her.

Her gaze assessed me. "He's not your cat, but you know he wasn't hurt?"

"No, he is not my cat. He simply lives with me and accompanies me wherever I go. That is all. Why is a Guardian pretending to be a Beloved and a nun?"

"Why is a Dark One abducting innocent people?" she countered.

I leaned over her in an attempt to intimidate. "Why did you climb over the fence when the signs clearly state that your presence is not welcome?"

She blinked those lovely soft gray eyes at me. "You're the one who put up the signs? Did you also chain the gate closed? We thought it might be the local authorities, although Teresa did show the police the documents the estate agent sent her, but you know how it is with Czech officials—they do love their paperwork—and Teresa figured she must have missed dotting an i or crossing a t."

"I am Czech," I said with much dignity.

"Really?" She tipped her head to consider me, not in the least bit intimidated by me, dammit. "You don't sound Czech. You sound British, like me. Who are you, exactly?"

"My name is Gray. Grayson Soucek, if you were going to ask, and I suspect you were, since you seem to ask everything else that occurs to you."

She giggled, and the sound went straight to my groin. I ignored the tightening sensation, grimly reminding myself that not only was she trouble, but even assuming that she wasn't really a nun, she was a housebreaker or, at best, a squatter, neither of which I intended on tolerating.

"Hi, Gray, I'm Noelle. I've always been naturally curious, and I found out a long time ago that if you don't ask questions, you won't learn the answers. I like your name, and it does sound Czech, but what are you doing here? And why have you abducted me? Why do you have a cat who isn't your cat? And why don't you think I'm a Beloved?"

You don't smell like one.

"That could be because the man I was supposed to end up with chose someone else over me," she said in a voice that had curiously lost its luster.

Startled, I took a step back. "What did you say?"

"You don't know him, do you? His name is Sebastian, and his replacement Beloved—who, I admit, is a very dear friend, and really, I couldn't be happier for them, especially now that they're expecting their first child, but still, you can understand how having your Dark One want someone else could wound your ego—his replacement Beloved's name is Belle. Ysabelle, really. We used to share a flat. Could you untie me? Your kitty wants me to pet him."

I took a deep breath, mentally shaking my head at both my surprise and the fact that I found this woman, this housebreaker and possible nun, more attractive with each word out of her delectable mouth. "No, I do not know a Dark One named Sebastian, not that I asked you about him in the first place. I will untie you, but if you make any attempt to escape, you will find yourself in a much worse position than you are currently in."

"You did ask me, you know," Noelle said as I moved behind her to slice the twine binding her wrists. "You said I don't smell like one, and I explained why I don't smell at all."

Again, I was aware of a sense of something profoundly unexpected happening. *I didn't say anything about you smelling.*

"Yes, you did. I heard you. Hullo, puss. Aren't you a big boy, then? What's your name?"

Johannes, I answered as I moved around to the front again, wondering to myself if I had suddenly gone insane.

"I'm afraid I can't answer that, not having known you for more than ten minutes, but I can say that it's not exactly normal popping out at people and Vulcan neck-pinching them. But outright insane? Hard to say. You are such a loving kitty, aren't you, although you have a very unusual name." Her head bent over Johannes as she murmured soft little words of affection to the cat. He'd eat up every word, I knew, and make everyone's life a hell until he finally grew tired of her.

"This cannot be," I said, shaking my head. "No. It is an aberration. You cannot hear me."

"I can, you know," she said, still nuzzling Johannes. *It doesn't make any sense.*

"What doesn't—oooh!" Her eyes widened as she realized that I had not spoken aloud. "You didn't . . . your mouth didn't . . . holy cats!"

Johannes is anything but a holy cat, I assure you.

Her eyes widened even further. "You did it again! Do you know what this means?"

I watched her warily as she took a step toward me. "Yes. It means that somehow I've . . . er . . ."

"Marked me!" she yelled, and with a whoop of joy, she leaped over Johannes and flung herself into my arms.

My mind may have known that the last thing in the world I should be doing was holding her, but my body certainly celebrated the fact that she was right where it wanted her to be—pressed tight against me, her soft, lush body stirring up all sorts of fires within me. Worse, her tantalizing scent woke the hunger I had just a few hours before sated, the gnawing, biting urge demanding that I dip my head and breathe deeply of her lilac-scented self.

It was madness to allow her to press kisses along my neck, but I couldn't seem to put her from me as I knew I should.

"You're my Dark One! I can't believe it! I never thought I'd find another one after Sebastian, especially since Allie and Belle kept trying to find him for me, but I never clicked with anyone else, and now, here you are, all mysterious and darkly handsome, and I love the cleft in your chin, and you have the most gorgeous green eyes, just like your cat's, and I'm your Beloved! You can brain-talk to me! I'm so happy!"

"No," I said at last, gathering every ounce of strength I had in order to put her at arm's length. It felt so wrong to do so, and yet I knew it was for the best. I had to stop this before it went any further, before she could be hurt.

"No what?" she said, her smile lighting up all the

dark places of my heart. The hunger grew, roaring inside me now.

"No, you are not my Beloved."

The joy so evident in her face faded. "But . . . I am. I know I am."

I shook my head, not wishing to cause this pain but knowing it was better to sever her hopes now, while they were still newly born and not yet grown to a point where it would devastate her. "We may have a sympathetic link somehow, but I cannot have a Beloved. I am vitiated."

"You're what?" The hurt in her eyes quickly faded to curiosity.

I was half tempted to explain the circumstances, but sanity prevailed. "All it means is that I can't have a Beloved. Now that we've dealt with that situation—"

"Have we? I don't think you saying you can't have a Beloved when you clearly can and do is dealing with it."

I ignored the interruption. "Now that we've dealt with that, let us move on to the part where you explain to me just what you and your cohorts in crime are doing to the Abbey, after which I will ring up the local officials and have them remove you from the premises."

She looked down at her hands for a few seconds. My gut tightened when I saw a glitter of tears in her eyes, but when she lifted her head again, her gaze was forthright and unwavering. "You want to have me arrested because I'm your Beloved?"

"You are *not* my Beloved. I thought I'd made myself clear—"

"Is it because you don't like me?" Self-consciously, she brushed a hand down the lightweight summer dress. "I'm sorry I can't change the way I look, but if I went on a diet, I could probably lose a few pounds."

"That would be a crime," I said without thinking, then mentally damned myself for saying it, then damned my damning, because women, it had been my experience, always believed the worst about their appearance, and I couldn't stand the thought of Noelle believing she was anything but a lovely, sensual goddess put on earth to tempt mankind. "On the contrary, I think your appearance is exquisite. It has, however, nothing to do with—"

"Do you hate Guardians? I can't leave the Guardians' Guild, because . . . well, I don't want to. I like being a Guardian, and I like helping people. But if there was some aspect of Guardians that you objected to, perhaps I could buffer that so it wouldn't annoy you."

"I don't care what the hell you do in your spare time, other than trespassing, that is."

"So there's nothing about me personally that you object to?" she asked with obvious relief. "I'm so glad. I have to say, if I was rejected by a Dark One a second time, I'd probably become a hermit and just give up on men. It's because you're . . . what did you call it . . . vitiated? That means marked, doesn't it? But that's silly. I'm a Guardian. If you're marked by a demon lord, then I'm just the person to help you. So, really, we're meant to be together."

She was back to looking happy again, dammit.

"There's quite a bit more to being vitiated than simply being marked. No." I held up my hand to stop her before she could start planning out our lives together. There was no future for us, period. "You are not my Beloved."

I think I am.

"I do not need a Guardian."

If a demon lord is after you, then you probably do.

"The only thing I want from you is the names of your cohorts and then for you to remove yourself from the grounds."

I really want to kiss you. Her eyes widened in horror as she covered her mouth with her fingertips. *Tell me you didn't hear that.*

Unbidden, my gaze went to her mouth as she dropped her hand. The hunger roared through me, shaking me with its strength, actually causing me to step forward until I realized what I was doing and stopped myself. I fought the hunger, fought the need to taste those lips, fought the urge to strip off that gauzy dress and lick every inch of the woman I'd just caught stealing into my grounds.

"I'm sorry if that offended you," she was saying,

her voice dimly audible over the growl of the beast inside me demanding that I take life from her. "I'm not normally the type of woman who falls instantly in love with the first devastatingly handsome vampire she finds, but I've heard from other Beloveds that they felt something right away, so I assume that's why I really want to kiss you. And touch your chest. And possibly your legs."

All too easily, the mental image came to mind of her kneeling on a bed next to me, her hand stroking its way up my legs, her lush, ripe body within my reach, waiting for me to taste it, to sate myself on her, to bury myself in her heat while feeding from her . . .

It was too much for me. Without another word, I turned on my heel and marched out of the room, my erection painful but not enough to distract me from the need to take her blood, to consume her, body and soul.

To make her mine.

Chapter Two

There you are. Where have you been? Miles and I have been going over the footage we shot yesterday, and he thinks we need to lose the Steadicam," Teresa said.

"It doesn't look Blair Witchy enough," a tall, elegant man insisted. "We want gritty. This isn't gritty, it's arty. How can I make people believe that they're really seeing the true me, the psychic me, the spiritual me, if it's visually pretty?"

"Arty is easier to watch, though. People get motion sickness with handheld cameras," the woman next to him argued before turning her gaze back to Noelle. "What do you think? Would you rather watch— Noelle? Are you all right?"

Noelle stopped in front of the three people clustered around a digital camcorder, their heads together as they watched a small video display. The two men dismissed her and returned to watching the footage, while the woman, petite and raven-haired, stood up to give Noelle a knowing look. "Something's happened to you. Did someone from the village say something about us filming here?"

"No, nothing like that, and the police promised that they'd keep an eye out for any more folks who try to disrupt the filming," Noelle replied, dropping onto a small packing box the backpack that she had retrieved from where it had fallen on the pitted gravel drive. "Teresa, what do you know about this place?"

Teresa looked puzzled. "What do I *know* about it? Other than it's haunted, you mean?"

"What do you know about the owners? Did the person you rented it from tell you anything about the family who lives here?"

At a sharp look from the elegant Miles, Teresa took Noelle's arm and moved off to the other side of the great hall, dark-paneled and prone to deep shadows that made one's imagination run wild. Right now, with one of the two double doors open to let in light, it looked less intimidating.

"Other than that it's owned by a very old man who lives in the south of France for his health, no. I take it there is an heir somewhere, but he doesn't spend time in the Czech Republic, so the house is available for rent. The agent did say that *Ghosts, Goblins, and Ghoulies* wanted to film here, but ever since the scandal with their host caught faking on-screen events, they haven't had the funding to do much but film in the same old tired haunted spots like the Tower of London." Her voice dripped with scorn, which amused Noelle no end, since she knew full well that there were two separate portals to Abaddon in the Tower grounds alone.

"The heir—do you know how old he is? If he has lovely green eyes and a chin dimple that makes you want to bite it and is tall and incredibly handsome and quite likely very dangerous?"

Teresa's eyebrows rose. "No, the rental agent didn't mention anything like that. I take it you've run into this tall, dark, and handsome man with a biteable chin?"

"I have," Noelle said with a loud sigh. She pulled forward one of the curule chairs flanking a stained coat of armor and pounded on the red-cushioned seat. A cloud of dust rose into the air, the sunlight streaming in through the door catching the dust motes and making a corona around her as she plumped down without ceremony. "I saw him, he kidnapped me, and then, when we were really having a quite interesting conversation, he ran away. It's the story of my life. I tell you, Teresa, it's almost enough to give me a complex."

"This handsome man kidnapped you?" Teresa's expression would have amused Noelle if she hadn't been so despondent. "You escaped?"

"No, he let me go." She sighed again. "It was all

so very romantic and somewhat mysterious, too, and you know how I love a good mystery. But then I think I scared him because I said I wanted to kiss him, and he ran away. Sometimes I really wish I could keep thoughts to myself."

Teresa blinked. "So you know this man?"

"Hmm?" Noelle looked up from where she'd been eyeing some faint tracks in the dust near the wainscoting. They looked like imp tracks. "Oh, no, I've never seen Gray before."

"Gray?"

"Grayson. Isn't that an interesting name? I like it. His cat had an interesting name, too. Unusual, rather."

Teresa passed a hand over her forehead. "The handsome kidnapper has a cat?"

"Evidently not, no."

"*Noelle.*"

At the note of frustration in her friend's voice, she made a mental promise to check the house for imps just as soon as she could. The last thing she needed was for Teresa to catch the little buggers on film. "Yes?"

"Start from the beginning. Don't leave anything out, not the kidnapping, or the cat who isn't a cat, or why you evidently told a complete stranger that you wanted to kiss him."

Noelle told the story, heavily edited, since Teresa hadn't the slightest idea of what Noelle really did or that there was such a thing as the Otherworld, which included all of the immortal beings who mingled with mortals. She also left out the fact that Gray was what most mortals referred to as a vampire, and that she worked with demons, and even that the spirits that Miles had spent the last four days communing with didn't actually exist.

". . . and right after I told him I wanted to kiss him, he had the most peculiar pained expression on his face, and then he just turned around and left. And the cat trotted after him. I tell you, it's like I'm a blight when it comes to men."

"I wonder who he is," Teresa said, a thoughtful expression wrinkling her brow. "You said he put a chain across the gate?"

"I assume it was him, since it wasn't there when I went to town early this morning, but it was when I came back."

"If the gate is chained, how are we to get out?"

Noelle shrugged. "I guess we'll worry about that when the time comes. You said you weren't going to leave during the two weeks you have the house, so it really doesn't matter, does it?"

"I suppose not, although it is annoying. Do you think he's the owner's heir?"

"Possibly." Or perhaps the owner himself, since Dark Ones frequently used such ruses as an absent parent to make it appear that property was being passed down through generations. "I wonder why he thinks we're trying to destroy the house."

Teresa made a face. "Who knows? He's probably

crazy, and I have enough of that on my hands with you-know-who."

Noelle glanced across the room to where Miles now stood, arms outstretched, head tilted back dramatically, a low chant issuing from his chiseled lips. Raleigh, the cameraman who was filming the pilot and first two episodes of *Haunted Miles*, stood with his back to the open doorway, filming the scene.

Miles turned his body just enough to make sure the camera caught his gorgeous profile.

"He really is shameless, isn't he?" Noelle whispered.

"Yes, but I'm willing to put up with that, and his insistence that he be allowed to hold séances every evening and all of the other shenanigans he pulls, because the public is going to eat this show up with a spoon and ask for more."

"I suppose so, although I wasn't aware that reality ghost shows were quite so popular."

"*Haunted Miles* will be different," Teresa said with complacency. "We have you."

Noelle wrinkled her nose. "When I told you I'd help you for a couple of weeks, I meant more along the lines of helping out with the production stuff, not wrangling ghosts for you. Not that Miles has found one yet."

"He will. While you were gone into town this morning, he said he had a run-in with a poltergeist in the east wing."

Now, that was interesting. "A polter? Really? How many arms did he or she have?"

Teresa stared at her as if she had turned into a five-foot-five rubber plant. "How many *arms*?"

"Four? Three? I assume if he had two, Miles wouldn't know he was a polter."

"What on earth are you talking about?" At a quick but pointed glance from her star, Teresa leaned in to Noelle and said in a softer tone, "I said a poltergeist, not a circus freak. You know, the noisy ghosts? The kinds that knock things around a room and rain rocks and stuff like that."

"Aports. The rocks are called aports, and—" Noelle bit off the rest, deciding that the truth about polters was probably not what Teresa needed to hear. "Never mind. So he found a poltergeist?"

"One who is very active, according to Miles. That's who he's trying to summon forth now." The two women watched for a few minutes before Teresa added, "Oh, so that footage we were just talking about, the one with you in the nun's outfit? We'll need to redo it tonight, if you don't mind."

Little nun. Gray had called her a little nun. Her lips quirked at the thought, even as a warm glow spread out from the depths of her belly. No one had ever given her a nickname, Guardians being, for the most part, feared or avoided by most folk of the Otherworld. "All right, although you have to be sure that it is very clear that it's being used as a re-creation and not doctored up to look like it's ghostly foot-age."

Teresa patted her hand. "I told you when you got here that this show is straight-up. We don't fake any-thing, not one single spooky minute. It'll all be real. That's why this house is so perfect." She looked around the hall and all but hugged herself. "It's so gloomy, so Gothicly eerie, it just can't possibly be without at least half a dozen ghosts and poltergeists."

Miles, now calling out an invocation to the spirits to come forth, moved toward the door and the better light, causing Raleigh to swing around and film him from the side. Teresa and Noelle hurriedly moved out of the range of the camera, toward the tall, curving stair that led up into the dimness of the second story.

"I am your friend," Miles said in a rich, BBC-newscaster voice that throbbed with sincerity. "I will listen to you. You are lost and alone, but now I am here. Speak to me. Tell me your tale. Show yourself to me."

Raleigh sidled out of the way as Miles stepped into the pool of light flooding the marble tiles nearest the doors, striking a pose that was meant to repre-sent humility and caring. Noelle was about to make a whispered waspish comment to Teresa when, sud-denly, Miles froze, his eyes alight with excitement as he said, "We have a manifestation! Right here! There is a scent that wasn't here before! It smells of . . ." He took a deep breath, his eyes closed. "It smells of hell-fire and demons, of the devil itself. It smells strongly of sulfur. It is a most powerful emanation. Hear me, oh being of the darkest bowels of hell! I feel your foul presence! I smell your nearness! Come forth and make yourself known!"

Noelle clapped a hand over her mouth to stifle the laughter that threatened to break free. Next to her, Teresa doubled over, her shoulders silently shaking, while Raleigh, with a mouthed "Sorry" to Teresa, waved a hand behind his rear.

"This is so juvenile, but I can't . . . can't . . . he smells s-s-sulfur," Noelle managed to whisper before having to clasp a hand over her mouth again.

Tears rolled down Teresa's face as she buried her face in the tail of her shirt.

By evening, Noelle could look at Teresa without the pair of them bursting into hysterical laughter, which made for a much easier time when it came to dealing with Miles, who was in one of his prima donna moods when Teresa told him she couldn't use the footage just shot.

"I don't see what was wrong with it," he repeated for the third time after viewing a playback of the footage yet again. "I wasn't making it up, if that's what you think. There was a foul odor there, something horrible and truly demonic."

Raleigh quickly left the room, his shoulders shaking with silent laughter.

Noelle had to bite her lip as Teresa, with a telltale quaver to her voice, tried to explain that the public might put a different interpretation on the scene, finding it comic rather than dramatic.

"Don't be ridiculous," Miles snapped. "How could anyone help but be impressed by the contact I've made so far? We have indisputable proof that some demonic being has been in our presence, and what's more, I fully intend to have a materialization at the séance tonight. Now, if you don't mind, I need quiet for my meditation time so that I may attune myself with the spirits found within this house."

Miles claimed the only comfortable (and clean) chair in the hall, closing his eyes and humming softly to himself. Noelle and Teresa exchanged glances and quietly walked toward the door, making it that far before Miles interrupted his communing to ask, "Where are we sitting?"

"I thought we'd try the west wing tonight, since we've been focusing on the east wing the last few days. Noelle thinks the west wing has a lot of potential."

He frowned. "Your friend is mistaken. This is what comes from letting amateurs mess around with scientific research; they meddle in things they don't know the first thing about. I will not have this show be made a laughingstock because of your shoddy research techniques and planning. You're the producer—produce! Leave the research to those of us who are experts."

Noelle bit her lip again as Teresa tried to calm him. "Noelle's family lives in a house that is supposed to be one of the most haunted in the county, so she knows all about ancestral spirits and gray ladies and all sorts of other things that go bump in the night."

All of which, Noelle thought to herself, were pure fabrication and imagination. She ought to know; her mother was perfectly capable of calling forth a spirit, had any lived in the family home.

Miles refused to be soothed. "The west wing is intact. No ghost in his right mind would stay there. I've told you before, woman, spirits love ruins, and it is in the ruined wing that we must look for them. The demonic presence in the hall excepted, all of our contact has been made in the ruined wing."

Noelle thought of pointing out the fact that Miles's idea of contact wasn't exactly especially valid but decided to leave the handling of the star to Teresa.

"We'll try the west wing tonight, and if we have no luck, we'll go back to the east side, all right?"

Miles harrumphed. "It will be an utter and complete waste of my time."

Teresa uttered a few more balms to his wounded pride before hurrying down the unlit hallway toward the inhabitable side of the house.

"Maybe I should bow out of being your temporary assistant," Noelle said as they passed the music room that presently served as a communal sleeping quarters, where, at Miles's insistence, they had all set up sleeping bags and air mattresses. Miles claimed it was to minimize their impact on the ghostly beings in the house, but Noelle couldn't help but feel he had a less noble reason for wanting to avoid sleeping alone.

"Not on your life! Just ignore Miles when he gets that way. He's rather protective of his role as ghostly expert. Now, let's see, what room looks good to you?"

The two women spent some time poking their heads into the various rooms on the ground and upper floors of the wing that remained mostly intact. Noelle kept a wary eye out for imps and other denizens of the Otherworld that she didn't wish brought to the attention of the general public, making note of which hallways and rooms showed signs of recent occupation by the little troublemakers.

Luckily, the imps had seemed to confine themselves to the first and second floors, not venturing farther upstairs to the servants' quarters. Noelle, dutifully trying to find the spookiest room possible, finally settled on a small attic room, once belonging to a housemaid and now containing nothing but a broken-down metal bedstead, a cracked washstand, and two partially broken wooden chairs.

"This is it," Noelle announced after having examined the heavy layer of dust for any signs of tracks. There were none, not even from four-legged rodents.

"This?" Teresa frowned as she looked around the dark, small room. "Are you sure?"

"Absolutely. This room is haunted right up to my armp—" Noelle had been in the act of raising her hand to gesture, when a man suddenly appeared out of nothing, grabbed her hand, and pressed a smacking kiss to it.

"Ah, me beauty, ye've found me at last, have ye?" the man said.

Noelle stared in shock at him, while Teresa, after freezing for a second, ran screaming from the room.

"Good Lord. There really are ghosts here," Noelle said, blinking in surprise at the somewhat transparent man. He was clad in a kilt and ruffled shirt, a broadsword strapped to his hip. Despite his ghostly state, there was a distinct roguish twinkle in his eye that left Noelle with the impression that he was greatly enjoying himself.

Teresa reappeared in the doorway, her eyes huge. "That's a . . . that's a . . . he's a . . . holy Mary, mother of God! That's a ghost!"

"We're preferrin' the term 'spirit,' ye ken, lass," the ghostly man said in a heavy Scottish accent. He waggled his eyebrows at Teresa, then made her a courtly bow, losing his translucence as he shifted to a solid form. It took him only a second to sweep up Teresa into a passionate embrace.

"Erm . . ." Noelle didn't know if it was polite to interrupt a ghost when he was kissing someone, but she knew this had to be a shock to Teresa. "Excuse me, but who are you?"

The man finished his kiss, setting Teresa upright on her feet again before saying, "Ah, but ye're a bonnie lass, too. I'm Jock, Jock McTorgeld. What be yer names, me beauties?"

"A ghost!" Teresa whispered, her eyes never leaving the man as she waved toward the door behind her. "I should film . . . Raleigh should be here . . . Miles . . . holy Mary, a real live ghost! Noelle! Can you see him, too? I'm not going insane, am I?"

"I can see him, too. That's Teresa," she told the ghost, "and I'm Noelle." It struck her that for a Scotsman, his accent was awfully broad, almost exaggerated in its rolling of Rs and gargling of vowels. "Do you . . . er . . . live in this room?"

"Here?" He looked around with a curl of his lip. "Nay, lassie. 'Tis but a servant's room, this. Jock McTorgeld roams where he pleases, when he pleases, and that's always where the bonnie lasses are." He leered at her, no doubt trying to drive home his point.

"Teresa," Noelle said slowly, having taken full measure of their new acquaintance. "Why don't you go get Raleigh and Miles so they can meet our friend from Scotland?"

"Yes," Teresa agreed, her eyes huge as she nodded quickly. "Yes, Raleigh, Miles. We should film Jock. A real ghost. We have a real ghost. Holy mother . . ."

Noelle closed the door as Teresa drifted off muttering to herself. She eyed the ghost, who was striding toward her with a devilish glint in his eye. "All right, she's gone. Now, who are you?"

"I've told ye me name, my heart. Now ye'll be

thankin' me, as is the way of me people, and if ye're as sweet as ye taste, I may be lettin' ye see what I've got on under me kilt."

Noelle had a hard time not rolling her eyes, but by dint of an almost superhuman effort, she managed it. "You can stop with the phony Scottish bit, too. I'm British, not Czech, and I know what a real Scot sounds like, and you aren't it."

The ghost came to an abrupt stop, his eyes narrowing on her. "Ye're daft, lass. I'm as Scottish as the wild thistle that grows above the burn."

"You're about as Scottish as my ass, and I'm not Scottish at all. Now, who are you, and what are you doing here?"

"Me name is Jock—"

"Right," Noelle interrupted, rolling up her sleeves. Before the ghost—who was in corporeal form and thus bound to the same laws as any other living being—could do so much as roll another R at her, she had a binding ward drawn and slapped over him. "Now, let's have the truth, shall we?"

"What the . . . Christos, you're a Guardian, aren't you?" the ghost said in a completely different voice, one that was slightly French. His form shivered and morphed into that of a tonsured young man in a faded grayish tunic, scapula, and cowl. He remained bound to the spot, held firmly by the ward despite his attempt to move out of it. "Just my luck, a couple of toothsome wenches finally show up, and you're Guardians."

"I am, but my friend is perfectly normal and doesn't know what a Guardian is, let alone what we do, so I'd appreciate it if you didn't mention that. Why were you pretending to be a Scot?"

The ghost sighed and shifted to his noncorporeal state, which left him partially translucent. "Women love a man in a kilt. I learned that . . . oh, must have been twenty, twenty-five years ago, when a group of women on a historical tour took the house for a week. They loved old Jock and his dashing accent. Tumbled more ladies that week than I did when I was alive."

Noelle couldn't help but laugh. "You're a monk, aren't you?"

"I was," he said, sighing. "Doesn't mean I didn't enjoy a lusty wench when I saw her."

"I think we'll just let that go. What's your real name?"

"Michel," he admitted. "Michel de Nostredame."

"Nostredame?" Noelle couldn't believe what she was hearing. "You're Nostradamus? I thought he died an old man?"

"He did. He was my cousin. I could have been famous like him, too, you know," Michel answered with an annoyed twitch of his head. "I had visions all the bloody time, but I never wrote the blasted things down like he did. If I knew then what I know now, I'd have been just as rich and famous as he was. More, because my visions were better than a bunch of vague mumble-jumble. I had visions of beauteous women performing many and varied acts of much interest. *Much interest!*"

"I just bet you did." Noelle considered the now-agitated ghost. "What are you doing in the Czech Republic, Michel?"

He grimaced, sat on the edge of the bed, sank through it to the floor, and got up, returning to corporeal form before sitting again. "Don't call me that, please. Michel is my cousin's name. You can call me Nosty. It's what all the dairymaids in Provence called me. As to your question, I was on a pilgrimage."

"In the Czech Republic?"

He shrugged. "I got sidetracked by a widow with the biggest—" He made a gesture that Noelle had no difficulty recognizing. "Somehow I ended up here with her. And then it turned out she wasn't a widow at all, and her husband found us in bed, and as it happens, he took me by surprise and gutted me before I could so much as explain that I was simply giving his wife a . . . er . . . blessing."

"Uh-huh," Noelle said, giving him a knowing look. "Well, it sounds like you brought that on yourself, but regardless, I hope you didn't suffer much. To be honest, I'm surprised we didn't see you two days ago, when we arrived and started filming."

"Filming? You're doing a movie?"

"You know what a movie is?"

"Of course. I'm dead, not an idiot," he answered with an irritated sniff. "There was a film crew here a few decades back. I learned a lot from them. And the young starlets."

Noelle ignored his lascivious grin and explained about the reality TV show and asked if he kept himself to the upper floors of the house.

"I wander all over. Normally, I stay around the grounds, because that's where you see the most people passing by. I've been over visiting her ladyship the last few days, though. I try to do that regularly, since it cheers her up."

"Her ladyship? Is there someone living on the grounds?"

"Lady Joan. She's a spirit, like me. She lives over in the cottage on the north side of the property. Very lonely and has many sad tales to tell of her life. A gentlewoman, she is, in case you're getting the wrong impression, not one who wants a quick tumble now and again, unlike some folks I could mention," Nosty said with a jerk of his head. "There's a couple of snooty Czech wenches living on the property next to ours who won't even pass the time of day with you, except when they have an itch that needs scratching, if you get my drift. Bah. Foreigners."

"Hmm." Noelle was in a quandary. Part of her felt obligated, for Teresa's sake, to present a bona fide ghost on *Haunted Miles*, but a sane inner voice warned her that revealing Nosty to the mortal world might cause more trouble than she could at that moment imagine.

She was just about to suggest a compromise when the ghost leaped to his feet, his eyes wide with surprise. "It is . . . it cannot be . . . no, it is him! What is he doing here? Now? *Nom de nom*, he is coming! You must away! *Dépêche-toi! Vite!*"

"Hurry to where? Who's coming? Miles? I assure you that he's perfectly harmless, if a bit naïve—"

Without another word, the ghost disappeared, leaving Noelle standing perfectly alone in the dingy attic room. She was still standing there when, a few minutes later, a breathless Miles skidded to a stop in the doorway, Teresa and Raleigh panting behind him.

"Where is the ghost?" Miles demanded, glaring around the room before narrowing his eyes on Noelle.

"He . . . er . . . left."

Miles's face turned red as he sucked in a large quantity of air. "Amateurs!" finally burst out of him. Then, turning, he shoved the others out of his way and stomped back down the stairs, a tirade about the woes of letting others meddle in affairs about which they knew nothing trailing after him.

Chapter Three

It took several hours of distracting business before I was confident that I could face the luminescent Noelle again without pouncing on her. I had also intended on feeding, to quell the hunger that had burst so insistently to life with Noelle's nearness, but none of the women in the small town outside the Abbey appealed to me. They were too tall, too thin, too blond or brunette, too . . . mundane. None of them had that little sparkle of amusement in her eyes, and none of them had silky-smooth skin that begged to be tasted.

None of them smelled of lilacs.

"I will not let this happen," I swore to Johannes as we approached the west wing of the Abbey, where my rooms had always been.

Johannes gave me a look that said he didn't

believe me. I ignored him, instead studying the house for a few minutes. I hadn't been to it since the night I had arrived to find the usurpers in possession, lest they were minions of Amaymon. But no demon in his right mind would consort with a Guardian, which meant they probably had designs on the house itself, rather than me. "Which is also not going to happen."

As I rounded what was once a sundial set in a small rose garden—but was now a sad jungle of weeds and rusted bits of metal strewn on the ground—the sound of voices had me ducking into the shadow of a wild yew hedge. Johannes marched past me to sit a few feet away, watching with interest the scene before him.

"No, no, no! She's ruining the whole thing, Teresa! Where did you find her, the local amateur theater group? Look, Noreen—"

"Noelle."

"Whatever. You're supposed to be a nun who's meeting her lover, the bishop, clandestinely here in the garden. You're ready to die for your love, not go for a power walk, for God's sake. You have to drift around slowly, as if you are contemplating the carnal act you are about to commit. Honestly, Teresa, I shouldn't have to produce the show and star in it as well."

The tone in the man's voice grated on my nerves, enough so that I moved into the shadows of the hedge to watch what the usurpers were planning.

Noelle was there, once again in a nun's habit, her

bright hair glittering and shining even when lit only by one lamp held by a slight man with a digital video camera. Not even the damned shapeless gray robe she wore stopped heat from pooling in my groin even as the hunger growled deep in my belly.

"I'm doing the best I can, but I'm not an actress," Noelle told the other man present. My eyes narrowed on him. He had a prancing, arrogant air that instantly annoyed me. "I will walk slower, but I don't know how I'm supposed to be contemplating having illicit sex with a monk—not a bishop, by the way, since the tale in question concerns a monk who was stoned for impregnating half the local countryside—without making all sorts of lewd gestures. I'll try to look contemplative about the joys of sex, but that's about all I can do."

A monk who was stoned for promiscuity? Dammit, Nosty must have been telling tales again.

"Teresa!" the arrogant man snarled. "She's ruining it!"

"Now, Miles—"

"Did I hear someone invoking my name? Or, rather, my tragic story?"

I groaned as a familiar form shimmered and appeared next to Noelle. The blonde who had attacked me the day before screamed and clutched at the arrogant man, who stumbled backward until he tripped over a stone bench overgrown with climbing plants. The man with the camera dropped it, shining a shaking light on Nosty, who, I noticed, was leering at Noelle in a way that made me see red.

"Nostredame, if you don't stop trying to look down her robe, I'll rip your nonexistent eyes out of your spectral head and shove them down your ghostly throat." I snarled as I strode forward, Johannes at my heels.

Nosty's eyes grew wide as he saw me. "Eep!" he said, and disappeared into nothing.

"Gray!" Noelle said at the same moment, emotion lighting up her face in away that had the fire in my belly sending out tendrils of warmth to all my limbs. "You're back. I'm so glad I didn't scare you off for good."

"What the hell?" roared the man on the ground as he let the female usurper help him to his feet. "Who are you? What's going on here? Dammit, Teresa, stop fussing over me. I didn't trip, I was thrown backward by some evil spectral force. You—yes, you—this is a closed set! We're making an important show here, and no one is allowed, especially not overzealous fans. Begone!"

"Fan?" I scowled at him. "Just what in the devil's name is going on here?"

"This is Gray Soucek," Noelle said, introducing me as the other three people eyed me curiously. "That's not his cat Johannes. Or, rather, that cat, which is not Gray's, is Johannes. And I'm pretty sure Gray's not a fan, zealous or otherwise. In fact, he's . . . uh . . ." *What exactly are you?*

A Dark One, dammit. You know that.

Yes, I know that, but what are you doing here?

This is my house.

I thought so, she said with a sense of satisfaction. "Gray is the owner of the Tomas Abbey. Gray, that's Teresa—she's my friend and the producer of a reality ghost-hunting show called *Haunted Miles*—and that's Raleigh, the cameraman, and over there is Miles."

"The star of the show," the arrogant man said with a disdainful look as he brushed off his jacket. "Yet another amateur. Just what we need."

"Oh, you're the owner," Teresa said with an odd look toward Noelle. "I think we've met. You . . . uh . . . you are the man I saw last night, aren't you?"

"The one you hosed down with pepper spray? Yes, that was me." My left eye twitched with the memory of the few hours that followed that experience. Johannes eyed the woman with interest.

She looked contrite, at least. "I'm so sorry. We've had a little trouble with some of the locals, you see, and when you popped up out of the dark like you did and demanded that Miles stop communing with the nature spirits, I thought you were one of the troublemakers."

"Communing with nature? He was taking a piss on a Sarazin statue of Leda and the swan. That was my mother's favorite, and I'll be damned if I'll let anyone defile it."

"He was?" Everyone turned to look at Miles.

"There are many ways to commune," he said with an irritated sniff. "The spirits wanted to speak to me, and I didn't have time to run back to the house. Besides, it's outdoors. It's had worse things on it, I'm sure."

"I'm sure that's not the point," Noelle said quickly as I took a step toward the bastard. She moved in front of me, her scent immediately wrapping around me, making my entire body tighten with need. "I don't blame Gray for being upset to find people at his house when he obviously didn't expect them. Did you?"

"No," I said, breathing deeply despite myself. Who knew that lilac could be such an erotic scent? "I seldom do expect to find trespassers at my house."

"I'm really sorry I didn't ask you who you were last night," Teresa said, making a vague gesture toward the others. "We'd just run off a fan earlier who tried to interrupt our filming and disrupt Miles while he was holding a séance, so . . . well . . . I'm just sorry about last night. I hope you can forgive me. But we aren't trespassing, you know. The estate agency rented the house and grounds to us for two weeks while we film the pilot of our show. I have the agreement, if you'd like to see it."

She pepper-sprayed you? Noelle squinted in the dim moonlight. *You don't look hurt at all.*

I'm not now. It wasn't any fun at the time, however.

I'm sure it wasn't. Why did you come back? Was it to see me? It was, wasn't it? I can feel how . . . um . . . hungry you are. Do you want to feed from me?

It took an effort, but I managed to think it. *No.*

One of her silky eyebrows rose. *Oh, really? That's why you're thinking about it right this moment?*

I'm not. And stop pretending you can read my thoughts.

I glowered at the pretentious Miles as he expounded about some foolishness or other, glancing at the papers that Noelle's friend had presented me with. "These look in order," I allowed, irritation lacing my voice. "I will have a word with the agent about leasing the house for such a purpose, but I suppose there's nothing I can do about it now."

"Oh, please don't throw us out," Teresa pleaded, glancing repeatedly at Noelle. "The Abbey is so perfect for us, and now that we've met the resident ghost, I know the show is going to break new ground and become a huge success."

I glanced at Noelle, who was watching me with quiet amusement in those soft gray eyes. *Why do I think you've had something to do with Nosty finding his way to the public's eye?*

Actually, it's just the opposite. She quirked her luscious pink lips. *I'd really prefer he stay hidden.*

Why? He can only do your friend's show good.

Yes, but I'm a Guardian. We try to keep all Otherworld beings from the attention of the mundane world.

I doubt if one ghost, even one as randy as Nosty, will do any harm. Now, stop talking to me in this manner. It does not mean you are my Beloved, and I dislike having you rummaging around in my thoughts.

I'm not rummaging, although I really do like that bit about licking me. I think I'd like you to lick me, Gray. I'd like to lick you, too. That chin dimple is driving me nuts. Would you be offended if I bit your chin?

With almost superhuman strength, I managed to keep from grabbing Noelle and carrying her off to the nearest bedroom. Yes, it would offend me to the tips of my toes. It would physically sicken me. It would be such a repugnant act I might actually vomit.

Her head tipped to one side as she considered me. You don't lie very well, do you?

I am a consummate liar! I thought with as much outrage as I could manage, and shoved down all the erotic thoughts of just what I wanted to do to her at that moment. You know nothing about me. And stop thinking about licking my belly and fondling my ass. Such things repel me unlike anything I've ever known.

I bet you have sensitive nipples, she all but cooed into my brain, making my groin tighten painfully.

I fought the image of her breasts, all satiny smooth and warm, plump little morsels just waiting for my mouth and hands, and for a moment, I couldn't even think. My nipples reject your desired attention. Please do not continue thinking about them. And stop this. I will no longer respond to you speaking to me thusly.

The others present had been discussing Nosty while Noelle damn near brought me to my knees with desire. With a strength of will I didn't know I possessed, I managed to drag my attention off the temptress and onto the others.

"Noelle and I saw him first upstairs, although he was in a kilt then, and later, after we had dinner, he appeared to Raleigh and me as we were setting up for this shoot and told us all about himself, how he suffered so horribly for love, and how the brothers eventually walled him up alive because he wouldn't renounce his love for a milkmaid." Teresa clutched the rental-agreement papers to her chest and sighed happily. "It's so very romantic. I just know the public is going to go gaga over him."

"I have yet to properly interview this so-called spirit," Miles said, obviously annoyed that attention was being drawn away from him. "I must speak with him first to determine the veracity of his claims. It could be a rival, you know, someone tricking us to make us believe he's a ghost, someone who wishes to see my downfall. I wouldn't put it past some of the other shows to send people here to deliberately try to destroy us before we've had a chance to even hit the air."

"I think he's real," Teresa said, looking to the cameraman for confirmation. "Raleigh saw him appear out of nothing, too, so he has to be real. He was really very interesting, although he seems to have a bit of a fixation on milkmaids. But other than that, he was most informative. He told us about this house and how your family has lived here for centuries, Mr. Soucek."

Acid filled my stomach; I'd swear vengeance on Nosty if he had been telling tales.

Noelle shot me a curious glance.

"There is nothing interesting about the Abbey. It is just an old house, nothing out of the ordinary. Part of it is falling down; the other part is unremarkable in all senses of the word." Even to my ears, the words sounded false and forced. I swore to myself.

Are you all right?

Yes.

You tensed up all of a sudden, as if you were worried about something.

"Unremarkable?" Teresa asked, gaping at me. "It's almost five hundred years old! It's gorgeous. Well, the part of it that's still standing is gorgeous. Not to mention it's haunted, which is just awesome. And of course, there's the secret treasure."

The acid turned to fire in my belly.

Gray?

The word was soft in my mind, filled with genuine concern, distracting me for a moment. How long had it been since someone felt anything but fear and loathing for me? How long had it been since someone was sincerely interested in what worried me, in what I wanted? How long had it been since someone cared?

I do care, you know. I was told once that it's hardwired into Beloveds and Dark Ones to be attracted to one another, but this is different. It's not just your adorable chin, and your nipples, and your stomach, and all the other interesting parts of you, it's . . . you're filled with so much darkness, Gray. So cold and alone, and you hurt. I want to change that. I don't want you to hurt any longer.

For one exquisitely painful moment, I let myself imagine what it would be like to allow Noelle to ease my pain, to fill me with her soft, gentle light, to warm me in the glow of her being. Her mind, I already knew, was unique, her thought processes endlessly fascinating. She would never bore me, never drive me away as mortal women had done over the centuries. I could at last experience the ecstasy so long sought by those of my kind.

And then the memories clutched at me, ripping such thoughts to shreds with little daggered fingers, tearing apart the finely spun web of illusion until I was left with nothing but despair.

No. I firmly pushed her from my mind. *I enjoy the cold and darkness and pain. I am giddy with happiness to experience them every moment of my endless life. I would miss them terribly if you took them from me. Begone from my mind, woman. I have no need for your concern or your warm, gentle feelings, just as I have no need for your luscious, silky-soft body.*

You are the strangest man I've ever met.

I am not a man. I am a Dark One. And I'm damned.

Only if you want to be. And she turned back to the others.

What the hell did that mean?

"What treasure?" the smug actor was demanding of Teresa. "Why didn't you tell me there was a treasure? That sort of thing is hugely popular with the public. They'll want me to find the treasure on air. Get that ghost back, and make him talk."

Do you seriously think I want to be a vitiate?

You're not talking to me, remember?

Do you have any idea what my life is like, being vitiated?

I would know if you were talking to me, because you'd apologize for shoving me out of your mind in such a rude and callous manner.

I am not rude and callous. I am not enjoying being a martyr, which is what you're thinking, isn't it? Ha! I can see you do think that!

Stop rummaging around in my mind. She cast my own words back at me, but I was too incensed to care.

I do not enjoy this! A demon lord has marked me for destruction. Every single member of his extensive legions of minions is sworn to destroy me on sight. Do you think you can live your life happily with imminent destruction at the hands of vengeful demons hanging over your head?

If you were talking to me, I would point out that I've mentioned repeatedly that I'm a Guardian and thus perfectly able to handle demons and even a demon lord, given enough preparation.

You're not my Beloved. I growled, desperately praying she'd finally have enough of my boorishness and spurn me as any sane woman would do.

She sighed. If I'm not, then this won't do a single thing for you, will it?

Before I could turn tail and run, she was there, in my arms, her warm, soft body pressed against me, her lilac scent filling my head. I had a brief glimpse of smoky gray eyes before she stroked her hands up my chest, digging her fingers into my hair and pulling my head down so she could kiss me.

Reject her! my mind demanded, even as I filled my hands with her delectable ass and hoisted her upward so she could better kiss me, angling her head just so, allowing me to take control of the kiss.

Dimly, I heard Teresa exclaim, "Noelle! What on earth are you doing?" and at the same time, the man Miles made a lewd comment.

None of that pierced beyond vague awareness; the only thing that mattered was claiming the sweetness that lay within Noelle. I nipped at her lower lip, causing her to giggle breathlessly against my mouth, her fingers tightening in my hair as she squirmed against my now painfully erect penis.

Stop that, I ordered, moaning when she parted her lips and my tongue swept into her warmth. *Christos, you are so hot, so sweet.*

So are you, she said, wiggling more until I hoisted her higher and she wrapped her legs around my hips.

"Noelle! Raleigh, do something!"

"What?" the cameraman asked.

"Well . . . I don't know. But surely we should be doing something? I mean, that man is kissing her like there's no tomorrow. We should stop him."

"Noelle went to him, Teresa. I think she's enjoying it. She's making happy noises."

"I am not going to stand around here wasting my time watching people snog each other," Miles said in an aggrieved voice. "Raleigh, come with me. I will attune with the spirits in the other garden, the one with the statue."

"Wait, guys . . . I can't leave Noelle. Can I? Noelle? Are you going to be all right? Moan twice if you are not being assaulted and are OK with this stranger kissing you like there's no tomorrow."

Noelle moaned twice.

"Oh, hell! I don't know what to do . . . dammit, wait up, Miles! I don't want to have to try to find you in the dark . . ."

Teresa's voice trailed off as Noelle's heat sank deep into my bones, driving out the chill that had gripped me for as long as I could remember.

All coherent thought ceased when Noelle's tongue swept alongside mine, twining around it, and when she actually began to suckle it, I thought my knees were going to buckle. I staggered over to a stone bench, sinking down gratefully onto it so I could further concentrate on kissing the very breath right out of the goddess in my arms.

Feed, Gray. Noelle gave another of those moans that had heat building in my groin. *I know you want to. You're hungry.*

I can't. My body was tight and clenched with need. *I cannot bind you to me. I am vitiated.*

Feed. I heard her siren's voice as she pulled her mouth from mine, turning her head to present her neck. *It will be all right. We were meant to be together.*

My gut tightened as the hunger swept over me,

consuming me, leaving me with little but the knowledge that I would cease to exist if I didn't take life
from her at that exact moment.

Feed, she repeated, pulling my head to her neck,
and my resistance slipped away into nothing. I licked
the pulse point that beat so strong just for me, my
mind filled with the taste and scent and feel of her.
Driven by a primal urge that wouldn't be denied any
longer, I bit the silken flesh, the taste of her driving
me almost beyond what I was fast realizing was a
tenuous grasp on control. I drank deeply, my body
clamoring for relief, demanding that I claim her even
as I took life from her.

She moved against me, her mind touching mine,
wrapping around me like velvet, her pleasure at feeding me burning along my skin. *Gray.* She was letting
me feel how aroused she was. *I really think I . . . I had no
idea . . . I had heard, the other Beloveds had said that feeding was
an erotic act, but this . . . oh, dear God, Gray, I'm going to go up in
flames if you don't make love to me right now.*

I was temporarily sated; the hunger had faded and
left only the desperate sense of unfulfillment that only
she could cure. But we were very close to Joining, and
that I could not, would not, do.

Nothing in my life had ever been as hard as gently
pushing her off my lap and walking away from her,
away from the warmth and light and joy she represented. I knew she'd think I was a bastard, a selfish,
soulless monster who used her without apology, and

I was glad. Maybe now she'd realize that there was nothing in my life that she could share.

Where are you going? she asked with a touch of desperation as I strode away, a sneering Johannes following me.

I have to go kill a ghost. After that, I will leave the country.

But . . . without me?

The pain that always held me in its grip tightened until I couldn't breathe. *Without you.*

Coward, she accused, and I knew I had at last hurt her.

If I'd had a soul, it would have wept at that moment. But I had no choice. I had to leave her in order to protect her. I was a man alone. I had no hope. No promise of relief. No salvation.

I had no future.

Chapter Four

I wonder if it's a crime to kill the undead," Noelle said aloud, then immediately qualified that thought. "Not that Dark Ones are undead. And Gray is very much alive." She spent a few minutes reliving the taste of him as he kissed her, the feel of him so hard and hot beneath her hands as she stroked his chest and back. "Very alive. But an idiot nonetheless." She shook her head and got to her feet.

Men were much more complicated creatures than she'd been led to believe. As she picked her way through the tangled and overgrown garden to the lower level, she tried to pin down just what it was about Grayson that attracted her. He was certainly sexy as hell, with that chin and those eyes and a classically handsome face. Her hands itched to touch his flesh, to stroke the long lines of his back down to his tempting behind, to feel the hard muscles of his thighs, to sculpt the swells and curves of his chest and abdomen. But it was more than his body that had her feeling that she was caught up in a whirlpool of emotions. He held so much darkness within him, such pain, bound together in a noble belief that he was destruction to anyone allowed near him.

"He has no faith," she told herself as she caught sight of Teresa and Raleigh filming Miles before the marble statue of a woman being wooed by a swan. "The problem is whether I can change that or not, and whether . . . oh, dear. That can't be good."

She stopped just outside the range of Raleigh's camera, watching with a slight pucker between her brows as the ghostly Nostredame, waggling his eyebrows at Teresa, allowed himself to be interviewed by Miles.

"—said there was a treasure here at the Abbey. Is this a treasure that you left when you were amongst the living?" Miles asked the ghost.

"I left many things behind," Nosty said with a look of smug maleness. "Both boys and girls."

Noelle rolled her eyes as she moved to stand next to Teresa, who asked her in an undertone, "Are you all right?"

"Of course."

"You two were going at it pretty hot and heavy," Teresa pointed out. "I'm assuming that is the man you said kidnapped you earlier? The one you just met?"

"Yes, that's him. Isn't he gorgeous?"

"His appearance isn't what was worrying me, although yes, he was pretty handsome. I've known you forever, Noelle, and you've never been the 'jump at a man you've just met' sort of girl."

Noelle smiled to herself. "Gray is different."

Theresa rolled her eyes. "That's what they all say."

"I know, but you have to trust me about this. When I say different, I mean *really* different."

Teresa said nothing more but gave her a knowing look that Noelle dismissed. Her attention turned to the scene in front of her, watching the ghost with a nagging worried feeling. What was it about Nosty that had Gray so upset? Was it the mention of a treasure? No, he'd tensed up when Nosty had first mentioned the history of the house, particularly Gray's family. Perhaps, in the interest of finding out what had happened to leave Gray vitiated, she would have to do a little investigating.

"Then who did hide the treasure in the Abbey?" Miles asked, trying manfully to keep the ghost's attention on himself. "Was it one of your ancestors who lived here?"

"I've told you, I don't know who left it. I was a visiting monk when this was an abbey, so I didn't really live here. The family who did live here later used to talk about the treasure and how someday they'd find it. No one ever did." Nosty shrugged. "I never looked for it myself. There were so many other things to interest me."

"How utterly fascinating," Miles said. "Now, tell us about yourself, how you died for love, and what happened to the nun you seduced."

Noelle tuned out the story that followed, certain that it would contain little actual truth and, most likely, a whole lot of fiction. Instead, she pondered the mystery that was Gray, what could have happened to him to leave him the victim of a demon lord's wrath, and how she was going to bring the infuriatingly obstinate man around to see reason.

Those thoughts were still with her two hours later, when Nosty had run out of both energy to remain visible and patience with Miles's endless questions about what life was like "beyond the misty veil." She lay in her sleeping bag in the communal music room, staring up at the patterns of shifting light cast from Miles's shaded camp lantern, wondering what Gray was doing at that moment. Gentle snores from both Raleigh's and Teresa's respective sleeping bags lulled her into a semisleeping state but still conscious enough to catch the whispered sound of cloth moving against cloth.

Careful not to move her body, she cracked open one eye and lifted her head, catching just the momentary flash of Miles's hand as he closed the door behind himself. That was odd. Miles didn't care for the dark and seemed to have an aversion to wandering the house by himself. Hmm. With a glance toward the other two sleepers, she slid out of her sleeping bag and silently made her way out of the room, pausing in the long, dark hallway to consider which way Miles would have gone. She didn't think it was likely that he'd go into another of the rooms that opened off the corridor, which left the main hall.

With a stealthy tread, she crept toward the hall, but it was as black as midnight. Frowning, she retraced her steps to the corridor, wishing she'd thought to bring her flashlight. She didn't want to risk waking up either Teresa or Raleigh with the noise of rustling through her bag for one, however, so she simply moved from door to door, alert for any sounds of movement as she opened each a crack.

It wasn't until she was on the second floor that she glimpsed a flicker of light under one of the doors. "Found you, Miles," she said softly as she opened the door, prepared to fire off a number of questions about just what he was doing creeping around the house.

The words froze on her lips as the sight of a naked derriere filled her vision. A wet, naked derriere, one belonging to an equally wet, naked Dark One. As her eyes grew round with the glory that was Gray, he spun around. Judging by the little wisps of steam coming from an adjoining room and a rumpled towel on the floor, he'd just had a shower.

"What the hell are you doing here?" he demanded.

Her gaze dropped to his genitals, her mouth going

suddenly dry as she let her eyes wander from his endowments to the strong line of his legs, back up to his stomach and chest, and then back to his groin. To her amazement, he was becoming aroused, an effect that left her staring with even more fascination. "Um . . . hmm?"

Hands on his adorable hips, he glared at her, saying, "Stop doing that!"

"Stop what?" she asked, unable to tear her gaze from him. "Staring at your privates?"

"Yes. Stop it. It's annoying me."

She entered the room and closed the door behind her, her eyes still on his growing length. "Actually, I think it's arousing you, unless you can be annoyed and aroused at the same time. Gray?"

"What?" he snapped, not moving to cover himself, a fact that Noelle highly appreciated. She was aware that Johannes was curled up on the bed, watching them, but she had eyes only for the tortured, delicious vampire before her.

"I'm not going to give up on you," she managed to say, which was a miracle considering that her tongue was glued to the roof of her mouth. "I know you're trying to drive me away, but I'm not going to let you do that. You need me. I can help you. I'm a Guardian, and your Beloved, whether you want to admit it or not, and you can either be miserable and irritating and unhappy and refuse to let me help you—which won't matter, because I'll help you anyway—or you can realize that you've been blessed and get down on your knees and thank me daily for making your life worth living again."

He looked for a moment as if he was going to explode.

"Was the knees bit too much?" she asked, worried for a moment that he might do himself some sort of damage if he kept all that anger bound inside.

"Yes," he said in a choked voice. To her surprise, however, he didn't scream and yell or deny any of what she said. He simply marched over to the bed, picked up the cat, and put him into the adjoining room before closing the door. He strode toward her, his eyes glittering, and before Noelle could ask him if he was really very annoyed with her, he scooped her up and tossed her onto the bed, following her down onto the mattress.

"Gracious me, what . . . oh, Gray!" Her eyes rolled backward as he pulled her sleep shirt over her head, leaving her clad in nothing but a scanty pair of satin underwear. His mouth descended upon one suddenly heavy, wanting breast, while his fingers stroked and teased the other one. She clutched at his head, her back arching up.

So soft. He groaned as his tongue tormented her breast, making it ache with a need she had never before known. *So warm.*

You're hungry again. She was amazed that she could form words in the face of such wonderful sensations.

It was as if his hands and mouth were made of fire, sending tendrils of heat radiating out of her chest and down her belly to deep, secret places.

I'm always hungry when I'm near you. The voice of his thoughts in her mind was as rough as sandpaper, his breath growing ragged as he switched breasts, his hand stroking downward, feeling her belly before sliding even lower to tease the source of her heat.

You may want to drink my blood, but I want to bite you all over, she answered, squirming when his fingers moved beneath her underwear to find sensitive flesh.

He lifted his head from her breast, an odd look in his lovely green eyes. "No one has ever bitten me."

She grinned and pushed at his shoulders until he obliged and rolled over onto his back, a quizzical frown between his brows. She got to her knees, quickly divesting herself of her underwear before leaning over his chest, taking a moment to swirl her tongue over his pert little nipples. He sucked in his breath. "Christos, woman!"

"You think that's good? Let's try this . . ." Her teeth closed gently around one nipple. Grayson almost came off the bed, his mind filled with a desperate need that was echoed in her own head.

"You're trying to kill me, aren't you?" Gray growled as he grabbed her by her hips and pulled her over his body. "Ride me!"

"I beg your pardon?" Noelle moaned and closed her eyes as the length of his arousal pressed along parts that were suddenly sensitized beyond human belief. *Goodness, Gray!*

He reached between them, shifting her upward and placing himself in position. "Ride me!"

She wanted to; oh, how she wanted to. There was nothing more she wanted at that moment than to sink down on the hard length of him, to taste him, to give herself up to the passion that only he seemed to be able to stir in her. But she had to be sure he wanted her, really wanted her.

"Yes!" he shouted, urging her hips downward even as he thrust up. "I want you, you delicious, seductive woman. I'll curl into a ball and dry up into dust, blowing away into nothing, if you don't take me into you right this second. Open for me, sweet. Let me into your warmth. Fill me with your light."

The images he was projecting into her head were too much. She sank down on him, her body welcoming the hard invader, muscles rippling around him in a way that had both of them moaning with ecstasy. And then he pulled her forward, down onto his chest, his mouth hot on her neck for a second before whitehot pain burst into a feeling so erotic that it pushed her over the edge into an orgasm.

She collapsed onto him, her body boneless, her mind so overwhelmed with their shared emotions that she could do little but attempt to breathe when he gave a hoarse cry of completion. She did manage to lift her head enough to press a kiss on his damp chest, but even that act seemed too much, because it took her a long, long time to recover.

Slowly, and with muscles that trembled from the unexpected activity, she sat up, her eyes immediately widening. "Dear Lord, you're still inside me."

"Don't . . . move . . ." Gray growled, clutching the sheets beneath him. "If you move, I'm going to make love to you again, and you've drained every last bit of strength from me. I am as weak as a newborn kitten, as soft as a bowl of jelly. I can't even make my brain work."

Noelle shifted her hips, just a little, just to see if she was going to be even the teensiest bit tender after holding him so deep inside her. But her muscles, slowly relaxing from the death grip upon him, sent up a little cheer of happiness and expressed willingness to regroup. "Goodness," she whispered, rocking forward, her eyes closed as she focused on the sensation of him.

Gray lurched beneath her, and suddenly, she was on her back.

"No," he said, pulling her legs over his shoulders as he thrust into her. "No, we are not doing this again. It is impossible to contemplate. Stop trying to seduce me, you vixen."

At the feel of him moving against her, her body tightened again, the pressure building quickly into another moment of rapture. "I've never been multi-orgasmic," she panted as his hips flexed with short, hard little movements that had her eyes crossing. "Oh, dear Lord, yes, do that again."

"I will not." He moaned, making the little swivel that hit all sorts of sensitive spots inside her. "I am going to sleep now. You have worn me out with your lusty demands."

"Glrn," she babbled, aware that she wasn't making any sense but unable to do anything about it. Her body spiraled into another orgasm that shook her to her toes, making her shout when Gray turned his head and bit the leg that lay over his shoulder. "I've got to . . . I have to . . . Gray, we have to Join. Now." Her voice trailed off into another moan of pleasure, the sensation of his own climax while he fed from her simply too much.

I can't do that to you.

You don't have a choice, she answered, grabbing his head when he let her legs slide off his shoulders, twining her tongue around his before nipping the end of it.

He jerked back, his eyes wide as she sucked the tip of his tongue, savoring the spicy, sweet taste of his blood. *Christ, woman, do you know what you've done?*

Yes. We've done all the steps of Joining except the sacrifice, and I'll do that just as soon as I figure out what sort of sacrifice I'll need to make.

She could feel the conflicted emotions within him—fear, anger, and a grudging admission that the attraction he felt for her was something more than mere lust. She drifted into a haze of sleepy satisfaction, pleasured to the tips of her toes, and was only half aware when Gray pulled the blankets of the massive bed over them, one arm around her waist as she lay limply against him.

He had accepted her. She just knew he had. Life was going to be wonderful now.

Chapter Five

I hate it when I'm wrong about things," Noelle told
Teresa a short eight hours later, as the two women
sat watching while Miles walked back and forth in
front of them, ranting about how he was simply trying to save them all, the TV show, and the house.

"No one will listen to me, that's the problem with
all of you," he snapped as he paced past them.

"What's wrong now?" Teresa asked in a low tone,
dutifully nodding when Miles demanded to know if
she was paying attention.

Noelle waited until he strode past, continuing his
rant, before answering in a whisper, "Well, for one,
Gray disappeared this morning. One minute he was
there, doing the most incredible things to me, and
the next he was gone, his side of the bed still warm."

"His side of the—Noelle!" Teresa gasped in an

undertone, shooting her friend an astonished look. "You didn't sleep with him? You *did*! You slept with him, and you just met him! That is so not like you!"

"I told you that we have a bit of an odd relationship," Noelle answered, unable to keep her cheeks from pinkening a little. "We have, for lack of a better word, a connection, and last night, Gray finally admitted it. Well, I thought he did, but maybe the fact that he disappeared this morning means he's still in denial. Although we did complete all the steps, so that must mean he can't go far."

"What steps?" Teresa asked, watching with a falsely rapt expression as Miles continued to expound about some theory of his regarding the danger they were all in from some facts he'd uncovered.

Noelle hesitated. She desperately needed someone to talk to, and since Grayson was hiding from her, Teresa was the only choice. "Gray's . . . er . . . people have a long tradition regarding courtship. There are seven steps that have to be completed before we're considered Joined."

"Joined?"

"It's another term for a couple."

"Huh. Odd family. Must be old Czech traditions or something. What are these steps?"

Noelle ran her mind over them, everything from the protecting her against the threat posed by the demon lord who had vitiated him, to the body fluid exchanges, right on down to the exchange of blood.

"Most of them are just minor things, like . . . erm . . . kissing and other courtship rituals, but that's really neither here nor there. According to the rules that govern his people, we're now officially a couple, and men who are part of such a relationship shouldn't just go haring off on their own."

Teresa giggled, then immediately donned a somber face when Miles, in full rant, shot her a suspicious look. "You really haven't dated much, have you? That's how men are, Noelle."

Not Dark Ones bound to a Beloved, Noelle thought, but she kept that to herself. Later, when Miles had stormed off in a hissy fit because Teresa insisted they stay for the remainder of their time on the lease despite his nebulous claims that the ghosts of the house posed some horrible, unnamed threat to them all, she spent a few hours ridding the house of the imp packs that had taken up residence. That she was also not-so-covertly searching for signs of the missing Gray was something she shrugged away. They were bound together now, whether he liked it or not.

She was in the garden when Nosty found her.

"There you are, my sweet one," he said as he sashayed up to her, making her a bow that was courtly despite his being clad in the worn gray habit. "Were you by chance waiting here for me?"

"No, I'm hunting for Gray. You haven't seen him today, have you?" She cast a glance upward at the cloudless sky. "Not that I'd expect to see him out in the sun, but I can't find him in the house and thought perhaps he'd come out into the garden for some peace and quiet."

"Eh," Nosty said, immediately looking bored. "He's probably gone to see Lady Joan."

"The ghost you visit?" Noelle frowned. "Why would he want to see her?"

Nosty's expression changed to one of impish amusement. He winked and moved off toward the house. "You'll have to ask the Dark One that."

"Really," she said slowly, sensing a mystery. She loved mysteries—loved unraveling them, that is. "Oh, Nosty, I meant to ask you, how many other spirits are there in the house? I have no way of sensing their presence, and Miles is making a nuisance of himself with Teresa, saying we're all in dire danger of who-knows-what if we don't leave the house to the ghosts."

"Other spirits?" Nostredame shook his head. "There are no other spirits but me in the Abbey. Lady Joan's domain is in her cottage, and the house dada has moved to another estate entirely because all of the decay here made him emo."

Noelle ignored the idea of a moody domestic spirit, asking only, "Are you sure? Miles seems very insistent."

"Do you think I would not know if there were others in my haunt?"

"Sorry, didn't mean to impugn your ghostly abilities," she apologized, which he accepted with haughty grandeur before moving off toward the house.

"Another mystery," Noelle said with satisfaction, shaking herself as she drew her mind back to the one that was most important: Gray. Perhaps he, too, was visiting the ghost Nosty had mentioned. If nothing else, she might have some idea of where Gray had gone.

Nosty had said that Lady Joan's spirit was confined to her cottage on the north side of the estate, but given how big the grounds were, it wasn't until the afternoon shadows had stretched long, inky fingers across the overgrown lawn and minute cottage garden that she found the place.

The cottage itself was mostly overrun with trumpet vines, wisteria, and honeysuckle, the thatched roof long since sunken into the center of the stone walls. One wall was entirely gone, the other three still standing but stained green and black with age. Noelle approached the tangled remains slowly, having to beat a path to the gaping blackness that was once a doorway. As she neared it, a profound sense of sadness seemed to leach up from the ground, choking her with its hopelessness. She stopped, goose bumps on her arms. Even the most unknowing of mundane mortals would know this was a haunted place.

"Hello? Lady Joan? My name is Noelle, and I'm a Guardian. I was told by Nostredame that you like to talk to people now and again."

Silence hung thick and heavy in the air, and it struck Noelle then that despite the cottage being nestled in a stand of willows, there was no birdsong, no distant drone of either cars or airplanes. Bees flitted around the honeysuckle and trumpet vine, but their hum, if any, was too muted to be heard. Quiet wrapped around the cottage as thick as cotton wool, merging with sadness and despair to make the hairs on the back of her neck stand on end.

Noelle shook her head against the fanciful thoughts. She was a Guardian, a keeper of a portal to hell itself. She had seen and bested beings much more frightening than one simple forlorn ghost. "Lady Joan?"

Tiny little motes of dust seemed to gather in on themselves, swirling around in the air and thickening until the figure of a spirit slowly resolved itself into that of a woman clad in a long, flowing gown, topped with a simple surcoat. "A . . . Guardian?" the ghost said after a moment of considering Noelle. Her voice was so soft that for a moment, Noelle thought she'd only imagined she heard the sound. It floated high, more like a gentle caress of the wind than an actual sound. "No, more than a Guardian. A Beloved."

"That's right. My name is Noelle, Lady Joan. I've come to talk to you about Gray Soucek."

"Grayson? You wish to talk about Grayson?" The ghost sucked in her breath, her form wavering for a moment before it solidified. "You are his Beloved?"

Noelle couldn't tell by her expression if the

woman was happy or angry about that. "Yes, I am. You do know Gray, don't you?"

Lady Joan gave a silent laugh that filled Noelle with more sadness than she thought possible. "He is my son, Beloved. He is my son, my only child, one whom I loved more than even the man I adored until the day I ceased to draw breath."

"You're his mother? Oh, then that explains how you knew I was a Beloved. You must be one . . . er . . . no, wait, that isn't right, is it?" Noelle frowned at her obvious faux pas. "I'm so sorry. I really put my foot in my mouth that time, didn't I? Gray is an unredeemed Dark One, which means you weren't his father's Beloved. How tragic for you."

The ghostly Lady Joan acknowledged this by closing her eyes for a moment, pain etched in her face. "I am bound to tragedy, Beloved, but you, at least, have brought me the joy of knowing my Grayson has a future where his father did not."

Noelle shivered despite the heat of the day, the shadows now consuming the cottage as the sun began to drop into the horizon. "I hope he does. I mean, he does, but right now he's being . . . well . . . I don't quite know what he's being. We've done the seven steps of Joining, so all that remains before he gets his soul back is for me to make some sort of a sacrifice for him, but I don't know what I'm supposed to do in order to achieve that. And Gray is being really tight-lipped because he didn't want to have a Beloved due to him being vitiated, which is understandable, although not at all necessary. Since I'm a Guardian, that is. Do you happen to know where he is?"

Lady Joan looked somewhat dazed by the wall of conversation that just hit her, but after a moment of sorting through it, she shook her head. "I have not seen Grayson since the day . . . since the day he left. He was so angry, so unyielding . . ." The ghost actually wrung her hands as she spoke, an act that made Noelle feel quite unnerved.

"What day was that, if you don't mind me asking? Or, rather, what happened that day? You don't have to tell me if it's too personal, although I have to admit now to being really curious about why you would be here in spirit form but your son wouldn't want to see you. It doesn't seem like Gray at all, because underneath all that denial, he's really a very nice person, but I'm sure you know that. Did you two have a falling out? Was there some sort of an argument? Was it about a demon lord, by any chance? Did—"

Before she could continue firing questions at the morose spirit, the sounds of a large body moving through the undergrowth disturbed the silence that hung so heavily over the cottage. Noelle stepped backward a few feet to eye the shadow that emerged from the trees, prepared for the worst—a demon—but filled with joy when she recognized the bulky shape as it stepped out from the darkest shadows.

"Speak of the devil. Well, not literally," Noelle told

Lady Joan, not wanting the woman to get the idea that she was bad-mouthing Gray. "Because obviously, Gray isn't the head of Abaddon, although I have to say that I've heard rumors that things are not going well for the demon lord who was in charge there."

The ghost blinked at her.

Noelle patted what would have been the ghost's hand if she'd been in corporeal form. "Don't worry, I won't let the overthrow of the premier demon lord Bael have any impact on Gray. I am quite capable of handling any demons or demon lords who decide to come after him. Not that I think they would, but in case someone does, I'm on it. So to speak. Am I confusing you? I think I am. You have the same expression that I've seen when I try to explain how you can destroy a demon's form but not the demon itself. Oh, hullo, Gray. I was just reassuring your mother that Bael isn't going to pose a threat to you."

Noelle couldn't help but notice the scowl that Gray wore like a badge of righteousness. "What the hell are you doing . . . did you say you were reassuring my mother?" he demanded to know as he stopped in front of her, careful to stand in the shadow of the house. The sun might be in the process of setting, but he was obviously wary of exposing himself to its still-potent rays.

"Yes. I think I may have babbled at her a bit. It's something I do when I'm comfortable with people. You probably haven't noticed that yet, because I'm still in the process of getting comfy with you, but you should be aware that I do that. So you won't be surprised, I mean. Where've you been? You were gone when I woke up. Well, the second time I woke up, since you were most definitely there the first time I woke up. Oh, dear." She looked from Gray to his mother. They both wore identical expressions of disbelief. "Now I've overwhelmed you both, haven't I?"

"Noelle," Gray said, taking a deep breath with the distinct air of someone who would be a likely candidate for martyrdom. His brow was still furrowed in a frown. "My mother is dead. She was mortal, and she died several centuries ago."

"Yes, I know, otherwise she wouldn't be a ghost." Noelle sent Lady Joan a reassuring *Your son may not be too bright, but he's sexy as hell* smile.

"She's not a ghost," he answered, and was clearly about to go into one of his denial lectures, but Noelle decided that this was a time when bud-nipping was most definitely called for.

"Gray, darling, I'm not stupid. Yes, I'm a Guardian, and yes, most of my experience is with demons, but I know a ghost when I see one, and your mother"— she paused to wave a hand at Lady Joan, who was gazing at her son with an expression of yearning that was painful to see—"your mother is most definitely one."

Gray froze, his eyes narrowed on her. "My mother is . . . *here?*"

"Yes." She looked more closely at him. "You don't see her, do you?"

He shook his head, pain and guilt gripping him with such strength that Noelle's knees weakened. She grabbed his arm, gasping for breath. "My God, what is it? Why do you feel that way? Why can't you see your mother's spirit?"

An inarticulate sob came from Lady Joan. Noelle, sharing Gray's pain, turned her head at the sound, the anguish on the woman's face so horrible to see that she fell to her knees.

Instantly, Gray was there, pulling her into his arms, tamping down the horrible pain inside himself until she could breathe again, the scent and feel of him so warm and alive wrapped around her like a soft blanket.

Are you all right, Beloved? I'm sorry that my emotions got away from me. I should have better shielded them from you.

"No, you shouldn't have," Noelle said, pulling herself away from the safe haven of his body in order to search his eyes. "I don't want to be protected from your emotions, Gray, not even the negative ones. What happened to you?" She took his face in her hands and gently kissed him. "What happened to your mother to leave her so devastated? Why can't you see her?"

Fresh pain lanced through him at her words, and Noelle swore to herself, damning her verbal clumsiness.

He rose to his feet, pulling her up at the same time,

his face shuttered, his emotions locked tightly away from her. "The past is in the past, where it should be. As for my mother . . ." He looked over her shoulder to the crumbling remains of the cottage. "If you can indeed see her and speak to her, tell her . . ." His voice cracked. It took him a few seconds to speak again. "Tell her that I am sorry."

Tears burned in Noelle's eyes as she glanced behind her to see Lady Joan, now seated on a fallen tree, weeping silently into her hands. *Obviously, whatever happened to you and your mother was a profound tragedy. But I don't get a sense of censure from her, Gray. I don't think she wants an apology from you.*

He stumbled away from her, pushing away her hands when she tried to grab his arm, his mind once again choked with so much guilt it almost strangled her.

Gray?

Leave me. Just . . . leave me. I bring nothing but sorrow to those close to me. You are better off without me, Noelle.

"Poor, deluded man," she said softly, watching his shadow flicker for a moment before it disappeared into the gathering darkness. "He honestly thinks that we'd be better off apart."

"He carries a great burden," Lady Joan said in her soft, whisper-thin voice. "He seeks to protect you from the darkness within him."

"But I can relieve him of that darkness, at least some of it. I can give him back his soul. Surely he must want that?" She turned to the ghost, who now bore an expression of hopelessness. "I'm going to be blunt, Lady Joan. Blunt and nosy. What happened between you that Gray feels such guilt?"

The ghost closed her eyes for a few moments. "He believes he is responsible for my death."

"Goddess! That would certainly account for his emotions. *Was* he responsible?"

"No, Grayson was not responsible." Lady Joan stood and brushed off her skirts before drifting toward the cottage, her visibility fading as she disappeared into the spirit realm. "It was his father who killed me."

Chapter Six

How did she find out? How the hell did she find out that Mother was here?" I spun around and glared at the cat, who perched regally on the tall four-poster bed. "You told her, didn't you?"

Johannes cocked an eyebrow at me.

"Oh, don't give me that look. I know full well that if you put your mind to it, you could speak. You damned . . ." Words failed me. I swore under my breath and stomped over to the window, jerking back the curtain to stare furiously down to the veranda. "If it wasn't you, it had to be that bastard Nostredame. I'll murder the bloody fool. Dammit, he's already dead. I'll . . . I'll . . . I'll call in a Summoner and have him removed."

Johannes got to his feet, stretched, then jumped off the bed and strolled to the door, giving me an imperious look over his shoulder.

"What, now I'm your personal servant?"

He just looked at me with half-closed wicked green eyes.

"One of these days, Johannes . . ." I flung open the door, yelling after him, "So help me God, if you say one more word to Noelle—don't give me that look, you could talk if you weren't so damned lazy. I swear to you by all that you hold dear, I'll send you back to Amaymon if you even think of meddling with my Beloved!"

The cat disappeared into the darkness of the hall-way, leaving me alone with the horrible knowledge that I'd lost even the brief glimpse of paradise that had descended so unexpectedly upon me.

I returned to the window, leaning my forehead against the chill of the glass, seriously considering drowning myself in the pond before I remembered that it had grown over decades ago. "You've made a bloody mess of everything," I told my reflection in the window. "Not content to screw up your own life, you ruined your mother's, destroyed any hope of a happy future, and now you're tainting the best thing that ever happened to you. You make me sick."

The face in the window stared back at me. I sighed at it. "Christ, I can't even be pathetically maudlin without sounding ridiculous."

A flicker from the veranda had me growling out oaths I hadn't used in a very long time, and without further thought about the reason I wanted to pummel

Nosty to a ghostly pulp when Noelle and I had no future, I found myself chasing after the blasted ghost. He didn't stay on the veranda long, leaving it before I found him. It took another twenty minutes before I finally pinned him down in the housekeeper's room in the basement of the east wing.

"There you are, you traitorous bastard!"

Nosty spun around at the sound of my voice, his gaze immediately flitting around the room, obviously in search of escape. "Er . . . Gray. Hello again. Long time no chitchat. I was just . . . uh . . . talking to Miles, here. Wasn't I, Miles?"

The mortal was sitting on a worn wooden chair in the middle of the room, lit only by a single candle that listed to one side, stuck into a broken saucer. "Who the devil are you?" He squinted at me for a moment. "Oh, you're that horrible actress's boyfriend. Well, you can leave, along with this chatterbox."

I ignored the ill-mannered man. Mortals, on the whole, were interesting. This one, however, I could quite happily never set eyes on again. I honed my glare on Nosty. "Don't try to weasel your way out of this. You know full well that I'm here because you've been telling tales."

"Hello! Am I suddenly mute? I just told you two to leave!" Miles sputtered.

Nosty edged away from me. "Tales? Me? I'd never do that, Gray, you know that. Especially not tales about you."

Miles breathed heavily through his nose. "The spirits sent me to this room so that I might commune with the deceased housekeeper. I feel that she has things she wishes to tell me, and she can't bloody well do that with you two standing there bollixing away."

"You told Noelle about my mother." I growled, stalking slowly toward the ghost.

Nosty gulped and backed up, his hands out in a placating gesture. "I didn't tell her anything about Lady Joan. Other than where she lived. But nothing else, Gray, I swear."

"I think I am being possessed." Miles, now swaying in his chair, his eyes closed, started humming to himself. "Yes, I believe the spirit of the housekeeper is merging with my consciousness. What is it you want, dear lady? You want these people out of your room? Yes, yes, I completely understand. You wish for your privacy to be honored."

"That was enough to send her running over to the cottage to speak with my mother, whose very presence you neglected to bother mentioning to me. Shall I tell you what I do to those who annoy me, Nosty?"

"You were never here!" the ghost shrieked, now backed up against the wall. He looked as if he was trying very hard to disappear into nothing, but I hadn't spent my entire existence coping with ghosts without learning a trick or two. I made sure he was grounded and couldn't dissipate his being. "How could I tell you if you never showed up at the Abbey?"

"You're bloody 'ere now, both of you, and you can just leave so I can get on with me 'ousework," Miles said in a strong Cockney accent as he glared at us. "I've got an entire 'ouse what to clean and feed."

I shot him a look. "The only housekeeper who ever used this room was Czech, not British, and she spoke no English."

Miles blinked for a second, then collapsed back onto the chair, slumped down, moaning. "The spirits, so many spirits here, they are fighting to speak through me . . ."

"If you so much as open your mouth to Noelle again—" I grabbed the ghost by the front of his robe and lifted him off the ground, shaking him as I did so.

"I won't!" Nosty babbled, his expression suitably frightened by my unspoken threat. "I swear by the saints, I won't say another thing to her! I won't tell her about Johannes, or Amaymon, or that night when your mother died . . . I won't tell her about any of that."

"See that you don't." I slammed him against the wall before I released my grip on his robe. He slid down the wall to the floor, where he crumpled into a ball before disappearing into nothing.

Behind me, Miles was humming softly to himself, occasionally tossing out a word of what was obviously tourist Czech. I turned to tell him he'd have to do better than that if he wanted to convince anyone that he was possessed, but the sight of the woman standing in the doorway, her arms crossed and one lovely sable eyebrow cocked in question, drove all lesser concerns from my mind.

"Johannes?" Noelle said, watching me avidly. *Amaymon? Is that the demon lord who vitiated you? Why did your father kill your mother, and more important, why do you feel so guilty about it?*

For a moment, for the time it takes for one synapse to fire at another, I thought of running. I'd run my entire life—why not now? But even as I stood tense and poised to escape, the warm lilac scent that seemed to be permanently imbued in her skin wrapped me in silken tendrils, pulling me toward her.

"I am now possessed," Miles announced loudly in a quasi-Czech accent as I walked past him to the door.

"Bully for you." I stopped in front of Noelle and looked down at her, trying to read in her eyes that which I so desperately wanted to see.

Her expression was inscrutable, although as I watched, the corners of her mouth began to curl up. I was distracted by the sight of her mouth, and the hunger within me came to life, swamping me with the pounding, insistent need to claim her in all the ways known to man and woman.

Instantly, I was ravenous with hunger and rock hard with baser needs.

"Oooh," she said as I scooped her up and lurched painfully down the narrow hall toward the back stairs. "I like what you're thinking. Feathers have been underused in sexual play, I've always felt."

I slid a glance down at her as I started up a flight of stairs toward my bedroom. "Just how much sexual play have you indulged in that you would feel so strongly about the subject?"

"Are you by any chance asking me how many men I've slept with?"

"Yes."

"I really don't think that's any of your business. I'm certainly not going to ask you how many women you've been with, so I don't think it's at all fair or even politically correct to inquire as to the number of my previous lovers. You do see, don't you, that it's what happens from here on out that's important, not what happened in our past?"

"Yes, I understand that."

She looked at me as I kicked open the door to the room that had been mine whenever I was at the Abbey, a little smile flirting with her lips. My erection went from rock hard to damn near impervious to a point-blank atomic blast.

"How many?" I asked, setting her on her feet and immediately stripping her of her clothing.

She giggled, damn her delicious hide. I had no resistance to such a feminine sound and only just managed to keep from pouncing on her. "Three. You?"

"Does that matter?"

"Oh, yes." She leaned forward to nip my bottom lip. "What's good for the goose and all that. How many, Gray?"

I sighed, checked the bathroom to make sure Johannes wasn't lurking about, then returned to find Noelle lying seductively on the bed. "Twenty-two, if you insist on knowing."

"Twenty-two . . . goodness!" She sat up, her breasts bobbing enticingly in front of me as I struggled to remove my trousers without simply shredding them off my body. "That's a lot of women, Gray. I don't think I like that number. When you compare three with twenty-two, well . . . that's quite a difference."

"I was born in 1664," I pointed out, finally wrestling my trousers off, eyeing her with indecision. Should I start with those delectable breasts and work my way down or begin at the shy, pink-tipped little toes and work upward?

"Were you? That's really neither here nor there, is it?" She did a little mental arithmetic. "Oh, I see what you mean. You've had relationships with an average of seven women every century."

"Whereas you've had three in less than approximately fifteen years," I said, crawling onto the bottom of the bed, taking one ankle in hand, the sensation of her smooth, warm flesh driving the hunger and passion inside me even higher, until I thought I might fall into the deep, red well of need.

"Twelve, actually. I'm thirty-one. Three makes me sound so very promiscuous," she said thoughtfully, watching with interest as I struggled with the hunger, keeping my bites to gentle little nips as I kissed my way up first one calf, then the other. "Wanton, almost. Are we going to have oral sex?"

I stopped licking behind her knee to look up as she lolled back on the pillows, her dark red curls tangled on the bed linens, desire mingling with expectation in her beautiful eyes. "We're going to do whatever you like. You may command me."

"Really?" She smiled. "Then you'll answer my questions about Amaymon and your parents and those other things that Nosty mentioned that had you looking like you wanted to kill him on the spot but knew you couldn't because, well, he's already dead, for one."

"You may command me in sexual acts," I said, biting a little harder on her thigh.

She moaned. "Oral sex, then."

"As you wish." I leaned forward to kiss a path down toward where shorter, darker curls shielded her intimate secrets, but she sat up, pushing me onto my back.

"You're going to be the recipient, though."

I thought, at least for an infinitesimal fraction of a second, of protesting that I wanted to be the one to give her pleasure, but there was no way on this good earth I was going to stop Noelle from doing what she so obviously wanted to do.

She laughed in my mind. *I don't think there's a man alive who would say no.*

I frowned as she moved my legs aside and sat on her heels between my calves. *It's not that. I simply do not wish to deprive you of the pleasure that you are so obviously anticipating.*

She looked pointedly at my erection, which, at that moment, had properties in tensile strength that were similar to titanium.

"All right. Perhaps I am anticipating them as well," I admitted.

"Tensile strength?" She giggled and stroked her hands up my legs, her touch like molten fire going straight to my blood and driving the hunger into a fevered pitch. "I like the way your mind works, Gray. Most men, most normal men, couldn't come up with phrases like 'tensile strength' at a time like this. Most men would be lying back, moaning, clutching the sheets with both hands, begging me to explore your titanium-like penis with my tongue and mouth and perhaps, if I'm very, very gentle, even a little scrape of teeth."

"I am not most—"

She bent over me, taking the very tip of me into her mouth.

The sensation of her tongue swirling against flesh that was suddenly sensitized beyond human bearing left me moaning, clutching the sheets with both hands, and begging her to never stop doing what she was doing.

I never thought I'd like this, she told me as she continued to torment me with her mouth, almost making me come off the bed when her hands joined in. *But with you, it's different. I think it's because I can feel what every little touch is doing to you. Now, how do you feel about this?*

It's too much. My back arched off the bed as my hips thrust upward into the sweet torment of her mouth. *You're going to kill me.*

You're immortal, my darling.

If it's possible to die of pleasure, I'll do it, I managed to get out before the hunger slipped control, and I was pulling her over me, thrusting up into her, capturing her cry of ecstasy in my mouth. Her fingers dug hard into my shoulders, her breasts, those delightful little strumpets bent on my utter captivation, tempting me with their silken warmth as she moved to a rhythm that was shared between us, her pleasure feeding mine, which in turn drove hers even higher. It was as if we were in a perpetual cycle of rapture, and it was only when her release claimed her that I let myself drink deeply, the skin of her shoulder a silken haven that I couldn't resist any longer. She was mine, and I knew at that moment that I would move the moon and the stars to make sure she remained that way.

It took a long time to recover, both physically and emotionally. I knew what committing myself to Noelle would mean, knew that it would require sacrifices from both of us, and was attempting to organize a number of arguments in favor of my point of view when she lifted her head and frowned at me. She was lying on top of me, our legs and arms tangled in a boneless, utterly sated manner. The fact that she had the strength not only to raise her head but also actually to frown annoyed me.

"You do not get to be annoyed," she told me, her frown deepening. "You have been sexed to your very limits, and if you don't like the fact that I, as a woman, can recover from such lovemaking faster than you, a mere man, then you can just pretend to be grateful that you have a Beloved as thoughtful and aerobically fit as to be able to withstand this sort of activity without actually dropping dead of pleasure."

"I am the one who told you that you were going to kill me with your mouth," I told her sternly. "I said it first, so you can't now claim that it was so good that it almost did you in, too."

She bit the end of my nose. "You were so good you almost did me in, Gray. You were like a titanium machine, a fabulously sexy, bitey, really, really talented machine whose touch makes me burn like a Roman candle."

I allowed her words to placate me, closing my eyes as I drew little contented patterns on her delicious ass. "You helped a little. You may take a tiny portion of the credit."

She pinched my nipple, giggling when I opened

my eyes and yelped in indignation. "Now," she said, stacking her hands and resting her chin on them, staring into my eyes. "We talk."

I closed my eyes and snored. "I'm sleeping. Good night."

"Oh, no, you're not that tired. You can talk to me for a little bit."

"Women talk after sex. Men recover."

You're immortal. You have nothing from which you need to recover.

I snored into her mind, but she was having none of it. "This is important, Gray. You know we're going to have to talk about it."

"Beloveds," I said, sighing and capturing her legs between mine. "My father always told me to stay away from them."

She cocked an eyebrow. "Would this be the same father who killed your mother?"

I frowned. "She told you that?"

"Yes. Look, I can feel that you're not happy about having to talk about this, but as I've said several times now, I'm a Guardian. I can help you with your problem, but I really do need to have all the facts before I decide what steps to take. Let's start with why you feel you were responsible for your mother's death. She says you weren't."

Pain clawed at my guts, a familiar pain that I was used to ignoring. "She's wrong."

"You killed her?" Noelle looked at me with a gaze

that stripped away all of the protective layers I'd built up over the years.

"Not physically, but if I hadn't left the Abbey, she wouldn't have died."

"Start at the beginning," she demanded, pulling the blankets over us and shifting until she was comfortable atop me, her gaze steady on mine as her fingers gently stroked my collarbone.

I didn't want to but knew that sooner or later, she'd breach the part of my mind where my secrets were hidden.

"The beginning goes back to before I was born. My father was the child of a Dark One and a mage. Such pairings are not common, but he was born with not only the nature of a Dark One but the drives of a mage. The Magisters' Guild wanted nothing to do with him, however, because of his dark origins, so he turned to a more sinister source of power."

"A demon lord," Noelle said, her eyes bright with interest.

"Not just one but two, actually. Amaymon and Ariton were thick as thieves, and when my father contacted them, they found in him a kindred spirit, albeit one who resided in the mortal world. They were inseparable for a time, according to all accounts, raping and pillaging and murdering at will. In addition, my father developed a taste for turning mortals, something the Moravian Council was and is quite against, except in extreme circumstances." It hurt to admit the truth, but I knew that she was correct about one thing: if we were to have a future together, she would have to know the worst.

"I'm sorry." Her kisses along my jaw were as soft as feathers, as gentle as the warmth she wrapped around my aching heart. *You're not responsible for your father's actions, though. Surely you must realize that.*

It's not quite that simple . . . A tapping noise had been slowly growing while I spoke, until it sounded right outside the door of my room. I cocked my head, listening for a moment. The tapping stopped, and the door opened, the thin, weak light from a pencil flashlight flickering around for a few seconds before Miles appeared in the doorway.

"Ah. Just so. Er . . . I appear to have been in a trance and lost my way. I'll return to my bed now."

The door closed softly behind him, and after a few seconds of silence, the tapping again sounded softly along the hallway.

"What on earth is he doing?" Noelle asked with a frown of puzzlement.

"Trying to locate the treasure."

"There's a treasure here?" she asked, curiosity gripping her.

"No, but he thinks there is. Nosty filled him full of some story he tells the tourists. Sooner or later, the mortal will find the hidden chamber behind the fireplace in the great hall and will realize that Nosty is unreliable as a source of historical information."

"Secret room, hmm? Sounds fascinating."

I smiled to myself as she began to plot a way to get me to tell her how to access the room.

"So your father was buddies with Amaymon and Ariton and raising hell, and you feel guilty about that for some reason. How does your mother's death fit into this?"

The pain that always accompanied that thought was just as sharp now as it had ever been. I wondered if it would ever dull. "I was powerless to stop my father's path of destruction. I tried repeatedly, we both did—my mother and I—but I think now that he must have been a little mad. He was certainly heartless. The last time I tried to stop him, he had Amaymon vitiate me."

She stared at me, clearly aghast, her jaw slack in surprise. "Your dad did this to you?"

"Yes. So I left the area, went to France first, later Italy, always hiding from the demons Amaymon sent after me. It wasn't until a year had passed that the truth reached me. The night I left, the night I was damned for all time . . ." I stopped, the memories choking me.

Noelle kissed me, her arms tight around me as she filled me with all her light and warmth and love, using it to battle the pain that was bound so tightly around me. *My darling, you're not alone anymore. Let me help you. Let me free you from the vitiation, at least.*

I held her, wanting to drink in her essence, wanting her goodness to erase all the stains on my life, but knowing I could taint her with my darkness. "The night I left, my mother died. By her own hand."

Noelle gasped and pulled back, her eyes filled with tears. "But . . . she said your father killed her."

"He did, in a way. He had a falling out with Amaymon—their relationship had begun to deteriorate for some unknown reason—and he went on a rampage of destruction. He blamed me for all the trouble that he himself had brought upon his head. Since my presence seemed to make things worse, I left, running from my responsibilities rather than facing them as I should. I told myself that things would improve if I were not around to remind him of his failures, and caught up as I was in my own fight for survival, I left the region. My mother saw what I did not: the only way to end my father's reign of terror was to kill him. I was gone, so there was no one left to do the job but her. He was taken by surprise. I'd tried to kill him twice before, so he knew to expect an attack from me, but she . . . she loved him, loved him with every morsel of her being. And she used that love to give her strength to stop him when I couldn't, taking her own life as penance for such a mortal sin."

Noelle clutched me again, her fury at my father surprising me, almost as much as the love she felt for me. It sank into my pores like water on parched earth, easing much of the pain that had for so long been a part of my life. She loved me! She loved me, and I would do whatever it took to keep her safe.

"None of that, now," she said, pinching my shoulder. "Perhaps I love you. I'm not entirely sure. It could be just indigestion. But even if I do, it doesn't mean that I'm suddenly fragile, or vulnerable, or anything different from what I was before. In fact, it's just the opposite. As a Beloved, I won't age and die. So you can just stop thinking those protect-me-at-all-costs sorts of thoughts and go back to being parched earth, because I'm not going to let you run away any longer."

I sighed and shifted her off me, getting out of the bed to open the door. Johannes sat outside it, giving me a smug look.

I stared at him, the taste of Noelle's sweet lips still on my tongue. "You have the worst timing."

Johannes strolled past me, tail held high, observing Noelle with interest as she clutched the blankets to her chest. He started for her, but I swore and picked him up, marching him over to the bathroom despite his yowls of protest.

"Go ahead." I snarled at him as I flung open the bathroom door. "You dig your claws into me, and you can spend the next few days locked in there."

"Gray!" Noelle gasped, sliding out of bed, winding a blanket around herself as she ran over to where the cat was spitting and hissing, trying to bite and claw me. "I know your emotions are running high right now, but you shouldn't take them out on an innocent cat."

"Innocent cat?" I spun around, holding Johannes

at arm's length, ignoring the pain when his back claws found my arm. "You didn't let me finish my story, Beloved. You didn't let me tell you what happened to my father after my mother killed him."

Her eyes were confused as she looked from the spitting, snarling ball of fur to me. "What . . . I assume he died."

"No. My mother killed him. Mostly. Amaymon may have washed his hands of Johannes, but his good friend Ariton was there as well, and he swore to my mother that he would not rest until my father was returned in one form or other."

Noelle's mouth formed an O of surprise as she looked at the cat, now making a low, ugly growl, his teeth bared at her. "He's . . . you mean the cat . . ."

"I have neglected to make the proper introductions, haven't I? Beloved, meet Johannes Horal, my father."

Chapter Seven

They came when Noelle was least expecting them.

Never, she said to Gray as Raleigh stopped filming Miles in order to gawk with an open mouth at the two men who had strolled into the great hall as if they owned the place. *Never have I known a demon who had good timing.*

Demon? Despite their distance, Noelle could feel Gray's sudden spurt of fury. *They are there?*

Yes. "Hullo," Noelle told the two demons.

Teresa, standing near enough to overhear, looked startled at the sight of the interlopers.

"Mortals," one of the demons said with a dismissive sniff as it looked around the room.

Flee, Gray demanded, even as panic for her welfare flooded his anger. *Run, Beloved. Do not, under any circumstance, attempt to deal with them yourself.*

Grayson, I am a Guardian, she reassured him.

"The spirits of the Abbey are uneasy, and thus their emanations—what the devil is going on now?" Miles glared at the interruption. "Who are these people? Dammit, Teresa, this is the last straw! I will not have this meaningful, important work documenting the existence of the spirit world put in jeopardy by your insistence on hiring every man on the street you can find!"

You're also my Beloved, and these demons are after me. It's my duty and right to protect you from them. Now, get the hell out of there so I can protect you.

She sighed even as she made a quick assessment. Although there were a pair of them, they were fifth-class demons, far from harmless but easily handled, even in a situation where she would have to protect the film team from exposure to beings of an Other-world nature.

"I asked them here," she said quickly in response to Miles's question, moving toward the demons, using her body to shield the fact that she was drawing a protection ward on herself. "They're some . . . erm . . . people I work with."

One of the demons, the shorter of the two, squinted at her. "It's a Beloved," the demon told its partner. "The Dark One must be here."

"Did he have a Beloved?" the first demon asked. "He didn't the last time we saw him, did he?"

Beloved?

"Could be he did and hid her from us," the second answered.

"I don't remember her."

"Noelle, I'm sorry, but we can't have your friends on set," Teresa said, giving her an apologetic glance.

The short demon shrugged. "Who cares, so long as we find him?"

Noelle!

"Oh, look!" Noelle interrupted, staring with wide eyes at nothing and pointing down a narrow side hall. "It's Nosty! Is that a box he's holding? A bound box? The kind treasure is kept in?"

"Treasure?" Miles slid a suspicious, narrow-eyed look at the others in the room before laughing heartily. "Ha ha ha. Treasure! Such a clichéd notion, one that naturally doesn't exist, but perhaps the spirit of the monk Nostredame has something importance to share with me. Er . . . the audience. I will go and ascertain just what that might be."

I demand that you answer me, woman.

I love you, Gray.

Bah! I'm turning around right now and will be there in five minutes. You are not to speak to the demons.

"You'd better go with him," Noelle suggested to Raleigh. "You might get Nosty on film this time."

"Oooh, that's true," Teresa said, and with a meaningful nod toward the two demons heading toward Noelle, she ran after Raleigh.

Did you dump your father off at the vet?

Not yet, but I'm going to, just as soon as I get you to safety.

Really, Gray . . . Noelle spun around to face the demons just before they reached her, slapping them both with lightning-quick binding wards. *I think we need to talk some more about this plan of yours to have your father neutered.*

It's the least I can do, he growled. *I can't kill him, and I'll be damned if I'll let him roam around on his own, causing who knows what sort of havoc. At least this way, I'll have some satisfaction.*

"A Guardian." The taller demon snarled, its face contorting with rage. "The Beloved is a Guardian!"

Punitive gelding is never the answer, she pointed out with what she felt was perfect sense. "You are correct. Would you like to tell me your names so that we can do this quickly, or are you going to make me drag it out, causing you untold torment?"

The demons looked disconcerted for a moment, before the smaller one snarled an imprecation that was not only obscene in its nature but also physically impossible.

She sighed. "Well, I can't say I'm surprised, but if that's the way you want it . . ."

Three minutes later, Teresa returned to the hall. "Noelle, I really think—oh." She blinked and worried her lower lip at the sight that greeted her. "What . . . er . . . what is going on?"

"Oh, hullo again. Well, as it turns out, the two men who dropped by were troublemakers, and not my friends as I thought. They came here to disrupt the filming, but you needn't worry. I have everything under control. One of them has already departed. I was just persuading this fellow to do the same." Noelle smiled again, wondering if she should dare try a little mind push on Teresa to make her forget she'd ever seen the demon hanging there, cursing and all but frothing at the mouth in its anger. The problem was, she'd never been very good at making people do things, so she preferred to avoid such situations. "But I suppose this is one of those times," she said softly with a sigh to herself.

"Troublemaker or not, don't you think it's a little harsh hanging him by his feet?" Teresa asked, stepping quickly to the side when the demon lashed out toward her.

Noelle moved between the demon and Teresa, glaring at it even as she quickly drew a second restraining ward on it. "Actually, I don't, but there's no way I'm going to be able to explain the whole situation to you, so instead, I think you should go check on Miles."

"Explain what?"

"Nothing," Noelle said, turning back to her friend with a calm smile and a concentrated mental push. "There's nothing happening here. Go see if Miles needs you."

"Miles?" Teresa looked confused.

"He may need something, and you know how he gets if you're not dancing attendance on him." Noelle gave her another mental push, praying that would do the job.

"I suppose I should." Hesitantly, Teresa started to cross the hall.

Noelle wasted no time in spinning around to pin back the demon with a stern look, and she quickly spoke the words necessary to banish it back to its master.

The demon's scream of frustration as it was returned to Abaddon echoed off the vaulted ceiling at the exact moment that Gray, with a spitting and furious Johannes in his arms, dashed into the hall. "Noelle!"

"Hullo," she said, love swelling inside until it threatened to burst out of her. She was just so incredibly happy, she felt like singing a grand opera or something suitably epic.

"Are you all right?" Gray swore when Johannes sank his teeth deep into his hand before leaping from his arms and hightailing it for the door, which had been left open. Gray ignored the cat as he studied her face, his concern swamping her and making her feeling even happier.

"Of course I am. The you-know-whats are gone." Noelle nodded toward Teresa, who was standing with a confused look on her face in the hallway that led off the main room.

"A temporary situation, since they'll simply tell Amaymon where I am." Gray's expression was as flinty as . . . well, flint. "We'll have to leave immediately."

"Do I smell demon smoke?" Nostredame hove into view, looking around the room before his gaze settled on Gray. "Ah. That would explain the smoke. Is everything all right?"

"No. Go away," Gray said curtly.

"Well!" Nosty said with an injured sniff. "It doesn't take an anvil to strike me on the head to know when I'm not wanted."

"Gray's a little upset because he doesn't like Guardians," Noelle explained.

"That's not the slightest bit true!" Gray protested. "Quite the contrary. I approve of Guardians, as a whole. I believe they provide a valuable service. I like, nay, I cherish Guardians and clasp them to the bosom of my . . . er . . . bosom."

"I love how he talks," Noelle told Nosty in a confidential tone. "It's like watching someone on the telly."

"I do not talk like a mortal actor!"

"It's all that time he spent on his own," Nosty agreed, waggling his forefinger in a circle. "Made him a bit squirrel-brained."

Gray glared at the ghost, saying with great menace, "Either make yourself useful by finding where Johannes has run off to, or I'll make sure that you are bound to the privy for the rest of your unnatural life."

Nosty's eyes widened. "I'm more than happy to help you and the charming Noelle, of course. I've always prided myself on my helpfulness where it concerns your family. If you recall the time when you had abandoned the Abbey, I was the one who kept up interest in it by appearing at opportune moments to the locals, so I'm quite happy to help now when you need me—"

"Go find Johannes and bring him back here!" Gray bellowed, pointing dramatically at the front doors, open to allow sunlight to stream into the dusty depths of the hall.

Noelle eyed him as he turned toward her and strode the few remaining feet to where she stood in the center of the hall. His frown grew at the sight of the circle drawn in the dust on the floor. "You have every appearance of someone who is about to lecture me for doing my job, but I know you won't do that, because you are aware that I would never tell you how to do your job, and thus, you'd give me the same respect."

"Taking care of you is my job!"

Noelle thought about that for a few seconds. "I'm not sure if that is flattering or annoying. On the one hand, I appreciate the fact that you want to protect me, because no one has ever wanted to do that before, and it's kind of a nice feeling. But on the other hand, I am a Guardian, and handling demons is what I do. I think all things considered, I'm going to stick to being flattered."

Gray had taken a deep breath preparatory to what was obviously going to be a pithy response when movement caught his eye. He tilted his head toward

Teresa and asked, *What is she doing just standing there staring at the wall?*

I tried to mind-push her, but I think all it did was confuse her. She was supposed to leave the room, but my mind pushes have never been what they should be, so she wandered off to the entrance over there and looked really confused by everything. She'll snap out of it shortly, I imagine. My mind pushes never last.

It's neither here nor there to me. What I wish to discuss is the fact that you disregarded my demand that you wait for me to help take care of the demons.

"Smoke," Teresa said, looking around with a puzzled expression.

I sniffed. The hall was still redolent of the demon smoke generated by the banishing of the demons. "As I told you, it's my job. If you held all Guardians to the bosom of your bosom as you said you do, you should be happy that I'm one and can quite competently perform my job. Do you smell something?"

"Smoke," Teresa repeated, right on cue. She passed a hand over her face, rubbing her forehead. "I could have sworn . . ." Her voice trailed off to nothing as she turned toward them.

"It's demon smoke, nothing more," Gray told her before taking Noelle by the arms and giving them a squeeze. "I don't care one iota that you are a Guardian, except when you put yourself in danger on my behalf—"

"Smoke," Teresa said again, this time much more forcefully. "I smell smoke. Noelle, do you—"

"Fire!" Miles unceremoniously pushed Teresa out of the way and ran into the hall, gesticulating wildly. "The Abbey is on fire! Everyone must leave immediately!"

"It's not on fire, that's simply smoke from . . . erm . . . another source," Gray told the frantic man, who was trying to shoo them all toward the front door.

"Don't be ridiculous, man, the whole place is about to go up in flames," Miles insisted, shoving Teresa toward the door before turning to Noelle. "It's as dry as a tinderbox here!"

"Miles, you're overreacting to nothing," Noelle said soothingly, even as she thought at Gray, *He really is such a drama queen.*

That's not all he is.

Noelle giggled in his mind, about to explain to Miles that the smoke he saw and smelled was nothing more than theatrical smoke, when a dark shape loomed up in the doorway.

"Where is he?"

The voice boomed across the hall with the impact of a bulldozer, causing not only the lamps nearest him to shatter but also several pieces of quite pretty crown molding to crumble and fall to the floor with deadened thuds. Gray stiffened for a moment before flinging himself at the man. Noelle, recognizing the aura that surrounded the stranger, yelled a warning and hastily slapped a protection ward on Gray when he reached his target.

"And just in time, too," she murmured as she watched Gray go flying across the room, wincing when he slammed into the wall, leaving a Gray-shaped smear as he slowly slid down the wood paneling to the floor. *Tell me you're not going to be prone to throwing yourself at demon lords, because if you are, we're going to have a very hard life.*

Gray moaned groggily in her mind as she helped him to his feet. *Stand back, Noelle. That's Amaymon, the demon lord who laid the vitiation upon me.*

So I gathered. That doesn't mean it's a smart thing for you to lunge at him. Demon lords tend to get snappish about that sort of thing.

"Where is he?" Amaymon demanded again as he strolled into the room, his aura blackish blue, little tendrils of which sparked with energy. He was a large man, not overly tall but heavily built, with black hair, dark eyes, and an unremarkable face . . . but even so, there was something about him that raised the hairs on Noelle's arms, warning her that he was the possessor of more power than she would ever wield.

"He's here," Noelle said, standing in front of Gray, her mind calm even if her heart was racing with fear and apprehension. "But if you're intending on doing something more to him, you should be aware that I'm a Guardian, and his Beloved, and I'll do whatever it takes to protect him."

Woman! You will cease trying to hide me. I am the Dark One, you are the Beloved. You will hide behind me, where you belong!

"Seriously?" Noelle asked when Gray tried to shove her behind him. "You're going to stand by that 'where you belong' comment? You wouldn't like to reconsider it before I have to explain to you the many, many ways that is so incredibly wrong?"

"What's a Guardian?" Teresa asked, moving a bit closer to Raleigh, who had been on Miles's heels. "Is this another of your friends, Noelle?"

We will discuss the issue later, Beloved. Until then, you will do as I say.

Noelle snorted in his mind. *Gray, I may love you, but that doesn't mean I've suddenly lost all my wits. You've indulged in the macho he-man stuff for long enough, so let's move on to the part of the day where you help me bargain with Amaymon.*

"Hello! Has everyone gone mad? The bloody house is on fire! We have to get everyone out. Now." Miles started to grab for Noelle, but a glare from Gray had him doing an about-face and more or less hustling Raleigh and Teresa out the door.

Bargain with him? Are you insane? He's a demon lord!

One who no doubt has a price. We just need to find out what that is.

"You are his Beloved?" Amaymon considered Noelle briefly before narrowing his gaze on Gray. "I know you."

"Well, I should hope you do, after all that you've done to him. No, it's all right, Teresa, you and Raleigh and Miles should probably leave the house. We're just going to have a wee little chat with this . . . erm . . .

with Gray's business acquaintance. Perhaps you should call the fire department while you're out there?"

"I don't like to leave you here," Teresa said, her face puckered with worry. "Fires can be dangerous in old buildings like this."

"We're fine. We're just a few steps away from the door, and if we see any sign of a fire, we'll leave immediately, all right?"

"I don't like it, but all right." Reluctantly, Teresa and Raleigh exited.

"It's not all right at all. You stupid woman, what part of 'the house is on fire and is going to fall down around your dense ears' escapes you?" Miles asked, storming toward Noelle. "I insist that you leave immediately."

"You are Johannes's son, the one who has drained my valuable resources for the last four hundred years," Amaymon said, his aura increasing.

Although Noelle knew that most mundane people couldn't see auras, they could feel them in close proximity, and when Miles passed the demon lord, a couple of the tendrils of power snaked out to sting him.

He yelped and leaped to the side, rubbing his arm while exclaiming, "A manifestation! I've felt a manifestation right here in the hall! The spirits are clearly restless, and they know the house will soon be destroyed and us with it. We must all leave!"

"No one is stopping you," Noelle told him, making shooing gestures. "We're fine. Although your little freak-out is getting kind of annoying. Isn't it, Gray?"

Gray didn't answer, being involved in a stare-off with Amaymon. "Yes, I am Johannes's son, the one you vitiated on his behalf."

Amaymon looked downright annoyed. "That's right, it was Johannes who demanded I do that. *Peste!* I knew he was trouble. I should have killed him when I had the chance. Instead, I gave in to his pleas to allow his potential the opportunity to ripen, and look how that ended. It cost me four hundred years of squandering resources by sending countless minions to track your movements, and for what purpose? It's all very irritating."

"If anyone has the right to be irritated, it's me," Gray protested. "I'm the one who has had to be on the run for all that time lest your minions find me. The blame for any squandering lies squarely on your head, thank you very much."

"You could have stopped it at any time by simply staying in one place," Amaymon answered.

"And let your minions hack off my head? I think not."

"They had much more important things to do than to give in to a pleasure trip. You, female, summon your Dark One," Amaymon told Noelle. "I would have my jeton returned to me."

Noelle glanced at Gray. *Er . . . what was that about the minions having more important things to do?*

I don't know, but he obviously thinks you are Johannes's Beloved, not mine. Gray's mind was forming and discarding all sorts of speculations. "Noelle is my Beloved, not my father's. As for this jeton you speak of, I have no knowledge of it."

What's a jeton?

I haven't the slightest idea.

"What exactly is a jeton?" Noelle asked Amaymon before leaning into Gray and pinching his side. *You're immortal and have lived a long time. You're supposed to know archaic things like that.*

I do not have the memory of an elephant, Noelle. I do occasionally forget things, especially if it's something I have no reason to recall for four hundred years.

"Fine, we'll all just stand here chatting while we burn to death," Miles said, throwing himself into a chair, coughing at the resultant cloud of dust. He waved casually toward the hallway leading off the main room. "I'll let you all know when I see actual flames, shall I?"

"Who is Johannes's Beloved?" Amaymon asked, ignoring both Noelle's question and Miles.

"He doesn't have one."

Amaymon's eyes narrowed on Gray. "There was a woman, a mortal—"

"My mother. She died when he did."

The demon lord's mouth tightened. "It matters not. Summon him to my presence."

"I like you," Miles told Amaymon in a chatty tone.

"You know how to deal with people. I'm going to have to use that line. Assuming we survive the fire that is even now bearing down on us, of course."

Gray?

If you're going to ask me if I'm thinking of handing over my father to Amaymon, the answer is, you're damned right I am.

Actually, I was going to ask if you thought we could use this jeton, whatever it is, to bargain with.

Gray stopped dwelling, with much enjoyment, on the act of handing Johannes over to Amaymon and mulled that thought over. *You mean, to lift the vitiation?*

Yes. He seems to want it quite badly. I mean, demon lords don't come into the mortal plain very often, since it costs them so much power to do so and leaves their legions vulnerable in Abaddon. So for Amaymon to come to see us himself says that this whatever-it-is that your father has is something he very much wants.

"What does the jeton look like?" Gray asked, crossing his arms over his chest and donning a nonchalant expression.

"Bring Johannes," Amaymon demanded again.

"If you tell us what the jeton is, perhaps we can find it without bothering to track down Johannes. Not that I'd mind bringing him to have a chat with you, because that would be something I'd likely enjoy greatly, but time is of the essence."

"It is a valuable token of my power! It needs no description!"

"Valuable, hmm?" Noelle turned to Gray. "Could it be hidden in the priest's hole?"

"What?" Miles suddenly sat up straight in his chair. "What . . . uh . . . priest hole?"

"There's one here, behind the fireplace," Noelle answered him, gesturing toward the far wall. "Could it be there, Gray?"

"There's nothing there but a few things of little value to anyone but family," Gray answered, shaking his head.

"Why don't we go look? Maybe it's there." Noelle started to cross the hall but stopped short when Miles leaped from his chair, a shiny black gun in his hand.

"Right, I've had enough of this farce. I don't know who he is or what he wants, but if he thinks he's getting my treasure, he's barking mad. You, you say you know where the priest hole is? Go open it."

"Oh, Miles, now is not the time for this," Noelle told him, exasperated that he had chosen this moment to continue his ridiculous treasure hunt.

"Do it," Miles told Gray, leveling the gun at Noelle. "Or I shoot her."

"That will serve no purpose," Gray said in a calm, apparently unconcerned voice.

Noelle knew otherwise. She could feel the anger in him at Miles's daring to turn a firearm upon her.

It's all right. He can't kill me, can he?

No. The Joining may not be wholly complete, but you are enough of my Beloved that a simple gunshot would do little to harm you.

Then stop thinking about stringing him up by his testicles and stay focused on the important matter at hand.

But I'm enjoying thinking about stringing him up by his nuts.

I know you are, and I admit, it is a tempting thought, but he's really nothing more than greedy and irritating and thus not really deserving of testicle-hanging.

You have no sense of adventure, Gray told her sternly, which just made her giggle at him. He strode over to the fireplace, pressing on a few ornate wooden wolf's heads that lined the mantel, gesturing when the panel alongside the fireplace slid back to reveal a darkened hole.

"Step back," Miles ordered, gesturing toward Noelle with the gun. "All the way across the room."

"You seem to forget who owns this house," Gray answered. "This is my priest's hole, and anything in it—not that there is anything—is mine."

"Take one more step toward it, and I'll shoot," Miles warned, turning the gun on him.

He really is such a drama queen, Noelle told Gray. I hate to admit it, but he's absolutely perfect for Teresa's show.

"That would be unwise in the extreme," Gray said, and stepped into the darkened hole.

Noelle knew the second before Miles pulled the trigger that he was going to shoot Gray, and despite the fact that she knew the shot would not kill him, despite all of her training, despite everything she'd ever learned while working with members of the Otherworld, a primitive part of her brain had her rushing forward to stop the attack.

"No!" she screamed, and flung herself on Miles,

her eyes widening in shock when a burning pain seared through her side.

Gray roared her name as the world seemed to spin around her, her legs suddenly feeling as if they were made of tofu.

He shot me, she told Gray, even as she was whisked off her feet. *He really shot me. Oh! You have your soul back! How nice. I think I'm going to faint. Do you mind?*

Not at all, he answered, and, happy despite the burning sensation that seemed to sweep over her entire body, she smiled as she gave in to the swoon.

Chapter Eight

"Are you sure you're all right now?"

"Absolutely. It was just the shock of actually being shot. But I'm fine now. You can untie Miles. He doesn't look very comfortable with that rope tied around his feet and neck. His face is bright red."

"He'll survive," Gray said, his face filled with grim satisfaction when he glanced at the man who lay bound at her feet. He rose and helped Noelle from her chair.

"If this little comedy is concluded?" Amaymon asked politely, but it was politeness edged with razor sharpness. "Bring me the jeton."

Gray met her gaze and then, with a little shrug, reentered the priest's hole, emerging a few seconds later covered in cobwebs but empty-handed.

"It's not there." He turned to Amaymon. "What does the jeton look like?"

Amaymon's jaw worked for a few seconds before he answered. "It is a small disc, about the size of a human fingernail, made of gold, and stamped on either side with my symbol of power."

Noelle drew in a deep breath. *The collar tag! He's talking about Johannes's collar tag.*

I remember now. Shortly before he died, Johannes gloated that he had a token of immense promise, one that would have beings everywhere bowing down to him because of who it represented. He led me to believe it was a statue, though. That sly old—Gray bit back an obscenity.

"What will you give us for this jeton?" Noelle asked, ignoring Gray's soft noise of irritation. "Will you exchange it for the removal of the vitiation on Gray?"

To her complete surprise, the demon lord waved a dismissive hand. "I care little for the squabble between a father and a son. The vitiation was useful only in finding the location of Johannes, since he was bound to you, Dark One. Give me the jeton, and I will remove the curse."

He never really wanted you. Noelle gave a little laugh. *It was your father he was after all along.*

He could have told me that! Gray snapped before saying aloud, "We accept. It will take me some little time to locate Johannes."

"I do not have any more time to waste on this. I have spent four hundred years waiting for my minions to recover the jeton. Bring it to me now, or I will simply take it and leave the vitiation as it is."

Miles grunted and made a few choking noises.

I think you're going to have to do something about him. Noelle nodded toward the bound man.

What would you like? I could sit on him, if he's annoying you.

How about cutting the rope that's choking him?

Why would I want to do that?

Because, my darling, he is the one responsible for your soul being returned. If he hadn't shot you, I wouldn't have reacted as I did, and that sacrifice is what completed the Joining and gave you back your soul. So, really, we owe him quite a bit.

Gray, with a tsk of irritation, flipped open a pocket knife and slit the hog-tie rope.

"Now, look here." Noelle addressed Amaymon, prepared to argue as long as it took to get him to see reason, which, upon reflection, might be decades, if not centuries, but luckily, at that moment, Nosty strolled into the door with a big orange cat in his arms.

"Found him! He was trying to get through the wards that someone drew on the front gate—mother of God! Demon lord!"

Nosty turned white, dropped Johannes, and, with a quick apologetic look at Gray, vanished into nothing.

"You almost killed me!" Miles gasped after he had

enough air in his lungs to speak again. He rolled over onto his back and glared at Gray. "You murdering bastard!"

"Johannes!"

Amaymon bellowed the name with such force that Noelle stumbled backward a few steps. Gray quickly wrapped an arm around her, holding her tight, as Johannes, his back arched and his mouth open in a silent hiss of fury, looked wildly around the room for an escape.

"Return to me the jeton which you stole!" Amaymon demanded, closing in on the cat. He raised his hand, power snapping and crackling around it.

Do something. Noelle prodded Gray.

What? Hold Johannes steady so Amaymon can smite him?

He's your father! You can't let him be destroyed right in front of us.

Why not? He destroyed my mother's life, not to mention mine. He deserves everything that is coming to him.

I agree, but let fate punish him, not Amaymon.

Gray sighed even as he strode forward, snatching up Johannes and whisking the leather collar over the cat's head. *You're not going to let me have any fun, are you?*

On the contrary, you're going to have so much fun you'll—

Get down on my knees every morning and thank the gods that you found me? he finished, laughing in her head.

Every morning and every night.

I accept your terms. "I take it that you didn't give this to Johannes to show he was high in your favor, as he claimed at the time?" Gray asked as he tossed the collar with its attached gold tag to the demon lord.

Amaymon looked with satisfaction at the disc, ripping it from the collar. "I did not. He has never held my favor, let alone earned this token. He stole it from one of my wrath demons." He flung the collar to the ground, glaring at the cat for a few seconds before turning toward the door.

"Hold on just one second," Noelle said quickly, coming forward to stand next to Gray, who was glaring down at the spitting, hissing ball of fur and claws in his hands. If the demon lord thought he could just walk out without fulfilling his part of the deal, he could just think again. "The vitiation?"

Amaymon paused, rolled his eyes, but turned back to draw an intricate symbol in the air that glowed black, then silver, before dissolving into nothing. "It is removed. Keep your father away from me, lest I regret my generosity in allowing you all to live."

"Generosity." Noelle snorted as Amaymon left the hall. "Without help from his minions, he doesn't have that sort of power in the mortal world."

"I'll get you both. See if I don't!" Miles snarled, spittle flying from his mouth as he scrabbled around helplessly on the floor. "You'll never work in television again!"

"Well, that's disappointing," Noelle said, patting the still-hissing Johannes on his head. "Still, the day hasn't been a total loss. I've had the experience of being shot and fainting, which I've never done before, and Gray has his soul back, thanks to you, Miles, and of course, the vitiation is gone, so we won't have to move every couple of weeks and can live here instead. Nosty will be thrilled with the company. I'll have to find someone to take over my portal in England, but I think that can be arranged. And now, I believe that a celebration is in order."

Gray smiled at her, his lovely eyes shining with so much love it took her breath away. "I couldn't agree more. Let me first lock this monster up in the priest's hole, and we can retire to my room, where I will celebrate you until your eyes roll back in your head and you can't do any more than lift a wan hand in praise of my manly prowess."

Noelle giggled. "I have a better idea of where we can leave Johannes so he won't get into any trouble."

"I swear by all that is holy that I will have my vengeance—you're leaving? You can't just leave me here like this! I demand that you untie me!"

As they strolled out the front door, Teresa ran up to Noelle. "Oh, there you are. I was just coming to get you. The fire trucks are at the gate, but we don't have the key to open the lock."

"The fire turned out to be nothing but Miles trying to get everyone out of the house so he could search the priest's hole for nonexistent treasure," Noelle told her as Gray dug into his pocket and handed Teresa a set of keys.

"Really?" Teresa frowned. "That's an underhanded thing to do. Although . . . I wonder if we could get a few shots of the halls filled with smoke. That would be very atmospheric. Where is Miles, speaking of him?"

"Inside," Gray answered, and reached into his pocket again, extracting his pocket knife and handing it to Raleigh.

"Er . . ." the cameraman said, gingerly taking it.

"It's a long story. Right now, we have to rehome Gray's cat. See you later," Noelle told them, taking Gray's hand.

"If you're going where I think you're going—" Gray started to say.

"It's the perfect answer, really, don't you think? Who better to watch over your father than your mother? Plus, she's lonely, Gray. Not that she'll continue to be now that we are going to move in, but still, having Johannes there will give her a reason to live. So to speak. And just think of what a fine sense of justice this is going to give her! He'll be dependent on her for everything."

Johannes howled, an unearthly, tormented howl that wasn't in the least bit feline.

Noelle watched with pleasure some ten minutes later, as Gray, for the first time since the vitiation had been bound upon him during that fateful night several hundred years before, was able to see his mother. She swallowed back a painful lump of tears as the two of them stared at each other for a few seconds, before Joan opened her arms and Gray clasped her to his chest.

"It really is the most touching scene," Noelle told Johannes, who continued to yowl and attempt to escape but was powerless to do so wrapped up in Gray's jacket. "You're very lucky. We both are, really. You get to be with your son and the woman who gave up her life for you, and I finally get to be a Beloved to someone who honestly wants me in his life."

I don't just want you, my love, I need you. You brought me more than just my soul—you brought me my mother's forgiveness, and salvation, and most of all, you gave me happiness in the form of a feisty, red-haired little nun.

Noelle smiled as Gray turned, his arm around the semitranslucent form of his mother. "Yes, indeed, we are lucky," she said softly, rubbing her chin on Johannes's head as she gazed with love at the man who gave her everything she wanted. "Now, about that visit to the vet—"

The birds, which had now returned to the trees around the derelict cottage after several hundred years, squawked in protest at the feline screech that filled the air.

Undead Sublet

Molly Harper

Beware of Jesting Vegetables

1

In retrospect, I should have known something was wrong when the arugula started telling knock-knock jokes.

Leafy greens rarely had a sense of humor. And yet there I was, standing in the bustling kitchen of my busy Chicago restaurant, watching the vegetables on the prep table perform their own vaudeville act.

When confronted by the comedic stylings of salad ingredients, most people would have maybe called it a night, taken a sick day. A normal person would have done exactly that. I was willing to admit that now, exiled from my kitchen and the city that I loved to the wilds of western Kentucky.

My only excuse was sheer exhaustion. The restaurant, Coda, had been overbooked since it opened four years before, far beyond even the wildest expectations of the owners. Six months in, the executive chef quit in a very loud, very public snit over farm-grown oysters, which I still didn't understand, so I'd been promoted to the head position on the fly. Changes I'd made to the menu caught the attention of some reviewers, which brought even more people through the door. The owners offered me a 5 percent share of the business because I'd been working eighteen-hour days for nearly three years and hadn't yet called the labor board. Even when I did manage to get a night off, some crisis would call me back into the kitchen, and before I knew it, I'd worked twenty-one days without a break.

I started making stupid mistakes, confusing sea bass with turbot and mistiming pasta. It was all fixable, but in my head, the mistakes compounded and made me a nervous, double-checking wreck. And yet I still kept up the schedule, only coming home to collapse for a few hours before rising again to scour the supplier markets for ingredients. Chefs who slept in missed the freshest produce and the choicest cuts of meat.

I ignored the signs that I was overworked every time I looked in the mirror. My hair was dark and thick but hung in a limp cloud around my face. It had no luster, no life. My skin was pale, pasty, and drawn. While I had a passably pert nose, my lips were far too wide and my blue eyes too large for my face, which was emphasized as my cheekbones became more prominent and the dark undereye circles spread.

I lost weight that I couldn't really afford to lose. I was short and small-boned but what one briefly employed busboy charmingly referred to as "stacked like hell." As if I needed another reason for men not to take me seriously in the kitchen, the distraction of an above-average rack meant I had to work that much harder, which led to more hours, which led to my interactions with giggling vegetables.

On top of the sleep deprivation, my vacation to London had been canceled because the restaurant's business manager, Phillip, booked a high-profile vintner's dinner for that week, deciding that I "wouldn't mind" putting off my trip for another year. That same manager, who also happened to be my ex-boyfriend, had asked me for "space" three months earlier and then had gotten engaged to the woman who cleaned his teeth. Who also happened to be his ex-girlfriend, something I didn't find out until after their engagement. No wonder he spent all that time flossing. And because I worked such insane hours, the chances of meeting a new man I was attracted to and didn't work with—trust me, I'd learned my lesson there—were practically nil. My rent was going up again, just as I was getting close to saving enough for a down payment on a townhouse. So if I wanted to buy my own home anytime soon, I was going to have to work more hours.

More. Hours.

I was contemplating how to bend the space-time continuum to make this possible, when the arugula shouted, "Knock knock!" When I answered, "Who's there?" that seemed to upset my coworkers. Joining the veggies in a full-on George Burns soft-shoe ensured Tess Maitland's place in the chronicles of "chefs who publicly flipped their shit."

The room tilted under my feet like a ship's deck, leaving me seasick and dizzy. I heard the disembodied voice of my mentor, Chef John Gamling, telling me that my hollandaise was gelatinous swill not fit to dress a McMuffin, which was weird, because I hadn't made hollandaise sauce that night. I tried to argue that I had people to do that for me, but then I collapsed on the floor in a heap.

And that's when the paramedics showed up.

Phillip, the ex-slash-manager, "strongly encouraged" me to take some time off. I said, fine, I would take the weekend. And then he made a noise in his throat that made it clear that two days was not what he had in mind. And then he used the word "sabbatical," which was international culinary code for "lost her fricking mind."

We cooks liked to pretend that our exiled brethren were touring northern Italy or southern France, collecting recipes and refining pastry techniques. But "on sabbatical" usually meant they were drying out in a facility called Promises or Sunrises or some such thing.

I responded by inviting Phillip to commit indecent acts upon himself with a lemon zester. Phillip suspended me without pay for six weeks, which was, I felt, an overreaction. By the time a dishwasher drove me home, the urge to sing and dance with garnishes had worn off. I sat in my living room, staring at the blank beige walls, and I got pissed.

"Coda" meant a satisfying conclusion—the slow build of a good meal brought to a delicious climax. Phillip had come up with the name. He could be a pretentious prick, but he knew about branding. Where was my coda? I loved my work. That kitchen was my life. But was I supposed to work myself into delirious zombiehood and then collapse dead on my stove?

The fact was, I needed a break. I needed to rest, to sleep, to have conversations with people that did not involve butter-fat ratios. I needed to get as far from Coda as possible so I wouldn't get sucked back into the kitchen and into that compulsive vortex of crazy. I made some arrangements online, packed a few essentials, and drove to Half-Moon Hollow, Kentucky, the only place I thought I'd get a welcome. Also, I may or may not have driven to Phillip's apartment and thrown a honey ricotta cheesecake at his front door.

Chef Gamling and his life partner, George, had retired to Kentucky a year before to be near George's family. Chef, my mentor in culinary school, was the only family I'd had in a long time. Never one to tolerate martyrs or kitchen drama, Chef had assigned himself the task of "whipping me back into shape."

Knowing Chef as I did, it was possible he would use a wire whisk.

So there I stood, on a dirt driveway in the middle of nowhere, outside the two-bedroom farmhouse I'd rented from late September to late October. It looked as if someone had been building a sturdy little farmhouse and at the last minute decided that Victorian gingerbread and frills were an absolute necessity. The house was halfway to restored, with recently painted lemon yellow siding and bleached white trim. But there were no flowers in the yard, no silly wind chimes laced through the gingerbread eaves, and I found that sort of sad. There were carefully mulched beds surrounding the house, but no one had bothered to plant anything in them. The house seemed ancient but somehow half-finished, a pall of failure hanging over it like real estate B.O.

I would fit right in.

My landlady, Lindy Clemson, had placed the house on a rental site after she and her husband filed for divorce. She'd told me she wanted to get some income out of it before she put it on the market in late October, when the divorce was finalized. Lindy seemed nice enough, if a little tightly wound. It was a real stroke of luck finding a landlord willing to rent for a term as short as one month, particularly in such a small town.

I heaved a sigh and adjusted the messenger bag on my shoulder, blowing the stick-straight dark brown hair from my face. Resolved, I tugged open the rear door of my SUV and hauled out my suitcases and boxes of kitchen equipment. The thought of using someone else's pots, pans, and knives was just ridiculous. I'd also packed coolers with the contents of my fridge—organic eggs, cheeses from Meroni's, asparagus from Sal (my asparagus guy), and enough wine to sink a ship. And of course, my travel-sized spice kit.

None of the food talked to me during the drive, which I took as a good sign.

Unpacking didn't take long. I hadn't brought many clothes, and I left my pans and knives in their special linen wrappings in the packing boxes. I explored the house, but once you got past living room, kitchen, dining-room-turned-office, two bedrooms, and bath, there wasn't much to discover. The basement, Lindy had explained, was being used to store her ex's belongings and wouldn't be accessible under my rental agreement.

The rooms were clean but bare. Lindy had left only the most basic of furnishings, the kind of stuff older relatives pawn off on college students and newlyweds: an old brown plaid couch, a sprung pleather Barcalounger, a chipped pressed-wood coffee table. Not to mention the bold brass and black laminate dining-room table that may have belonged to a villain on Miami Vice.

A few pictures decorated the walls, but squares of unfaded wallpaper revealed where other frames had hung. Other rooms were freshly painted or, like the pretty little kitchen with its cheerful white and blue tile, had recently been refloored. The house smelled pleasantly of linseed oil and sawdust. I explored the rooms, pleased to find the odd window seat or corner bookshelf here and there.

While I was happy with the house, it didn't matter much. I could live without cubbies and comforts. I just wanted to do my time "on sabbatical" and get back to the city to reclaim my life.

The main problem was, without the grinding routine of the restaurant, I had no flipping clue what to do with myself. There was TV, but it only had basic cable, and I didn't feel like sitting down for the farm report. I hadn't thought to bring any books with me, and the only selections to be found in the house were a bunch of John Jakes paperbacks. I wasn't even hungry. Ever since "The Incident," my stomach fought against anything but chamomile tea and toast. So I did something I hadn't done in almost ten years: I treated myself to more than four hours of sleep.

I put fresh sheets on the lumpy little double bed in the master bedroom, pulled the shades tight, and went to bed at 7:30 P.M. I slept deep and dreamless, even with the occasional creak of the house settling against a backdrop of blissful country silence.

The first order of business the next morning was to drop by my landlady's office with my deposit and rent for the month, then to visit Chef Gamling. It shocked me to find that Chef Gamling was well and truly retired. Like most of his students, I believed he would die with a spatula in one hand and an unruly saucier's collar in the other. Now he ambled around his house all day in yoga pants while George taught chemistry at the community college. He was taking up gardening and painting abstract watercolor landscapes that looked like extremely depressing Rorschach blots.

George, a sweet man with fading cornsilk-colored hair and shoulders as broad as a barn, insisted I was too skinny from the moment I walked through the door of their cute little ranch house. Before ushering me to the back porch, George loaded me down with a bowl of something called monkey bread (a local specialty, I assumed). It was basically blobs of biscuit dough shoved into a Bundt pan and doused in caramel syrup. I don't believe monkey was an actual ingredient. I didn't want to ask.

I think this lump of sucrose-soaked carbs was supposed to serve as a comforting buffer for when Chef lowered the boom on me. It did not work.

"Any proper student of mine would know better," Chef growled without preamble, glaring down from his easel, a paintbrush hanging loose in his hand. Chef was a stocky, mustachioed bull of a man with salt-and-pepper hair and deceptively steely gray eyes. And because I knew he loved me and I deserved the ass chewing, I contritely sipped iced tea, trying not to feel like an ill-behaved third-grader called to the principal's office. The hint of a German accent made the admonishments seem even sterner than he intended.

"A chef must be sharp, reacting to a multitude of crises with calm and confidence. In order to do that, you need rest and proper meals. Did I not tell all of my students that ignoring your body's basic needs was a one-way ticket to addiction, exhaustion, and disaster? How are you to maintain quality and prevent mistakes if you can't remember orders? What good are you to your staff if you have run yourself down like a soggy dishrag? How are staff to respect you if you are singing and dancing like the puppet show—what's it called, with the chicken and the vampire?"

"*Sesame Street?*" I suggested.

"Yes, *Sesame Street.*"

"I don't think Big Bird is a chicken," I grumbled petulantly.

"Yes, I'm so sorry. You clearly have the expertise in performing figments of one's imagination. And sassy-mouthing your mentor."

"You're going to make me peel potatoes again, aren't you?" I groaned.

Chef Gamling did not, in fact, make me peel potatoes, as he would have when I made a stupid mistake in school. He gave me several Tupperware containers full of his special *maultaschen*, a German dumpling dish that he only made for me when I was sick in school.

His eyes softened as I bobbled the containers. "I worry about you, *süße*." My throat caught at his rare use of a German endearment. He pinched my cheek gently, as if gauging how much weight I'd lost over the last year. "I don't hear from you in months, and you show up at my door looking like this? Pale, skinny, big dark circles under your eyes. You look like you're going to drop at any moment. And George is no good with first aid."

"You wouldn't be performing mouth-to-mouth on me in the 'dropping' scenario?" I asked, squinting up at him.

He shook his head and hugged me fiercely. "I have heard the foul words that mouth is capable of producing. Lips that dirty shall never touch mine."

"Hey, you were the one who told the female students that professional chefs 'often season the food with salty language,' so we couldn't afford to become ladylike and offended."

"Yes, but I didn't expect you to embrace the concept so wholeheartedly." He sighed.

And so I was instructed to go home, sleep, eat, and then sleep again. If I didn't finish the *maultaschen* within three days, he was going to add malted milkshakes to my "regimen." Also, I was supposed to meet him at the HMH First Baptist Church the next Saturday. The last time I'd seen the inside of a church, a funeral was involved, so this was not a good sign.

George caught me on my way out of the house and gave me a tire-sized chunk of monkey bread to call my very own. I couldn't help but accept it, because the gesture was so sweet. So very, very sweet.

George was a veritable font of information about local quirks and perks. When he heard where I was staying, he'd clapped his hands together like a little kid and demanded to know all of the details. When I gave him nothing but a confused smile, he told me that "the Lassiter place" had quite a reputation. "Everybody knew" that the house was rife with ghostly lights and strange noises. Before Lindy's husband bought the place, teenagers used to sneak out to the property and dare each other to knock on the door and call out for the original owner, John Lassiter.

"You're saying my house is haunted?" I asked.

"More like cursed," George told me. "Ever since poor John Lassiter built it for his wife-to-be in 1900. He was one of those confirmed bachelors who suddenly decide to get married in their fifties. His fiancée was young and fickle. Elizabeth Early didn't really want to marry John, so she kept finding reasons that the house wasn't ready. She wanted the kitchen to be east-facing, she wanted a water closet, she wanted gingerbread and bits of flotsam all over the eaves. Finally, her father put his foot down and told her to quit stalling and put poor John out of his misery. The morning of their wedding, they woke up to find Elizabeth had run off with a peddler."

"Tacky."

"But effective," George conceded. "John never heard from her again. He died a few years later, alone in that little house. He could have sold it. There were plenty of young men who would have given him good money for a pretty house to offer their brides. But he wouldn't budge. He didn't want a happy couple living in his house when he was so alone. And ever since he died, any couple who has lived together in that place has either died or had a marriage so miserable they wished they were dead."

"So there's no such thing as divorce in backwoods ghost stories?" I deadpanned.

"Laugh all you want, smartass. The only reason you're renting the house is that Lindy Clemson's husband died unexpectedly. It's cursed, I tell you."

"Lindy told me she was getting a divorce."

George blanched, as if he regretted revealing the information. He cleared his throat. "Well, in her case, it's a little bit of both."

"How could it possibly be both?"

"Things are different here, honey. This is Kentucky."

"Oh, fine, so my house is cursed." I sighed. "What are the terms?"

"Terms?"

"Every curse has terms. You know, sleep a hundred years and kiss a prince, you're in the clear, that sort of thing. So what did John want from the couples who lived in his house? How can they get back in his good graces?"

"I don't think he set any terms."

I sniffed. "Well, then it's more of a jinx than a curse."

"Semantics."

"I will try not to provoke the spirits of the epically lovelorn while I'm in town," I promised.

"See that you don't, sweetie."

The Travel Wok—
When Pepper Spray Just Won't Do

2

There it was again!

The soft thump down the hall had me sitting up in bed, blinking into the black quiet of my room. My sleep-blurred brain tumbled to George, his stories about poor, lovelorn Mr. Lassiter, and the possibility that said deceased bachelor could be wandering around my house in spectral form.

This was what I got for going to bed so early. My internal clock was all wonky. Thoroughly chastised and toting Tupperware and a bowling-ball-sized chunk of monkey bread, I'd found myself back in my house with nothing to do. No dishes to prep. Nothing to chop or sauté. No pans to wash. No knives to sharpen.

The highlight of the evening was tripping and falling flat on my face as soon as I walked into the living room. The coffee table seemed . . . off. I remembered it being a little farther away from the couch. Then again, I was still adjusting to, well, everything, so who was I to think I'd already mentally mapped the living room?

I settled for more sleep. It seemed the more I slept, the more I needed to sleep. My body had been running on fumes for so long it was as if it was soaking up all the rest it could because I couldn't be trusted to sleep decently again when I went back to my life. The house was so quiet, a far cry from the traffic noises and sirens that bounced around my city apartment. I didn't need a white-noise machine here. The silence of the house seemed to wrap around me like a sweet cocoon, helping me ignore my ailing stomach and table bruises.

The only hitch in my "sleep the month away" plan was that the extreme quiet made every creak, every groan, of every board echo like a gunshot. I didn't know much about old houses, but it seemed this one spent a lot of time settling. At times, it almost sounded like footsteps falling softly against the hardwood floors—ridiculous, as I'd triple-checked the locks myself, a habit I'd carried with me from Chicago.

The Clemsons' debris was strewn across the house like broken toys. Lindy left a bunch of men's plaid flannels and Clemson Construction T-shirts in the closet. A manly bar of plain yellow Dial still occupied the little soap dish in the master bath. When I opened the coat closet, I had to dive out of the way to avoid the avalanche of blueprints and graph paper that came tumbling from the top shelf.

And now, on top of these depressing relics, I had to deal with things that went bump in the night? I tilted my head, like a dog listening for its master, and it happened again. The weird noise echoed down the hall. It didn't sound like the house creaking. This time, it really did sound like footsteps, distinct movements on the floor. As if someone was walking around in the kitchen.

Slowly, my hand slid down the side of the mattress, reaching for the Louisville Slugger I kept under the bed in my apartment. But of course, it wasn't there. Why would I bring a weapon to a nice, safe country cottage?

Something in the other room hit the floor with a muted thud, sending a cold, watery flash through my belly. I'd seen *Straw Dogs*. I knew this scenario wouldn't end well for the out-of-towner.

I jumped out of bed, carefully moving to close the door with a soft click. I leaned against it, both palms pressed to the wood, as if my scrawny self could be any kind of barricade. Forcing myself to take slow, deep breaths, I stepped into my sneakers and a hoodie.

Options! I barked at my brain. *Give me options. You can panic later.*

I needed to call 911. But Lindy had taken all of the landline phones with her when she'd moved out. My cell phone? In my bag, on the TV table next to the front door. The front door, which was right by the kitchen. That was very poor planning on my part.

I would kick myself later, I promised. OK, I couldn't call for help. I couldn't get to my car keys. Could I run? My nearest neighbors were three miles away, but if I cut across the cow pasture that bordered the property, I could make that distance pretty easily. I could run in my pajama pants. It would mean leaving my purse behind, but at this point, I was willing to live without my cell phone and the fourteen Chap-Sticks rattling around in my shoulder bag.

I crept over to the window and tried to shove the sash up. Nothing. It didn't budge a millimeter. Planting my feet, I tried again, shoving with all my might. Nothing. Being low to the ground gave me proper leverage, but I was also skinny, malnourished, with no weight-lifting regimen.

I leaned closer to the sill. "What the hell?" I hissed. The windows had been nailed shut from the outside. "Who does that?"

Were all of the windows nailed shut? Why would Lindy do that? I considered throwing my nightstand through the single-pane window and making a break for it, but having no idea who was in the house or why, I preferred to get away without calling attention to myself.

I need more options, Brain!

But Brain was ignoring me in favor of regurgitating random soup recipes. Because knowing the exact amount of mushrooms in the porcini bisque special from the previous week was super-useful at the moment. *Stupid Brain.*

OK, the back door was near the kitchen, which was clearly not a viable route. If I was very quiet, I might be able to sneak past the kitchen, grab my purse, and get out through the front door, calling the cops while I ran for the neighbors'. It was better than cowering in my room, waiting for some unknown intruder to decide whether he wanted to add murder to his criminal résumé.

I listened at the door, unable to hear anything on the other side. I touched the knob with shaking fingers, forcing myself to grasp it and turn. I could do this, I told myself. I was a city girl. And I would not let some hillbilly housebreaker intimidate me. I eased the door open. This was my house, damn it, however temporary. I didn't let people intimidate me in my kitchen, much less my house. Giving up the relative safety of my room, I took a few resolute steps out into the hall.

I was Tess Maitland, terror of junior line cooks everywhere. I wasn't afraid of anything.

Except for heights. And sharks. And backwoods burglars.

My bravado deflated to nil as I neared the kitchen. If I could just sneak past unnoticed and slip out the front door . . . If I could grab my keys and make it to my car, all the better.

My favorite wok—fourteen inches in diameter and

carbon steel, nice and heavy—sat on top of a box full of kitchen supplies I'd left in the hallway. I slipped my fingers through the smooth wood handle. Now if he got in the way, the home intruder was going to get a nice, solid whack.

From the kitchen, I could now hear the low hum of the microwave. My arms fell to my sides, wok bumping against my leg.

Who the hell breaks into someone's house to use their microwave?

Believe it or not, this actually made me feel better. For one thing, someone who was warming up ramen in a stranger's house probably wasn't planning the dismemberment of said stranger. And the microwave had probably covered the sound of my approach. As long as I didn't—

I moved my left foot, wincing as the board beneath it squeaked.

Damn it.

The microwave stopped, and swift footsteps moved toward the kitchen door. I threw myself against the wall, hoping to make myself invisible.

The kitchen lights were flicked off, and something was coming my way. My hands shook as I gripped the pan tightly.

As the dark shape moved toward me, I raised my weapon high over my head. In front of me, white hands came into view, and a clear, low voice said, "Wait a min—"

Without waiting for the rest of his speech, I did what any reasonable person would do. I brought the steel pan crashing down on his head.

"Ow," the shape growled, although he did not drop to his knees.

I shrieked and whacked him again, a nice uppercut swing that landed across his face. Enough moonlight spilled from the window that I could just make out the slim build, long limbs, dark hair, and darker eyes.

"Stop that!" he spat, sounding rather annoyed now. And I found the tone of his voice really pissed me off. He was in my house. He was skulking around in my kitchen, cooking what I assumed was my food, and he was annoyed with me for interrupting him? He grunted when I swung the pan down on the crown of his head, but he still didn't drop.

"Screw this, I'm going to get my knives," I hissed, stomping toward the kitchen.

This was stupid for two reasons. One, I could have just walked out of the house unscathed. Also, I'd just broadcast my plans to my opponent. The moment I moved past him, his arm shot out and caught me by the hand, squeezing with enough force that I cried out. Twirling the wok with my free hand, I smacked his arm away with the edge of the pan.

"Stop hittin' me with Asian cookware!" he shouted, shoving me away, sending me skidding into the fridge.

"Get the hell out of my house!" I shouted back.

He backed toward the doorway. "Look, I'm going to turn on the lights. And when I do, please don't swing any other kitchen stuff at my head."

"Did you miss the part where I said 'Get the hell out of my house'?"

"Well, that's the thing. It's not your house, it's mine."

I squinted as he flicked on the lights.

Holy hell.

My deluded burglar was sex in a pair of Levi's. He was tall and lean, with the exception of a well-developed chest and arms under a worn True Value Hardware T-shirt. His eyes were a warm teak color with dark chocolate centers around the pupils, which complemented the mussed dark hair nicely. He had high cheekbones, marked with a little triangle of freckles at the corner of his left eye, which shouldn't have been adorable on a burglar, but it was.

The most unusual thing about him was his skin, which was paper-pale. No one I'd so far seen in this town was pale, particularly the young men. People here spent so much time outdoors, doing farm work or yard work or hunting or fishing—everyone I'd seen had a healthy windburned glow. But this guy's skin was like polished marble, smooth and white, with a faintly iridescent shine. He flashed me his best winning smile, a blinding white with prominent canines. I stepped back instinctively.

"Oh, come on! You're a vampire?"

He grinned nastily, dropping his fangs.

"Damn it."

Contrary to popular legend, vampires didn't have to wait to be invited into your house. They could walk through any human's door any time they wanted. They just chose not to out of politeness. This was one of the many, many misconceptions that had been blown out of the water when vampires came out of the coffin in 1999.

Believe it or not, even living in a big city, I hadn't come into contact with vampires often. Unable to digest human food, they didn't exactly flood my restaurant with business. We had a vampire dishwasher for a while. The hours suited him perfectly, but being around that much silver, to which vampires were severely allergic, had him on edge for his entire shift, and he quit after three weeks. We tried to point out that our silverware was actually stainless steel, but Bruno couldn't be persuaded. It was a shame. He was the one guy we could count on to show up on time.

I'd always figured that vampires had centuries under the radar to sink their teeth into anyone they wanted before the Coming Out, so why would they pick off random bystanders now that they were under media scrutiny? At least, that's what I thought before one of them slunk into my kitchen and used my microwave without permission.

What the hell did a vampire heat up in a microwave, anyway?

"Whatsa matter?" he asked, the faint bluegrass

twang rising and falling like ripples in bourbon. "Cat got your tongue?"

Despite the panty-dropping lilt of his voice, he touched the nerve that hadn't sparked since Phillip had uttered the word "sabbatical." I grabbed for the canvas carrying case that protected my ungodly expensive ceramic knives.

"Oh, put the knives down," he said, moving around me at lightning speed and pushing the case out of my reach. "Gosh darn hysterical female."

"Look, pulse or no pulse, you are breaking and entering. You need to get out, right now, or I'll call the Council hotline."

"Call V-one-one," he said, referring to the nickname for the World Council for the Equal Treatment of the Undead's national hotline for humans with vampire problems. "I have every right to be here."

"I have a rental agreement in my bag that says otherwise," I shot back.

"My name is Sam Clemson. I've lived here for the last five years. My wife and I are in the middle of a divorce. Until it's final on October 28, I have the legal right to be here."

"Tess Maitland. Wait—" I clapped my hand over my face. "Lindy's husband? George said her husband died!"

"Well, to be fair, he wasn't wrong," he admitted. "I was turned about two years ago."

"Show me some ID," I said, holding out my hand

imperiously. I would think about exactly how stupid it was to order vampires around at a later date.

The corners of his lips quirked. "What?"

"How do I know you're not just some crazy who wandered into the house? All vampires are required by Council to register after they're turned and file for their vampire identification card."

"Congratulations, you've read *USA Today*."

"Show me the card, Mr. Clemson."

"Sam, please. Mr. Clemson was my father."

"Are you sure about that?" I retorted.

"Haha, I'm a bastard, clever." He grumbled as he pulled his wallet out of his back pocket and handed me the little green card. He was indeed Sam Clemson, and this was his address. And contrary to all laws of DMV logic, Sam took a damn fine ID picture.

"So, you've been here this whole time? How? Where have you been sleeping—" I gasped. "Is that why I can't get into the basement? You're locked in there during the day?"

"I don't think I should tell you where I sleep during the day," he said, lifting an eyebrow.

My lips wanted to twitch into a smile, but I clamped them tightly together. I supposed I couldn't blame him for being cautious. Some paranoid humans spent the first year "postvampire" finding any reason possible to drag vampires out into the daylight or push them onto handy pointy wooden objects. The Council formed to "formally interact with human governments and facilitate open, cordial communication." In other words, they busted their way into the homes of presidents, prime ministers, and dictators around the world and told them, "Quit killing us off for your twisted amusement, or we will FedEx you pieces of your beloved Robert Pattinson."

And then a thought occurred to me.

"Wait, did Lindy know you were still staying here?" I demanded. He nodded, stepping away from me and my kitchen implements. "She rented this house to me knowing there was a vampire sleeping in the basement? That bitch!"

"Hey," he objected. "That's my—well, my ex-wife you're talkin' about. Do you always cuss so much?"

"Aren't you the least bit upset about this?" I yelled.

"Of course I'm upset about it," he shouted back. "Do you think I'm happy that my wi—Lindy thought it was OK to open our home up to some stranger, without tellin' me? I didn't even realize you were here until yesterday, when I tripped over your stupid box of kitchen stuff. How early have you been goin' to sleep, woman?"

"Beside the point."

"I was still tryin' to figure out how to get you out of the house without talking to you, when you came in here swingin' that wok. Who travels with a wok?"

"You, don't talk anymore," I snapped at him. I snatched up my purse from the hallway and grabbed my phone. I didn't feel bad about calling, despite the fact that it was after 11:00 P.M. Even if Lindy was in bed, I thought she owed me an explanation. She didn't pick up, and the call went to voice mail. I hissed out very specific instructions to call me as soon as she got my message, no matter what the time.

I slammed my phone onto the counter and let out a vicious stream of anatomically detailed curses.

He pulled those full, pale lips into a sneer. "You are just a big ol' ball of sunshine, aren't you?"

"The better to melt your face with, my dear," I snapped. I took a deep breath and tried to remember that even if this guy was being a bit of a dick, it wasn't his fault that his ex-wife had taken the last of my cash reserves under false pretenses. I was ashamed that I'd been conned by that little bumpkin bimbo. Clearly, a perky blond ponytail and a great big Jesus fish on one's car didn't make a person trustworthy.

I sighed. "OK, calling the cops is out, because you apparently live here. And I really need to take full advantage of my lease. I'm only here for a month."

"I will not leave my house for some random stranger."

"So, I guess we're at an impasse," I said.

"Yeah, if 'impasse' means 'the foul-mouthed human moves out as soon as possible.'"

I crossed my arms under my chest . . . and realized that sort of pushed my boobs up into this weird cleavage popover. I dropped my arms. "I'm not going anywhere."

"Fine, you don't have to leave," he said silkily as moved toward me. His body language suddenly shifted into a predatory lean, his tall frame looming over me, trapping me against the counter. "By all means, please stay. It gets so lonely out here when I'm on my own. I could use some . . . companionship." He dropped his fangs and bared them dramatically.

And because the bad-decision-making lobes of my brain were in charge, I giggled instead of cowering against the counter. I stepped forward, into the cage of his arms.

"I'm sorry. Are you trying to intimidate me?" I scoffed. "You're about as threatening as the cornfield chorus on *Hee Haw*. Do you have any idea what it takes for a woman to work her way up to head chef at a fine-dining restaurant in a major city? Or what kind of bullshit I've had to put up with over the years from chauvinist pigs who didn't think I should be able to tell them what to do because I lacked the requisite testicles? I'm going to tell you the same thing I told them. I own thirty different types of extremely expensive knives. And I know how to put each of them to creative use. Try to intimidate me again, and you will wake up next to a beautifully plated medley of freshly sautéed vampire bits."

Slightly boggled, Sam stared down at me, horrified, and backed away. "You're crazy."

"You'll find that all chefs are a little unstable." I offered him my scariest smile, the kind that made waiters cringe away like frightened deer. "Normal people don't like to play with fire and raw meat all day."

He grabbed his mug of what I assumed was blood and stalked toward the basement door, glaring over his shoulder.

I grinned to myself. "I think I won that one."

With the (disturbingly attractive) interloper holed up in his basement, I made a huge pot of coffee and retreated to my room. I threw my blinds up so the minute the sun rose, my room would be bathed in light, and crouched on my bed.

I had a vampire roommate. This was just the cherry on the crap sundae of my life.

Was this even legal? Could Lindy rent the house to me when it was already occupied? Vampire property rights were still a little vague. After the Great Coming Out, the Council wrangled with the human governments over financial issues. Vampires became the answer to a dwindling economy, an untapped taxable workforce capable of launching untold cottage industries—blood banks, all-night shopping centers, fang-friendly dental clinics.

But there were problems. Recently turned vampires weren't eager to take back the credit-card balances they'd left behind when they'd "died." Other vampires hadn't paid taxes in centuries and deeply resented the idea that they'd have to file 1040s. This reluctance led to some resentment from the humans, which led to some "less than friendly" policies toward the undead when it came to mortgages, leases, and probate laws. After all, vampires weren't technically alive, so how could they have property rights?

Even after the Undead Civil Rights Act, there were still loopholes of which humans took full advantage. Landlords suddenly aware of why some tenants only came out at night kicked vampires out of their apartments over the slightest infractions. Home loans to vampires came with outrageous interest rates. And when they divorced, they were lucky to get away with the clothes on their backs. I couldn't imagine a judge in semirural Kentucky giving Sam a fair shake against sweet little Lindy.

Was this rental scheme some sort of revenge against Sam? They'd been married for three years before Sam had been turned. Clearly, Lindy had skinned him in the divorce. She'd taken all of the good furniture, whatever had been hanging on the walls. There wasn't anything in the kitchen cupboards but lint and the groceries I'd brought. I was surprised she let Sam stay in the house.

I didn't have the luxury of sympathizing with Sam. Maybe it was selfish, but I wasn't in a very stable position myself. I'd cleared out my checking account to put down the rent on this place. I had a healthy savings account, but it was earmarked for my new apartment. And I didn't know whether I had a job to return to after my "sabbatical." My contract with Coda was performance-based. I got a share in the business, but the owners didn't have to keep using me in the kitchen if I was unable to fulfill their expectations. If I didn't have a regular paycheck, I would need every penny when I got back to the city.

I didn't have the available cash to travel somewhere else. I couldn't go home. I lived right around the corner from Coda. The temptation to go back to check on my kitchen would be too great. I could stay with Chef Gamling and George, I supposed. But it would prick my pride. It was bad enough that Chef felt he had to nurse me back to health like some emotionally stunted kitten. Plus, Chef's house didn't even have a guest room. The second bedroom had been converted into Chef's painting studio. I would be reduced to a couch surfer. A big pathetic couch-surfing loser who talked to vegetables.

Still, I wouldn't stay in a house with a strange man, much less a man who saw me as his favorite food group.

I didn't want to leave the house. Hell, if I had the money for a vacation home in the sticks, I would buy the place. I liked the weird nooks and crannies in the design. I liked the quiet and the way the light came through the kitchen windows in the morning. I could sleep there, and I couldn't seem to sleep anywhere. I wasn't going to give that up. I needed the Lassiter place to get better. If Sam was going to get in the way of that, he would have to go.

Blinded by the Brine

3

My new landlord did not appreciate my predawn call.

"Is there a problem with the house?" Lindy asked, all guilelessness and concern.

I huffed out an irritated sigh. She was honestly going to make me say it. She was going to plead ignorance, just in case I was calling about a leak in the roof or a plumbing problem.

"Yes, you didn't make it clear in the rental ad that the house came with a fully furnished vampire lair in the basement," I snapped.

"Oh, that."

"Yes, that. Your vampire ex-husband is sleeping in the basement. That would be pertinent information to give a prospective tenant, I think, before renting out the house."

"Look, this really isn't my problem, Tess."

"You rented me a house that someone was already living in!"

She yawned. "Technically, no one is living there."

"Don't you argue semantics with me. You either get your vampire ex out of here, or you refund my money."

"You'll find I don't have to do either. You signed the paperwork. The house is livable. Besides, I don't have your money anymore."

It was all downhill from there. Lindy said the house was my problem now and told me I had to deal with it. I told her to do a lot of things, most of which were not anatomically possible. She called the cops and reported me for harassment.

It turned out that there was very little that local law enforcement could do to help me resolve my dispute with Lindy. Until the divorce was final, Lindy was technically entitled to rent out the space as she chose, according to Half-Moon Hollow Police Sergeant Russell Lane, although he said it in a tone that gave me the distinct impression that he was guessing. The good news was that as far as the police were concerned, I hadn't violated my rental agreement. I hadn't actually threatened Lindy, just annoyed her. So she couldn't force me to leave just because she was upset with me.

"Don't I have the right to a house without undead occupants?" I'd asked Sergeant Lane.

He shrugged. "You are free to take her to small-claims court."

Considering that the case would likely be called months after I returned to Chicago, I decided against that. I also passed on Lane's suggestion that I could move into a motel in town if I was so uncomfortable with Sam's presence in the house. I saw a few of those establishments on my first drive through town. Unless I was an out-of-state fisherman or an adulterer, I didn't think I would be comfortable at the Lucky Clover Motel.

Given the choice between sticky sheets and bedbugs versus a vampire, I would take my chances with the vampire.

My day did not get better. Despite my extreme fatigue, I couldn't get any rest. I tossed and turned, but I was too keyed up from my visit from the fuzz. There was this weird gnawing sensation under my breastbone that kept me from relaxing.

How had I become so uncomfortable in my own skin? I used to be such a physical person. When I was in school, everything seemed easy. When I was hungry, I ate. If my body felt too soft, I exercised. And the sex. Everything you've heard about the stove being a hotbed for sexual tension is completely true.

But when you reach a certain level of success in the kitchen, everything becomes so competitive—

who gets the best reviews, who gets their photos taken with celebrity diners, who gets guest spots on the Food Network. Because of my schedule, I rarely spent time with nonculinary "civilians." I couldn't date other chefs, because they became insecure if they felt they were the "beta" in the relationship. Even Phillip, whose image and income *depended* on my success, seemed uncomfortable with the idea of a girlfriend who was "high-profile." He wanted to conduct the front of house like a maestro with his orchestra, not answer diners' questions about his girlfriend. No wonder he'd gone back to the dental hygienist. No one wanted to discuss flossing in detail.

So for months, there had been no sleep *and* no sex. Clearly, I was lucky I hadn't taken out bystanders in my vegetable-based breakdown.

I stretched. I popped a few antacids. I opened my laptop, checked my e-mail, and was shocked to find a dozen or so messages from restaurant owners around Chicago. Most of them were the standard "get well soon" messages one would expect from a colleague, even a competitor. But others seemed to be fishing for information. Was I leaving Coda? Was I really having health problems, or had the gossip mill blown that out of proportion? What were my immediate plans when I got back into town? There were a few subtle hints—that if my sudden decline was simply an excuse to get away from newly engaged Phillip, that several establishments would be more than willing to hire me.

The fact that I didn't immediately delete the e-mail was a bit shocking. For years, I'd devoted every waking hour to Coda. Could I really leave the restaurant? I would have to move. It would be too awkward, living so close to the restaurant. If I was going to do this, I wanted a fresh start. I would need a new apartment—maybe I'd even indulge in something with a view of the Chicago skyline that didn't involve the guy across the street practicing nude yoga in front of an open window.

Before I'd left, the owners at Coda had made it clear that if I wanted to sell out, they would be happy to reclaim stakes in their business from a potentially crazy woman. They'd only offered the small share I held to appease me. If I sold out, I might have enough to put the down payment on a modest townhouse in a semisafe neighborhood.

I would check the apartments across the street for nude yoga enthusiasts before I moved in.

That night, I sat at the kitchen counter with some jasmine tea and waited, feeling like a teenager on her first job interview.

I tried to focus on the positive steps I'd taken that day—unpacking, finding a store that sold Amish breads and sweets, buying a very large lock for my bedroom door at the hardware store. Lindy would just have to deal with the fact that her master bedroom now had a brand-new mental-hospital-quality dead-bolt.

But I was about to have a potentially unpleasant conversation with my new vampire roommate, and I just couldn't seem to shake the feeling that it was going to end badly—or bloodily—for me.

The sun dropped behind the horizon, leaving the kitchen purpled and shadowed. Just as I flipped the light switch, I could hear footsteps lumbering up the basement stairs. I took a deep breath, willing myself to be calm, cool, civil.

At the very least, I would not threaten him with Asian cookware.

Sam stepped through the basement door, just as tall and broody as I remembered. Pulling a faded blue T-shirt over some pale but nicely defined abs, he started at the sight of a human sitting at his counter. He frowned, shifting the donor bag of blood between his hands. "Oh, you're still here."

"All of the awkwardness of a one-night stand without any of the fun," I said, trying desperately to look anywhere but at the half-buttoned jeans. It didn't work. It was as if there were some sort of vision magnet embedded in the little metal rivets. *Don't look, Tess. Don't loo—*

Damn it. I looked. And he caught me.

Sam smirked, a devilish little dimple winking out at me as he crossed to the microwave and heated a mugful of synthetic blood. With his jeans still undone.

At this point, I was pretty sure he was refusing to button them, just to mess with me. So I stared at the wall and forged ahead.

"Remember that impasse we discussed? Well, I had a conversation with your ex this morning . . . and the police. And it would appear that Lindy doesn't have to repay my money, but she can't force me out, either. So I'm here to stay."

"Why don't you just go back home? There's nothing for you here."

"Because I'm supposed to be 'recuperating.' If I go back to Chicago, I will end up somewhere I don't need to be."

He turned his head sharply, glaring at me. "Hold on, are you a drug addict?"

The flinty tone of Sam's voice, the command, set my nerves on edge. Chef Gamling was the only one allowed to use that tone with me. I took a deep breath, forcing myself to exhale slowly.

"I am not a drug addict," I said through clenched teeth. "I'm a workaholic. You probably figured out from all of the kitchen equipment that I'm a chef. I had a bit of a setback at my restaurant, and my boss put me on leave. If I go back before I'm supposed to, my manager-slash-ex will probably fire me. I'll be humiliated, again, and probably won't be able to find work. My point is, I'm not leaving. Can't you just go stay with one of your vampire friends for a while?"

Sam scowled. "I haven't been a vampire long

enough to have a 'crash pad' in the undead community. And my wife got all my living friends in the divorce."

"Well, I'm sorry that your being antisocial has worked against you. But I am not going to share a house with you. And that's not because you're a vampire. It's because you're a strange *male* vampire, who could be a tutu-wearing serial killer for all I know."

His dark brows drew together as he shook off that visual. "I guess one of us is just going to have to leave."

"Yeah, I guess *one of us* is," I shot back. "In case you missed it, 'one of us' translates to the one not freeloading.'"

"Freeloading?"

"I'm paying my way here. You have no job that I'm aware of. You have no decent aboveground furniture. You're riding out the time left on a divorce settlement before Lindy puts this place on the market."

I should not have said that. Even before the words came out of my mouth, I knew I shouldn't have called him out on his broken marriage. Why didn't I just go drop-kick a baby polar bear and then poke its mama with a stick?

He muttered something along the lines of "She's that sure I won't get the money, is she?"

Given the sharp expression in Sam's dark eyes, I had no choice but to backtrack. "Look, I'm really sorry about your marital issues, but it doesn't change the fact that I'm staying. I've paid to stay the month, so I'm not going anywhere."

"You may be paying your way, but that doesn't make this your home," he hissed, gripping the counter with those strong white hands. "You can pack up and leave anytime. And trust me, I'm going to do everything I can to try to make that time come sooner than you expect."

"Are you threatening me?" I asked, a sly grin spreading across my face as I looked up at him. I couldn't help it. I couldn't think of the last time a man challenged me like this. For the first time in a long time, I felt a frisson of . . . something there were no clean words for. "I bet you I can make you run screaming from this house like something out of *The Amityville Horror*."

"You sound awfully confident for a mortal without superpowers." He growled, leaning ever so slightly closer. His nostrils flared as if he was taking in my scent. "You won't make me move an inch."

I showed off my own teeth in a sharp, wicked smile. "You will run screaming into broad daylight like a little, tiny girl."

"First one to fold leaves for good?" he asked, licking his lips.

"Agreed."

Sam offered his hand to shake on the deal. "Bring it on, cupcake."

I smirked, grasping his cool hand tightly. The slight wince he gave showed he didn't expect me to have much of a grip. "Sweetie, you're already standing in the middle of it, and you're too dumb to see it."

One Epiphany, Hold the Pimento Cheese

4

The next twenty-four hours were tense, the long, silent wait for the first shot in a battle.

Sam's first efforts at "pranking" me were the stuff of summer camps and middle school sleepovers. While I was asleep, he sneaked into the bathroom and Saran Wrapped the toilet. He also switched all of the staples in the kitchen. There was salt in the sugar canister, baking soda in the can of baking powder, that sort of thing. It might have confused someone who hadn't taken professional baking courses.

After visiting an establishment called Bubba's Beer and Bait, I responded by drilling a little hole in the basement door and gently coaxing two containers of live crickets through a funnel and onto the basement steps. I corked the hole and wedged a towel into the crack under the door so they couldn't escape. The best part was that Sam would never find all of them. They would crawl under his bed and into corners, and he would drive himself nuts trying to find the source of their annoying little cheeps.

I was careful to lock myself in my room by sundown that night, just so I could listen to his irritated yelps as he woke up to hundreds of chirping bunkmates. The combination was downright musical.

I was having fun. For the first time in a long time, I felt challenged by a man, and not just in a "You can't tell me what to do!" rebelling-against-Daddy sort of way. Sam was playing with me, sometimes in a meanspirited, irritating fashion, but he was devoting a lot of time and effort to keeping me entertained. And that made me like him just the tiniest bit.

But then the sawing started. Nights at the house went from blissfully quiet to my own personal construction zone. Sawing, hammering, drilling, and some sound I could only identify as a cat getting stuck in a dishwasher. I never knew when it was going to start. And some nights, I would sit up until the wee hours of the morning, waiting for it, only to be treated to a quick fifteen minutes of audio torture before dawn.

I would wake up every morning, unlock my bedroom, and find some project half-completed that made my life more difficult. The tub was left stripped and half-caulked, meaning that I couldn't bathe without doing permanent damage to the surrounding drywall. The hardwood floors in the hallway were refinished, meaning that if I wanted to leave my room, I had to choose between climbing out the windows or walking across the fresh sealant and ruining his work. He knew I liked the house too much to want to hurt it. Damn him.

One morning, I found that he'd removed all of the knobs from the house. All of the knobs. The faucets, the doorknobs, the drawer pulls for the bathroom vanity, the stove and oven knobs, and the volume knob for the TV. Yes, I was shocked that Sam's TV had a volume knob. Let's just say that Lindy didn't leave him HDTV-ready.

I launched a reciprocal offensive. I roasted a turkey and placed an oscillating fan so that it blew the delicious Thanksgiving fragrance toward the basement door. I baked fragrant cinnamon rolls and lasagnas redolent with garlic and herbs. This gastronomical warfare worked on two fronts, physical and emotional. One, human food smelled spoiled and rancid to vampires. They lacked the enzymes to process solids, so exposure to most "regular" food resulted in projectile vomiting. And two, Sam would be reminded of all of the things he missed about eating as a human and—in my mind—would wind up weeping in a little pile of soggy vampire on the kitchen floor.

It seemed to be having some effect on him. Every few days, I would find a cheap discount-store sauce-pan in the kitchen sink, burned black and coated with some unidentifiable oily substance. Was he trying to retaliate?

I supposed I went too far when I made my special peanut-butter-cup brownies and left them under a glass dome on the counter. I even left a little card next to the display that read, "Enjoy!" The next day, I woke up to find that he'd shut off the gas connection to the stove, rendering it unusable. Clearly, he didn't expect me to know how to fix that.

Amateur.

While the pranks kept my mind active and dis-tracted from the potential disasters looming when I returned to Chicago, the sleep deprivation from the constant power-tooling was taking a physical toll. I was getting even less rest than when I was living at home. I took naps in the afternoons, just to keep alert during Sam's active hours.

My routine was changing—again—and I was feel-ing it. What little progress I'd made health-wise took a distinct slide in the opposite direction. Chef was pleased to see that I was keeping the weight I'd gained from forced helpings of dumplings and milkshakes, but he tsked over the reemergence of dark circles under my eyes. I'd looked forward to jogging on some of the green-canopied country roads that surrounded the house, but I didn't have the energy. I became snappish and grumpy, even with Chef, earning me a ten-pound bag of potatoes to peel.

After I'd reconnected the stove's innards, I went back to bed and tried to think calm, happy thoughts. I needed to sleep if I was going to come up with an appropriate and painful rebuttal to this abuse of my domain. Striking at my stove was a new low for Sam. How would he like it if I went into his basement and melted down all of his precious tools?

Hmmmm.

"Oh, come on, Tess, where are you going to get a smelter?" I said to myself, sighing and rubbing at the persistent ache in my middle. Perplexed, I sat up in my sad, lumpy bed and realized I was hungry. Not just a little peckish. I was seriously, feeling-my-belly-button-rub-against-my-spine starving. I hadn't been this hungry in years, certainly not this early in the morning. I was usually just hungry enough to need a snack by the end of a dinner shift, meaning a lot of midnight carbs. I usually skipped breakfast in favor of running five miles to make up for the late-night eating.

I thought back to the last time I'd actually made breakfast for myself and couldn't remember what I'd eaten. And now that I was hungry, what did I want? Waffles? Frittata? Crepes?

Those things were all well and good, but what I really wanted was Lucky Charms. I hadn't had sugary cereals since culinary school, when I'd regularly carried those mini-single-serving boxes around for snacking between classes. My pastry instructor found a box of Sugar Smacks sticking out of my purse in class one day and embarrassed me so thoroughly for my "toddler palate" that I'd lost my taste for them. But now I wanted a bowl of marshmallowy, sugar-coated goodness—badly. But what I had was fancy cheeses, eggs, and brioche.

So, instead of Lucky Charms, I had a spinach and feta omelet.

This just wouldn't do.

On my safari into the Shop 'n Save, I grabbed my Lucky Charms, and some Cap'n Crunch for good measure. I bought Oreos, Pop-Tarts, and the makings of Fluffernutter sandwiches—things I'd loved as a kid but had abandoned for the sake of refining my palate. After recovering from the shock of how little I'd spent at the register, I tucked the grocery bags underneath the front seat of my car and cast a longing glance down the quaint little street. It was one of those old-fashioned Main Street arrangements, skinny two-story buildings all bunched up against one another—a hardware store, an antiques store, one of those old-fashioned ice cream parlors, and a sandwich shop called the Three Little Pigs. The cars lining the parking lots were older but well maintained, and the people milling around did it pretty slowly. This was not the place for the Hollow's young and hip to do their errands.

Did the Hollow have a young and hip crowd?

I didn't want to go home just yet. So I walked. I window-shopped at the antiques store and browsed the selections at the ice cream parlor for later reference.

I walked past the Three Little Pigs, a snug little brick building with a ridiculously charming cartoon sign. Catching sight of a patron chowing down on a triple-decker ham sandwich through the front window, I seemed to be moving over the threshold before I could stop myself. I was just in time for a late lunch, and I was hoping that whatever I ordered incorporated cheese fries in some way. I hadn't had cheese fries in years.

The interior was done in dark panels and black-and-white hunting photos, presumably of the owner's family. The menu was scrawled on a chalkboard in bright colors. The smell was incredible, so many layers of scent—fresh bread, frying bacon, melting cheese. I had to catch myself to keep from drooling all over the floor. This might be even better than Lucky Charms.

With an emphasis on carnivorous delights, the Three Little Pigs seemed to be primarily a sandwich shop. If it once had a pulse, it could be grilled, fried, braised, or roasted, then slapped between two slices of bread and delivered to your table. I was trying to decide between the house specialty—pork chop on wheat, topped with grilled ham and bacon—or starting off small with a turkey club, when a dill pickle flew over the opposite side of my booth and smacked me square in the eye.

"Sonofa—" I yelped, turning to see the adorable strawberry blond toddler who had blinded me with dill brine. "Gun," I finished lamely.

"I'm so sorry!" a beautiful auburn-haired woman gushed, stepping around the booth and handing me a napkin to dab at my stinging, stinky eye. Her tinny country twang contrasted sharply with the fierce elegance of her face, but I doubted the sandy-haired man sitting with her minded all that much. "We're still workin' on hand-eye coordination and table manners. Trust me, they normally don't waste a bite."

"That really stings," I marveled as she hovered.

"I know, it's the vinegar," she said, clucking her tongue and offering more napkins. "I'm so sorry."

I snorted a little. "That's OK. 'Blinded by flying pickles' goes nicely with the rest of my week."

"I'm Jolene Lavelle, and this is my husband, Zeb." She gestured to the sandy-haired man, who was currently scrubbing barbecue sauce from the boy twin's face. "And these are our twins, Janelyn and Joe."

"Nice to meet you," I said, swiping at my eye one last time. "Tess Maitland."

"You new in town?" Jolene drawled.

"Yeah, how can you tell?"

"The accent. You don't have one."

I chuckled. "I'm from Chicago. I'm just visiting the area for a while."

"And you're not having a very good time?" Zeb asked, his big brown doe eyes sympathetic. "You said a pickle to the eye went with the rest of your week. That can't be a good vacation."

"Come on over here, honey, and tell us all about it," Jolene said, dragging me out of my booth. Geez, this girl was crazy strong for someone so slight. As she pushed me into the seat opposite Joe the pickle flinger, she yelled for someone named Maybelline to bring her a "tall blue."

I really hoped that was some sort of home-brewed moonshine, because I could have used a drink right about then.

Imagine my surprise when a tall blue turned out to be a large blue glass bottle of homemade root beer, which Jolene swore would cheer me right up. It was tasty, with strong undertones of sassafras and ginger. The lack of carbonation was a little weird, but it settled my stomach almost instantly, and the lift in blood sugar helped my outlook considerably.

Jolene took the kids behind the counter and handed them off to two equally pretty waitresses, who bore a strong resemblance to my new friend. The ladies bobbed the babies on their hips and fed them bits of smoked sausage, which could not possibly be good for them. Then again, those kids seemed to have a lot of teeth.

Jolene snapped me out of my thoughts by sliding onto the bench seat next to me. "OK, now you have my full attention. Let's hear it." I lifted my eyebrows at her commanding tone. "Oh, come on, you look like your head's about to pop off. You're dyin' to talk to someone. Now, spill."

I looked to Zeb, who smiled at his wife fondly. "It's best to just do what she asks. She'll get it out of you somehow."

I sighed. "It's just, this house I'm renting, I have an 'unexpected' roommate. I would feel sorry for him, but he's kind of rude and prickly. And I can't get rid of him because I don't have superstrength."

On and on, I rambled about the house, which I loved, and Lindy, whom I didn't have any fond feelings for, about Sam and Phillip and talking arugula, until I finished with "My professional reputation is in shreds. I haven't had sex in six months, and I'm starting to think that after a certain period of disuse, everything grows over down there. Plus, I don't know if I have a job or health insurance to go back to, so how am I going to afford the reconstructive hooha surgery?"

"Wow," Jolene marveled. "That was an impressive rant." She shot a look to her husband. "That was a Jane rant."

Zeb grinned and shrugged, as if answering some unspoken question from his wife. There was a non-verbal coziness to their communication that made my chest ache a bit. I'd never had that kind of intimacy with any of my boyfriends.

"It's all going to be just fine, Tess. You'll see. You just relax now, while I get us a little lunch."

Jolene returned to the table with two trays piled high with all sorts of foods that I didn't recognize—colorful casseroles and fried mystery items and ribs.

"There's no way the three of us could eat all this!" I cried, rising to help her heft the trays. "Please let me know what the check total is, so I can cover my share."

"Pay?" Zeb scoffed. "McClaines eat free at the Three Little Pigs. Otherwise, we wouldn't get access to Aunt Lulu's special seven-layer salad. She doesn't give that to just anybody."

Without responding, I poked at the mayonnaise-covered bowl skeptically. "Why don't I see any green vegetables in that salad?"

"Surrounded by beautiful smartasses, that's my lot in life." Zeb sighed, lifting his eyes to the ceiling.

"Everything you see here was made by my family, except for the pulled pork and the ribs," Jolene said, unloading her culinary treasures with a practiced hand. "It's on special, provided by the Volunteer Fire Department. They're hosting a barbecue booth at Burley Days, and they needed the practice. My uncles don't handle barbecue very well, which is why they don't usually serve it here. Something about the smokers and fire—they get all wound up bein' manly men and end up overcookin' the meat."

"Outdoor cooking has been known to do that. So, seven-layer salad?" I said, lifting a brow and staring at some well-disguised romaine lettuce that seemed to be topped with mayonnaise and bacon.

Jolene shook her head in a maternal fashion. "Hold on, sweetie, we have to start you out slow. We'll work you up to seven-layer salad. You're new to this whole Southern comfort food thing, and I don't want you to get sick off your first try."

I scanned the table to try to find something I recognized. "How is it that I grew up just a few hundred miles from here and I've never heard of these dishes?"

"We have a recipe-hoarding border patrol at the Illinois state line," Jolene deadpanned.

"We can't possibly eat all of this."

"Just watch," Zeb muttered. "Jolene will mow through this in no time flat."

I wondered at the crack on Jolene's eating habits, particularly from Zeb, since she didn't have a spare ounce on her *and* she'd recently given birth to his twins. But there was no malice in expression or tone. It was fond, as if he was just waiting for the word to run and get another tray full of food. The silly, love-struck look on his face made my heart ache a little.

Jolene began systematically loading my plate with little scoops of every dish. I sampled a few familiar things—potato salad, corn casserole, three-bean salad. But when I got to the orangey-yellow substance that sort of resembled scrambled eggs with little red bits, I poked it with my fork. "I'm sorry. But what the hell is this?"

"Homemade pimento cheese," Jolene said. I took a little bite. "Velveeta, pimentos, and mayonnaise. Oh, and bacon. It's Aunt Vonnie's recipe."

I swallowed, then took a huge gulp of water to wash down the gelatinous mass of funk. "Is Aunt Vonnie here?" I asked. And when they shook their heads, I shuddered, wiping at my mouth with my napkin. "Why? Oh, my God, why would anyone do that to an innocent processed food product?"

"I believe that pimento cheese was invented as a practical joke by two mean old church ladies, but they died before they could get their laugh in," Zeb told me. "We are left with their legacy of mean-spirited hospitality."

"I'm going for the seven-layer salad," I told Jolene, aiming my fork for the bowl of lettuce, peas, bacon, shredded cheese, and purple onions, covered in a dressing consisting of mayonnaise, parmesan cheese, and sugar.

"Don't say I didn't warn you," she retorted as I forked a healthy sample into my mouth.

Seven-layer salad was freaking amazing. Simple, fresh, and green, with a series of flavors tumbling against my tongue like dominoes. "This should not be as good as it is," I told her, taking another huge bite.

"It's the great mystery of Southern cuisine," Jolene intoned.

"And what's that?" I asked, stabbing through a

cornflake crust to find a bubbling mixture of cheese and potatoes.

"Hash-brown casserole—hash browns, cream of mushroom soup, cheddar cheese, and a couple of other things."

I put a scoop into my mouth. It was everything that was good about comfort food, warm and cheesy and gooey and savory. I tucked more into my mouth, moaning indecently.

"Would you two like to be alone?" Zeb asked, eyeing the casserole.

"I think so," I said, sighing happily as I swallowed another bite.

"Easy, girl." Jolene chortled. "Pulling the full Meg Ryan is not a good way to introduce yourself to Half-Moon Hollow society."

"I'll try to contain myself," I promised.

This was what food was supposed to be. This was satisfying, filling, comforting. Food was supposed to feed you, body and soul. It was so simple that I felt stupid for not seeing it sooner. Pink Himalayan sea salt? Was just freaking salt. Black truffles? Stinky mushrooms, and I really never liked the taste of them anyway. Smoked extra-virgin olive oil? Well, that was pretty awesome. I couldn't really give that up.

Food could be simple. Food could be anything you wanted, whether the ingredients came from a farmer's market or a convenience store. Food could be fan-freaking-tastic.

I shook my head, as if to clear it, and took another bite of cheesy potatoes. Maybe Jolene had slipped some sort of hallucinogen into my portion.

I didn't care all that much.

Zeb unwrapped a steaming aluminum-foil packet the size of a basketball. "Now, this is pulled pork shoulder. We're going to give it to you straight, no sauce, at first, because I figure you'd appreciate it by itself. But there are three levels of sauce here in these little cups. Mild, which is basically ketchup, the sort of thing we give to the kids. Hot, which is more of a Tabasco-sauce level of heat. And nuclear, which I do not recommend, even if you enjoy spicy food. There are some intestinal consequences that cannot be undone."

"Ew!" Jolene squealed. "Zeb!"

"She ate pimento cheese in public. Her threshold for gross is pretty high," he said, shrugging.

"He has a point," I conceded, placing a small bite of the pink-gray smoked meat on my tongue. I gripped the picnic table for support as a shudder of pleasure rippled up from my throat. Everything that was good about meat was currently in my mouth.

I sincerely hoped I hadn't just said that out loud.

"How have I never had barbecue like this before?" I demanded, forking more meat onto my plate. I could taste garlic, white pepper, paprika, the smoky essence of cumin. My mind immediately began scanning my internal wine list to select which vintage would offset the tangy hickory flavor. "I thought barbecue was supposed to be all gloppy sauce and burned ends. But this is like a meat marshmallow, slightly caramelized on the outside, and bursting with soft, moist flavor inside. This is—" I paused to lick my fingers. "How do they do this? What temperature do they use? For how long? Are they just using hickory, or do I detect a note of applewood, too? The smoker, is it aluminum or cast-iron?"

Because she had no answers for me, Jolene simply led me over to the booth where most of the Half-Moon Hollow Volunteer Fire Department was having lunch and introduced me to the cooks, Anna and Joe Bob. They were more than happy to discuss the ins and outs of the smokers, the hickory wood used to smoke and flavor the meat as it cooked, and the base for the sauces. Joe Bob promised to show me which cuts of pork shoulder worked best and how to keep the ribs from drying out before they cooked completely.

"We're firing up another batch at dawn if you wanna come by," Anna offered cheerfully, her round, cherubic cheeks smudged with soot from the smoker. "You could see the whole shebang from start to finish."

"I would love to!" I exclaimed, clapping and hopping up and down like a cranked-up game-show contestant.

"Are you going to keep doing that?" she asked, lifting her eyebrow.

I bit my lip and stopped with the hopping. "No."

"We'll get along just fine, then."

Now, That's a Spicy Vampire!

5

It was a matter of timing. Sam never left the basement door unlocked while he was awake. So in the window of time between his warming up his "wake-up" blood and showering, I managed to slip into the basement to do my dirty work and ducked out the front door before he saw me.

Jolene had invited me to join her book club for the evening, despite the fact that I hadn't read *The Night Circus*. I'd expected a bunch of frustrated housewives slugging back wine in some well-appointed suburban living room. And while there was wine, the group was made up of open, friendly gals who met at a funky little bookshop called Specialty Books.

The interior of the shop was a cheerful mix of paperback pop culture and antique tomes. The walls were painted a cheerful midnight blue, with a sprinkle of twinkling silver stars. There were comfy purple chairs and café tables arranged around the room in little conversation groups. The leaded-glass and maple cabinet that held the cash register displayed a collection of ritual knives and candles that I didn't quite understand. I was OK with not understanding.

The store had an impressive selection of cookbooks, everything from Introducing Variety to the Undead Diet to Food Gifts for Faerie Folk. I found a deeply discounted title on drinkable sauces for vampires, but Jane, the shopkeeper and book club organizer, warned me against it. It turned out the recently turned French chef–author had not bothered to test his recipes, and his use of eggs, flour, and purees had made several hapless vampire customers quite ill. Jane only kept the book on the shelves because it was something of a cookbook cautionary tale.

Jane was a vampire, as were her manager, Andrea, and several members of the club. At first, I worried that it was a setup, that Sam had somehow managed to round up some of his undead friends to strongarm me out of town. But then Jane referred to me as Jolene's "pocket-sized new friend," and I figured that was more humor than one usually found in a paid assailant.

Jane and Andrea were funny, smart, and snarky as hell, having both been turned in the last five years and having a more human perspective than most vampires. Although they were obviously close, the ladies were polar opposites on the vampire fashion spectrum. Titian-haired Andrea was polished and perfect in a peach sweater set and pearls, while tousled brunette Jane was wearing jeans over her impossibly long legs and a T-shirt touting "Dick Cheney for President—2012." When I asked her about it, she grumbled that she'd lost a bet with Andrea's husband.

After paying lip service to the book of the month, the women broke up into smaller "discussion groups," and I learned all about Jane's sordid history in the vampire community, including the fact that she'd been turned after a local drunk mistook her for a deer and shot her. A vampire, Gabriel, to whom Jane was now married, saved her by turning her, and they lived happily ever after. Sort of.

"Isn't that an unusual way to be turned?" I asked, sipping the surprisingly tasty latte Andrea had prepared for me. "I mean, you'd think you guys would make it into the news more often if 'mistaken for a deer and shot' was the average vampire experience."

"Yes, Jane is very unusual," Andrea said, rolling her eyes. "But she was given a choice about whether she wanted to be turned, which is the norm nowadays. Despite the fact that it's illegal to turn a human into a vampire against their will, some of us weren't afforded that luxury. But we make the best of it."

I noticed the slightly pained expression on Jane's

face as she gave Andrea's shoulder a little squeeze. I got the feeling there were details about Andrea's transition that I was missing, but it would be rude to ask. Andrea shrugged and handed Jane what looked like a mochaccino.

"Wait a minute," I said. "I thought you guys couldn't eat human food."

"We don't. But Andrea and I have been experimenting for years with all those fancy coffees that folks can't seem to live without, trying to find ways to make them more palatable for vampires."

"Interesting!" I exclaimed. "Would you mind if I asked you about your techniques?"

"Tess is a chef," Jolene said proudly. "In one of those big-city restaurants where the paparazzi lie in wait for celebrities."

"Jolene made friends with a chef, color me shocked," Andrea said, smirking and shaking her head.

Again with the cracks about Jolene's eating? Had Jolene recently lost a bunch of weight? She'd eaten a pretty hefty lunch at the Three Little Pigs, so she wasn't dieting. Either way, it was sort of shitty for her friend to poke fun at her.

I was about to jump to her defense when Jane piped up in a desperate tone, "So, Tess, I'm always interested in how people ended up in their professions. Why did you start cooking?"

"I'm good at it," I said, shrugging.

Jane didn't seem satisfied with this and leaned a

bit closer, staring into my eyes as if there were secret messages written on my corneas. "But you didn't know that until you started. And that's what I was asking, how did you start cooking?"

A bit rattled by Jane's gaze and feeling very much like a lobster over a pot of boiling water, I blurted out, "Cooking made sense, even when I was a kid. You put eggs, milk, and cinnamon on bread, you got French toast. As long as I followed the rules, I knew what the outcome would be. It was one of the few areas of my life that was predictable. And most of the time, if my parents were eating something I made, their mouths were too full to bicker. It was quite the incentive."

My mouth snapped shut like a steel trap. I stirred my cappuccino, shocked that I'd said so much. I rarely talked about my parents, even with Chef. Hell, in those two sessions of therapy I'd attended, I hadn't said more than, "My parents were well-intentioned but selfish people who would probably be making each other—and me by extension—miserable today if they hadn't died."

"Do you mind if I ask why you're so curious about vampires?" Jane asked, sensing somehow that I needed a change in topics. "Jolene said you would probably have some questions for us."

I cleared my throat, commanding my brain to produce more polite conversation. "Oh, I live with one. Not quite voluntarily."

"Anyone we know?" Andrea asked.

"Sam Clemson," I said.

Andrea and Jane both tilted their heads and gave me the "aw" face. "Poor Sam." Jane sighed.

"Why 'poor Sam'?" I asked. "I mean, other than he's married to a ring-tailed bitch."

Silence. My comment was met with complete, stone-faced silence. I bit my lip, afraid that I'd offended my new acquaintances. But then Jane burst out laughing and exclaimed, "Thank you!" while Andrea rolled her eyes.

Andrea said, "Lindy's not that bad."

"She tricked Tess into renting her house without telling her Sam was sleeping in the basement," Jolene informed her.

"Oh, then she's an evil she-beast," Andrea conceded. I chuckled, and she shrugged. "My opinions are very adaptable. They have to be when you're married to a vampire named Dick Cheney."

Jane's T-shirt made much more sense now.

"I actually meant 'poor Sam,' as in he was one of the vampires we were talking about, the ones who don't get a choice about whether they were turned or not," Jane said. "You know Sam was a contractor, right?"

I shook my head. "Actually, I don't know anything beyond Sam's the cranky guy who lives in my basement."

"Sam was pretty well known around here for being

a trustworthy guy," Jolene said. "He did quality work at a fair price, and you didn't have to worry about him raiding your jewelry box while you were out. We hired him to finish up our house after some, uh, other companies failed to do the work they'd been paid for."

Jane smirked but didn't elaborate. "Sam and Lindy moved here about six months before Sam took a job for an old-school vampire who'd just moved into the area. The vampire—his name was Hans something—asked for a light-proof sleeping compartment to be added to his bedroom closet. When Sam finished it, the vampire decided he didn't want a human knowing where his evil lair was and drained him."

"I thought it was illegal to forcibly turn a human."

"Technically, he didn't turn him. Hans just drained him until it would be impossible for Sam to survive and dumped him in the woods behind his house to let nature take its course. Fortunately, Hans was already under surveillance for some suspicious feeding activity over in Murphy. When the head of the local Council, Ophelia, saw him tossing Sam's body, she stepped in and had one of her Council goons turn him. Ophelia would do just about anything to avoid scandal for the vampire community. Draining innocent human temp workers would qualify as a PR disaster."

"Of course, Lindy pitched a fit, told everybody in town that Sam had gone off the deep end, had an early midlife crisis, fooled around with some vamp-tramp, and got himself 'infected,'" Jolene said. "Oh, and because of the physical trauma he'd been through, it took Sam nearly five days to transform into a vampire, which is practically unheard of. The Council admitted that it was possible that Sam might not make it through the transformation to vampire, and Lindy managed to get some judge to declare him too dead and/or incompetent to handle his own affairs, which was a legal first. There was no will, and Lindy got everything. She controls every bit of their money until the divorce goes through. Sam gets an allowance for his blood and utilities."

I mulled that over for a moment. Part of me felt sort of bad for him, in love with a woman who couldn't see him as the same person she'd married, just because his diet and waking hours had changed. And then I remembered the previous Tuesday, when he'd hidden every product I had that contained caffeine—after keeping me up until 3:00 A.M. with the melodious screams of a jigsaw. My sympathy was short-lived.

"Honestly, I think he just hasn't adjusted to unlife yet," she said. "Sam seems like a do-it-yourself kind of guy. And those first few months as a vampire, all you need is help. You feel like you're losing your connection to the human world and your place in it. You need someone to help you figure out your new schedule, how to feed without hurting your human donor, to vampire-proof your house. Sam went through all that alone."

A strange, hot sensation twisted in my belly. What

if Sam felt like that? What if he was lost and alone? Here I was making life that much more difficult for him, taking away from what little time he had left in his own home. I felt something shift inside me, a little spark of empathy I'd been missing for a while.

I jumped to my feet, nearly knocking over the little café table and our coffees. "I've got to go."

"What? Why?" Jolene's surprised expression morphed into wary resignation. "What did you do?"

I cringed, thinking of the various traps I'd left around the house for Sam. Suddenly, Jane burst out laughing and clapped her hand over her mouth.

My own jaw dropped. Could Jane read my mind?

Jane winked at me and nodded.

I would worry about that later.

I dug my keys out of my bag. "Someone may have sprayed down the basement steps with high-viscosity cooking spray, making them superslick."

Jolene sighed as Jane struggled to cover her snickers with her hand. "Tess."

I held my hands, defenseless. "No, I said *someone*."

"Don't you think you've taken this prank thang a little too far?" she asked. "I mean, some of these tricks are sort of stupid and juvenile, not to mention sort of mean."

I dashed toward the door. "This was really the least stupid or juvenile idea I had. You should have seen what I had planned with a can of Sterno and a jar of pineapple jelly."

Jolene slapped her palm over her face as I opened the door. Over the tinkle of the little cowbell above the door frame, I heard Jane say, "I really like her."

After driving across town in record time, I dashed into the house just as Sam opened the microwave. The house was still standing, which was a good sign. Sam was in the kitchen, apparently uninjured, also a good sign. What was not good was that he was making his dinner, tossing a warmed bag back and forth between his hands to settle the red cells.

"Look, I've had a bad night at work, and I really don't want to deal with you right now." He sighed, his shoulders sagging underneath his faded John Deere T-shirt.

Stalled midwarning, I raised an eyebrow. Work? Since when did Sam work? And where? Was that where he was all those nights when the construction noises didn't start until the wee hours? I thought he was slow-playing me, depriving me of sleep with the anticipation of torture. Had he been out on a job? This new perspective changed the way I'd looked at a lot of the stunts I'd chalked up to Sam's mean temper. Maybe he was leaving the chores around the house half-finished because he didn't have the time he needed, not because he wanted to the leave the house unlivable. Then again, that didn't explain the Saran Wrap. Or the stove.

"Sam, you really don't want to do that," I cautioned as he reached toward the cabinet where we kept the coffee mugs. In my haste, I bumped into a saucepan I'd set on the stove. The handle came away in my hands, and the metal bowl clattered to the floor. I gasped in horror as the pieces of my dismantled darling came clattering to a standstill. I shot him a murderous look. He smirked at me, his dark eyes twinkling. I jerked open the drawer where I kept my pots and pans. Everything I touched came apart in my hands. Somehow Sam had managed to remove the rivets from my pans.

I whirled on him. "You no-good, undead douche!"

"You know, with those dulcet tones, it really is surprising that some lucky man hasn't snatched you right up," he said, smirking.

Snarling, I whipped the pan handle at him. He used his unnatural speed to duck out of the way, which was fortunate, because I threw it so hard that it broke through the plaster behind his head.

"You!" I growled. "What the hell is wrong with you? Do you have any decency? You wanna hide my stuff? Fine. Use sleep deprivation to drive me into a psychotic episode? All righty, then. But when you mess around with my pans, that's going just one step too freaking far!"

"Really, this is what pushed you over the edge?" he asked blandly as he poured his warmed blood into a mug. "I messed around with your cookware?"

"You don't touch a chef's pans!" I shouted as

he took a long drink, wincing as the blood rolled down his throat. I smiled sweetly, pulling a carefully wrapped dropper bottle from my pocket and placing it on the counter in front of me.

"What the?" he asked, clearing his throat and pulling at the collar of his plaid work shirt. By now, he was feeling that tickle of discomfort near the back of his tongue, that feeling that something was definitely not right with his evening meal.

"Ever hear of something called the ghost chili?" I asked, rolling the plastic-wrapped extract bottle between my thumb and forefinger. "In the pepper family, it's basically the crazy cousin who just got out of prison, around a million units on the Scoville heat scale." He gave me a confused frown, and if I wasn't mistaken, there was just the hint of sweat popping out on his upper lip. I didn't know vampires could sweat. "That's about four hundred times hotter than the average jalapeño pepper."

"What did you do?" he demanded, rubbing at his throat. With the rush of spicy blood to his cheeks, I could see what he had looked like as a human, ruddy and virile, like something out of a "Hunky Farmhand of the Month" calendar.

I cleared my own throat, forcing myself to focus. This was war, damn it. Dirty, nasty, nonsexy war.

"Well, I called my friend Sakar, who works in my favorite spice shop, and asked him where I could find something special." I grinned nastily. "For my roommate. He just happened to know a store about forty miles from here that carries extract of ghost chili."

"You put it in my blood bag?" He grunted, coughing and spluttering as the capsaicin set flame to his tongue. He reached into the fridge, tore open another bag, and dumped the still-cold contents into his mouth.

I snickered. "Not just that bag."

"Augh!" he cried, dropping the doctored bag and running for the faucet. He stuck the sprayer into his mouth and turned it on full blast. When that failed to quell the heat raging through his mouth, he ran for the shower.

"Did I mention that water only makes the oil spread around?" I called. I dropped the bottle into the trash. Thinking better of it, I fished the bottle out, emptied it, and buried it in the backyard so he couldn't use it against me later.

When I came back into the house, a very wet, very red Sam was practically vibrating with rage. His fangs were down, and he looked every inch the dangerous vampire. I suddenly wondered about the wisdom of this weird little war. And it occurred to me that I should have had those worries before I pranked someone with superstrength.

"So, no yelling?" I asked, faking bravery as he glowered down at me. "No calling me names or making empty threats?"

"No." He scooped his hands under the lines of my jaw and dragged me to him. I squeaked as his mouth clashed with mine, pulling my tongue into his mouth to dance with his. I braced myself against his bare chest, fingertips digging into the cool flesh. His lips dragged across mine, and his tongue rippled over every ridge and bump of my mouth. He bit harshly down on my bottom lip, drawing just the tiniest bit of blood to the surface. I could feel my nipples blossoming into little points through my shirt as he pulled blood from the wound. It was like some warm thread was running directly from my thighs to the flow of blood, and every time he pulled on it, that thread drew across my nerves with a luxurious tension.

I was panting as if I'd run a marathon by the time he pulled away.

"What the hell was *that*?" I demanded.

He leered, halfway between self-satisfied smirk and impish grin. "I just wanted to share."

And that's when the tingling started.

"Oh, motherf—" I gasped as the chili oil that now coated my lips and tongue began to burn. I clapped a hand over my aching, searing lips. "You!"

Sam laughed while I ran for the fridge. I felt as if I'd swallowed about a hundred yellow jackets and they were all stinging the absolute shit out of my tongue.

I reached into the fridge for the only solution I knew of: dairy and popsicles. I ripped the lid off a container of plain Greek yogurt and started licking the contents while I unwrapped a Fudgsicle. I alternated between the two, cursing at him the whole time.

Because cursing sounds superintimidating when it's muffled by a Fudgsicle.

"Give up, you crazy woman," he growled out. "And could you please, please watch the cursing? This isn't a truck stop."

"No!" I pulled the Fudgsicle out long enough to shout. "You apologize for dismantling my kitchen!"

"It's not your kitchen!" he spat back. "You apologize for giving me doctored blood. No wonder you got fired. You're like some sort of evil comic-book villain. You—you're the Joker!"

"Oh, all I did was respond in kind. Look, I felt a little sorry for you earlier tonight, because of your bad luck and your tragic marriage. Clearly, empathizing with the enemy was a mistake. Now, either you fix my pans, or I will find brand-new places to put that chili extract, jackass." I growled, backing out of the room and stalking toward my bedroom.

He called after me, "I'd say this one was a draw, wouldn't you, sweetheart?"

Here in Lunch Lady Land...

6

Jolene was not impressed with my vampire-provoking shenanigans.

"Have I not explained how dangerous it can be to spend time with vampires when they're in a *good* mood?" She sighed, frowning at me in that way that only mothers could master.

Jolene's powers of emotional concentration would have been more impressive had she not been staring me down while turning her van into a dry cleaner's parking lot. I was trying to treat the still-tingling nerves of my lips and tongue with a strawberry milkshake from the Dairy Freeze. I was starting to suspect that it was more than just physiological, because nothing was working. It wasn't even unpleasant anymore, just a lasting, warm tingle over my skin. This couldn't be normal. "I thought you were goin' home to prevent your pranks from 'goin'' off on Sam."

"I tried to stop it," I said lamely, clutching the door frame for all it was worth, so I wouldn't smack my face into the window. "And then he took apart my pans and said mean things to me, and I sort of stopped myself from stopping it."

"So he slipped down the basement steps?" she said, cringing as she pulled to a screeching stop.

"I forgot about that," I said. "It would explain the loud thump I heard before bed."

Jolene gave me a withering look.

"What?" I grumped, crossing my arms.

"Have you thought about the fact that under the fangs and the bluster, there's a person with feelings?"

"I don't really care how he feels, Jolene," I protested. "I'm sorry for what he's going through. But he's not the only one out there in pain. I—what is it we're doing here, again? I thought we were going to Jane's shop."

"I need to make a quick stop first. I work part-time for a vampire concierge service here in town. My boss, Iris, asked me to pick up some of her clients' dry cleaning. Vampires are hell on clothes, let me tell you. I'll just be a minute. Do you want to come in?"

I glanced around the busy corner of Main Street, right off the memorial square of downtown Half-Moon Hollow. There was a classic white gazebo in the center, flanked by golden ginkgo trees and statues of Civil War soldiers. There was a huge plastic banner stretched across the street, advertising "Burley Days! Food, Frolic, and Family Fun!" starting in two weeks.

"No, I'll just wander around, if that's OK. I'll meet you back here in a bit."

She glanced down the street at the small-town oasis drawing me in and grinned broadly. I was stunned for just a moment by the sheer brilliant expanse of that smile. There was a fierce quality to Jolene, something not quite human rippling under that beauty. I started to wonder whether the reason she was so comfortable with the supernatural was that *she* was something supernatural.

Not that I'd let something like that get between us. Other than Chef and George, Jolene was the only real friend I'd made in years. I was determined not to care about it. If she felt like it, she would tell me in her own time.

"You do that," she said. "I'll catch up to you."

As Jolene ducked into AAA Cleaners, I perused the posters for Burley Days hung in various shop windows. "Family Fun" apparently included rides, game, a parade, street performers, and something called the "First-Ever Faux Type O Bloody Bake-Off!" which sounded absolutely disgusting. I would be skipping Burley Days.

I wandered down the street, staring at the old 1930s architecture. In Chicago, these buildings wouldn't be anything special. The Second City prided itself on preserving anything that had survived the Great Fire, the Depression, and both Richard Daleys. But it was clear that these old banks and general stores were the pride of the Hollow, lovingly restored and newly painted— all except this white and pink two-story building wedged between what were now an antiques shop and a florist. The windows were blocked over with soap, but I could still make out the faded paint reading, "HOWLIN' HANK'S BBQ, Est. 1968."

The white paint flaked off the brick front like falling snow. The door handle was damaged, as if someone had tried to kick it in. Someone had replaced the old faded Realtor sign with a new one: "A Honey of a Deal! Call Sherry Jameson, Hometown Realtors!" with Sherry's contact information spelled out in bold red print. Another poster for the Bloody Bake-Off had been tacked over a broken pane in the front door but was now hanging loose at the upper right corner, giving me a glimpse inside.

Someone had loved this place once but gave up a long time ago. The maroon pleather booths were cracked and peeling. The napkin dispensers consisted of paper-towel racks mounted against the oak paneling. The tables flanked a stout oak bar/counter. Old neon beer signs still hung on the walls, the tubing broken in places; one particularly ornate Budweiser sign was home to a rather large bird's nest. I could barely see the kitchen through the dining room, but I could make out a huge brick pit in the middle of the space.

I could see that the dusty tables had been intricately carved with messages. "Marcy Loves Joe Lee, 1976," or "Petey and Maybelline, First Date, 06/23/81," or a heart carved around the initials "MH + DW, 1992." It was sort of sweet, all of these couples marking their lives together on the tables where they'd shared meals. And I was sad that those people, who most likely still lived in the Hollow, couldn't come back there to visit their little milestone markers.

I rattled the doorknob, wondering if it counted as breaking and entering if the building was already "broken." The knob twisted in my hands, and—

"Kind of sad, isn't it?"

Jolene's voice sounded just behind me, making me jump and smack my head against the decorative rack of ribs hanging low over the doorway. "Ow!"

Jolene continued as if I hadn't just beaned myself with plaster-of-Paris pork. "This place was a Half-Moon Hollow institution until about ten years ago. Hank Fowler died, and his kids just didn't have the business sense or the flair for the kitchen that their daddy did. They limped along until a couple of years ago. They just couldn't keep the doors open anymore. I don't know why they've never sold the place."

"Too many prospective buyers injured themselves on the low-hanging decorative pig?" I said, rubbing my head. I nodded toward the poster. "OK, explain this Burley Days thing to me."

"It's the highlight of the Hollow social calendar,"

Jolene said, feigning distress at my ignorance. "It goes back to when burley tobacco was the big crop around here. Local farmers would bring their harvests to the brokers and get paid on one particular weekend each fall. They'd have money to spend, so vendors and carnies showed up every year to take it. It became a big party. Farmers around here have moved on to soybeans and such, but we've kept the tradition alive with funnel cake and ring toss. It's a hoot."

"How does a Bloody Bake-Off figure into this?" I asked, cringing.

Jolene wrinkled her nose. "Jane says that Faux Type O is sponsoring some sort of cook-off, asking people to come up with recipes using synthetic blood."

"Why would the company want to do that?" I asked as we ambled back toward the van.

"Newer vampires miss human food," she said. "They want more variety in their diet. Rather than lose their audience, Faux Type O is lookin' for ways to incorporate its product into the sort of 'cravin' foods' that new vampires will want. They're going to put the winning recipes into a cookbook. So if you win, you're basically selling the rights to the recipe for your prize money.

"They're hosting the contests all over the country. Ophelia, the head of our local Council office—she's really scary," Jolene said. "She has connections at the beverage company, and she's good at intimidating city officials. She said she wants to, quote, 'integrate the undead community into the Hollow's traditions.'"

"She gets a cut from the company, doesn't she?" I asked.

"Probably."

"Is Jane going to enter?" I asked.

Jolene stopped in her tracks, spluttering and choking, nearly doubled over in laughter. When she finally straightened up and wiped at her eyes, she wheezed out, "Jane's first few solo attempts at serving coffee at the shop sent people into convulsions. I don't think she's willing to do that, even if it means winning twenty-five thousand dollars."

Now it was time for me to splutter. "Twenty-five thousand dollars! You're telling me some vampire could win twenty-five thousand dollars just for making up a recipe?"

"Doesn't have to be a vampire," Jolene said, giving me a pointed look. When I scoffed, she cried, "What? You cook all the time."

"Yes, for people with pulses and the ability to process solid foods," I said. "There are some dietary restrictions even I can't work with."

"Fine, leave the vampire judges to deal with Jane's mama's Bloody Pot Pie." Jolene sighed as we climbed into the minivan. "Jane's mama seems to think she can force Jane into eating human food again if she just gives her enough pot pies. If she figures out a way to put

Faux Type O in a pot pie, I pity those poor volunteers—
including Jane."

"Why would Jane volunteer for something like
that?"

"Like I said, Ophelia is scary," Jolene said, shrugging. "So, are you ready for tonight?"

"What's tonight?"

"I'm droppin' these clothes off, and then you, me,
Jane, and Andrea are goin' out for a girls' night. Jane
hasn't made any of the plans, so we should be safe.
Think you're up for it?"

I snorted. "I think I'm ready for whatever nightlife
Half-Moon Hollow can dish out."

I was *so* not ready.

Girls' night, apparently, meant The Cellar, where
it was "Country-Western Night," and Jane never paid
for drinks, because she'd rescued the owner-bartender
during an attempted robbery a few years ago. So we
had not only unlimited alcohol but also access to a
mechanical bull.

One of the few things I could remember clearly
about the evening was being grateful that Sam wasn't
home when I stumbled through the front door around
2:00 A.M. and broke my fall with my face. But according to the pictures Andrea saved to my phone, I had
not only ridden the mechanical bull, I'd borrowed a
stranger's cowboy hat to make my experience more
authentic. I thought the hat went very nicely with

Andrea's sparkly black tank top. And the western-wear lover's phone number appeared to be scrawled on my arm, next to "Call me, Cowgirl!"

Oh, well, at least he was cute, according to the picture that showed me returning his hat and giving him a big wet kiss on the cheek.

The rest of the pictures included various shots of Jolene attempting karaoke, Jane hugging Norm, the cuddly bartender whose life she'd saved, and the four of us gathered at the bar, shot glasses in hand, giggling our asses off while Jolene tried to fit all of us into the frame.

At some point, my friends' husbands dropped by to scrape our inebriated asses off the barroom floor and drive us home. I'd met Zeb before and liked him. Underneath his oily charm, the vampire Dick Cheney was a really sweet guy who clearly loved Andrea and his friends with the ferocity of a pissed-off honey badger. I sort of recalled that the one guy who tried to hit on me in his presence was given the scariest stink-eyed glare this side of a correctional facility. Jane's Gabriel was more of a mystery, all brooding silence and stiff upper lip, until Jane made some ridiculous joke and he smiled like a man seeing boobs for the first time. But in a really romantic, courtly way.

The final picture was a group shot taken by Norm. Somehow I ended up in the middle of all of those couples without sticking out like the sore single thumb. I looked happy. Not just drunk-giddy or relaxed but genuinely, no-holds-barred happy. I couldn't remember seeing that expression on my own face since . . . I couldn't remember seeing that expression on my face.

Still, it was the deepest night's (and most of the morning's) sleep I'd had since I arrived in the Hollow. I rolled onto my back, and the reverberating pain in my head made me instantly regret moving. Zeb, my designated driver, had apparently left a glass of water and some Advil next to my bed when he'd dropped me off. I lifted my head from the pillow, just barely, to look at my alarm clock and saw that I was supposed to be meeting Chef Gamling at the Half-Moon Hollow First Baptist Church in less than an hour. Moving gingerly, I eased up from the bed and reached for the water glass. It only took me three tries to pick it up.

After scrubbing off eau de barroom, I discovered that Sam not only had soaked all of my clean bras and put them in the freezer, but he had also destroyed yet another cheap pot and left it in the sink. After preparing my traditional hangover cure of a bacon, egg, and tomato sandwich, I barely had time to Super Glue Sam's car keys to the counter before I was due to meet Chef.

The Half-Moon Hollow First Baptist Church was one of those classic brick churches with stained-glass windows. I felt nervous walking through the back entrance of the fellowship, as if God would reject my hungover presence in his house like a faulty kidney. But he let me walk all the way into the industrial-sized kitchen unscathed, so figured I wasn't his top "smiting" priority.

Chef Gamling was already stationed at the counter, shredding cheddar from a block the size of a football. A gigantic stock pot boiled on the stove, while another pot held a huge batch of green beans with bits of bacon. I could smell ham baking and the cinnamon-spice mix Chef used for his special apple pie recipe.

"Are we catering a party?" I asked.

He turned and leveled a critical gaze at my clean jeans and T-shirt, the sensible shoes and tight ponytail. He tossed an apron at me. "You'll do."

My transition back to Chef's galley slave was made with alarmingly little force. He had me chopping veggies, straining pasta, making a roux for the basic white sauce he needed. Dealing with hot butter fats was particularly cruel given my hungover state, but I think that was probably the point to Chef's exercise.

"What exactly are we making?" I asked as he added the shredded cheese to the white sauce.

"Macaroni and cheese," he said. "Ham. Granny Houston's famous green beans—a recipe I had to barter a Le Creuset casserole for, thank you—and apple pie."

"For what?"

"The church has Saturday-afternoon fellowship meals. Everybody from the community is welcome, whether they pay or not, whether they're members of the church or not. The pastor thinks it's important for everybody to gather for a good meal, for no other reason than to spend time together. Usually, they play board games or volleyball, depending on the weather. I think the plan for today is an Uno tournament. "

"You're going to all this trouble—aged cheddar, sauce from scratch, what appears to be green beans combined with bacon, butter, and brown sugar—so you can feed a church crowd mac 'n' cheese before a card game?"

"These people deserve good food, carefully prepared, whether it's simple fare or a wedding feast. They're going to share a meal, something to bring them closer together. That's the point of what we do, Tess. Not the reviews or the interviews. Good food. Happy diners. That's all there is."

He pinned me with that frank gray gaze, and I felt a little ashamed of myself. "Now, be a good girl and stir the sauce."

With that, he popped me on the butt with a dish-towel and returned to his nutritionally bankrupt green beans.

When I was in college, I saw cafeteria serving as the last stop before culinary oblivion. I had nightmares in which I woke up patting my head to make sure the hairnet wasn't really there. But now I found that I liked greeting people as they came through the kitchen line for their lunches. I liked being able to talk to friendly faces as they moved by, complimenting the colors of the food or the delicious smells wafting up from the steam table.

I'd never had this sort of contact with customers before. Phillip did his damnedest to make sure I was insulated from dealing with overenthusiastic customers. I rarely left my kitchen, just in case.

But because these diners liked Chef, I was accepted as his little helper, greeted warmly, and complimented for my addition of smoked paprika to the macaroni and cheese. After we'd fed everyone, some of them twice, Chef made me sit at the counter and eat a huge helping of everything. I wasn't gaining weight back fast enough, in his opinion. Overall, it was a very pleasant way to spend an afternoon.

I guessed Chef didn't have more Kitchen Yoda wisdom to impart, because he joined the Uno games—leaving me with the dishes, thank you very much. I was up to my elbows in bubbles when a trilling feminine voice behind me cried, "Hi there!"

Jumping and nearly dropping a sixty-four-ounce glass measuring cup on my foot, I turned to see a pretty, slender woman with a brown bob and mischievous hazel eyes. The shape of her mouth reminded me of someone.

"Aren't you Tess?" she asked, smiling broadly.

"Um, ye—gah!" I yelped when the woman threw her arms around me and squished me to her bosom.

"Oh, honey!" she exclaimed. "I'm so glad my Jane has a friend who goes to church!"

Well, I was standing in a church building, so I guess she was technically right.

"I'm Sherry Jameson, Jane's mama." She sighed, giving me one last squeeze. "But you can call me Sherry. All her little friends do. Jane told me you'd be here today, and I just couldn't wait to meet you! Now, don't get me wrong, I love Andrea and Jolene, but it's just so good to know that my daughter spends time with a nice girl. I mean, just look at you, cooking up a storm in the Lord's kitchen."

Now was so not the time to whip out my phone and show her the pictures of Jane and me running tequila boat races. So I settled for a bland smile while Mrs. Jameson pressed a heavy Saran Wrapped package in my damp hands.

"I made you my special peach cobbler. Jane mentioned you're a cook, so I knew you'd appreciate a little something sweet. Don't you worry about sugar or calories, all right, honey? You need a little meat on your bones," she said. "I used to make this for my Jane all the time, but you know, she doesn't eat anymore."

"Thank you," I managed to say before Sherry crushed me into another hug, my arms flailing against her back.

I glanced down at the package in my hands. Mrs. Jameson had cooked for me. I didn't even know if it was any good. But it was thrilling to have someone else cook something for me, not because she was trying to impress me or drill me for information but for no other reason than that I was a friend of her daughter's and she thought I needed it.

Hungover or not, I was going to go home and eat every bite.

Somewhere in the back of my pickled brain, a switch labeled "Sherry Jameson" flipped into place. Now I knew why Sherry's name sounded so familiar.

I smiled brightly, though it sort of hurt my cheeks. "Aren't you the Realtor selling Howlin' Hank's?"

Two hours later, I was in love with the Howlin' Hank's building.

Miss Sherry was honest with me. Hometown Realtors had assigned her this building to test her newly official salesman skills. The agency had been trying to offload the place for years and hadn't had so much as a nibble. The idea that she could be the one finally to sell it had thrown Sherry into warp speed, as Jane put it.

Chef Gamling accompanied us as my "anti-life-ruining-decision lifeguard." Before she let me in the front door, Sherry went in to turn on all of the old beer signs and the jukebox. The current selection was a Hank Williams Jr. song made overtly off-key by the warped 45. That's right. The jukebox was so old it played actual records. Still, the electric display gave me a better idea of what the place had looked like in its heyday.

Chef Gamling didn't comment on the dilapidated condition of the building or the sheer amount of beer and/or NASCAR memorabilia on the walls. He simply wandered around the kitchen, his hands clasped behind his back, while he chewed on his lip. The kitchen was in surprisingly good shape, albeit seriously outdated. I would need to replace all of the appliances, but the traffic flow of the room was pitch-perfect for maximum efficiency from the stove to the pass to the dishwashing area.

The dining room's open floor plan, the old oak bar worn satiny smooth by countless hands, the wide, spacious booths—it was the perfect setup for a small, informal restaurant. Before I'd even put down my purse, I'd started making plans in my head. I'd keep some of the more retro beer signs, but I would paint the walls a soft denim blue. I would have to replace the tables. But I might be able to preserve the carved tabletops and use them as wall panels.

I would keep the view to the kitchen open, so the customers would get the feeling that they were just hanging out at a friend's place, waiting for their meals to be finished. I would replace the battered dartboards with photos of the original Hank's and maybe a few of the remodel—something to show that I appreciated the history of this place and wanted to be part of it.

Oh, how I wanted to be part of it.

I rubbed at my sternum, praying for the acidic roll in my stomach to die down. Could I really do this? Could I stay in the Hollow and open up my own restaurant? Chef Gamling was here. My friends were here. What did I have waiting for me in Chicago?

I had acquaintances and colleagues in the city but nobody who would take me out for drinks and mechanical-bull rides. I had Phillip, who was waiting for his marriage-license paperwork, not for me. I had my reputation, but that wasn't exactly keeping me warm at night. It couldn't even give me the warm sense of fulfillment that it used to.

I sat down at one of the booths, leaning over to put my head between my knees. Across the table, I could hear the sound of old leatherette crackling. I looked up to squint at Chef, grimacing. "Am I completely insane?"

"Why would this be insane?"

"Because I've only cooked. I've never managed a restaurant. Because of the risks involved. Because these are disastrous economic times to strike out on my own."

"This is all true," he conceded. "But do you want this?"

I chewed on my lip, nodding. It scared me how much I wanted this. I didn't think I'd ever wanted something so badly in my life. Sure, I'd wanted to leave my hometown. I'd wanted to graduate. I'd wanted the job at Coda. But this was a different level of desire.

I had to have this place. I could feel the desperation down in my bones, crushing my stomach with the anxiety that I might not be able to make it happen.

I had a place in the city. I had a routine. But I could have a life here. I didn't exactly fit in, but I could love people here. I was well on my way to loving a few already. And those people could love me if I let them.

I could do this. I could make a life here. Hell, I already had a life here.

I wanted to feed people, not just because they had showed up for a business meeting or to be seen. I wanted them to leave my dining room happy. I wanted to cook and not think about whether the ingredients were exotic enough to please the customers. I wanted to serve food that nourished people, that made them feel comfort, whether it meant using Velveeta or ungodly expensive Jarlsberg cheese.

"Yes," I whispered. "I really want this."

"Then you are insane," Chef said, shrugging. "But it could be just the kind of insane needed to run this place."

"Not helpful." I groaned, dropping my head back to the table.

I felt a cool, damp cloth pressed to the back of my neck and heard a fond tsking sound just in front of me.

Sherry pressed her handkerchief to my temples and smiled gently. "Jane felt the same way just before she decided to renovate her shop. She was so afraid of making a change, so afraid that she would fail. But she couldn't stand not to try to make a go of it. She's always been my brave one, you know. Though if you tell her that, I'll deny it just to keep her on her toes. The bottom line is, life is for living, sweetie. It's for taking chances and trying to grab up every little piece of happiness you can latch on to. And I say that as a mama and a friend and not someone who stands to make a very healthy commission if you agree to take this place on."

I laughed and handed the damp handkerchief back to Sherry.

I stood and took another look around the restaurant. While my savings were not enough for the real estate market in Chicago, I had more than enough for the down payment on the building. Heck, given Hank's kids' desire to unload the building, I might be able to buy it outright, if Sherry and I were clever enough. The problem would be the cost of renovating; I would have to figure out a way to pay for that.

I needed to make this change. I needed this town. I needed the slower pace, the quiet. I needed the people here. This was my place now.

I edged toward the dusty old chalkboard behind the bar, advertising the specials and "pie du jour" in place when Hank's had closed. I took the eraser and carefully swiped off the old chalk marks. The brittle white chalk nearly crumbled under my touch, but I was able to scratch out what I wanted. "Honey-smoked pork with apples," I wrote. "Corn fritters with spicy relish. Dessert of the day: raisin brioche bread pudding."

I stood back and admired my handiwork.

"I would have served a chutney with the fritters," Chef said, sniffing.

My lips twitched. "Well, it's not your restaurant."

He sighed, rolling his eyes heavenward. "Sassy-mouthing again."

Sherry grinned at my very first selection of specials. "I take it you've made a decision?"

I turned and threw my arms around her and squealed, a very un-Tess-like squeal. She laughed again and patted my back. "Is it OK to hug your Realtor?" I asked.

Sherry gave me a very momlike little squeeze. "I'll allow it this once."

Poaching Territory

7

I sat on the front porch, under a purpling sky, mulling over the paperwork for Howlin' Hank's. I teetered between giddy joy and abject horror over signing a letter of intent to buy the building. What was I thinking? What had I done? What would I serve? What would I call the place?

I should have considered that before I signed the papers.

I made calls to Chicago as I drove, shell-shocked, back to the house. Phillip was very gracious about accepting my resignation and agreed that it would be too awkward to work with me while planning his wedding to someone else.

As expected, Coda's owners jumped at the chance to buy me out and promised to deliver a cashier's check within forty-eight hours. While their offer was generous, considering the economy, it left me with two options: Take out a mortgage for the building and a second loan to cover the costs of renovating, or pay cash for the building and leave myself with a practically nonexistent budget for the facelift. Neither seemed like the ideal situation. While the building was structurally sound—with the exception of some storm damage to the roof—it would need some serious cosmetic work. Key changes usually translated to "expensive" in construction-speak. The whole prospect made me nervous. Thanks to some youthful indiscretions with a Visa card, my credit wasn't stellar. Damn my addiction to fancy Belgian knives.

Giving up my apartment would be shockingly easy. I'd barely spent enough time there over the years to make it a home. I hadn't decorated or added any personal touches. Everything was beige, for cripe's sake. But the thought of giving up the Lassiter place was singularly depressing.

Sherry had shown me the apartment above Howlin' Hank's and it was perfectly adequate. Or would be, after the renovations that would jack up my construction budget even further. But ultimately, I had enough on my plate taking on the restaurant. I wouldn't have the time, money, or energy to take on a fixer-upper house.

If I could find a way to stretch my budget another twenty thousand dollars or so, I'd have enough breathing room to do what I hoped to with the restaurant. But I did not, in fact, have naked pictures with which to blackmail Bill Gates, and I didn't have anything else to sell, unless you counted my car or a kidney—and I would need both.

The sun slipped over the horizon, leaving long lavender shadows in its wake. I buried my face in my hands and groaned. I leaned against the porch railing and looked out over the velvety green lawn. I would miss this place. I would miss having my own quiet space. I would miss waking up every morning to plot revenge against Sam for his pranks, even if I did sort of regret dosing his blood with essence of third-degree tongue burn. Then again, that had led to receiving the hottest kiss of my life, in every sense of the word, so it couldn't have been a terrible plan.

A soft thump sounded behind me, making me turn toward the front door. Speak of the bewildering devil. Sam was standing there, framed behind the screen door, his dark hair tousled. He was staring at me, his head tilted at a quizzical angle. I simply stared back, unsure of what else to do. I supposed I should have been nervous, caught in the sights of an apex predator, but there was nothing threatening in his gaze. He seemed curious, a little irritated, as if he were looking at some overpriced abstract painting he couldn't figure out . . . because he probably wasn't supposed to. I tilted my head to mirror his posture, because, frankly, I doubted I'd ever interpret Sam correctly, either. I wanted to. I just didn't know how to reset our relationship from minor domestic booby-trapping to "let's be friends."

What could we have been, if we hadn't started off so badly? If we'd just met walking down the sidewalk on Main Street, would we have been friends? Would he have asked me out for coffee, or whatever vampires did for awkward-first-date beverages? It was sad that I would never know. Part of me—a teeny, tiny synapse in the dimmer region of my brain—would even miss Sam when I moved out. Yes, he pissed me off. And yes, he had hurt my pans. But he kept things entertaining. And I couldn't deny that through the frustrations and near-injuries, we had chemistry. The sort of chemistry that seemed to be melting holes in the screen door at the moment.

Blinking slowly, Sam seemed to come to his senses and backed away from the screen, closing the front door behind him.

Well, that was weird.

It struck me that it wasn't a great idea to start my new life in the Hollow with a local vampire pissed off at me. Maybe as a going-away present, I could make something nice for Sam, some variation of whatever he was trying to do with those burned-out saucepans, only edible. He obviously missed real food, and I had sort of tortured him with the lasagna and the brownies. That seemed less OK now that I would probably bump into him at Walmart at some point.

But where would I start? How did you make blood more palatable? Add other, tastier bloods? Herbs and spices? Make it into gravy? Blood pudding?

I slapped my hand over my face. How could I forget about something called the Bloody Bake-Off? If I entered the contest and won, the grand prize was $25,000. That would pad my construction budget considerably. And frankly, I didn't think any other gourmet chefs of my caliber would be entering. My chances of beating Jane's mom were pretty high. Plus, it couldn't hurt my reputation locally for word to get around that I was a good enough cook to make vampire food palatable.

I pulled out my phone and dialed the number listed in my contacts under "Jane, if you're not calling for bail $$."

"Hey, Jane, it's Tess," I said. "Do you know where I sign up for this vampire cooking contest?"

My approach to the contest entries was simple. I wanted to make something that reminded the judges of their human days—assuming they remembered them—but still appealed to their vampire palates. Clearly, all of the ingredients had to be liquid. I didn't even want to risk purees after what Jane had told me about the French cookbook.

I tried to stay with familiar flavors, nothing too exotic. Hell, I even made a very thin marinara from tomato juice, but I needed some feedback before I decided which entry was the best. I tried tasting a few of my samples, but the weird metallic aftertaste of the Faux Type O overrode any other flavors.

This brought my favorite vampires, Jane, Gabriel, Andrea, and Dick, to the recently cleaned bar in the Howlin' Hank's building. (I was really going to have to come up with a name for the place soon.) The family was more than willing to let me "play" in the space while the final sale paperwork was ironed out, as long as I paid cash. I was so confident in my ability to win the prize money that I'd agreed. I bought the building outright, saving just a few thousand for the renovations and new equipment.

The dining room was still pretty beat-up, but I'd done a thorough cleaning. I'd found and washed some shot glasses, then used them to set up a tasting session at the bar.

"Are you sure it's safe to eat anything prepared here?" Gabriel asked, obviously trying to keep his tone in the "nonpanic" range as he eyed the defunct beer signs and broken chairs. "Did you say you only had the electricity turned back on this morning?"

"I didn't cook this here," I assured him. "I cooked it at home, but I didn't want to stir up my cranky roommate by inviting a bunch of people there. I thought this would be more fun."

"She clearly has Jane's idea of fun," Dick muttered to Gabriel.

"So, when are you going to start work on this

place?" Jane asked, elbowing Dick as I poured shot glasses full of a warm, deep-red concoction.

"I'm not sure. I have to find a contractor who's willing to work with my budget."

"Why don't you talk to Sam?" Andrea asked as I sprinkled a tiny bit of rosemary oil over each shot.

"Because I don't want my lower lip nailed to the bar at some point during the construction process?" I asked. "I mean, I've done things to him that the Geneva Convention would frown upon. I don't think he's going to give me a fair and accurate estimate, Andrea."

"I might know someone," Dick said before the other three cut him off with a chorus of "NO!" Dick huffed and crossed his arms over his chest. "Fine."

"Jolene will help you find someone. If she doesn't have a cousin who will do it for you, she has a cousin who knows someone who will do it for you," Jane assured me, lifting a shot glass and sniffing. "So, what do we have here?"

I wiped my hands on a dishtowel and did a small curtsy behind the bar. "OK, this is a red-wine reduction with shallots—well, shallot juice—and a few other goodies, and, of course, Faux Type O. It's basically the go-to sauce for any chef auditioning for a job."

The vampires sniffed the glasses and then, giving one another subtly wary looks, knocked back the shots.

"So, what do you think?" I said, bouncing up and down on my heels. "Should I stick with this one as the contest entry, or do you want to taste more? Because I'm pretty sure this is the best selection."

They stared at me, eyes unnaturally wide. That's when I noticed that they weren't smiling. Most people smiled when they were eating my food.

Dick swallowed heavily, grimacing. "Taste more?"

"This is the *best* one?" Jane said, dabbing at her mouth with a napkin.

My eyes flicked to each vampire's face and their expressions of strained, polite discomfort. They hated it.

A cold flush of shock and panic skittered down my spine. My brain kept screaming, *Impossible!* I didn't make bad food. Even when I made blue-box macaroni and cheese, I did it with flair. And this was my red-wine reduction. Everybody loved my red-wine reduction, even Chef Gamling.

I'd tasted this batch myself just before adding the blood. It was the perfect mix of sophistication and Southern comfort. Except it wasn't, because Dick seemed to be trying to scrape his tongue with a napkin without being obvious about it.

"Does synthetic blood curdle?" I reached for the shot glass and sniffed. It smelled fine to me, a little coppery under the peppery tang of the sauce, but fine.

Gabriel cleared his throat. "No, no, it's fine. It just a little . . ."

Dick murmured, "How can we put this delicately?"

Jane took my hands in hers, looked me straight in the eye, and said, "It tastes like old sandals and feta cheese."

"*That* was delicately?" I deadpanned.

"For Jane, yes, it was," Andrea informed me.

"OK, what could I change?" I asked, my voice hitching slightly. I took a deep breath to stave off the worst of my panic. "Should I season it differently? Change the consistency?"

"I don't know," Jane said. "It's not even an issue of spices or texture. It just tastes . . . wrong."

"OK." I whisked another set of shot glasses off the counter, the one containing my second choice, an attempt at masking the taste of the blood in an Asian-inspired plum sauce. "Try this one."

Dick couldn't hold the glass to his lips for more than two seconds before shuddering, giving me an apologetic look, and placing the glass back on my tray. When Andrea lifted the glass to her mouth, Dick's hand shot toward her and pulled the glass out of her grasp. Jane sipped, gagged, and spat the sauce back into her shot glass. Gabriel, who seemed to feel sorry for me, downed the sauce in one gulp. He paled, which was saying something, mumbled "Excuse me," and ran for the bathroom.

"What am I doing wrong?" I exclaimed.

"I don't know," Jane said sympathetically. "But you'll get it. Don't worry."

But I *was* worried. I refused to subject my guests

to further gastronomical torture. I went home to my kitchen and went over my recipes one by one. These were my tried-and-true recipes. I used versions of them at Coda every day. No one hated these. I'd done my research. I'd broken down the flavor profiles on a molecular level to match the right sauce to the right blood type.

If I didn't win this contest, I would barely have enough to make Howlin' Hank's habitable. I'd been so stupidly confident in my skills, in my ability to blow the locals out of the water, that creating something inedible hadn't even crossed my mind.

I felt like such an idiot. Did vampire taste buds really change so much after death? Gabriel described the taste issue as the vampire body's method of digestive self-defense. The vampire's brain instinctually knew that solid food would make them sick, so it sent messages to the body that human food was rancid and disgusting. Maybe if I could trick the vampire's brain into thinking it was just enjoying another cup of blood, I wouldn't serve them something that tasted like the inside of Mike Tyson's gym bag.

"I can fix this," I assured them. I grabbed the spices and herbal oils I'd brought with me to garnish the shots and went to work doctoring the remaining entries. Dick grimaced but gamely stepped up to the bar. Gabriel rolled his eyes but clearly didn't want to be outdone in the chivalry department. He stepped forward, too.

"I haven't thrown up in more than a year," Andrea told me, taking her own shot glass in hand. "You break my streak, and I'm going to be pissed at you."

I'd broken Andrea's streak and then some. My poor ladies' room would never be the same.

Hours later, I sat at the Lassiter house's kitchen counter, my face buried in my hands. I'd never cooked anything bad before. When I was a culinary student, I'd gotten cocky with the seasonings and turned a simple roast chicken into a garlic-soaked mess. Even then, I'd managed to turn the carcass into a palatable soup and gotten partial credit.

"What did I do?" I groaned, thunking my head on the counter. I let it rest there as hot tears tracked down my cheeks. If I didn't come up with a prize-winning entry, I had no shot at the money I needed for renovations. Who would want to eat in a restaurant with a semiprivate bathroom?

A cool hand awkwardly patted my head, followed by an arm slipping around my shoulder. I glanced up through my hair to see Sam sitting next to me, stretching his body as far away from me as possible, as if he was cuddling up to an incendiary device.

"There, there," he said, his voice resigned and sheepish as he patted my head. "I'm sorry I hurt your pans."

"What?" I exclaimed, snorting far too loudly as my head popped up.

Sam looked stricken, his cheeks pale(r) and his brown eyes clouded with concern. His lean frame was curved around mine almost protectively, and I found I didn't want to move away. Hell, I wanted to move closer. I sniffed, offering him a watery smile.

"Don't flatter yourself. This is not about you." I waved a hand at my tear-stained cheeks. "This is just . . . everything. I've been on this roller coaster, feeling like a failure, feeling almost normal, feeling I've got it all figured out, and then right back at failure again. Only this time, I don't know if I can bounce back. I have hubris-ed myself right into a corner, and I don't even think that's a verb."

"Psfff." He snorted, pulling a bar stool close to mine and sitting. "Failure. Trust me, I know failure. Whatever this is, it's just a bump in the road. I moved here to try to save my marriage. And livin' here is what destroyed it."

"I'm sorry," I said. "I heard that Lindy didn't handle your, er, transition, very well."

He scoffed. "You know, her brother was one of my best friends. He warned me against her, and not just in that 'friends don't mess around with their friends' sisters' way. He told me Lindy was a 'wanter.' She planned and prayed, but then once she had whatever 'it' was, she didn't want it anymore. She got a degree in marketing but decided she wanted to be a medical coder. I rented us an apartment, but she wanted out of the lease by the third month. She went through three wedding dresses before I even proposed.

"I thought she would settle down, be happy, once we were married. We were living in Nashville. I was workin' as a project manager for this big construction firm. Lots of hours, lots of travelin'. I hardly ever saw Lindy. She's the one who pushed for us to move. This house, in this town, was supposed to save our marriage. A quieter life, less stress, more time together."

"And it didn't work?"

He grimaced, that cute little constellation of freckles disappearing into the creases under his eyes. "It turned out that not spending time together was what held our marriage together for so long in the first place."

"Ouch."

"I fit right into the Hollow. There are nice people here. It was a good place if we wanted to raise a family. My business picked up faster than I expected. Lindy just sort of drifted, which was unusual for her. She couldn't find friends. It was too quiet for her. She didn't like livin' in a work in progress. When she saw how happy I was, I think it pissed her off. I think she decided that I was the latest thing she just didn't want anymore.

"I wasn't perfect," he admitted when I made a derisive snorting noise. "The more Lindy tried to tell me what I should and shouldn't do, the more I dug in and did what I thought I needed. I thought that once the place was finished, it would get better. Livin' our life in this house, livin' up to its potential, was supposed to fix things. But then I took that job for Hans and got turned. I know it was scary for her, not knowing if I was dead or not, not knowing what it would be like, married to me. But hell, it was scary for me, too. I woke up, and she was gone. Our life together was gone. And when I tried to talk to her about it, well, she freaked out. Called me a monster, told me to stay away from her. And I . . . may have gotten Hulk-angry and thrown a couch through a window."

"Wow."

"Not my finest moment," he admitted, running his fingers through his unruly hair. His mouth formed a slanted, rueful grin. "Lindy, of course, insisted I was too dangerous to be around normal people. Called her family, our friends, my friends here in town, to 'warn' them about my new nature and how fast I could turn on humans. Damn near ruined the life I'd built here, but she was scared and confused, and I guess I can't blame her."

I muttered, "I can." He frowned at me, making me shrug. "I'm a grudge holder."

"She's puttin' the house on the market on October 28," he said, his voice toneless and resigned. "All the property went to her when I died. But thanks to the Council's intervention, I got to stay here, and she had to return the holdings for my construction business—the business account, the tools, equipment, and such—and I have until October 28 to buy her out of the house. I've been working a little, doing nighttime projects for one of our neighbors, Mr. Calix. He's added a fence, an outbuilding, and a finished basement to his house in the last few months. I think he's just doin' it because he's tryin' to help me out, but he's too nice to say anythin' about it. It hasn't been enough to save what I need."

I muttered, "That explains why the drills didn't start until the wee hours some nights."

"I had to squeeze annoyin' you in where I could," he admitted, grinning sheepishly. "I am sorry you got pulled into this mess. Lindy was using you, leasin' the house to you while I was still here. She was countin' on something called the Vampire Squatters' Act. Right after the Comin' Out, human mortgage companies and landlords got tired of newly turned vampires just walking away from their homes, figurin' that mortgages and leases didn't apply to them anymore. So the government declared that any vampire who left their property for more than thirty-two days had abandoned it.

"She must have a buyer lined up already. If I raise the money before the deadline, she has to sell me the house. That's why she rented it. She thought if some tenant annoyed me enough, I would move out for the length of the lease, and the house would be considered abandoned to her. She'd be free to sell it without giving me a dime."

"So I was her backup plan? I think that hurts my feelings," I mumbled, my face flushing hot with shame. No wonder Sam had put up such a fight against leaving, despite my campaign against him. I hated the idea that I'd been helping Lindy, albeit unwittingly, try to drive Sam away from this place. The manipulative little wench would pay for that.

"I'm really sorry about the crickets," I said, my voice soft. "And the ghost chili. And gluing your car keys to the counter. Well, I'm pretty sure you deserved the chili thing, but—this is not how a normal person behaves. I'm sorry. I can't leave, but I don't want to be this crazy wok-swinging whackaloon anymore. If we could just find a way to share the house for just a little while longer, I swear I won't attack you again. I'm supposed to be resting, not plotting."

"I don't want to do this anymore, either. I'm afraid we're going to escalate to the point where one of us is left with a permanent limp," he said. "And to my everlastin' shame, between the two of us, your pranks seem to be more effective, so I'm all for a ceasefire."

"It's not even that I don't like you," I said, wiping at my dripping nose with my sleeve just as Sam tried to hand me a red bandanna from his back pocket. "There's nothing specific about you not to like. Other than your mere presence.

"I will stay out of the basement," I swore. "If you agree to stay away from my cookware."

"Agreed," he said, patting my shoulder again.

"We're goin' to be OK. When I'm not actively tryin' to get rid of someone, I'm actually a very easygoin' roommate."

"Oh, sure, you're a charmer." I lifted my head and looked directly at him for the first time since the conversation started. It amazed me that I could move it so easily. My neck felt as if it had had a bowling ball lifted off it.

"If we're going to make an honest go of this, we're going to have to abide by some rules."

"More rules? I've already agreed not to attack you with kitchen implements!" I exclaimed, feigning indignation.

He gave me a withering, and somehow incredibly sexy, glare.

"Such as?" I asked.

"I stay out of your room," he said. "And you stay out of mine."

"Like I wanted to visit your lair." I snorted.

"I think a part of you is a little curious about it," he said, grinning cheekily.

"I'm a little curious about tattoos," I shot back. "Doesn't mean I'm going to get a tramp stamp."

"I think you'd look hot with a tramp stamp," he said, tilting his head and giving me a long, speculative look that made a shiver ripple up my spine. "A cute little kitten . . . wavin' a very sharp knife."

"Funny," I retorted. "And on that note, I promise that I won't threaten you with my knives anymore. No more hitting you with pans. No more tainting your blood with evil pepper juice. If you're civil to me, I'm civil to you. It's what I should have said in the first place."

"Agreed. And I will stop callin' you a psycho."

"You called me a psycho?"

He shrugged. "Not to your face." He took a long pull from the bottle of synthetic blood, the faintest lines of a grimace crinkling the corners of his mouth.

"Not as good as the real thing?" I asked.

His brows drew up in surprise. "You offering?"

"No," I said, shaking my head emphatically. "No, no, no. I'm just curious about what that tastes like to you. What would make it taste better, that sort of thing. I'm trying to enter this cooking contest for vampires—"

"The Bloody Bake-Off?"

"Yes, and I can't quite get a grasp on what I'm supposed to be doing. It's more than that—I'm, aw hell, I'm just sucking beyond the telling of it." I unwrapped the remnants of the red-wine reduction sauce and held it up for him to sniff. "I've done everything I can to cover up the taste of the synthetic blood, but all of my efforts made my vampire friends sick. And if I don't figure out what I'm doing wrong, my life here in the Hollow is going to be . . . well, less than I'd hoped."

He brought the sauce up to his face and winced.

"You're probably lookin' at it from your own perspective, what tastes good to you. You make something that sounds good for a human palate and then add some blood. You need to think about what tastes good to a vampire, start with the blood, and work from there." He held up the half-empty bottle of synthetic blood. "This doesn't taste like anything. For vampires, it's not so much bein' hungry as bein' really, really thirsty. You can't think of anything else until you feed. Human blood, donated or live-fed, answers that thirst and lets you think clearly again. This? This is like drinkin' water when you could be havin' an ice-cold lemonade."

"Hmmph."

He snickered at my distaste. "I take it that you've never thought about being turned into a vampire?"

I pulled a frown. "Well, everything I cooked would taste spoiled and rotten to me. Not exactly a great career move."

"Good point." He sighed, pushed to his feet, and wiped his hands on his jeans, as if his palms had been sweating. "OK, get up, wash your face, and show me some of these samples that made your friends upchuck."

I sniffed, more than a little startled by his friendly tone and the way he stretched his long fingers toward mine. I was sure I'd misheard him. "What?"

"Look, I've tried coming up with a contest entry of my own, but I can't boil water without startin' a fire.

And you can't seem to grasp the whole vampire-taste-bud thing. But if we combine our efforts, we might have a chance at winnin' this thing."

"That's why I've been finding the burned pans? You were cooking on your own?"

"Sadly, yes."

I cackled, making him pout a little. "What temperature setting were you using on the stove?"

He frowned. "There are different settings?"

I rubbed my temples. "I weep for you, I really do. But I have plans for that prize money, as much as I want to help you stick it to Lindy."

"I know, you just bought Howlin' Hank's, and you need the money to fix it up," he said. When my jaw dropped, he added, "It's a small town. Word gets around, even to the hermits."

"So if you know I need the money, why are you asking me to do this?"

He dropped to bended knee in an exaggerated show of chivalry. He took my hand in his cool, slim fingers and pressed both over his still heart. His dark eyes twinkled as he looked up at me. "Because I have a proposal for you. I'll help you perfect the recipe for your entry. If you win, you give me the prize money so I can buy the house from Lindy. In exchange, I will do all of the renovations on your restaurant, for the cost of materials."

"You're screwing with me," I scoffed. "If I helped you, and I'm not saying I will, you would run off with the money, leaving me with squat."

"I wouldn't," he swore. "I may be a lot of things, but I'm a man of my word. And if it makes you feel any better, I'd sign a contract with you, guaranteeing my services. We could file it with the Council office."

I pinched my lips into a prim expression to prevent the crazy grin that threatened to split my face. "I have other vampire friends who are willing to be my guinea pigs."

"None of them can hang drywall like I can."

Why did that sound slightly dirty when he said it? I eyed him suspiciously. As much as I wanted to rain some sort of biblical vengeance upon Sam's snotty blond ex, I didn't really want to be pulled into their marital drama. I did not need to take on other people's stress when I was just learning to manage my own, and I found angry-married-people baggage to be particularly distasteful. But Sam had been honest with me, more honest than my last three boyfriends. And frankly, he did do some very nice work around the house. I would love to see what he could do for the restaurant.

"Come on, Tess, what do you say?" he said, the sound of my name on his lips making my stomach do strange, flippy things.

I shuddered but managed to maintain what little composure I had left as I said, "I don't even know if I want to use you as a contractor."

"Aw, come on, you can play dirty all you want, but don't play dumb," he countered, sounding miffed at the slight against his abilities.

Snickering, I reached out my other hand for an official shake, then retracted it, narrowing my eyes at him. "This isn't another prank?"

He dropped my hand and held up his own in a mockery of the Boy Scout oath. "I promise."

"I'm going to need some time to think about it."

He rose to his feet, standing a little closer to me than I was comfortable with. I backed up, only to bump against the counter. "I understand. And while you're thinking, I just want you to consider one thing."

"What?"

He grinned at me with those sharp white teeth, making my knees wobble a bit. I held on to the counter for support as he leaned closer and whispered, "How much it's going to piss Lindy off when she realizes her 'renter' is helping to snatch the house out from under her."

Blending Oil and Water

8

"ey, Sam!" I called. "Would you come taste this?"

I hovered over the rust-colored mixture bubbling merrily in my saucepan, waiting for just the right moment of consistency to remove it from the heat. I whisked the pan from the stove and stirred it carefully before noting the time and cooking temperature in my little recipe notebook.

On the other side of the house, I heard the whining peal of an electric drill. But this time, instead of attempting to drive me insane, Sam was putting up a heavy-duty curtain rod for sunproof shades.

In the last week or so, we'd developed a routine at the Lassiter house. I would visit Jolene, nap, or experiment with new recipes during the day. Then I'd make dinner and warm up some blood just in time for Sam to rise. We'd eat together, hold completely ridiculous conversations about '80s music, our favorite tacky monster movies, and whether reality television would be the social factor that finally triggered the apocalypse.

Sam would work through the samples I'd prepared that day, and—depending on whether or not I'd made him violently ill—we'd spend the rest of the night making small changes in the recipes.

While we talked about movies, music, food, sports, and any number of pop-culture phenomena, we rarely ventured into territory as personal as his revelations about his marriage to Lindy. It seemed to have made him uncomfortable, being that open, and he'd retreated to safer topics. That was fine, as long as we kept talking. Now that we were on the same team, I was seeing a whole new side to Sam—funny, laid-back, sensible, easy with a smile, and quick to admit when his cooking advice went horribly awry. I didn't feel I had to play down my accomplishments, as I had to with so many men I'd dated before. I didn't have to pretend to be a delicate little flower who rarely ate more than a salad with dressing on the side. Because Sam knew I was neither delicate nor flowerlike. And he'd seen me eat an entire quart of Three Little Pigs hash-brown casserole in one sitting. I could be myself with Sam, the unglossed, cooking-in-a-wife-beater-and-yoga-pants, "real" version of me that Phillip hadn't met until we'd been dating for six months. We'd barely lasted seven.

I would miss our evenings together when I moved into the apartment over my as-yet-unnamed eatery. Maybe we'd arrange some sort of vampire-food-for-maintenance-work barter system after I opened, just so we could keep in touch.

I spent several afternoons helping Chef Gamling with the church dinners. On the rare evening I didn't spend with Chef or Sam, I was with Jolene and her friends. Jolene was very quickly becoming my first meaningful friendship outside of the kitchen. She was funny, warm, smart in a no-nonsense, "don't try to screw with me just because I'm gorgeous" way that sort of made me want to have her babies. Not that I would, because (a) science wasn't quite there yet, and (b) she seemed pretty attached to Zeb, for whom I also had very fond feelings.

I'd found a circle of friends here. And I was really enjoying my time with them. Jolene had talked her uncles into letting me shadow them in their kitchen at the Three Little Pigs. Jane had invited me to one of her infamous girls' movie nights, which guaranteed that I would never look at Jane Austen adaptations ever again.

Sam's voice behind me drew me out of my musings. "You hollered?"

"Did you like Italian food when you were human? Because this has chicken stock and Marsala wine. The cooking process should have left a result that won't make you sick."

"Should?" he said, eyeing the shot glass suspiciously.

Without responding to his concerns, I added, "Just try it." I pushed the shot glass toward his lips.

"But you said you weren't sure about it," he protested.

I took the shot glass out of his hand and pressed it to his lips.

"That's not bad," he said.

"No nausea?"

"Can I have another?"

"Try this one," I said. "It's like barbecue sauce. Honey, liquid smoke, pork stock, and other by-products you may not want to know about."

"There's pig's blood in here?" he said, wrinkling his nose.

"How is it different from drinking human blood?" I asked. "Besides, if you ate bacon in life, it's a little hypocritical to turn your nose up at pig's blood now."

"Oh," he said, sighing, after knocking back the shot. "Now I just really miss ribs."

"My blender cannot handle rib bones," I told him.

"This," he informed me, lifting the barbecue sauce, "is awesome. If you could bottle this, you would kick the crap out of Paul Newman and his salad dressings."

"Paul Newman's dead," I reminded him, narrowing my eyes. "Unless there's something you and the vampire community have to explain to me."

"That's not nice," he said. "You could be the first

celebrity chef for vampires, like Rachael Ray or, if Mr. Gamling keeps giving you those dumplin's, that Paula Deen chick."

"Thank you for reminding me why being nice to you is never a good idea, you ass."

He leaned in close, his brown eyes twinkling. "Oh, come on, Tess, I'm sorry. You can be as nice to me and my ass as you want."

"I'm not touching that one."

He smirked. "You know you want to."

"Do you want to go back to cricket warfare again? Because I'm feeling a trip to the bait shop coming on."

He shuddered, giving me the vampire puppy-dog eyes, which was just disturbing. "Please, ma'am, don't unleash your biblical plagues of bitchery upon my household."

I laughed, shoving at his shoulder. He was so close, and my arm was pulled flush against his chest. I closed my eyes, enjoying the vibrations from his laughter traveling from his chest through my fingertips, all the way up my arm to my heart. It was like feeling the pulse he no longer had. I felt my lips part in a smile so wide my cheeks ached. This wouldn't do. I couldn't let him see that smile and know what a big part he played in it. I dipped my head, glancing down at the feet so closely arranged we could have been dancing. My forehead brushed against his shoulder. He tucked his fingertips under my chin and tilted my head toward his. His eyes were hooded and dark and stared right through me. His lips looked so soft, even turned into that slightly mocking grin he was giving me. I could stand up on my tippy-toes, or maybe on a chair, and kiss him so easily.

But I didn't.

Smiling awkwardly, I stepped away and took a deep breath. He wasn't ready. And no matter how loudly my raging hormones screamed, *You moron, do you realize how long it's been since anyone has gone near your forbidden zones?* I couldn't be the one to decide that he was over his ex-wife.

He was going to have to make the first move. And considering the fact that I was standing immediately lip-adjacent and he didn't give me a 20 percent lean-in, I didn't think he was going to be doing that anytime soon.

"So, the barbecue sauce, huh?"

He nodded, taking a step back. "That's your winner."

The nights went by faster than I imagined they could. We focused our efforts on perfecting the barbecue sauce. We experimented with cooking times, temperatures, spices, sauce bases, until Sam pronounced it almost as good as eating real food when he was human. Sam and I visited the restaurant and discussed the changes he would make, including improvements to the apartment upstairs. My calendar filled up with closings with the Realtor, appointments with the bank, and drinks with the girls. Before I knew it, we were bumping down the country road toward town in Sam's truck, with our contest entry carefully balanced on my lap.

"Don't be nervous," Sam told me.

"Can't help it," I said, leaning my head back against the seat rest. "There's a reason I hide in a kitchen all day. I'm not good with crowds."

He nudged me with his elbow. "You're going to be fine."

"Liar." I sighed.

Sam's truck smelled nice, like Murphy's Oil Soap and piña colada air freshener. This was a very different vampire from the one I'd been pranking. He was relaxed, if not quite happy, as he hummed along to George Strait. He actually smiled at me when he emerged from the basement earlier and complimented me on the little red sweater I'd paired with jeans. It felt natural driving along with him like this, almost like a date, if one's first date involved hauling several servings of synthetic blood around in a warmer.

Sam pulled the truck to a stop in front of an old bank building, near Howlin' Hank's. While I stared, bewildered by the sheer number of cars parked in front of the darkened buildings, he pulled me out of the truck and helped me with our parcels.

While parents hauled sunburned, exhausted children to their cars, the "night shift" for Burley Days was arriving in droves. The town square was bustling with laughing humans and vampires toting an odd assortment of cheap stuffed animals. Red, white, and blue twinkle lights hung from every stationary object, giving the square a festive glow. Gleeful screams echoed over the insistent country and western music pumped over the PA system.

We carried our sauce samples in a foam chest lined with warming gel packs. As we walked, I noticed several people watching Sam, flashes of recognition flitting across their faces before they averted their eyes. They were human, I could tell by their tans, and they refused to make eye contact. They didn't exactly turn their backs, but they definitely weren't giving him manly fist bumps. Were these people Sam's friends and clients before he was turned? What had Lindy said to them that would make them retreat this way? My irritation with Sam's ex ratcheted up to "bitch-slap on sight" levels.

When Sam took my hand to lead me through the crowd gathered in front of the dunking booth, I gave his a little squeeze. He dropped it as if I'd burned him, but I tried not to take it personally. Earlier head patting aside, it must have been strange to have me touching him after I'd done everything in my power to injure him.

We spotted the garish black and red Faux Type O booth near the center of the square. Two tall black columns flanked a long red-swathed table. A black banner proclaimed Half-Moon Hollow's historic participation in the first-ever Bloody Bake-Off. A handful of people, human and vampire alike, were lined up at the registration point, holding various containers. One woman, with heavy circles under her eyes and a cigarette dangling from her lips, seemed to be holding a pitcher of bloodred margaritas. She actually had me worried. But we registered our entry, which we were calling "Blood Creek Barbecue Sauce," with little incident. A registration number kept our entry anonymous and prevented bias from the judges. That made me feel a bit guilty, considering that Jane had helped me taste-test. But she'd never tasted the final sauce. Heck, the fact that she'd tasted my lesser efforts would probably keep her from guessing which one was mine.

We were given a goodie bag courtesy of the local Council office, just for participating. The contents included a sample of Solar Shield SPF 500 Sunblock, iron supplements, a six-pack of Faux Type O, and a to-go-sized container of Razor Wire Fang Floss.

"I'm just going to let you hold on to that," I said, handing the tote to Sam.

"Probably for the best," he said, peering into the bag. "They make mouthwash just for vampires?"

"You have so much to learn about your own culture," I said.

"A bag full of blood and dental supplies is culture?"

"It's some culture. Speaking of which, what do we do now?" I asked. "We've got an hour before the results are announced."

"Now we explore the magic and mystery of Burley Days."

Sam led me through the rows of food vendors and rigged games and a particularly bewildering antiques mall. We stopped in front of a table where a dozen grown men were participating in a Frito-Pie-eating contest. I watched in horror as they dove face-first into a combination of corn chips, chili, and cheese, lapping it up like ravenous dogs.

He chuckled, dragging me away from the carnage. "This must be hell for you."

"No, but it will be when the first 'loser' sicks up his efforts," I said, shuddering. "Haven't you people ever heard of fruit pies?"

"No," he said, laughing harder. "I meant there are no fancy food emporiums, no Apple Stores, only one Starbucks within a fifty-mile radius. Growin' up around that sort of thing, you probably take it for granted until you end up in a place like this."

"I didn't grow up around it." I scoffed. "I grew up in Hader's Knob, Missouri. Population five thousand thirty-four."

He frowned as he seemed to mentally review all of the conversations we'd had over the last few nights. "I just assumed."

"You never asked," I said, smirking. "It wasn't the

greatest place to call home. The liquor stores and the pawn shops were the only businesses that did well."

"Do you ever go home to visit?"

I shrugged. "No reason to. My parents were killed in a car accident when I was in college. Chef Gamling was the one who drove me home from school to help me arrange my parents' funeral. He was the one who helped me figure out how to handle their mess of an estate. And he's right here in the Hollow, so where else would I go?"

"So you're a small-town girl," he said, eyeing me speculatively. "Bein' a small-town boy myself—Mount Pleasant, Tennessee, thank you very much—I can appreciate that. How'd you end up in Chicago?"

"Culinary school," I said. "My dad thought it was nuts, but Mom said I should follow my dream, even when that dream led me about four hundred miles away from them . . . which was half of its charm."

He made a waving motion with his hand, as if to say, *And?* When I didn't respond, he nudged my ribs with his elbow. "Woman, I've seen you weepin' over maimed kitchen gadgets. You know about my torpedoed marriage. And I've made out with you under the influence of evil peppers. We have no secrets."

"My parents didn't fight, exactly. They bickered a lot, but I can't remember them ever really raising their voices. They were locked in this bizarre constant battle for who was *winning* at the relationship. One of them was always leaving the other one, demanding apologies, demanding that I take sides one way or the other. They separated, they got back together, they separated, they got back together, over and over." The words seemed to rush out of my mouth like water. And when they'd finished, I was a bit out of breath but felt lighter. I frowned, mulling over what it meant that I could say those things to Sam in the middle of a crowded street but not to my mentor or licensed psychiatric professionals.

"That must have been . . . confusin'?" he suggested, with a wary expression on his handsome face, as if he wasn't sure if I was joking, but he knew he wasn't supposed to laugh.

I shrugged. "They always said they were staying together for my sake. Because clearly, it would traumatize me if my parents got a divorce, but telling me every other month that 'this time it's over for good' was OK. Frankly, I would have been relieved if they'd just made a clean break of it. Lived separate lives. Maybe they would have been happy apart. Maybe it was selfish of me to want to get away from that. And believe me, the fact that they died with so much between us unsettled—there isn't a day that goes by that I don't regret that. But I had to have my own life. I just couldn't spend another minute mixed up in their drama. Either you love somebody enough to spend the rest of your life with them, or you don't. In my mind, there's not much room in between."

"I'm sorry," he said, closing his hand around my shoulder and pulling me into a sort of side hug.

I nodded, once again marveling at the loose, relaxed feeling in my chest. "And now the only real family I have is a cranky old German professor and his life partner, both of them trying to fatten me up with dumplings and monkey bread."

After a long, contemplative pause, he nodded and sagely observed, "I thought I noticed a little more junk in your trunk."

I took a swat at his shoulder. "Jerk."

"Ouch!" He dodged and cackled at me, drawing the eyes of several curious bystanders. "It's not right that someone so small can hit so hard. I'm going to miss your gentle, delicate mannerisms after you move out."

"Oh, come on." I snickered. "You know you'll miss me."

His smile faltered. His lips parted as if to say something, but before he could, I heard Jolene cry, "Tess!" from across the square. I turned to see her dragging a bemused Zeb in her wake. Jolene threw her arms around me in an enthusiastic, if slightly painful, hug. "Are you excited about the contest?"

"Nearly wetting myself," I assured her, patting her back. "Sam, I think you know Zeb and Jolene Lavelle. Zeb and Jolene, my, uh, roommate, Sam Clemson."

"Nice to see you again, Sam," Zeb said, holding out his hand.

Sam smiled, almost shyly, and shook it. "Good to see you two. How are the kids?"

As Zeb whipped out a cell phone full of photos, Jolene launched into a story about little Joe the pickle flinger and his attempts to chew his way out of his crib. Sam listened with interested amusement, oohing and aahing appropriately at the cuteness of my friends' offspring. This kept us all sufficiently distracted until we heard, "Ladies and gents, if you'll proceed to the center stage, we'll announce the results for the Hollow's First-Ever Bloody Bake-Off," from a human man in his forties shouting into the microphone near the Faux Type O booth. A teenage girl dressed in a red gingham picnic dress—whom Jolene identified as the scary teen-vampire bureaucrat Ophelia—shrank away from him, as if his loud "yee-haw" was going to make her ears bleed.

As the crowd milled over to the main (and only) stage, Ophelia snatched the mic out of his hands and eyed the poor, unsuspecting man in a way I'd only seen diabetics case the dessert cart. She sighed and turned to the vampires wearing "official judge" sashes. All of them, including my hapless friend, Jane, had their arms crossed over their middles and looked slightly ill.

"We were very pleased to receive such a wide array of entries, everything from a Chum Cherry Slushie to a Bloody Pot Pie," Ophelia said, smirking at Jane, who sent her a hard look in return.

Even in this crowd, I could hear Sherry Jameson saying, "Well, she used to love them when she was human!"

Poor Jane.

I found it a little disturbing that Ophelia hadn't mentioned the barbecue sauce. Did that mean something? Did that mean that my entry hadn't been memorable enough to mention? I'd felt pretty comfortable with my submission when I got here, but now, seeing those nauseated expressions on the judges' faces— Oh, my God, what if I lost a cook-off in small-town Kentucky to a bunch of homemakers? What if I failed, leaving Sam without a house and myself without a construction budget? The sudden rush of cold, hard fear up my spine had me bending slightly, bracing my hands against my knees.

I felt cool, insistent pressure at the base of my neck. It rubbed in soft circles over my nape, and I realized it was Sam's hand. I peered up at him through the haze of hair that hung over my face.

"It will be OK," he promised. "Now, suck it up, people are starting to stare."

"Got it," I said, clearing my throat and straightening to my full (though not impressive) height. "Thanks."

I rolled my shoulders and took a deep breath. I noticed that Sam's hand remained on the back of my neck, his thumb occasionally sweeping over my vertebrae. I shivered a bit, but Sam kept his hand there.

"Now, before I announce the award winners, which will be included in the first-ever Faux Type O cookbook, *Blue Ribbons with Bite*, I'd like to announce the honorable mentions. First, we have Rita Scott with her Chum Cherry Slushie, a delightfully pulverized mix of blood blended with cherry syrup and ice."

A plump, pretty blond woman in a bright pink church dress squealed joyfully and went to the stage to accept her yellow ribbon and certificate. Jane turned slightly green around the gills. I gave her a sympathetic look but then started to giggle. She made a very rude gesture behind the thin shield of her left hand. When Ophelia announced the second honorable mention as Ginger Lavelle with her Bloody Mary Margarita, the haggard chain-smoker I'd seen earlier launched herself at Ophelia and snatched her victory ribbon, waving it like a war banner. Ophelia stepped out of range, an unimpressed grimace twisting her young features.

"Lavelle?" I looked to Jolene. "Any relation?"

Jolene huffed out an irritated sigh. "That would be my mother-in-law."

We watched as Ginger Lavelle did a victory shimmy that looked like something from a burlesque performance. "Wow," I marveled.

"Well, she stuck with her area of expertise," Jolene grumbled. "Booze."

I expected Zeb to take offense at this, but he just

nodded. "It's possible she would have stumbled upon this recipe without the contest."

Ophelia moved on to the prize winners. Third place and a thousand-dollar check went to a blood-and-beef-broth concoction created by Martha Hackett, a sweet-looking elderly lady I'd assumed was human until she grinned and flashed her fangs at the crowd. The fact that another name was called filled me with equal parts dread and hope. If I hadn't placed third, it was likely that I'd placed second or first. Then again, I might not have placed at all. I imagined the humiliation of explaining to Chef Gamling that I hadn't . . . and there I was, bent over hyperventilating again.

"Would you stop that?" Sam exclaimed, pulling me upright and pressing me against his side.

Second place went to Lulu McClaine's Thinned Blood Pudding, a "charming drinkable dessert that tickled each judge's palate." Jolene whooped and cheered for her aunt before giving me an apologetic look. "Sorry, family loyalties."

I groaned. I knew I should have made blood pudding!

"This is what we want," Sam reminded me. "We've still got a shot. And if you throw up on me, I will get seriously pissed at you."

I kept my face buried in my hands as Ophelia built up to the announcement of first place, describing the fabulous photo spread each prize winner would receive in the cookbook, the cash prize, and, of course, "the knowledge that the winner had helped new vampires adjust to their new diet." Finally, Ophelia felt that she'd tortured us enough and exclaimed, "Every judge was pleased with the first-prize winner. For our recently turned panelists, it was everything good about summer cookouts, without the regrets of solid food on the vampire digestive system. Ladies and gentlemen, the winner of the Faux Type O Bloody Bake-Off and the twenty-five-thousand-dollar grand prize—Blood Creek Barbecue Sauce by Tess Maitland and Sam Clemson!"

If there was applause, I couldn't hear it. I was frozen, unable to move or see anything beyond Sam's face and its elated expression. His bright, unearthly smile lit up the town square. We'd done it. We had the money to buy the house out from under Lindy. I could stay in the Hollow and live in the place I loved. For the first time, everything I really wanted was in my grasp.

Jolene hugged me, and I shrieked, hopping up and down like a maniac. Sam laughed, watching with amusement as I seemed to lose my mind. I threw my arms around him and squeezed until he made a wheezing *uhf* sound. I beamed up at him.

Well, maybe not *everything* I wanted. But it was a good start.

"You put my name on the entry slip?" Sam asked as we made our way to the stage. "I didn't see you do that."

As an overenthusiastic well-wisher slapped me on the back, nearly bowling me over, Sam caught my elbow and shot the guy a dark look. I laughed, waving off the back-slapper's apologies. "Of course I did. You were just as much a part of the creative process as I was. Without you, the vampire judges might have ended up in the hospital with food poisoning."

He gave my arm an affectionate squeeze. "Thanks, Tess. I mean it."

"I meant it, too," I countered. Sam leaned in closer to me, his eyes intent on my upturned mouth. I smiled up at him, my hand slipping over the fingers gripping my arm.

From the stage, we heard a none-too-subtle throat clearing. Ophelia stood there, holding an oversized novelty check, her eyebrows arched. I blushed, and Sam gave her an apologetic shrug. We crossed the stage and claimed the giant check and the blue ribbon. We shook the judges' hands. And while Jane was clearly trying to maintain the appearance of objectivity, the excited squeeze she gave my hand nearly brought me to my knees.

"I didn't know it was yours, I swear," she whispered. "After all, your first efforts were so . . . uh, raw. I thought you'd made the Valentine's Day Massacre Marinara Sauce."

"That's so wrong," I whispered back.

Jane shuddered. "Yes, it was."

Ophelia motioned for me to join her and Sam at

the mic. I blinked at the sheer number of people gathered in front of me. *Oh, hell.* This was why I hid out in the kitchen at work. I was not great in front of crowds. Ophelia gave me another nudge toward the mic, where I spluttered, "Um, th-thanks. Thanks so much for this. I'm thrilled."

Ophelia looked less than impressed with my oratory skills, and when I tried to back away from the mic, she looped her arm through mine and kept me in place. "Tess is a recent addition to Half-Moon Hollow. One of our judges has informed me that our winner will be opening a restaurant here in town soon. And I'm sure she will have a wide selection of vampire menu items."

Ophelia gave me a pointed smile, which I supposed deserved a response. "Uh, sure."

"What are you going to call your establishment, Tess?" Ophelia asked.

I floundered, my cheeks hot. I couldn't believe I still hadn't come up with a name for the place yet. Stricken, I looked up to Sam, who leaned into the microphone and announced, "Miss Maitland's new restaurant will be called Southern Comforts."

"Yes," I squeaked. "Southern Comforts."

"Well, I'm sure we're all looking forward to the opening," Ophelia said, smirking. The crowd applauded, and I waved halfheartedly. Ophelia leaned closer and whispered, "You should go now."

Still a bit rattled, I nodded, and Sam led me off-stage. Ophelia's assistant gave us paperwork to sign and details about collecting our winnings. We also received a large cast-iron pot full of Faux Type O products to "continue our experimentation."

After we thanked Jane again, she warned us to beware the unexpected gift basket and the potential trouble it could bring into our lives. Explaining that Jane had "issues" with gift baskets, Jolene and Zeb helped us lug the check and the cast-iron albatross to the truck. Then they insisted on taking us for drinks over at the Fraternal Order of Police beer garden. I noticed that Sam snagged one of the "special occasion" bottles of Faux Type O High Life before walking back with us.

"Thanks for naming my restaurant for me," I told him as we took our seats at a picnic table near an improvised stage, where the night-shift sergeants picked out old country-western standards on acoustic guitars.

Sam grimaced. "Yeah, sorry. You just had this frozen deer expression, and I didn't know how long it would take you to snap out of it."

"Or Ophelia could have snapped on you," Zeb observed.

"It's OK, I like it," I said. "Southern Comforts has quite the ring to it. And it fits with the theme I'd planned." Sam sipped his drink, looking pleased, so I added, "Of course, you're going to have to be my guinea pig."

He chuckled, then straightened his expression into a frown. "I never agreed to that."

"I think you'll be willing to renegotiate," I said, arching my eyebrows into a supervillain expression. "Or I will lace every bottle of blood in that gift basket with ghost chili oil."

He narrowed his eyes at me. "You are the most twisted, evil little thing."

"Why does that sound all sexy when he says it?" Zeb asked his wife.

Shaking her head, Jolene raised her cup of beer in a toast. "Here's to your first Burley Days."

"So far, it hasn't sucked," I added, clinking my cup against hers. I caught Sam's eye before repeating the gesture against his blood bottle. "To ceasefires."

Sam's lips quirked into a grin. "To ceasefires."

A few beers later, Sam decided it was time to leave. I kept lingering, discussing plans for the restaurant with Jolene, until Sam and Zeb shared a determined "manly men together" look and dragged us away from the table.

"You know, if you make too much of a show of this, some very ugly rumors about vampire brutality on tourists will start spreading around town," I told Sam, snickering as he slung me under his arm like a football and carried me down the darkened sidewalk to his truck.

"Yeah, because I have such a great reputation." He

grunted as he hauled me toward the truck. "My God, woman, how much funnel cake did you eat?"

"Nice." I barked out a laugh while he opened the truck door for me. He grinned down at me, giving me a boost as I climbed into the passenger seat. His hands were resting on my hips, and I had the strangest urge to map that little constellation of freckles on his cheekbone with my tongue. His lips parted, and I leaned forward just in time to hear—

"Sammy?"

Breaking a Few Eggs

9

The spell broke as we turned to find Sam's ex-wife standing on the sidewalk, gaping at us.

"Sammy, what are you doing here?" Lindy demanded, shrugging off the insistent arm of a blond, tan man in jeans and pink polo shirt. The guy was in his midthirties and had intentionally popped his collar.

An unfiltered expression of pain flashed across Sam's face, particularly when he saw Mr. Popped Collar's arm around Lindy's shoulders.

"You know it's not a good idea for you to be out in public." Lindy sighed, as if she were scolding a small child. "You know how you are. What if you hurt someone?"

"I'm fine." Sam growled, ever so subtly stepping away from me. I looked to Popped Collar, to gauge how he felt about interloping in the Clemsons' bizarre marital drama. He appeared to be playing Angry Birds on his phone.

"Still, maybe I should take you home," Lindy fussed. "You know how you get around humans. This has to be pushing your control to the limit. Let's just get you home before you hurt someone."

"Don't you worry about me!" Sam barked. "You owe Tess here an apology for dragging her into our mess. How could you rent the house without even talkin' to me? That's out-there, even for you, Lindy."

"Sammy, I didn't want to rent out the house, but I needed the money," she said, her voice rising to a wheedling, babyish tone that grated on my nerves. "You know how expensive it is to start up with a new apartment. I just need a little extra to put down the security deposit."

I huffed. "Oh, come on!"

Sam turned to me with a weird, glazed expression, as if he'd almost forgotten I was there, despite the fact that he'd just spoken about me. "Could you just give me a minute?" he asked.

I sighed. "Fine."

I climbed into the truck and slammed the door. Unfortunately, Sam's windows were pretty solid, and I couldn't hear what was being said on the other side of the glass. That was a shame, because Lindy appeared to be wailing like a banshee, and Sam was waving his arms to an invisible orchestra.

Sam's fangs kept popping down, which was a problem for new vampires not quite in control of their emotions. Of course, every time it happened, Lindy flinched dramatically, which only made Sam more upset. Popped Collar remained blissfully uninvolved.

When Lindy started screaming, her face flushing red while she jabbed her finger toward Sam's face, I'd had enough. I didn't want to get pulled into the middle of this, but damn it, she didn't get to talk to Sam that way. Not after what she'd pulled, not after leaving him without money or friends or the house he loved. I threw the truck door open, hauling the heavy cast-iron pot with me, just in time to hear Sam exclaim, "You're going to have to deal with it!"

The next five seconds were a balletic comedy of errors. Sam slammed the truck door just as I started to climb out, shutting it on my foot. I yowled in protest, and when he realized that he'd hurt me, he turned toward me, which irritated Lindy. She swung her purse at his head. Sam ducked just as I pushed my way out of the truck and stepped right into Lindy's swing. Her (fortunately, very soft) quilted Vera Bradley handbag landed broadside across my cheek, leaving me with a resounding thud bouncing around my skull.

"Here," I said, and handed the pot to Sam's ex. She blinked at me, confused, as I drew my hand back as if I was going to slap her. She shrieked, dropping the handles to cover her face with her hands. The heavy iron pot crashed down on Lindy's foot with a clang. She howled, hopping up and down on her good foot.

"That's for screwing me over on the lease!" I shouted.

Lindy lunged for me, claws out. Sam threw me over his shoulder, turning to plop me back into the truck, only to smack my forehead across the edge of the door. I yelped, he spun around too quickly to see what had happened, and my sneaker whacked Lindy across the mouth. Lindy wailed, but I was too busy nursing my aching temple to laugh.

"Your vampire reflexes suck." I groaned as Sam threw me unceremoniously into the passenger seat while Lindy continued to berate us both.

Sam rounded the truck, jumped into the driver's seat, and gave me a long, incredulous look. "Did you just drop a pot on my ex-wife's foot?"

As he turned the key in the ignition, I shook my head, wincing at the pain in my temple. "Technically, she dropped the pot on her foot."

"You're a scary woman."

And through it all, Popped Collar continued to kill those little green pigs.

I stood at the back door, sipping jasmine tea and watching the late-afternoon sky shift into an angry, bruised green. The trees danced so violently in the wind that I was afraid the limbs would snap off and come crashing into the house.

With that in mind, I stepped back from the windows a few paces.

It had been a very productive couple of days. The beverage company had wired the prize money into Sam's account, allowing Sam to file papers with the bank. Sam and I had finalized blueprints for the changes to the restaurant. I had started making arrangements to move out of the house.

Somehow the sky went even darker, casting the house in purpling shadows as roiling clouds gathered overhead. I was wondering whether I should go look for a flashlight when the electricity winked off with a snap of ozone.

I groaned. Perfect timing.

There were no flashlights, of course. Lindy had probably run off with them when she left. I lit a "Relaxing Seascape" pillar candle on the mantel.

"Yep, I'm more relaxed already," I muttered.

The house was getting darker and darker as sheets of rain lashed against the windows. Even though we were reaching "house sucked away by a cyclone" levels of interior shade, Sam wasn't due to wake up for a few more hours.

I was trying to figure out what my dinner options would be without power or a manual can opener when I heard a strange thumping noise from the side of the house. I rushed to the window and saw that one side of the in-ground double door to the cellar had come loose and was flapping in the wind like a particularly heavy flag. Had the latch slipped out of place?

Oh, shoot. The cellar, where Sam was sleeping. Rain was pouring into the open door.

The second I stepped outside, my brain shouted, *Error! Error! Get your ass back inside!*

The rain felt like being slapped around by quick, icy hands, soaking through my T-shirt and stinging my skin. A wind gust knocked me back against the porch railing. I tried to take a step toward the banging noise, but I couldn't keep my eyes open against the force of the wind and the water.

I scrambled back through the door, slamming it behind me. I flicked my hair out of my face, slinging water across the room. I looked out the window, and through the blurred, rain-spattered glass, I saw that the other door was now waving back and forth. "Well, that was stupid."

I couldn't just leave it like that. I didn't know where the cellar door opened in relation to Sam's resting place. The storm could pass through quickly, and if Sam was sleeping anywhere near the door and sunlight suddenly broke through the clouds, he could end up a little pile of dust. Candle in hand, I traipsed through the darkened kitchen. The basement door wasn't locked, which I thought was a nice sign of trust.

The candle was warming in my hand, the wax softening and releasing its strange sharp-clean scent, as I carefully made my way down the stairs. While the walls were lined with neatly hung tools and clean, orderly worktables, the floor space was open. At least I wouldn't trip over anything. The noise of the door flapping was deafening, but I couldn't see Sam anywhere. There was another door at the other end of the cellar, a solid metal door surrounded by new brick. It reminded me of one of those old-fashioned walk-in bank safes.

Of course, Sam had built himself an actual lair. I laughed, shoving my hair back from my face and setting the candle aside on a worktable. It took me a few tries to get the doors shut, particularly when I found that the latch had broken off. I had to secure it with a shovel through the door handles. And thanks to additional rain battering, my white T-shirt and khakis were now completely transparent, which was a fun look for me.

I took the still-burning candle, and I swear, I meant to just walk out, but there was that door at the end of the room. Beckoning. A mental itch I couldn't ignore. All these nights, I'd been staying in this house, and I'd never seen where Sam slept. It couldn't hurt to look, right? I mean, he was technically dead at the moment. He'd never find out.

By the time I'd reached the door, I'd rationalized it seven different ways. The vault door featured a traditional combination dial, set to the combination and therefore unlocked. It made me feel equal parts guilty and happy that he trusted me enough to sleep unguarded.

The space was small. Sam had bricked in just enough room for a bed and a dresser. Now that I'd opened that door, it felt so intrusive and wrong. But I couldn't help but look at the slim form sprawled across the bed. It was one of those lovely old-fashioned wrought-iron numbers with curlicues in the headboard and a feather tick mattress. How had Lindy missed this? Had Sam sneaked it down here before she started her ransacking of the house?

I moved closer, the small flame from the candle casting a dancing orange light across Sam's pale face. He was handsome when he was awake. He was absolutely beautiful in sleep, all white angles and smooth skin. His long lashes rested against high cheekbones. He was relaxed, not quite innocent, but definitely not the angry, sad guy I'd met weeks ago.

Also, Sam slept naked.

Panic bloomed in my chest. This was so wrong. He was lying there, naked and vulnerable, and I was peeping at him. I was going to be listed on some sort of Council sex-offender list. Just then, hot wax dripped down the side of the pillar candle and burned my fingers. I hissed in pain, bobbling the candle and spilling even more wax, dripping it right onto Sam's chest.

And that was the moment I remembered the story about Cupid and Psyche. I'd become painfully familiar with Greek mythology while planning a "themed meal" for one of my culinary-school projects. I'd chosen "A Feast for the Gods." Spanakopita. Never again.

Psyche was told never to bother Cupid while he was sleeping, but she couldn't help her curiosity and sneaked into his room with an oil lamp, dripping oil on his shoulder and burning him. He was furious and left her shortly after, and she had to perform several dignity-defying tasks for the gods before he would come back.

Shit.

Sam didn't seem to be stirring. I stepped back, slowly pulling my arm and the candle out of reach. A hand shot out to clamp around my wrist. Sam's eyes were open, hungry, and dark. I pulled frantically at my wrist, barely keeping the candle upright as he dragged me down to the mattress.

"Sam, I'm sorry, I just wanted to make sure you're OK. There's a storm—mmph!"

His mouth closed over mine, pulling my bottom lip between his teeth and nibbling it. He pulled the candle from my hand and placed it on a bedside table. He yanked me close, rolling over me and pressing me into the mattress, plucking the buttons of my wet shirt like guitar strings. His hips pressed into mine, pinning me down. He was so solid, so sure, over me, when my head seemed to be running on its own roller-coaster track.

He pushed the wet shirt from my shoulders, running his hands under my back until they cupped my butt, and rocked his hips. I groaned shamelessly, throwing my head back against the pillow. He rained kisses down the line of my throat. I could feel his wicked smile against my skin when I didn't so much as tense when his teeth skimmed over my jugular.

His fingers worked over my collarbone, tickled the rim of my belly button, and traced my hips. Somewhere in the course of this, my pants seemed to have disappeared. I glanced down, transfixed by the sight of Sam's hard length slipping between my thighs.

I gasped. I would worry about the pants later.

The storm died down. I had no idea when, but by the time I collapsed back against the mattress, sore, sweaty, and a little dizzy, the wind had dwindled to a dull roar. We could still hear the rain spattering against the siding. It was nice, sprawling out on the bed, the light low, and what sounded like ocean waves beating against the walls.

Sam's arm was thrown over me, his face pressed into the mattress. I didn't want to brag, but I was pretty sure I'd broken him. Toward the end, I'd taken his power of speech and the ability to control his eyelids. But he'd done his damage, too. The pretty iron curlicues on the headboard now looked like something from a Tim Burton movie.

His head rose, and his eyelids twitched slightly as he gave me a lazy smile. He grabbed me and pulled me close.

"I was wonderin' how long it would take you to come down here," he murmured against my mouth. "Really, woman, how many hints do I have to give you?"

"H-hints?" I sputtered

"I left the doors unlocked."

"That's not a hint. That's inattention to personal safety."

"Says the woman who spilled candle wax on a sleepin' vampire," he whispered, biting lightly at the place where my neck met my jaw. "Kinky girl."

"Nice." I rolled my eyes and made myself more comfortable, balancing carefully on his chest. My knee hit the mattress wrong, and the bed sagged in the middle. As pretty as it was, the mattress was lumpy as hell, and the springs squeaked every time we moved. But I was so comfortable. And I loved the feeling of Sam's hands slipping along my spine, tracing each vertebra with his fingertips. I lay there, my head tilted sweetly against the ridge of his collarbone, completely relaxed.

"So, what happens now?" he asked.

"I think that's my line," I said without looking up.

"You know what I mean," he said, poking my ribs. "When you move out, will I see you again, or will I just be part of the Half-Moon Hollow welcome wagon package?"

"I'll give you a good review on Yelp, if that will make you feel better."

"Oh, you're funny, you are."

"I try." I was so tempted to tell him I was staying right there with him, in this very house, as long as he wanted me. And I would be willing to sleep in this freaky Tim Burton bed if he would keep rubbing my back like that. But for now, that sounded a little psycho. So I gave him a Cheshire Cat smile and said, "I'm not quite sure yet."

"Oh, that's mean." He groaned.

I slid my arms around his neck and rolled over him. "Maybe I should take another spin on the welcome wagon before I decide."

I nipped along the line of his throat, leaving a deliberate mark on his collarbone with my teeth. It faded in seconds. I was going to have to find a way to make those stick.

"That's so wrong." he said, sighing.

"You want more genteel pillow talk, get a more genteel girl."

The next thing I knew, I startled awake in the bed, alone. I could hear footsteps above me, making the floorboards creak. Sam was pacing upstairs in the living room, and I could hear his hushed tones even in the basement. I blinked blearily at the alarm clock on the bedside table. It was after 10:00 P.M. Who would be visiting here at this time of night?

I slipped into my shirt and jeans and crept quietly up the stairs. The kitchen was dark, but the lights in the living room were blazing. I could hear Sam yelling, "No, I don't have to explain that to you!" followed by tinny babbling. Was he talking on the phone? I hovered near the door, watching as Sam paced back and forth over the worn rug.

"Lindy, that was the amount agreed upon in the settlement. I have a promissory note to show the court. I've made the deadline. If you're not happy with the payment, talk to the judge about it."

More squawking on the other end of the line.

"No, you don't have the right to ask that," he spat. "Because it's none of your—no!" He sighed. "No. I'm not sleepin' with her. Lindy, she's not even my type . . .

"She's a friend!" he yelled in response to something Lindy had asked. "She's just a friend. She's a nice girl you took advantage of. I felt sorry for her after what you did, so we made an effort to get along. Stop gettin' away from the point. I'm gettin' the house fair and square. You need to deal with it . . .

"No, I don't want to meet up to talk about it!" he barked. After a long pause, his voice softened as he said, "Look, Lindy, please don't cry. Please, just stop. No, I don't hate you. No, I'm not mad anymore . . . You know I do."

I backed away from the door, feeling as if I'd been punched in the stomach. Was that really how he felt? I was just a friend? He felt sorry for me? Was I a "friend with benefits" now? A rebound lay? I didn't want to be boxed into some "friend zone" category of women Sam liked enough to sleep with but not enough to date. And I wanted a relationship with Sam, a real one. I hadn't realized that until I heard him describe me in such bland terms.

Why would he say I was "just a friend"? Because he didn't want to hurt Lindy? Did he still love her, despite everything? Was he going to end up going back to his ex like Phillip? Would I get sucked into another bizarre cyclical marriage trap like my parents' relationship hell? Would any progress I made die as Sam yo-yoed back and forth between the two of us?

My breath came out in a painful little hiccup as I found my shoes and purse. I threaded my fingers through the handle of my bag. I couldn't be here for this. I couldn't listen to him talk this way. I couldn't stay in the house, knowing that he might come down the stairs and find some gentle, "friendly" way to ask me to go upstairs to my own bed. The rational, reasonable part of my brain seemed to be on vacation—again—while the more primal portions yelled for me to get out. *Get out now! Get out before he gives us the "I need space" speech!*

My keys jangled slightly, and I caught them before Sam overheard. I approached the living room. His back was turned to me as he growled into the phone, "Fine, call your lawyer! He wrote the agreement in the first place!" Hands shaking, I slipped from the kitchen to the front hall in a few steps, launching out the door as if I were on a catapult. As I revved my engine and sped down the drive, I glanced back in the rearview mirror and saw Sam framed in the doorway.

That night, I cried the whole thing out to Jolene, curled up on her couch.

"It's just so embarrassing." I sighed. "I don't get caught up this way, all emotional and crazy and snotting all over my friends' sofas. It's not the first time I've slept with a man who didn't love me. Hell, Phillip made it clear he didn't even like me toward the end of our relationship. But it's never hurt this badly before."

"Maybe that's because you didn't care about any of those guys before," Jolene said, offering me a tall glass of liquor, the origin of which I chose not to question. "And you may be overreacting, you know. You never actually heard him say he still wanted her around. All he said was that he didn't hate her. It's not exactly a declaration of love."

"No one likes a smartass, Jolene," I informed her, wiping at my wet cheeks.

Zeb, who had disappeared like a cartoon coyote when he'd opened the door and saw my tearstained face, crept quietly into the living room, placed a beer and a plate of chocolate-chip cookies in front of me, and dashed to the safety of the twins' room.

"I hope that's not true, for your sake," she muttered. "So, what are you going to do now?"

I swiped at my cheeks. "Go ahead with my plans. This doesn't really change anything, except that I need to move out of Sam's place ahead of schedule. I think we both need to figure out what we want. I don't think we can do that if I'm living in his back pocket. I'll just have to find a new contractor. And a bank willing to give me a very low-interest loan—or maybe I'll just rob a bank, I haven't decided."

"I have some cousins who work construction," Jolene offered.

"Of course you do." I snorted into a tissue. "So, Jolene—my best friend, my right hand, the only person I know who loves food as much as I do—would you like a job?"

Jolene frowned at me. "I will not track Lindy down and kill her for you. I mean, I know how to hide a body, but I've got kids now."

"No!" I exclaimed. "I mean a job at the restaurant. Would you like to manage it for me?"

"Well, I already work part-time for Beeline, and I work some days at my uncle's shop."

"Exactly. You know how a restaurant works, and you know the people here much better than I do. If you see me doing something stupid, you'll tell me, loudly."

"Would you actually listen to me?" she asked dryly.

"At least half the time," I promised. "Come on,

how would you feel about dropping the part-time jobs and working for me? I can offer you a pitiful salary and all of the free food you can eat."

"You may want to rethink that!" Zeb called from the back of the house.

"I don't think my uncles would like me working for the competition."

"That's just it. I don't plan on competing with your uncles' place. They do beautiful sandwiches and deli selections, mostly lunch and breakfast. I'm aiming more for comfort foods, slightly upscale, but not so much that you wouldn't be comfortable there in jeans. A lunch and dinner crowd."

"I'd still want to check with them first. And my dad."

I raised an eyebrow.

She nodded. "We're a close family."

I muttered, "Must be a Southern thing."

Jolene helped me get the apartment above Southern Comforts into a somewhat livable condition over the next few days, cleaning and making small repairs. After retrieving my stuff from Sam's house, Jane and Andrea showed up with an enormous care package stocked with housewarming gifts such as a new shower curtain, cleaning supplies, and a great big bottle of vodka. I loved Jane and Andrea. I really did.

Sam called, but I didn't pick up the phone. His messages were increasingly apologetic, which just made me feel worse for hurting him. He was sorry I woke up to his conversation with Lindy, he said. He didn't know what I'd heard, but he wished I would talk to him so we could work this out. One message had him sounding so worried, so lonely, that I nearly hit "end" so I could dial Sam's number, but then he said, "I thought we were friends." And that kept me from checking my messages for the next two days.

By day three, the words "just a friend" kept running through my head on a loop, making me cringe and cry and occasionally throw a pot at a wall.

I was really going to have to stop doing that.

On October 28, the day Sam was supposed to reclaim his house, I sat in my new restaurant with a perfectly nice lager resting on the bar in front of me. Jolene had finally agreed to take the job at Southern Comforts. But her uncles had warned me that if they caught me duplicating from their menu, I would be in for an old-fashioned ass-whupping. But I hadn't had any luck finding a contractor to do the repairs I needed. I was having trouble narrowing down which human and vampire menus I wanted to use for the restaurant. I couldn't even decide on a color scheme for the menu.

For the first time in my life, I truly had no clue what to do. Even when I had my meltdown, I'd had a plan—visit Chef Gamling, get my life back in order. But now, even though I knew what I was doing in the long term, I was completely paralyzed by indecision over what to do in the next few days, in the next few hours.

I toyed with the cap from a Faux Type O bottle. There were so many things I could do with this place, but I wasn't sure of any of them now. Did I really want to save the tabletops as wall displays? Could I refinish the bar to its original oaken glory? How much additional storage space could I allow myself in the kitchen? I wanted Sam's input in these decisions, his sensible contractor's brain. But it seemed that John Lassiter's curse had killed my pseudo-relationship before it even got off the ground, taking my construction plans down with it.

I took a deep breath and a deeper draw from my beer. This stopped now. The time for useless pouting and self-flagellating was done. I was a homeowner, sort of. I owned my own restaurant. I had friends, real friends who liked me, despite my basket-case tendencies. I'd managed a semifunctional relationship for a few days, which was a personal record. My life was so much better than it was when I'd rolled into town.

The first order of business was turning off this playlist, because Adele's gorgeous emo postbreakup music was killing me.

I scrolled through the lists on my iPod until I found some Lynyrd Skynyrd and filled my kitchen with the sounds of "Sweet Home Alabama." I pulled out a notebook and pen and began painstakingly writing text and printing instructions for the menu of my new restaurant.

Coda

10

"Jolene, put the green down, and step away from the wall."

"But it's so cheerful!" Jolene protested, holding up the paint can labeled "New Leaf."

"It's neon!"

"It is rather, er, bright," Chef Gamling told her gently.

Jolene chucked a fork at my head. "It is not!"

"Yipe!" I cried, ducking out of the way. "Hey, you left the kids at home to limit the number of items thrown at my head tonight. And giving me a fork-related head contusion will not change the fact that our color scheme is white and blue."

"Actually, we left the kids at home because we're

spending the evening in a construction zone," Zeb said. "A construction zone with a bar in it."

"Just give the green a chance!" Jolene begged.

"Are you going to be this stubborn about every-thing?" I groaned.

I shot a pleading look at Zeb, Jane, Gabriel, Dick, and Andrea, who were sitting at the bar, watching the exchange gleefully. Apparently, whatever instinct they may have had to protect the "new girl" in the group had evaporated over Halloween, when I beat Jane at quarters while dressed as Wonder Woman. Vampires seemed to take drinking games very seri-ously.

My eyes narrowed. "Oh, you guys are no help whatsoever."

"Just be glad it's not peach," Gabriel said.

Jane cackled when she saw my confused expres-sion. "Someday, I'll show you pictures of the brides-maids' dresses from Jolene and Zeb's wedding."

"I didn't even pick out that color!" Jolene retorted. "That's not fair."

"I'm just here for the free eats," Dick said, raising a shot glass full of the Blood Creek Barbecue Sauce. Although Faux Type O technically owned the recipe, the company was so impressed with my plan to open a vampire-friendly restaurant that they'd let me keep the rights to serving it. We were calling the special menu Southern Comforts Blood Shots, to prevent confusions with the liquor menu or the human menu. My resident vampire friends were helping me tweak the recipes with another taste-testing.

Chef Gamling, who had agreed to work part-time in my kitchen when the restaurant opened, was leading them through the "appropriate tasting process" and recording their comments.

Since he didn't drink blood, Zeb was content to sample the various pie concoctions we'd come up with—caramel apple, peppermint cream with a crushed Oreo crust, and a mixed fruit involving strawberries, cranberries, and raspberries. And, of course, he enjoyed my attempts to control his wife's horrendous decorating skills. Is there a color-sense equivalent to being tone-deaf?

With the endless details I was juggling, I worried that I would be too busy to maintain my new-found connections with the group. But they simply wouldn't let me quietly fade into my work as I had in Chicago. Jolene was with me at every step of setting up shop, whether I wanted her opinions or not. Dick had offered to help me find dishes and equipment through his "connections," while Gabriel stood behind him and shook his dark head vehemently. Jane had offered her advice on starting a small business in the Hollow, the chief of which was to avoid the local Chamber of Commerce like the plague. Andrea's help had been invaluable while I waded through the complicated licensing process for blending and serving human donor blood. I supposed it shouldn't be easy to serve human blood to an unsuspecting public, but the red tape was a serious pain in the ass.

"Isn't it premature to start picking paint colors when you have so much structural work to do around here?" Gabriel asked, a concerned expression wrinkling his brow.

"Why don't you just ask Sam to help you?" Jane asked.

"You know why," I shot back, making her raise her hands defensively.

"I tried to help Tess find a contractor," Dick protested. While the girls tried to nurse me through my confused post-Sam feelings with ice cream and Jane Austen movies, Dick's method was taking me to The Cellar and getting me hammered. Which made Dick my new favorite guy ever.

I shot my new drinking buddy the stink-eye. "Dick, it only took me two 'laying pipe' innuendos from your handsy plumbing guy to decide that I will only use contractors I find through the Yellow Pages."

"Hey!" Dick exclaimed. "That wasn't my guy, that was a cousin of my guy. Doesn't count! And didn't he come back to apologize?"

"Yes, black and blue, he came back to apologize, which meant I ended up feeling guilty because you beat the tar out of him."

"Gabriel helped!" Dick protested. "If I knew he would go in for a boob grab in lieu of a handshake, I never would have recommended him. The beatin' was deserved."

Dick turned as the battered cowbell above the door jangled and Sam stepped through.

Well, I could at least take comfort in the fact that he looked as bad as I felt. The last two weeks of radio silence had not been kind to Sam Clemson. He looked as if Dick and Gabriel had gotten a piece of him, too—dark bruiselike circles under his eyes, paler-than-usual cheeks, and thin, pinched lips. Something seemed lodged in my throat, a weighty lump that kept me from breathing or swallowing.

Seeing him, all wretched and drawn, made me feel a bit ridiculous for being so angry with him. He hadn't hurt me intentionally. The f-word he'd used wasn't an insult. And he wasn't the first guy to have lingering feelings for his ex-wife. Don't get me wrong. The fact that I seemed to feel more for him than he felt for me still hurt. But I didn't feel the urge to damage him or my drywall, which felt like progress.

I finally choked out a profound "Sam?"

The awkward silence continued for a few more agonizing seconds before Jane announced, "Well, kids, I think we should be going now."

"But we'll miss the fireworks," Dick protested, then saw Andrea's stern expression. He sighed. "Fine."

Jane edged Gabriel off his stool while Andrea bumped Dick out the door. Jolene was so busy glaring at Sam that Zeb had to walk around the bar and literally drag her out. Chef Gamling gave Sam a long, speculative look before following the thundering herd out the door. I heard it shut just as Dick said, "If she throws knives and we miss it, I'm going to be pissed."

Sam looked around the ruins of the dining room. "I like what you've done with the place."

"Well, I've had a little trouble finding reliable contractors," I said, crossing my arms over my chest protectively. I wanted to round the bar, sit next to him on the stools. But I needed space. I needed a physical barrier to keep from making a complete fool of myself.

He nodded and picked up a shot glass from Andrea's plate. He smiled. "You're really going through with it, huh? The vampire menu?" .

"I don't see why not. I want to feed people. Whether they have a pulse is irrelevant," I said, fidgeting with a dishtowel.

"So, I've been callin' you. A lot."

"I know."

He frowned. "Oh, so there wasn't some tragic fire that destroyed your phone . . . which means you've just been ignorin' me. That makes me feel better."

"I haven't been ignoring you. I've been giving you space," I countered.

"The difference is that when you give someone space, you tell them ahead of time. Otherwise, it's just ignorin' them. Look, I know you overheard me talkin' to Lindy. I don't know what I said that upset you, but I take it back. I take it all back. I just want you to talk to me again. I tried stayin' away . . . after the eighth straight day of you not returnin' my calls. But the house is just empty without you. There's no light, no music, no weird smells coming from the kitchen. I can't take it anymore."

"You told Lindy I was just a friend. You told her you felt sorry for me. You said you didn't hate her."

And yes, I did realize how lame that last bit sounded, but I wasn't about to weaken my position with logic.

"Well, I don't hate her. I never hated her. I just don't want to be married to her anymore." Sam rounded the bar, advancing until his hand ghosted down the length of my arm, never quite touching. He smirked down at me. "Besides, what was I supposed to say? 'Hey, Lindy, I know we still have a real estate and divorce settlement pending, but I want to let you know that I just had awesome sex with that woman who whacked you with a cast-iron pot. Yes, the same woman who helped me swipe the house out from under you, ruining your plan to sell it and keep the money for yourself. And by the way, I also think she's prettier and far more interesting than you'? Lindy was already ranting and raving like a crazy woman about you, saying you'd ruined her plans to sell the house to some doctor from Louisville. The last thing I wanted to do was give her more reasons to hate you. The fact that I couldn't wait to get back downstairs because your skin was soft and warm and smelled like honeysuckle was definitely going to make her hate you."

I glared up at him, but inside, I was doing the tiniest victory dance. "But what about 'You know I do'?" I asked.

He blinked a few times, as if trying to operate on the same insane wavelength as my brain. "You mean the part where she said, 'Are you sure you want to go through with this divorce?' And yes, I do. It was just like her to ask that right before the divorce was final. This is just another case of Lindy getting what she wanted and then not wanting it anymore. So, am I glad the divorce is final? Yes, I am. Am I glad the bank papers are signed and the house is mine? Yes, I am. And am I willing to call Lindy right now and describe our awesome sex in detail? Yes, I am."

My lips twitched as I squinted up at him. "You know, when I was a little girl and I dreamed of a man declaring his love for me, it did not involve the words 'Let's call my ex-wife and give her details about our awesome sex life.'"

"I didn't say I was declaring my love for you."

"Oh, please." I snickered, rolling my eyes. "I've owned your ass since the moment you kissed me."

He pulled me closer, settling his hands at the small of my back. "Oh, you mean the night you tainted my food supply with a dangerous substance?"

"Uh-huh," I said, grinning, pressing my lips to his. His whole body seemed to relax, to sag against mine as he pulled me closer. I murmured against his chest, "I think you need some time to be alone, to get over Lindy. I don't want to be that rebound girl who helps you heal up for your next 'real relationship.'"

"Honey, it doesn't get any more real than the girl who pepper-sprays my insides and drips hot candle wax on me while I sleep. Frankly, I have to make up with you. I'm afraid of what would happen if you were angry at me much longer. I don't need to get over Lindy. We were over a long time ago. I've been ready for a new life for a while now. I just needed everything else to catch up."

"I don't want you to rush."

"We won't," he promised. "We'll take it slow." Then he added under his breath, "As soon as we move your stuff back in."

"What?"

"I was thinking, it's pretty silly for you to live here, in a crappy little apartment, when there's plenty of room at the house. Besides, we should do it just to prove Lassiter wrong."

"So we should live together to break a hundred-year-old curse? That's a line I haven't heard before." I rolled my eyes at him. "So have you told Lindy I'll be moving in?"

He ducked his head. "Not important."

"She hit you with cookware, too, didn't she?"

"Not important," he insisted.

"Can I hit her with cookware?" I asked.

"If you keep doing that to people, someone's going to file charges against you." He sighed into my neck. "We're not going to do anything to Lindy. She's not an issue for me anymore, and she shouldn't be one for you. We're not going to devote any more energy to her. And swinging that wok of yours takes a lot of energy."

I supposed that was fair. But I would keep my wok handy.

I laughed as he squeezed me tight. "Well, I have to warn you, there will need to be some rules."

"Such as?"

"Personal space is overrated. I want to be able to see you at least a few hours a night, even if we have to move around our work schedules."

"Sounds reasonable," he said. "And I promise, I will only remove parts from the doors and cabinets when they need to be fixed, not just to amuse myself."

"Very reasonable," I told him. "I will only threaten you with pans and pepper extracts when you really deserve it."

"And the vampire issue," he said. "Any idea where you stand on that?"

"I don't know," I admitted. "And I don't know if I'll be able to give you an answer anytime soon. But for right now, I want to be with you. Bad furniture and all.

Besides, I need a contractor, and you're the only one I know who doesn't make my skin crawl."

He gave me a quick flash of a grin, then covered it with a mocking frown. He slid his arms around me. "I don't know if you can afford me."

I kissed him, pinching his butt just a little bit. "I think we can work out a barter system."

Faux Type O Sangria

1 bottle St. John's Red
¾ cup huckleberry syrup
¾ cup mango, peach, and orange juice blend
1½ cups orange juice
Cherries and orange slices for garnish

Mix liquid ingredients. Serve chilled.
Makes 8–10 servings.

(Courtesy of Glisson Vineyards and Winery in Paducah, Kentucky.)

Out with a Fang

Jessica Sims

Chapter One

"Hi there." A woman with short, perky blond pigtails stuck out her hand in greeting. "I'm Ryder Anderson from Midnight Liaisons. You must be Ruby Sommers."

"That's me," I said firmly, shaking her hand. Her grip was wimpy, like most human women's, and there was an odd scent to her that I couldn't place. Maybe it was just my nerves. I was so anxious that I felt like throwing up or running out the door. Possibly both.

Ryder gave me a cheery smile. "It's so nice to finally meet you. Your date isn't scheduled to arrive for another ten minutes, so I thought I'd finish going over a few things about the dating service with you, if that's all right?" Her voice was incessantly bubbly.

"Okay," I said, feeling overwhelmed despite her efficient attitude. When she waved me forward, I followed her like a lost baby duckling, and I hated myself for it.

The restaurant she'd picked for the date had a cozy, publike atmosphere. It was dark and intimate, with a small flickering oil lamp on each table. The booths were surrounded by tall wooden panels with green ivy growing over the edges, making each section private.

I sat down at the table she led me to, tugging my chair in and then wiping my sweating palms over my green linen retro dress. It belted at the waist and had a cute flared skirt. My sister, Jayde, had picked it out when she learned I'd planned to wear jeans and a sweater. "You'll never catch a man like that," she'd told me.

Maybe she was right. It shouldn't be hard for me to catch a man at all. As a shifter female, I should have my pick, right? Yet here I was, lonely and desperate and set up on a blind date through a dating service. Maybe it *was* how I dressed. I eyed Ryder's attire. Her polo top was bright pink and belted into white capris with pink piping. Pink-and-white heeled sandals completed the outfit. She looked as if she was ready to go to the country club, and she looked really eager for my date.

I didn't feel half as excited as she looked. Instead, there was a pit of dread in my stomach telling me this wouldn't end well.

"So," she said with a big grin. "Here's how this

works. I'm going to go sit on the far side of the restaurant. It's like a chaperoned date, but I won't listen
in." She pointed at her ear. "Humans can't hear across
noisy rooms. It's just to observe and make sure you
feel safe and comfortable. The date will begin and end
here at the restaurant. If you wish to meet him again,
it won't be chaperoned, though we will ask you to log
each date so we can keep track of where you're at and
any interspecies information you might wish to share
with the agency."

"I see." This all sounded a little controlled. I just
wanted a date with a nice guy. A little conversation
and maybe some flirting to break up the monotony
of my life. Someone to talk to who wouldn't make me
feel so alone.

Someone who would wipe the memories of my
last relationship from my mind, because I couldn't
seem to forget about Michael.

"Now, do you want me to set up a rescue call?"
Her blue eyes focused on me.

"Rescue call?"

"In case the date is going badly," Ryder said, pulling out her phone and typing. "I can call you forty-
five minutes into the date and say that you're needed
at work. You can choose to answer however you like,
but it'll give you an out."

"No, that's okay. I think I'll be all right."

She winked at me cheerfully. "I think you will be,
too. Everyone loves Valjean."

"Valjean?" I laughed. "You mean, like the one from the musical?"

"Musical?" She looked confused.

"Never mind." I guessed perky Ryder didn't spend much time listening to anything she couldn't work out to. "I just thought it was a weird name."

She grinned. "We'll get to him soon enough. But first, I need to finish filling out your profile. Can I see your Alliance ID card?"

I pulled my wallet out of my tiny clutch. Another one of Jayde's brilliant ideas—a teeny, tiny matching green purse instead of my normal serviceable brown satchel. "Here you go."

Ryder peered at it, then typed something else into her iPad. "Okay, good. It looks like you didn't fill out your profession on your profile."

"Oh, yeah." I could feel my cheeks flush. "That's because I really don't have an official one."

Ryder tilted her head at me, confused. "You don't have one?" She looked down at her notes on the iPad, then back to me. "But I show here that you're twenty-six and have some college education. What do you do for a living?"

I hated this question. "I'm a security guard at an Alliance storage facility."

She blinked at me as if it did not compute, and her gaze flicked over my five-foot-nothing frame and my slightly too curvy body. Her response was a polite "Oh?"

"It's the nose," I said lamely, gesturing at my face.

Ryder looked even more confused.

"My sense of smell," I clarified. God, this was so embarrassing. "They hired me because of my predator instincts. We're good at chasing things down in shifted form. Hunters. Apex predators," I mumbled.

Ryder's smile was brilliant once more. "Oh. Of course."

God, I felt stupid. And short.

"Sooooo," Ryder continued cheerfully, tapping her fingers on the iPad. "You also left number twenty-five blank. 'What made you decide to contact Midnight Liaisons?' It's a purely optional question, but we like to get an idea of what brings people to the service. I hope you don't mind me asking."

What made me decide to contact a supernatural dating agency? I was twenty-six and alone and couldn't date humans because of Alliance rules. I worked in a dead-end job and saw no one except my boss when we switched shifts. At the few places I did go to on a regular basis—the library, the movie theater, the grocery store—I couldn't just pick a guy up on the fly. He had to be vetted by the Alliance before I could date him. Men in my life had to have a tail or fangs or both. And since supernaturals lived on the down-low, I was essentially limited to my circle of friends.

Which pretty much left my sister and my boss. I didn't meet new people easily, and were-jaguars were loners by nature.

But there was a difference between loner and lonely. "My sister suggested the service. She says she's met a lot of guys through Midnight Liaisons, and it's been a while since I dated."

"Of course," Ryder said sympathetically.

"I had a long-term boyfriend, but it didn't . . . work out," I added, feeling the need to explain or she'd think something was wrong with me. "We sort of broke off on an ugly note."

She made sympathetic noises in her throat, nodding at me. "Of course. Men can be such dicks."

Such a vehement phrase from such a perky human. "Actually," I said, feeling my heart squeeze painfully for the thousandth time since that day, "he was a really nice guy. I broke it off."

"Why is that?"

I couldn't tell her that I'd been dating a human, since that was forbidden. Humans weren't supposed to know about people who grew tails and things that went bump in the night. A human might freak out and tell others, and then we'd show up on the pages of the Enquirer. Dating a human put everyone in jeopardy.

But I'd been so very in love with Michael. Handsome, funny, sexy. God, so sexy. He'd had a sweet smile that would come over his face slowly when he saw me, as if the sight of me instantly made his world a better place. I'd been addicted to him and spent half of my senior year practically living in his dorm.

Once my father had found out, he'd been furious. Not over the classes I'd been skipping or my slumping grades but because I'd broken a sacred rule. Humans were a one-night stand, and only if it couldn't be avoided. And what I had with Michael could not be construed as anything but a relationship.

My father had threatened me, and when I'd ignored his threats, he'd threatened Michael's life instead. I'd had no choice but to end the relationship, and quickly. I'd ended it badly enough to make sure that there was no chance of us getting back together ever again.

"It wasn't his fault," I said. "He caught me with another guy."

"Oh," she said slowly. "I see."

Why couldn't I keep my nervous mouth shut? "It was a long time ago. Four years. Not a big deal."

"Of course," Ryder said soothingly, then patted my hand. "So, are you ready to hear about your date tonight?"

My stomach gave a little lurch in protest. "Sure."

Ryder practically wiggled in her seat with excitement. "Now, you did say you were open to dating all kinds of men."

I didn't remember that, since I'd filled it out in the groggy post-work-shift state. Lord only knew what I'd written down. "That's fine. I don't care what breed of shifter he is."

Ryder smiled. "Let me tell you a little bit about Valjean. He's a more recent member of the Alliance.

He went to the same university as you, which is a great common ground. I think you're really going to like him."

"What's he do for a living?"

She glanced down at her sheet. "I'm told he's an investor. He loves to travel. I think he recently spent a few years in Europe."

Envy flared through me. I'd always wanted to travel to Europe, back before real life beat me down and smothered my dreams. "A world traveler? I don't know how much we'll have in common, then. I never travel."

Ryder smiled brilliantly. "Then you'll enjoy his stories! I'm sure you two will get along just fine."

"What breed is he?"

"Welllll." She tilted her head and lifted her shoulders a little. "He's a vampire."

I blinked. "You set me up with a vampire?"

"An Alliance vampire," she clarified, then raised a hand to stave off my objections. "I know what you're thinking, but when vampires join the Alliance, they have to sign strict nondisclosure and nonharassment policies. I assure you that he's very safe."

I rubbed the side of my neck. "You know, I'm not really sure a vampire is a good idea—"

"Well, you did mark 'anything' on your form," Ryder said in a businesslike tone. "After this date, you can revise your form as you feel necessary, but until then, I think you should give him a chance."

I sighed. It wasn't Ryder's fault, I supposed, but I didn't like the thought. Undead was just kind of . . . not my type. "It's fine."

"Good!" Ryder pulled out a silk scarf and laid it on the table between us. "There's another condition to this date that I haven't told you about."

Oh, no. "What?"

"He's a little uncomfortable with the vampire thing. Says the fangs bother people, and they stare at his mouth when he talks. He says he won't be able to relax unless you can't see him."

I stared at her, then at the black scarf. "You're joking."

This was going to be a literal blind date? I growled low in my throat.

"It's just for tonight," Ryder hastily said. "I know it's a weird request, but he's a really nice guy, and I'm going to be in the room the whole time. You're a shifter, and you go by smell anyhow, right? So the blindfold thing should be trivial."

"It's not trivial," I snarled. "You have got to be kidding me."

"I wish I was," she said with a patient little sigh. "But unfortunately, Valjean really wants you to wear this. I've got you two a private table at the back of the restaurant, and no one will see that you're wearing it but Valjean. I promise you that it's totally safe."

"No," I said flatly.

"He's just nervous about his teeth," she pleaded.

Her eyes were wide, as if I were somehow being unreasonable. "You can understand that, can't you? This is the first date he's had in a very long time, and he's anxious about meeting you."

I wavered.

Sensing my hesitation, Ryder pounced. "How many Saturday nights do you get to spend with an immortal millionaire who wants to buy you dinner? Doesn't it beat staying at home?"

She nudged the scarf at me.

Damn it. I stared at it for a moment longer, then glared at her. "He'd better be hot."

"He's gorgeous," she assured me, standing up. "Come on. I'll take you to your table."

I clutched my tiny purse and, with Ryder at my side, approached the table as if it would bite. I sat with a thump, my heart hammering. She was right; the table was in the farthest corner of the room, dark and secluded and tucked away from the other tables.

My nostrils picked up the scent of the last couple who'd sat there—both human. No vampire in the proximity, either. I'd smelled two of them at Alliance meetings once; they had an odd, spicy scent that was impossible to get out of the nose. I'd have noticed if he'd been there. I set my purse on the table and put my fidgety hands in my lap.

Maybe I should back out. I wasn't really ready to date again, even after four years. Michael had been perfect for me, except that he hadn't been a shifter. If I was still thinking about him this much, I wasn't ready to move on.

But backing out now would be rude. Maybe I was just being a chicken. Maybe this Valjean would be really nice.

But he was *undead*. I mean, I was desperate, but I didn't think I was *that* desperate.

Ryder lifted the scarf toward me just as a human waiter set a glass of water on the table and smiled at me. He glanced at the blindfold, and his smile faded a little. "Are you ladies ready to order?"

I slid the glass closer, not making eye contact. I guess I was going to do this after all. My stomach quivered uncomfortably. "Not yet. I'm waiting for my date."

He nodded and moved to the next table, his gaze flicking over Ryder again.

After he left, I sighed. "He thinks we're weird."

"Just tip him well. He won't care."

I glared at her as she handed me the blindfold again.

"I really appreciate you being such a sport about this," she said, her smile evident in her voice as she covered my eyes with the blindfold. Combined with the dim lighting, it ensured that I wouldn't be able to see anyone. *Great.*

"Okay, how many fingers am I holding up?" Ryder asked, waving her arm in front of my face and making her powdery perfume waft through the air.

I sighed. "One."

"Three. Good. I'm going to be just on the other side of the room, so don't worry in the slightest. This is all totally safe."

"What if I have to go to the bathroom?"

"Oh. Um." She thought for a moment. "Just don't drink a lot."

So much for the thought of loading up on fortifying alcohol. I drummed my fingers on the tabletop, tempted to tear the blindfold away. If he had weird protruding teeth, I'd want to see that, right?

But I'd agreed to this, and Ryder was right—I was lonely. I didn't have anything better to do tonight than curl up with a movie. The thought was depressing.

"Go get 'em, tiger," Ryder said, and patted me on the shoulder. "I'll be across the room if you need me."

I'd heard enough cat jokes to last me three lifetimes, so I said nothing. I heard her shoes tap on the hardwood floor as she moved to the other end of the room. With my eyes covered, my other senses, already acute, flared to life. Someone at the bar was laughing in a low, husky voice that wobbled as if she'd had too much to drink. A man murmured in the drunk woman's ear. I could hear the tap of Ryder's fingertips hitting her phone as she texted someone. Heard another person drop a fork from across the room. Heard someone at the closest table—still a good distance away—whispering about stock portfolios. My sense of smell was heightened, too, although I was doing my best to ignore that. The scents of everyone who had walked past the table recently all mixed into an overwhelming cocktail that my brain couldn't process without becoming overloaded, so I focused on small things. The sizzle of fajitas at a table somewhere in the room. That smelled good. Maybe I'd order that, provided I could eat anything while blindfolded. God, this was so stupid.

Well, it was just one date. I'd politely get through the evening, and then we'd go our separate way, and maybe I'd date a nice were-hyena next.

Or maybe not. That was the problem with being an apex predator. Smaller creatures had dominance issues. When I'd been around other guys, they hadn't been interested in a shifter who was dozens of times stronger and more dangerous in cat form than they were. It did terrible things to the male ego. And I sure as hell wasn't going to play down my strength or pretend to be a simpering female to appease some guy's insecure ego.

I'd never been able to just be me with a guy. I'd had to keep a distance on so many things, even with Michael. I hadn't introduced him to my family when he'd asked. They were complicated, I'd told him. When he'd invited me to move in with him, I'd declined. I needed the ability to come and go as the predatory instinct struck me. I'd been such a shitty girlfriend to him, yet he'd been patient and understanding.

Until the day my father told me to end it with

Michael, or he'd end Michael to protect me. It was Jayde's idea to have him catch me in bed with another man, and she'd volunteered her sometime-boyfriend, Thad. Then Jayde had set Michael up, inviting him to go to my dorm that evening for a surprise.

He'd seen a surprise, all right. He'd thrown my key down, declared that we were through, and slammed the door. Seeing his face stark with betrayal had destroyed me. He hadn't heard my sobs as he'd stormed down the hall, sobs that any shifter would have picked up. And I'd known that, even as I'd known it was for his own good.

I took a gulp of water, trying to dislodge the knot in my throat. Four years, and I still hadn't moved past it. Maybe because I spent so much time alone at my job. In the slow moments, I thought about Michael. I wondered what he was doing. I had searched for him online at every social-networking website, but he was nowhere to be found.

Maybe if I could find him, his hair receding, his gut paunchy, in a picture with a wife and two kids, that would cure me of my obsession.

I scowled. How sad and pathetic I was to be mooning over a human—a human! Maybe I needed to be more like Jayde. At least she got around. And she dated everything—wolf, lion, tiger. You name it.

Well, I thought with a grimace, not vampires. Jayde drew the line at that.

I heard footsteps, then the swish of clothing that

told me someone was approaching. The air shifted, and I caught an appealing new scent: spicy, with a hint of sweetness, mixed with the perfume of human flesh. I immediately stiffened.

My vampire date was here.

"Your hand," a low voice murmured. There was an odd quality to his voice, as if it were somehow modified.

The fangs? Maybe he was newly turned and struggled with controlling them? I pictured a vampire with buck teeth and quelled the hysterical giggle that rose in my throat.

He waited, so I raised my hand and was surprised when he leaned over it to kiss the back of it. I felt the brush of teeth and jerked away.

"I wouldn't bite you without permission," he rasped, his voice a bare whisper.

"You'll have to forgive me for being nervous," I said dryly. "I'm not a fan of the blindfold bit."

"Yet I appreciate the gesture."

"You should," I said, my tone sharp. "Sorry. I'm a little on edge. I've never dated someone who refused to let me see his face."

I heard his chair being drawn out, and his clothing rustled as he sat down. His hand touched mine on the table, as if he meant to hold it.

I pulled away, noticing that his skin was cooler than mine. "That's a little forward for a first date, isn't it? How about we talk first?"

Man, vampires were weird, and I apparently had a handsy one.

"You look very nice tonight, Ruby."

I tilted my head a little, puzzled. His tone sounded a little more intimate than a stranger's should. Or was I just imagining things? "Thanks. I'd say the same to you, but . . ." I gestured at the blindfold.

He chuckled, and the sound made my body prickle with pleasure. *Whoa. Down, girl.* I'd heard that vampires could be very enticing, but that was . . . alarming.

An awkward silence fell again. "Tell me about you," he finally said. "Please."

Did he have a hint of a British accent? How had I missed that? I deflected, wanting to hear him talk more. "Oh, I'm just your average girl with a tail."

He chuckled again. "I believe I'm supposed to ask for your ID to confirm that."

I flipped my purse open, running my fingers over the cards in my wallet until I found one that had no raised numbers on it and offered it to him. "That's either my driver's license or my ID. Are my eyes open in the picture?"

"They are." He sounded amused.

"Then that's my Alliance ID."

There was a moment of quiet. "Were-jaguar?"

"Yes," I said, getting defensive. This was what usually made men run out the door. It was hard dating when your shifter side was at the top of the food chain. "Is that a problem?"

"No, just surprising. I'd have thought you were something smaller . . . softer. Like a were-bunny."

I bristled. Who did this guy think he was? "Not funny."

"Then I apologize," he said in that same odd voice I couldn't figure out.

"Uh-huh. I'd ask for your ID, but that seems useless, seeing as how I'm blindfolded."

"Ryder has vetted it prior to our date. And the ID would do you no good. Vampires don't photograph, and my sketch does not do me justice."

"How can I confirm that you are one?"

"Give me your hand again, and you can tell."

Despite my unease with him, I stretched my hand over the table, palm up. He'd have to place his hand in mine, not the other way around. There was that apex predator in me again, always needing the upper hand.

To my surprise, he placed his hand in mine and waited. His fingertips were cool against my skin, his scent enveloped me, and it was impossible to think that he was anything but vampire.

His thumb grazed the inside of my palm in a caress.

Startled, I jerked my hand away. Were all vampires so grabby? I resisted the urge to flick out my claws to scare him and instead put my hand in my lap. *Be nice, Ruby.* I cleared my throat. "How long have you been a vampire?"

"Four years. How long have you been a were-jaguar?"

I forced a smile to my face, still feeling a little annoyed. "I've always been one. Most of us are born shifters. It's rare that anyone is turned."

"I see," he said in an odd tone.

There was something he wasn't telling me, but for the life of me, I couldn't figure out what it was. It was as if he knew something I didn't and was judging my answers according to that. I didn't like it. Plus, the damn blindfold was driving me crazy. I tugged at the scarf. "Can I take this off so we can have a real conversation?"

"I would prefer you kept it on," Valjean said. "As a favor to me."

Again, that odd lilt that seemed to come and go. Something he'd picked up in Europe?

"Fine," I said after a moment. "But I just want you to know I'm not enjoying this. I can't get comfortable with my eyes covered."

"I think you'll be more comfortable around me with it on," he said cryptically.

A twinge of sympathy shot through me. "If it's about the teeth, I assure you that it's not a big deal to me. I'm used to big canines hanging out of my own mouth."

"Still, this is what I prefer. It allows me to feast my gaze upon you without worry."

I squirmed uncomfortably, my nipples pricking at the thought. I hoped he didn't notice that. I also hoped he wasn't spending the whole evening staring at my boobs.

"You are very beautiful," he said in a soft, husky voice that sent a shiver through my body. "Any man would consider himself lucky to be sitting in my chair right now."

"Thank you, but I can't date any man," I said, a hint of bitterness in my voice. "I have to date Alliance."

Awkward silence. Probably not the wisest thing to say. *This is why you're single,* I could hear Jayde saying. *You're too hung up on that human guy. Forget him.*

"So tell me about you," I said, rushing into the awkward silence. "Is Valjean a family name? A nickname? Do you have a thing for musicals?"

"It is a name I chose. It seemed appropriate."

"How so?"

"A man betrayed on all sides, forced to live a double life . . ." He trailed off.

"Betrayed?" I had to ask.

"It is a long story, and one for a different day."

I rolled my eyes under the blindfold. This Valjean guy needed to get over himself. "Just thought I'd ask. It's an unusual name."

"Didn't you know? Vampires assume new identities. It helps us break our ties with our old lives."

There was something about him that bothered me, even as I found him appealing. I tilted my head, trying to put my finger on why his responses were unsettling to me. As I moved, I heard him inhale sharply across the table.

I froze. Was he turned on by the sight of my neck? My entire body tingled with alarm . . . and a hint of arousal. That my slightest gesture could turn a man on so much was bizarre and heady.

Not *a man*, I corrected myself. *A vampire*. That changed everything.

Perhaps I'd misunderstood his reaction, though. The blindfold made it difficult to trust my senses, since there was context that I was missing. As a test, I tilted my head further and brushed my long, curling hair over one shoulder, baring my throat. I tilted my chin slowly, working over to the other side as if stretching.

I heard the barest hint of a groan, and he shifted in his chair, adjusting his clothing. As if it had become suddenly . . . too tight in one area?

That pervert! "Okay, that's it," I said firmly, getting to my feet. I tugged at the knot at the back of my head. "I can deal with a lot of things, but I'm not going to sit here in the dark while you're getting turned on by this freaking blindfold—"

"Ruby, don't—" the vampire began, his accent suddenly gone, his voice sounding oddly familiar.

I popped my claws, sliced through the fabric, jerked the blindfold away, and stared at my date.

Michael.

Chapter Two

When we'd first started dating, Michael had been this gorgeous, geeky god, and that hadn't changed. Inky black hair covered his head in a rakish, thick swath. It was always a little too long on top, and when he dragged his hand through his hair, the black locks stuck up like wild spikes on top of his head. I'd been infatuated with those spikes; they made him look untamed. His face was as perfect as I remembered it, too—his cheekbones defined and arching, his brows dark slashes in an otherwise pale face, his jaw narrow but firm and currently clenched with anger. His eyes were beacons of pale green, and his mouth was full and sensual. He was every bit as muscled and hard as he was back when he was playing football in college. In the past, he'd always had a bit of a five o'clock shadow—that was gone now. His chin was completely smooth. He'd always had a tan in the past, too; that was also gone.

He was a vampire.

Michael was freaking *undead*. The blood drained from my face as I put things together. *Four years*, he'd told me he'd been a vampire. He must have been changed right after we'd broken up.

My gaze narrowed, and I focused on his teeth. There was nothing wrong with them. Nothing at all.

This date was all a setup. He hadn't wanted me to see that it was him. He'd been sitting there, laughing at me as I was blindfolded and trying to act as if it was a real date. Disguising his voice so I wouldn't be clued in that it was him.

Why would he do such a thing? Just to mess with me? To get the upper hand and make me look like a fool?

Fury pulsed through me. "What the fuck is this, Michael? Some sort of sick little game?"

He stiffened in anger. "So what if it is, Ruby? Is it so different from the tricks you played on me when we were together?"

So it *was* just to fuck with me. I threw the scarf at him, smacking him in the chest with it. "I never played games. I was always straightforward with you."

"Didn't you? Because I seem to recall that your last words to me were 'It's not what it looks like, Michael.'"

"Fuck you, Valjean," I said coldly. I scooped up

my clutch purse, which would make a great projectile when I launched it at his head. "Find some other woman to ogle while she's blindfolded. I refuse to go along with your sick, perverted little vampire game."

I pushed my way through the restaurant, ignoring Ryder's questioning call. So much for a little companionship. I was done with this. Out of here. Waiters and customers scurried out of my way as I stomped to the door, bristling with outrage.

Outside on the sidewalk, I inhaled sharply, breathing in the clear night air. Odd how I'd enjoyed the slightly spicy, sweet vampire scent. I'd heard that was part of their charm, so attractive and appealing that normal, sane people let their guard down. I took a few steps down the street, stretching and letting the night air brush over my shoulders, and headed for the bus stop.

"Stop!" Michael called. "Ruby, stop! I want to talk to you."

This evening was a waking nightmare. How many times had I dreamed of seeing him again? Of confessing my horrible misdeeds and having him forgive me? Of telling him that I'd always loved him and having him say the same back to me? The only thing Michael wanted was to fuck with me. I walked even faster.

A cool hand grasped my arm.

I turned and snarled. "What?"

The wind ruffled his thick, unruly hair. He loomed over my smaller form, and I was struck anew at how beautiful he was. His features seemed refined in undeath. It suited him.

I hated that.

"Where do you think you're going?" he said.

"I'm leaving," I bit back, jerking my arm away from him. That was the good thing about being a were-jaguar. He wasn't stronger than me. "This was obviously a mistake. I'd say it was nice to see you again, but we'd both know that was a lie, right? So I won't even bother."

"Don't you think it's unfair for you to leave so quickly?"

I stopped and turned, furious. "Exactly *how* is this unfair?"

"Don't I get a kiss good night?"

"Not as long as you have fangs in your mouth." I stomped away. God, what was wrong with him? With *me*, for dreaming about him for so long?

"Good-bye, Ruby," he said softly, so softly I almost didn't catch it.

The bus pulled up to the curb in a noisy squeal, drowning out anything else he might have said. I paused. Why had his voice gotten so soft and thoughtful? Was it a vampire lure? I peeked over my shoulder and caught a man turning into an alley. Michael must have decided to stick to the shadows for his walk home. *Valjean*, I corrected myself with a curl of my lip, and turned to the waiting bus. Just then, a heavy shuffling and the sound of flesh striking flesh pricked my ears. A fight? It was coming from the alley.

A trick?

The wind shifted, and along with the heavy scent of car exhaust, I caught the smell of something odd and pungent. I scanned the strip of restaurants nearby. No Italian. How odd that I'd caught the thick scent of garlic—

I gasped, then raced for the alley.

Two men fought there, and I saw Michael slug a guy in a polo shirt. The other man reeled at the hit. Michael growled low in his throat—strange how sexy I found that sound—and pounced on the man.

Irritation flashed through me. Was he taking out some hapless passerby in an alley out of a pissy fit of temper, or worse, because he was thirsty? I put my hands on my hips and tapped my foot. "Michael, this is so *not* cool."

Michael whirled around, and his eyes were so dark that for a moment, I thought there was something wrong with him. A hypodermic needle was sticking out of the side of his neck, and he yanked it out and tossed it to the ground. He staggered forward a step and raised a hand out to me. "Get out of here, Ruby," he said in low, angry growl. "Leave!"

Behind him, the man leaped onto Michael's back and pushed another hypodermic into his throat. Michael shuddered, his eyes rolling back in their sockets, and he collapsed to the ground. The smell of thick garlic filled the air.

I took a step forward. "What the hell is going on?"

The man crouching over Michael stood. He was tall, with broad shoulders, a scruffy beard, and cuts on his face from where Michael's fists had clearly done some damage. A dark sleeve of tattoos covered each of his arms. This didn't seem like a botched feeding.

"What are you doing?" I asked, approaching.

He stepped in front of Michael's sprawled form. "Collecting a bounty. Move along."

"Bounty?"

"You need to mind your own business, lady. Move along," he repeated, cracking his knuckles in a menacing way.

I raised an eyebrow. "Maybe I should stop you."

"Now, sweetie," he said, staring condescendingly down at me. "I'd hate for you to break a nail on one of your cute little hands."

Oh, was that how it was going to be? I moved forward, letting my eyes flash with moonlight like a cat's.

Recognition dawned on his face, along with a slow, evil smile that showed a pair of extremely long fangs. "What are you, a were-bunny? I've never tasted one. Tonight might be the night."

God damn it, why did everyone think I was a were-bunny? I dropped my purse onto the ground and began to unbutton the front of my dress, letting the change ripple through my insides. "Try again."

"Were-kitten?" he said with a leer as I dropped my nice new dress to the ground and stepped out of it, then my shoes. "Or maybe a cute little were—"

The words choked in his throat as I dropped to all fours and black-and-gold-spotted fur sprouted all over my body. My lashing tail distended immediately, and thick, curving claws grew from my fingertips. My teeth elongated and extended into sharp predator teeth. My shoulders hunched low, my hips sliding back to adjust for powerful hindquarters.

"Oh, fuck," he swore under his breath.

And there it is, I thought smugly. Then the change fully overtook me, and my thought became of nothing but my jaguar until the transformation was done. When I opened my eyes and took a prowling step forward, he bolted down the alley.

My inner cat went wild. I gave a chuffing little cry and sprang after him. As he raced down the alley I swiped at his back, toying with him. He yelped as my claws ripped his shirt open, exposing a back full of more tattoos. I sped up, nipping at his heels. I could break his neck and play with him, spring onto his back and sink my teeth into the fragile bones at the base of his head. A broken neck wouldn't kill a vampire, but it'd be really fun to see the fear in his eyes as he realized he'd be mine to play with and destroy at my leisure.

Sometimes there was a big upside to being an apex predator, I thought with a gleeful rush.

A groan sounded behind me, and I skidded to a halt, flattening my ears, listening for another breath of sound.

The tattooed man sensed my distraction and sped up, heading toward traffic.

I could still catch him. If he got toward one of the main streets, I'd have no choice but to abandon the hunt. A big cat roaming downtown Fort Worth? Kinda noticeable. But he wasn't faster than me. I could still spring on him, knock him to his back, snap his neck—

The groan sounded again. *Michael.* I gave another chuffing cry of anger and turned back toward him.

I'd deal with that tattooed vampire later. I had his scent now, and I'd be able to pick up his trail if he didn't get into a car.

I padded to Michael's side and placed my damp nose against his skin. Flushed with heat. That wasn't good for a vampire. The garlic must have given him a fever.

I touched him with the tip of my tongue. He was still unconscious, his hair spilling over his forehead and sticking to his skin in sweaty spikes. His eyelids fluttered rapidly, his breath rasping, quick, and shallow.

I nudged him. He didn't move. Another low moan escaped his throat. He was in pain, and my heart clenched in response.

Shit. I couldn't leave him there. What if humans

found him? I couldn't take him to the local Alliance doc; he only treated shifters. And if one vampire was looking for him, there might be more. If I left his side, he'd be vulnerable.

I looked at Michael's big body, slumped on the concrete. I could probably carry him in my human form, but that would draw too much attention, given our sizes. Maybe I could find someplace safe nearby. Then I could leave him and scout out the area.

The vampire couldn't have gotten far, and I wanted to know what exactly this "bounty" was about.

I dragged Michael a short way and then got him onto my back—no mean trick without hands, let me tell you. It wasn't easy keeping him balanced there, and he was probably going to have knuckles full of gravel when he woke up from his hands dragging on the ground, but I made it a few blocks away from the restaurant. My progress was slow, but I knew the area well. With some creative thinking, it wasn't too hard to keep out of sight, going down alleys, cutting through overpasses, and keeping to the shadows. I was spotted once or twice, but most people rubbed their eyes and stared, not believing the sight. There might be some odd calls to the police, but I'd be long gone by the time a patrol car got there.

I kept my head low, looking for a safe place to bunk down and check out Michael's injuries. My night vision showed me a massive, looming building in the distance. The old abandoned meatpacking plant. It sat in the heart of Fort Worth, a ghastly eyesore that was only opened up at Halloween to run a haunted house.

I circled around to the back of the building, where the shadows were heavier, and dropped Michael off in a dark corner. I paced around the side of the immensely long structure, examining the rows of windows. I had no idea how protected the building was. If there was security, we'd be toast.

Well, there was only one way to find out. I flung my jaguar body through a lower window and waited.

No alarms. *Perfect.* I jumped back out the window again, shifted quickly to my human form, cleared the glass, and proceeded to shove Michael through the window.

Haunted-house props littered the bottom floor, so I carried Michael deeper in until there was nothing but broken equipment and storage crap, all covered in a thick layer of dust. I laid him in the corner of the room behind a couple of empty cable spools. He was still—too still. I hesitated, then forced myself to get up. I had to make sure he was safe first.

Since I'd carried him through the old warehouse and through most of the city, anyone looking for him wouldn't find his scent unless they were practically upon him. That was good. I dragged props and crates around him, making a small fortress to protect him. He'd be safe there, as long as we hadn't been followed.

In case we *had* been followed, I transformed back to my shifter form and paced through the inside of the old plant, leaving a scent trail that crossed and crisscrossed itself to confuse any trackers. Vampires couldn't track by scent, but I didn't trust anything to chance. Then, when Michael was as protected as I could make him, I slipped out the window and headed back toward the alley. I needed my dress, and I needed to scout the area for answers.

The alley was choked with the thick, spicy scent of the tattooed vampire, who had indeed returned. I clung to the shadows, my tail twitching as I watched my prey.

The vampire had a phone raised to his ear, and he squatted to pick up my dress. "You didn't tell me he was with a big goddamn shifter," Tattoos said.

"I didn't know. He must be getting desperate for blood," said the voice on the phone. "Angelo's got him on the run. Serves him right."

Tattoos snorted. "It's not his fault Mariah's so hot for him."

"Doesn't matter," the phone voice said curtly. "Angelo still wants him dead. You said the shifter ran off with him? See if she's abandoned him nearby. Look for clues."

"I'm not Scooby-Doo," Tattoos muttered, pulling a gun out of the waistband of his jeans and glaring down the alley.

A gun? *Damn.* I sprang away, climbing up a nearby awning and then jumping to the top of a building. I circled back to the abandoned warehouse slowly, thinking hard. Someone named Angelo wanted Michael dead. What was I supposed to do with that information?

I slipped back into the warehouse and padded to where I'd left Michael. His scent was thick and strong, mixed with garlic. It made the spice in his vampire scent turn sour and wrong. Garlic was a poison for the undead, and Michael had gotten a massive dose.

He was delirious and weak, his eyelids fluttering as I crouched next to him and shifted back to my human form. I leaned over him and pressed my fingers to his forehead, gauging his temperature. Still hot and damp with sweat. What was I supposed to do with a sick vampire?

Michael's eyes opened, so green they almost glowed in his flushed face. To my surprise, he reached out and gently touched his fingers against my cheek, then traced my jaw.

"Dreamed of this," he murmured. "So beautiful."

Then his eyelids fluttered shut, and he went limp, leaving me alone, naked, and very, very confused.

Chapter Three

Throughout the night, Michael twitched and shivered, caught up in the throes of the poison. I could smell garlic seeping from his pores as he sweated, delirious.

I paced, feeling helpless, my thoughts a confusing swirl.

Michael is here.

Michael is a vampire now.

And vampires aren't off-limits to shifters. I felt a flutter of hope and quickly squashed it. He'd had four years to hate me. Our reunion had been horrible, and when I'd accused him of messing with me, he hadn't denied it. He'd been deliberately cruel.

But he'd touched my cheek so tenderly, had whispered, "Dreamed of this," when he'd seen me. What did that mean?

Even though our blind date was worse than awful, seeing him tossing and turning in the moonlight brought all my emotions back to the surface. I couldn't abandon him. Not while he was vulnerable and alone and hunted. I knew a thing or two about hunting and protecting. That was my job, after all. I could protect him until he was back on his feet.

Provided I could find some clothing, of course.

I prowled through the broken-down plant, looking for something to cover up my nudity, but there was nothing. The tattooed vampire had taken my dress and my purse, and I was essentially trapped with no wallet, no cell phone, and a vampire who was delirious with fever.

All in all, not a great date.

I crept over to his side again, worrying about the dawn creeping through the nearby windows. I'd moved him to the darkest corner of the warehouse and arranged tarps over the stacked crates to give him a shelter from the sunlight, but what if it wasn't enough to protect him?

It wasn't. Although the sun wasn't hitting him directly, as soon as light filled the windows, his tossing and turning became more frantic. Sweat beaded on his skin, and his breathing came in harsh, shallow pants.

I stroked a hand over his forehead, concerned.

His eyes flew open, his pupils dilated to pools of black. His lips parted, and his fangs elongated, growing to four times their size. I stared at them in revulsion. Movie vampires had tiny baby fangs. The reality was more like a goddamn saber-toothed tiger.

"Just what we needed," I muttered to myself.

At the sound of my voice, his eyes rolled back in his head, and his eyelids fluttered, his body arching as if in pain.

"Michael?" I laid a hand to his cheek, alarmed. "Are you okay?"

He turned toward my wrist, and his nostrils flared like a shifter's did when on a scent. Did he smell my blood? My skin prickled with alarm, but he didn't move. The pulse in his neck fluttered weakly, and his mouth went slack. His lips looked cracked, and even the sweat that had been rolling off him was drying.

This wasn't good.

His tongue touched his dry lips, and I heard the barest hiss of a word. "Blood."

I squeezed my eyes shut . . . and pushed my wrist against his mouth.

This time, he bit down.

The pain was excruciating. It felt as if twin nails had been hammered through my wrist; I could feel his teeth scrape my wrist bones. I jerked, trying to pull away from the pain shooting up my arm.

He wouldn't let go, though. His hands locked around my wrist, and he began to drink, each pull feeling as if he was sucking on a straw. I jerked again, but he was strong in his need, his skin hot and dry against my own. This was not worth it.

Except . . . that sick flush in his cheeks seemed to be fading a little. The fevered chills were gone. He wasn't moaning with pain from the sun any longer.

I gritted my teeth, prepared to endure it for his sake. I supposed I owed him that much.

Michael continued to drink as if instinct had taken over to save his life. I let him, occasionally reaching over to stroke his hair.

Even as a weird, undead, saber-toothed vampire, he was still incredibly beautiful to me. My heart swelled with longing, and I smiled down at him.

The room tilted and wobbled, just a little. Light-headed. He was taking too much blood. I tugged at my wrist. "That's enough."

He continued to drink, his throat flexing with each gulp.

"Michael," I gritted, bracing my other hand against his shoulder and pushing. When that didn't work, I tried yanking at his fingers, still locked around my wrist. "I said, that's *enough*."

But he was beyond hearing me. I had to stop him before he killed me.

I placed one foot against his jaw and pushed hard. His teeth finally came free, and he flew backward, his fangs gouging my arm. I cried out in pain and clutched my wrist to my chest. Ow.

He landed in a pool of weak sunlight, and his skin

immediately began to smoke. I groaned and dragged him back to the shelter again. My wrist was bleeding profusely, so I ripped a strip from his shirt for a bandage.

"Totally crossing vampires off the dating list," I muttered as I bound my wrist.

The day passed slowly. As the sun grew higher in the sky, the warehouse became oppressively hot. I didn't mind it, because of my cat nature, but I did mind the stagnant, dirty air. Michael's phone was nowhere to be seen, and I didn't even know if he carried one. Mine had been taken with my purse, so we were effectively stranded. I longed to go check on my apartment, to see if they had raided it after discovering my purse, but I couldn't exactly cross town naked—or in my jaguar form. I could get away with being a big cat in the night when the shadows hid me, but in the daytime, people tended to call animal control on you.

Plus, I was tired. I'd been up all night watching over Michael, and my strength was sliding away. I curled up near his body and catnapped through the day, waking at the slightest sound. Shifters had incredibly keen hearing, so I'd be alert the moment someone came near the building.

I woke up late in the afternoon to the sound of a rat scurrying over the floor in the next room. I sat up, and my stomach growled, reminding me that I hadn't eaten in almost a full day. The rat moved again, and my stomach rumbled once more in response, reminding me that if I was in my cat form, vermin made a nice snack.

I decided I'd go without for a bit longer.

I did shift to my cat form to do a quick reconnaissance of the area while waiting for the sun to go down. No new scents in the area—good. Our hideaway had yet to be discovered.

I returned to Michael's side as soon as the last of daylight disappeared. Not wanting to startle him, I shifted back to my human form and waited for him. Would he wake up? What if he'd died while sleeping? I placed my hand to his forehead, which felt cool to the touch. That was a good thing for vampires, right?

At my touch, his entire body jerked, and his eyes flicked open. He grabbed my bandaged wrist before I could pull it away. His nostrils flared, and I watched his teeth extend out of his mouth, as if the very scent of blood made him lose control.

I twisted my wrist in his grasp, gently but firmly. "Let go of me."

He did so at once, his dilated eyes blinking rapidly. Then his teeth retracted, and he looked at my face for a long moment, as if struggling to comprehend where he was.

"You're awake," I said, hiding my relief.

His gaze slid to my bare breasts. "You're naked."

"Long story. We can get to that after you tell me why you're being chased by a bounty hunter."

He continued to stare at my breasts, as if entranced

by their close proximity and their free-hanging state. "Bounty . . . hunter?" he repeated slowly. His fingers twitched, and I wondered if he was wanting to reach out and touch me.

The thought made unwelcome heat flare through my body, making my nipples tighten. I snapped my fingers in front of my face. "Eyes up here."

He broke from his trance, looking up at me. Then he looked a bit chagrined. "Sorry. You were saying . . . bounty hunters?"

I nodded. Would it be totally obvious if I pulled my long, curly black hair over my shoulders to cover my breasts? Probably. I resolved to ignore his fascinated gaze, which was even now creeping back to my naked body. "Do you want to tell me why other vampires are trying to kill you? It's put both of our lives in jeopardy."

He frowned, thinking, and sat up in the little fort I'd made him. Michael ran a hand down his face. "All I remember was heading down the alley. Someone jumped down from the roof and landed on me and jabbed the needle in my throat. I think we struggled. The last thing I remember is pain." He grimaced, placing his hand on his neck. "Lots and lots of white-hot pain."

"So you don't know who he was," I stated.

"No."

"Or why he came after you?"

This time, he was silent.

"You *do* know why he came after you?" A surge of

irritation flared through me. "What were you thinking, going out on a date in public if you knew someone was hunting you? How could you put my life in danger like that?"

"I didn't know that part," he said, raking a hand through his hair and making it stick up like a sexy tumbleweed all over again. "I didn't know that Angelo was actively seeking to have me eliminated because of Mariah's infatuation."

I crossed my arms over my chest, both gratified and annoyed that his gaze immediately went there. "Who are Angelo and Mariah?"

"Other vampires."

"The ones who turned you?"

"No, the one who turned me was Gemma."

A pang of pain shot through me. A woman had turned him? "But you know why you're being hunted?"

"Angelo wants Mariah to be his blood partner." At my blank look, he continued. "Blood partners are a symbiotic couple—they need nothing but each other and can feed on each other eternally. Mariah doesn't want that relationship with Angelo, and the best way to send a message that you're not interested? Acquiring a blood partner."

"You?" I guessed, my tone scathing.

I could have sworn he looked a little bothered. "Not everyone finds me as repugnant as you do."

Repugnant? Did he really think that? Flustered, I

pulled my hair over my breasts, not caring if the move was obvious. "So this Mariah wants you to shack up with her, and her wannabe boyfriend is trying to kill you?"

He nodded. "A blood partner is greatly prized, and Angelo's had his eye on Mariah for a long time. I guess he feels that he's put in enough time that he doesn't want to lose her to someone else. I don't think it's love as much as pride."

"And did you sleep with this Mariah?" I asked, and then was glad the darkness hid the uncomfortable flush on my cheeks. Why did I care if my ex-boyfriend slept with some skanky vampire chick?

"I have never approached her," he said in a low, soft voice. "Never had any interest at all, never encouraged her. Nothing. This is all Mariah. I changed my name and went into hiding, figuring that if she had a few decades to forget about me, then I could reenter vampire society, but she is making things . . . difficult."

"I'll say," I said. "And this Angelo guy, is he powerful?"

"He's the head of the vampire clan in this area."

"That's a yes, then."

An awkward pause fell. After a moment, Michael peeked up at me again. "You saved my life? How?"

The gleam in his eyes was a little disconcerting. Was that affection? Lust? Unrequited love still burning after four long years of misery? Or was I just imagining it?

"I heard you gasp, and something told me to check it out. So I did what anyone would do—changed to my shifter form and scared him off."

He reached out to brush a stray curl off my shoulder, his cool fingertips gliding over my skin. "Not anyone. He could have hurt you."

"Actually," I said in a light, breathless voice as his fingers moved down my bare arm, "he probably couldn't. Apex predator and all."

Michael snatched his hand away from my arm. "Of course. Were-jaguar." He glanced around the warehouse. "And you somehow managed to bring me here?"

"I did," I replied firmly, wondering why it bothered me so much that he'd jerked away as soon as the were-jaguar thing was mentioned. I mean, heck, he was freaking undead, and you didn't see me panicking and going all to pieces, did you? No, you did not.

"I owe you a debt of gratitude," he said in a soft voice.

I squirmed a little, uncomfortable at the thought of him owing me. Me, who had kept secrets and stomped on his heart. "Don't be ridiculous."

"At the very least, I owe you an apology," he said softly. "I wasn't kind to you at dinner. The blindfold was cruel. I'm sorry."

I waved off his apology. "I've hurt you, too. I guess we're even, right?"

"I don't want to be even," he said in a low, husky voice.

"Yet you wanted to hurt me once you found out that I was in the agency database. When you figured out I had lied to you about what I was."

"I did," he admitted, his green gaze on me. "But I've changed my mind."

I raised an eyebrow at him. "Already?"

He brushed his fingers over my cheek, confusing me with flutters of feeling all over again. "You saved my life. And what we had before . . . it was good. I've missed you. I want to be friends again."

My heart skipped an excited beat even as I was crestfallen. After all the heartbreak and the agony, all he wanted was to be friends? Could I be friends with a man I'd once loved?

And really, had I ever stopped loving him at all?

"Friends," I repeated with a forced smile, and stuck my hand out.

He looked at my extended hand in surprise. Then he smiled and shook it. "Friends, then."

My heart felt as if it was breaking into a million tiny pieces.

Chapter Four

Michael was still a little weak and slow-moving because of the poison, but he didn't like that I was stranded there naked and that his bounty hunters likely had my ID and home address.

"We can go to my house," he said. "I've been living under an assumed name for quite a while now. I doubt they know it."

"They know something about you," I pointed out. "Otherwise, how were they able to find you at the restaurant?"

He shrugged. "Dumb luck? They know I'm in the area, they just don't know where."

I frowned at him. "Then why don't you leave the area and go somewhere safe?"

He shrugged, glancing away. "I like it here. It's home."

"Not if home gets you killed," I retorted, and got to my feet. "What's the plan?"

His gaze strayed back to my nude body, pale in the moonlight, and then quickly flicked away again, as if he couldn't help himself but was trying to be polite for the sake of our friendship. Already I hated that word. "We should scout the area, see if they're still nearby. If not, we can head out."

"And go where?"

"I have multiple safe houses in the area," he said calmly. "One of them is bound to be secure."

We didn't have any other options that I could see, but I didn't like it. It felt like tempting fate. "Fine. I'll scout the area, and once I know it's clear, we can go."

"I can scout, too," he said. He jumped to his feet and immediately swayed, reaching for a nearby crate to hold himself up.

I went back to his side. He leaned against me heavily. "What's wrong?" I asked, worried.

He shook his head and righted himself. "Just a little residually weak from the garlic oil. It'll be fine once I feed again." He gave me a hopeful look. "Don't suppose you'd volunteer for the task?"

I shuddered, remembering those enormous teeth sinking into my wrist and the excruciating pain. "No, thank you. It's not my thing."

"Most people enjoy it," he said, his tone light and cajoling.

I waved my bandaged wrist at him. "I already did my good deed for the week. Find some other sucker to drink from. It's not my idea of fun at all."

Michael looked stricken, grabbing my wrist and pulling it forward to inspect the bandages more closely. "When did I do this, Ruby?"

"When you were sick and the sunlight hit you. I thought you were going to die, so I offered my wrist." A tiny shudder went through me again.

He saw my reaction, his face pale and dismayed. "And it hurt?"

"Yes."

He released my arm with a small sigh. "Then I owe you another apology."

"Don't worry about it," I said, not liking how hard he was taking this.

"I must not have prepared you. I'm sorry."

No amount of preparation could have prepared me for four-inch-long fangs sinking into my wrist. "Like I said, the vampire thing just isn't for me."

He looked tense. "No, I guess not."

Again, the uncomfortable silence fell. I gestured at the moonlight streaming in through the dusty windows. "I'm going out to have a look around. It's safest if I go alone. You stay here."

He stripped off his jacket and began to remove his shirt. "Here. Take my clothes, at least."

I put a hand on his chest, stopping him. Okay, I hadn't needed to touch him, but I couldn't seem to help myself. "You keep it. I'll just tear it when I shift."

He looked at me in surprised fascination. "Are you going to shift right now?"

"I am. You might want to turn away," I said, then stepped away a few feet and behind some boxes to prevent him from seeing the worst.

A lot of people find shifting hideous. As we move from one form to another, our muscles bunch and redirect. Our bones become almost bendy and shift and flex with our bodies. I don't know how it works in a scientific way—all I know is that our entire being rearranges itself, and it's probably something straight out of a horror movie unless you're expecting it.

I looked over midchange and noticed that he wasn't looking away. He'd moved so he could get a better look at my shift, leaning heavily against one of the nearby crates.

When I was done, I stretched in my cat form, my tail flicking.

Michael looked impressed. "That was amazing."

Flatterer. I blinked my cat eyes at him, then went back to his pallet, circled there twice, and then stared at him.

"All right. I'm going," he said, unable to keep the smile from his face as he sat down.

Although the night breeze was brisk, the air was warm and carried with it numerous scents. I could smell exhaust and hear the movement of cars in the distance. I also smelled small rodents, reminding my rumbling stomach that I needed to eat just as badly as Michael did.

I also smelled something else—a spicy, enticing smell that I was becoming all too familiar with.

Vampire. And not Michael.

I found the scent on the far side of the building and tracked it, but I could find no other traces of his scent in the parking lot. I checked the loading-bay doors on this side of the building, but the lock and chain were undisturbed. The windows were unbroken there, but on the other side of the building, where Michael and I were hiding, I'd broken a window. He'd be able to get in through it.

I moved to the far side of the building and picked up another scent, and this one made my blood run cold.

Werewolf. The vampire was using a tracker to hunt us.

Shit. We were in trouble. The wolf would smell jaguar all over this building and know that I was hiding here. I padded back through the parking lot on quick, silent feet, heading for the window that led me back to Michael.

A dark form crouched close to the window. I gave a low, chuffing cry of warning and watched the canine head turn toward me. The wolf raised his head, scenting the air. He hadn't yet seen me, but he'd heard my warning and smelled me on the wind. I stalked out of the shadows and let him get a good look at my size. At my long, pointed teeth. I hissed, baring my teeth, my tail lashing.

The wolf took one look at me and ran like the wind. He didn't stand a chance, and he knew it. Wolves were strong when they were many in number.

I was strong just being me.

That took care of the bloodhound. Now to find the other vampire before he shot Michael full of garlic again—or worse. I climbed up to the ledge of the broken window, then dropped inside. I immediately lowered myself to my belly, tail twitching as I scented the area.

I smelled Michael, his scent far too obvious. I also smelled a faint vampire spice with a different flavor to it, coming from my right. I moved through the shadows, grateful for the haunted-house props that let me slink through the room unnoticed.

Against the wall, I heard a piece of wood shift and fall.

I heard Michael stiffen, his clothes rustling as he moved. I heard something rasp against his hand—a weapon, I hoped. "Ruby? That you?"

I saw a figure rise from the shadows, raising something long to his shoulder. My haunches tightened, and I readied to spring.

"Not Ruby," the man said, and when he tilted his head, I realized he held a crossbow. I sprang with a cry, claws extended.

My heavy weight dropped onto him, and I heard the singing whizz of the crossbow as it released. Something thunked into plywood nearby, and I heard Michael swear. The vampire beneath me struggled hard, and I smelled blood under my claws as I bent my head to break his neck, instinct strong.

"Please," he whispered. "Don't kill me."

I stopped as my front teeth brushed against his cold flesh. I couldn't kill a man in cold blood, however much of a danger he presented to us. I lifted my head, sniffing the air for other vampires as he squirmed underneath me.

I smelled no one else, so I turned my attention back to the vampire below me.

"Ruby?" Michael called again. "Ruby, where are you?"

The vampire below me gave a violent twist, and I put my mouth against his neck in warning.

He raised his free hand, and I saw that he'd somehow produced another gun. With a cold smile full of fangs, he held it against my shoulder and fired.

I waited for the pain of the bullet to hit me, but all I felt was a sting. Then I saw the tranquilizer sticking out of my shoulder, two seconds before the world slid to darkness.

Screw mercy. Next time, I was totally killing the

bad guy. My last view was of Michael snarling, fangs extended, as he leaped onto the vampire.

"Ruby," a voice said, patting my cheek. "Wake up."

I groaned at the throbbing headache behind my eyes. My mouth felt dry, and I was dying for a drink of water. I cracked one eyelid open and stared around.

Michael hovered over me, his face lined with concern. His mouth had a cut in the corner, and there was a scrape on one cheekbone, as if he'd been brawling. He frowned down at my face, and I felt his fingertips stroke my jaw. "Are you okay?"

I was back in my human form, which meant that I'd been out for a while. I sat up, wincing, and rubbed my shoulder, remembering the dart. "He tranq'd me," I said peevishly. "Like a fucking zoo animal."

"I know," he said, sitting back on his haunches. His lips twitched as if he was trying not to laugh. "I was there."

I peered around. The shadows seemed deeper than before. How long was I out? "Did you kill him?"

"No. After he tranquilized you, I pounded him until he reached for his crossbow. Then I grabbed it and smashed it. I think he was out of weapons after that, because he ran like a coward. I had a choice between following him and tending to you, and I chose you."

I wasn't entirely sure that was the wiser choice, but I said nothing. My arm stung, but otherwise I felt fine, just a little sluggish. "So that was the bounty hunter again?"

He nodded. "He'll be back, but not tonight."

"Why not?"

"No vampire wants to be caught out close to daylight, and that's less than an hour away."

"Oh." Had I been asleep for that long? That was depressing. I noticed Michael no longer wore his shirt, and it had been pulled over me. "Thanks for the clothes."

"Tempting as it was to let you lie around naked, I felt it wasn't fair to you, since you'd lost your clothes defending me."

He found me tempting naked, did he? A sliver of pleasure cut through me, but I ignored it, getting to my feet. "We should get out of here."

"Like I said," he began, "no vampire is going to be caught out near sunlight. That includes me."

Right. Damn. "So we're stuck here another night?"

"You're not. I appreciate the assistance, but you're not required to help me anymore. I can take care of myself now."

I frowned. Was this an attempt to ditch me? Was he counting the hours until I left? "But you'll be vulnerable."

"I'll be fine."

"And can you defend yourself when the sun is up?"

He crossed his arms over his chest. "The other guy's a vampire, too. I don't need to worry about that."

"Wrong. He's working with a werewolf. You'd be a sitting duck if *he* found you."

He said nothing.

"I thought so," I replied, my tone crisp. "So I need to look after you until you can get somewhere safe. That's what a friend would do."

He smiled at me then, slow, sensual, and my insides turned to mush. "Thank you, Ruby. I'm sorry you're stuck with me for a bit longer."

His tone implied that he wasn't sorry at all. I smiled back at him.

My smile faded a little when he began to unbutton his pants. I found myself staring at his fingers as he slid his fly down, my throat suddenly dryer than dry. "Um, what are you doing?"

"A convenience store can't be far from here. You need to eat something. I can hear your stomach growling from over here. And if you're going to be my bodyguard, you need to keep your strength up."

"There's a few rats in the building," I joked.

"You might have to leave those for me."

"Funny," I said, then realized he was *not* joking. Ugh. I hated the thought of fighting him for rats. "All right, then. Give me your pants."

If the guy behind the counter at the 7-Eleven thought it was weird that a woman would show up at four in the morning dressed in a man's clothing and buy six hot dogs, all of the beef jerky on the shelf, three bags of chips, and two gigantic bottles of water, he didn't say so. He simply took my cash and went back to watching the movie on his monitor. I trotted back to the plant with my stash swinging from my hand. I didn't like leaving Michael alone, but it was either that or starve to death.

I ate all of the hot dogs before I even made it back and was polishing off the first bag of chips by the time I crawled back through the window. Michael looked relieved at the sight of me, devouring my body with his eyes.

"You look ravishing in my clothes," he commented.

"Aren't you supposed to tell me that I look better out of them?" I teased, stripping off his pants and handing them to him. He wore tighty whiteys that outlined far more than I remembered, and I blushed every time I looked at him.

It should be sinful for the undead to look that good.

I sat cross-legged (my borrowed shirt covered plenty) and offered him some of my haul. "Can you eat human food?"

He shook his head at me. "I'll be fine."

"How often do vampires need to drink?"

"Not often."

Huh. That surprised me. Shapeshifters had high metabolisms because of our supernatural bodies, and I had assumed it'd be the same for vampires. But perhaps not.

I gestured at the nearby window. "Sun's coming up soon. As soon as it goes down, we'll get out of here, since they'll be back tonight."

"One of my safe houses isn't far from here."

"Sounds like a plan," I said, getting to my feet to adjust the tarp over the crates, just in case they'd shifted during the fight earlier.

He stood, too . . . and stumbled.

I automatically reached out to steady him, alarm pounding through me. "Michael? You okay?"

He sat back down again, leaning heavily against one of the crates. "Yeah, just give me a second."

"Is it the poison? Are you still sick?"

"I'll be fine," he said in a hard voice. "Leave me alone, Ruby."

"Oh, sure," I said sarcastically. "Because I know when I'm fine, I fall over and have to support myself on furniture. That's totally what fine people do, right? How silly of me to be concerned."

His mouth quirked on one side. "You're concerned about me?"

He was about two inches away from getting a fist in his mouth. "Don't try to change the subject on me."

"I'm just a little weak still," he said, raking a hand through his hair. It stood a little higher. "It'll go with time, and I imagine it'll be gone with the next feeding."

I crossed my arms over my chest, a sinking feeling coming over me. "Tell me the truth—how often do vampires need to feed?"

He gave me a rueful smile. "How often do you need to eat?"

"Michael," I said in an exasperated tone. "Why didn't you tell me?"

"Because there's nothing to do about it."

But there was. I was full of nice, fresh blood, and he wasn't asking. I knew it would be kind of me to volunteer, but the memory of how horrible it was still made me shudder with distaste.

But I didn't want him to starve, either. I sighed.

"It's okay, Ruby," he said, straightening his shoulders. He rubbed his head, making that crazy hair stand up on end. "I'll be fine. I just need to sleep it off."

"Actually, I know what we can do," I said, rolling up one of the long sleeves of my borrowed shirt.

I almost hated the hungry flash that crossed his gorgeous face. "You're going to feed me?"

"No, I'm going to go catch you one of those rats." At his startled expression, I rolled my eyes. "Of course I'm going to feed you." I finished rolling up my sleeve, my movements jerky. I was nervous and more than a little wigged out. After vowing never to feed a vampire again, here I was, offering up my good wrist like an idiot.

Michael's fangs elongated as I stepped toward him, and the look in his eyes grew sleepy with desire. "I won't hurt you, Ruby. I promise."

"Don't make promises you can't keep," I said in a

hard voice, and shoved my wrist forward, offering it to him. "Let's just get it over with."

He took my uninjured wrist tenderly, his thumb brushing over the soft skin. Then he looked up at me, and his pupils were nearly black, they were so dark with hunger. But he only pressed a kiss to my palm. "You don't believe me when I say I won't hurt you? I vow it."

"Says the man with four-inch fangs."

He grinned, and the fangs seemed even larger. "Two inches. But you flatter my ego."

I flushed at the innuendo and turned away so I wouldn't see him maul my wrist. "Just get it over with."

He reached for my chin and turned me toward him, his expression puzzled, the hunger dilating his eyes abating a little. "Did . . . did I hurt you badly last time?" He looked miserable at the thought. "When you fed me?"

It *was like having my wrist torn from my arm.* I nodded, unable to stop the trembling in my body.

His free hand brushed over my cheek, and he looked at me tenderly. "And yet you would feed me again?"

I shrugged, averting my eyes. "You'd do the same for me."

"I would," he said, and the words seemed to have more weight than a simple meal should involve.

He snared me around my waist and tugged me

close, and I fell forward into his arms. "It's not sup-posed to hurt," he murmured. "The bite is pleasur-able."

I said nothing, but my expression must have said volumes.

Michael tugged me closer. My breasts pressed against his upper body, and he released my hand. It instinctively went to the firm wall of his chest. His skin felt cool against mine but not unappealing. Instead, his hand slid to the collar of my shirt, tug-ging it away from my neck. "Do you believe me when I promise you that it won't hurt?"

I froze, instinct and memory warring against the feel of Michael against me. My sex had started to throb with need, my nipples scraping against his chest, hard little pinpricks.

"Do you trust me?" he said.

My fingertips twitched against his chest, and then I nodded slowly.

He leaned in so close that I thought he might kiss me, but he just ran his lips over my jawline.

I shivered against him, my fingers curling just a little.

"The trick with vampires," he said as he breathed against my throat, "is that our saliva is a bit of a won-der drug. It's a coagulant and an aphrodisiac all at once."

I stiffened in his arms. "Aphrodisiac?"

He pulled my hair away from my neck with one

hand. The way he held it, I was forced to tilt my head a little, exposing my neck.

"Let me show you," he said softly. He leaned in and licked my neck at the curve of my collarbone.

The sensation was ticklish and sexy and sent another pulsing flare to the junction of my thighs. That was nice, but it didn't feel like anything special. "I'm not sure that I'm feeling anything. Maybe shifters are immune—"

"You're not immune," he said with a chuckle, and licked the same spot again.

"I still don't . . . ohhh . . ." The spot he'd licked felt amazing. Tingly. Warm. Delicious. My sex suddenly felt hot and slick with need, and my nipples ached, they were so tight. I reached for him, tangling my fingers in his hair. "Oh . . . I see what you mean."

He licked at my throat again, more languidly, and I couldn't stop the moan that rose from my throat.

"We don't drink from the wrist," he said against my throat. "Too many delicate bones there packed close together. Not enough surface area. The neck is so much more pleasurable, wouldn't you agree?"

My hips rose involuntarily, and I dimly realized that I was straddling him. Didn't care. God, he felt good. My skin felt flushed and hot with need. "Oh, *Michael*."

He groaned against my throat. "I love hearing you say my name, Ruby." He drew in a ragged breath and then nuzzled at my neck once more. "I'm going to drink now, sweetheart."

My body tensed a little at that, my heart fluttering with fear. Before I could protest, though, I felt his tongue press against my throat once more. Then there was a tiny pinch, and I felt his teeth sink into my throat, felt him pull hard, sucking at my blood.

God, it felt as if he'd thrust deep inside me. I whimpered, and my free hand went to my sex, finding it soaking wet and aching with need. This was such a bad idea, but I didn't care. I rubbed myself as he drew from me, and I heard a low groan low in his throat. His fingers curled into the curves of my ass as he drank, and I moaned, needing more. Wanting more. My hand slid away from my sex, and I fumbled with the zipper of his pants. His cock was hot and hard under me, and when I ground my hips down on his, he thrust against me with equal heat. He wanted this, too. I didn't care if it was just the aphrodisiac of his tongue or my own desperate, lonely need, but I needed him deep inside me.

"Ruby," he whispered softly against my throat before sinking his fangs in again and drinking once more. He lifted his head, and I felt those long fangs slide free of my skin once more. "Are you sure—"

"Yes. I want you," I whispered. I pushed at his head, encouraging him to return to my neck.

His tongue traced the spilled blood on my skin, licking it away, and then I felt his fangs return, felt his teeth sink deep.

I moaned. My fingers found the hard, velvety

length of him. It sprang free from his trousers, and I felt his grip tighten on my hips. I wrapped my fingers around that hard length and sank down over him, my breath sucking in as he seated himself in my tight warmth. It had been a long time since I'd had sex, and he was big—had he always been that big? I whimpered again as his hips gave a jerky thrust and his tongue moved against my neck. I couldn't tell if he was still sucking, but it didn't matter. He was deep inside me. I rocked my hips, moaning at how good he felt filling me. *My beloved Michael.*

He thrust up into me, and I cried out at the delicious sensation. His tongue lapped at my neck as I leaned forward, brushing my nipples against his chest. His hands tugged me down hard every time he thrust upward, and I heard him whisper my name. I rode him, need overtaking me, until I was rocking atop him savagely, heading for a climax, his thrusts becoming just as frantic and jerky as my own. His fingers dug into my hips harder, pulling me down on him with each wild, rough thrust. Just when I was close to hitting the peak, he bit my neck once more. I cried out at the pure, piercing pleasure, my entire body stiffening, and felt him tense underneath me in orgasm. Waves of ecstasy rolled through me, exploding through my shuddering body, until I returned to earth and found myself panting, sweating, and weak in Michael's arms.

His hands slid up my back, and he pulled me close for a long, hot kiss that tasted of my own blood, his fangs now retracted. I kissed him back, heat flaring anew as his tongue rubbed against my own. The kiss seemed to last forever, and he pressed repeated smaller kisses on my mouth as if he was unable to stop tasting me.

I suddenly thought about what we'd just done and flushed with embarrassment. We'd been reunited for a blink of an eye, and here I was climbing all over him like a jungle gym. Since I wasn't a one-night-stand type, this might complicate things.

"Thank you, Ruby," he whispered against my mouth, and pulled me down under the small shelter with him as he moved toward day-slumber.

Those three little words echoed in my head, taunting me, as Michael fell asleep.

Thank you, Ruby.

Thank you? As if I'd handed him a sandwich or something? I'd let him drink from me! We'd shared wild, orgasmic sex! And I got a pat on the shoulder and a thank-you?

Like a friend.

Chapter Five

I decided to sleep in my jaguar form so I would be ready for any surprises. When the sun was about to set, I scouted the area once again, looking for hints that the vampires would be back as soon as the sun went down. When I saw no traces of trouble, I headed back in, shifted to human, and demolished the rest of the food as I waited for Michael to awaken.

After we got out of there tonight, my life could go back to normal. Quiet job, quiet days, quiet nights alone. Normal and lonely. Michael would continue running, since the vampires knew he was in Fort Worth. He'd be gone again just when he was back in my life. Now, when I could date him. Could sleep with him. Could touch him and not worry about endangering others with my lust for him. I touched my mouth, thinking of his kiss. My fingers strayed to my neck, where nothing indicated that I'd been bitten. He'd been right—it had been wonderful.

How many women had he bitten since we'd broken up? I hated that I even wondered, as if I had any claim on him. This was just a hookup with an old flame. I could blame it on the aphrodisiac, but the truth was, I'd wanted him and I'd taken him. Simple as that.

This evening when he awoke, his eyes were bright and his smile brighter. He looked over at me and reached his hand toward mine. "Ruby."

I stood up, straightening my borrowed shirt. "No time for chitchat. We should get out of here while it's still early. We can get a head start on the bad guys."

Michael sat up, the expression on his face inscrutable. "We should talk—"

"Not right now," I said in an exasperated tone. "Michael, please. I don't want to live in this dusty old meatpacking plant forever."

"Of course," he said in an angry, stiff voice, clearly taking my actions as a rebuff.

And maybe they were. Friends didn't get all sappy with friends after they had sex, right? I began quickly unbuttoning my shirt. "Where is your closest hideaway?"

"Southwest side of I-35. Other side of downtown. Not a great neighborhood, but that's what makes it ideal for a hideout."

"Okay, we'll go there for now. Then we'll decide

what to do." I took off the shirt and handed it back to him. This time, his gaze was carefully averted from my nakedness, and for some reason, that hurt. Why did sex have to ruin everything? "I'm going to go in jag form. You're going to be my owner. I found a strip of fabric that can pass as a collar and some rope, so I'm going to be your exotic pet, all right?"

He frowned. "But that's demeaning to you."

"It doesn't matter," I said. "It'll give me a chance to protect you if I need to and allow me to use my animal senses. Plus, it'll be easier than strolling through the street naked." I dropped to my knees to change again.

"Ruby," he began thoughtfully.

I shot back upright, my heart hammering with hope. Was he going to tell me how he felt? "Yes?"

He smiled at me thoughtfully. "Thank you. For everything."

I could have cheerfully strangled him. I dropped back to my knees and began to shift.

People swerved off the sidewalk at the sight of my jaguar form. Michael just smiled and acted as if he always took a massive feline out for an evening stroll. I hoped the bright pink bow collar I'd fashioned out of discarded costume parts would alleviate some of the fear. It looked ridiculous, and I felt ridiculous wearing it, so I hoped it took away a lot of the scariness.

We turned down an alley, and I kept guard as

Michael slipped a key from his wallet and then punched in a key code. The door clicked open, and Michael nodded at me. "Come on in."

I quickly changed back to human form and followed him inside.

We entered a butcher's shop, and my mouth watered at the overwhelming smell of meat. Even though it was put away in refrigerated cases, I could still smell it, the blood soaking the paper, everything. It was like walking into a buffet.

"It's back this way," Michael said, going behind the counter.

I stared up at the security cameras and crossed my arms over my breasts. "Are those going to be a problem?"

"Oh, uh." He paused, scratching his head. "I guess they will be. Don't worry. I'll leave a note for the manager."

"Won't he wonder why you're not on the camera and I am? Totally naked, I might add?"

"A long note," Michael amended, then gestured for me to follow him. "Come on."

Reluctant, I followed behind him.

Michael entered the meat freezer, and I tiptoed in behind him. He moved to the back of the freezer and began to run his hand along the back wall. I glanced at the gigantic sides of beef hanging from the hooks, the pork, the splayed racks of ribs. Wow. It all looked . . . juicy. The thought revolted me even as my stomach growled. My jaguar half wasn't picky, but the human part didn't like the thought of gnawing on raw meat.

"Here we go." Michael's hand found a seam in the metal wall, and he pushed at an invisible panel. The wall clicked and opened a crack, revealing a dark room on the other side. I followed Michael in and was surprised to discover that this was just a small antechamber, equally as cold as the meat freezer. The room was empty of everything but a windowless door on the far side and a numbered security panel set into the wall.

"The code is eleven twenty-nine," he said, punching in the numbers. "Just in case you need to get back in while I'm unconscious."

"Eleven twenty-nine? That's my birthday."

He glanced over at me, a hint of a smile flicking over his face. "Coincidence."

Yeah. I gave his back a skeptical look as he turned toward the door. The panel beeped, accepting the code, and the door clicked, unlocking. Michael held it open for me.

If I was expecting something amazing on the other side, I was sorely disappointed. There was an easy chair, a flat-screen TV mounted on the wall, a game system on the floor below it, and a single bed on the far side of the room. The blankets were mussed, and the room was small, maybe twelve by eight feet across.

It wasn't warm, either. I rubbed my arms, looking around. "This is your safe room?"

"One of several." He moved forward, grabbing DVDs off the seat of the chair and placing them on a nearby rack. "I've been moving around in the hopes that Mariah would think I was gone and would get the picture, but she doesn't seem to be paying attention."

"She doesn't seem to be very good at that," I agreed, then rubbed my arms. "Clothes?"

He looked stricken. "None here. It's a fairly new setup for me."

I tried to ignore the chill. As a shifter, I was fairly immune to cold weather, but I was naked, and it felt a bit nippy even to my metabolism. "Mind if I get under your blankets, then?"

"Be my guest."

I crawled under the covers and wrapped them around my body, noticing that his gaze followed me. "You hungry again?"

"I'm okay," he said, too quickly. "You?"

"Hungry," I admitted. "All that meat two rooms over isn't helping."

He grinned. "You like your meat raw?"

"Not *that* raw, but if I get hungry enough, it'll do."

He gestured back to the freezer. "There's ready-made sandwiches out in the deli fridge."

"Now you're talking," I said, smiling at him.

We retrieved a few sandwiches and another bottle of water, and I wrapped myself up in the blanket, crossing my legs and sitting up.

While I ate, he turned the easy chair toward me

and watched as I devoured sandwiches. "You want my shirt again?"

"I'm good for now." Plus, his shirt would smell way too much like him, and having it rub against my skin again might give me ideas. Time for a distraction. "So," I said between bites, "you going to tell me your story?"

"My story?" He looked blank for a moment, then laughed.

He was so handsome that I stopped chewing just to stare at him, my heart pounding. That laugh brought back so many memories and filled me with intense longing.

"You mean how I got turned?"

Not trusting myself to speak around the knot in my throat, I nodded.

He raked a hand through his hair, and it stuck up. "Well. After I, uh, dropped out . . ."

When we'd broken up . . . I said nothing, letting the awkward silence fill the room. What could I say? *Yeah, when you caught me banging that guy? And then you quit school?*

"I decided that I should see the world," he said. "Took my Pell Grants and decided to tour Europe."

"Don't tell me," I said. "Transylvania?"

"Madrid, actually. I met a very lovely English-woman named Gemma who was touring the Continent. We took to spending time together while I was in Spain. She was fun and carefree and loved to laugh. I needed that, back then."

Fun and carefree English Gemma. I hated her. *That bitch.*

"I spent most nights drunk, trying to for—" He shifted in his seat and paused. "Well. I wasn't in a good place, so I didn't much care what happened to me. Gemma was a bit of a party girl and a drinker, so I partied and drank with her. One night, I was on a bender, and I passed out in her room early, skipping the party. When I woke up the next evening, I found out that she had turned me into a vampire."

"Turned you against your will? That's awful!" I immediately burned with hatred for her. *That bitch.*

"Well, she hadn't meant to," Michael said with a rueful, affectionate smile that made my heart thump with a different kind of beat—jealousy. "Turns out she'd been sipping from me here and there when we were necking, and I'd made her drunk. Too much alcohol in my blood, and she lost her inhibitions. When I passed out in her room, she'd been unable to resist and drained a bit too much. I was in danger of dying, so she turned me instead."

"This is a pretty rotten story," I told him. "Did you hate her?"

He shook his head. "Nah. She was truly apologetic. Anyhow, she took me under her wing and taught me how to survive as a vampire. Then, when I had the hang of things, she gave me a nice settlement and sent me on my way."

"You should have staked her," I muttered.

"It's not like that," Michael said. "I like being a vampire. The feeding's tricky at times, but it's opened up an entire new world that I didn't know even existed. I have new abilities, and I've met fascinating people I would have never met otherwise. I don't regret it."

I regretted it for him, though. He should have been living in the suburbs by now, with 2.5 kids, a dog, and a cubicle job or something. "You didn't stay with Gemma?"

He shook his head. "Not long. She didn't want a partner, just a drinking buddy. We parted on good terms. After she left, I traveled through Europe and Asia, visiting some of the vampire havens along the way. After a couple of years of that, I got bored and decided I wanted to come back to the States. And since I'm new to the area, I joined the dating agency." He shrugged. "It's uneventful, I'm sorry to say."

He'd traveled the world and been turned into a vampire. I'd been working at the local storage unit and wishing I'd had the guts to stand up to my parents back when I had the chance.

He smiled over at me. "What about you? Living it up since college? What did you get your degree in?"

I chewed on my lip. *Tell him the truth? Lie?* I sighed after a moment and decided to go for the totally unglamorous truth. "I dropped out a few days after you did. I was . . . struggling."

"I see," he said, but it didn't sound judging. "You didn't go back?"

I shook my head, regret washing through me. "No. I didn't know what to do with myself, so I decided to work instead."

"Where do you work?"

"Cool Storage," I said, and then snorted. "I'm a security guard. Funny, huh?"

"Why? I think you'd be amazing at whatever you put your mind to."

His admiring tone bothered me. I gave him a bitter look and flicked my fingers, as if brushing off his compliments. "No, you don't. You think I'm a loser because I've been stuck in a dead-end job in the same city since you last saw me. I didn't get a degree, I don't have a family, and I'm resorting to meeting men through a dating agency, even though I should be able to find someone easily since shifter women are rare. Yet here I am, on the lam with a vampire on a date that won't quite end. A vampire who dumped me four years ago, I might add." I tightened the blankets around my body and resisted the urge to turn my face to the wall. "Kind of a shitty date, if you ask me."

Silence. He raked his hand through his hair again, then scratched his head. "I'm sorry, Ruby."

"Don't be sorry. I'm the one who's being unreasonable and ridiculous."

"You're not unreasonable. Or ridiculous," he said vehemently.

"No?" My tone was bitter. "You, of all people, should find me so."

. "I would never think that about you," he said, his eyes going black with emotion. "I loved you," he said, and my heart stuttered for a moment. ". . . back when we were in college."

My heart stopped stuttering.

"You're just as warm and funny and strong now as you were back then, and I still want to be your friend. You are the furthest thing from unreasonable that I could imagine."

My cheeks pinked a little. I was having mixed feelings about the way he kept tossing "friend" out there, as if he were trying to remind me that our relationship was now platonic. Well . . . maybe not so platonic. Friends with benefits.

Speaking of. "So, um, do you really need to drink three times a day?"

He shrugged, raking a hand through his spiky hair again. "We can skip meals, but, just like regular people, we start to feel light-headed and weak."

"Huh. Any other stuff about vampires I should know?"

He gave me a thoughtful look, then leaned forward, elbows resting on his knees. The casual pose was so utterly Michael that my heart gave that crazy little flip again. "Let's see. The garlic thing works. Holy water, yes, crosses, yes. Can't see reflection in mirrors. There's an old tale about not being able to cross water, but that's not true. Oh, and we can't turn into bats. Sunlight will supposedly fry us to a crisp in about ten minutes, and I've never felt the urge to test it."

I was distracted by his long hands and the tilt of his body as he shifted closer. When he leaned forward, he was almost touching my foot with his fingers. It wouldn't take much for him to slide his hand under the blanket, where I was naked and waiting for him. "And your heart?" I asked lightly. "Does it beat?"

"Nope," he said, and a boyish grin crossed his face. "Want to hear?"

"Is it weird if I do?" I sat up straighter on the bed, clutching the blankets close.

"Nah. It was the first thing I wondered about, too. Well, that and the bat thing." He got up from the chair and sat next to me on the bed. "Come listen."

He lay back, and I crawled forward, hugging the blanket to my bare breasts. He smiled at me, and I felt that same weird little surge. It felt as if time hadn't passed and we hadn't spent four years apart, wishing things had been different. I could almost imagine that we were together again.

I laid my ear against his chest and waited. And waited. And then I realized I would keep waiting, because I wasn't hearing anything. It was like pressing my ear to a block of wood.

"Wow," I said, a laugh surging from me. "That's kind of freaky."

"Not that freaky. If you can overlook the cool skin, you can overlook the heart thing, right?"

I felt his hand touch the strands of my hair that spilled over his chest. Desire flashed through me, and I sat up, looking down at him. His pupils had darkened again, the laughing smile gone from his beautiful face.

I let the sheet drop, exposing my breasts to his gaze. "Thirsty?"

The Adam's apple in his neck bobbed. "Always."

The fangs sprouted from his mouth, and I watched them descend, so long that they practically scraped his chin. I touched one with my finger, curious, and enjoyed his shudder.

"Do my . . . changes . . . frighten you?" He gestured at himself, his voice thick as if it were difficult to speak around his fangs.

I shrugged. "You're talking to a were-jaguar. You're different but not frightening." My smile curved, and I leaned in to run the tip of my tongue over one tooth. "Besides, I think my teeth are longer in my cat form."

"Ruby," he said with a groan, and his hand reached for the back of my neck, as if he wanted to pull me down against him. "You don't have to do this. I know you don't want to be here."

"If I didn't want to be here," I said softly, "I'd have changed and left two days ago."

When I leaned in to kiss him, his arms wrapped around my waist, and he pulled me against him. His fangs retracted when my mouth touched his, and his tongue darted to brush against my own. Immediately,

I felt that wonderful blossom of pleasure from his mouth, the languid kiss of the aphrodisiac. I fell onto him, my breasts pressing against his shirt.

He gave a low growl of frustration and, with supernatural speed, flipped me to my back on the mattress.

I laughed. "Now, that was a neat trick."

He grinned back at me, tugging his clothes off. "I'm about to show you another."

When he'd removed his shirt and jacket, I reached for him, running my hands over the cool pads of muscle. He'd always had a trim, muscular body, and I loved that it hadn't changed. I sighed at the simple pleasure of being able to run my hands down his chest.

He leaned in and kissed me, the kiss increasing in intensity and longing. When it broke, I was panting for breath. His hand slid to my breast and cupped it, and then he moved lower, until his mouth hovered over my nipple, the other gently teased to a peak by his hand. I could feel his breath over the tip of my breast. "Ready?"

I writhed under him. "Ready for what?"

He didn't respond, just leaned in and licked my nipple. I sucked in a breath at the feel of his mouth on the sensitive tip . . . and then the aphrodisiac kicked in. I moaned as intense pleasure spiraled through my body, the nipple growing hot and hard with desire. I surged up under him.

"Oh, my God."

"I know," he said smugly, and then licked my breast again. The second lick felt as if it were pulsing directly to my sex, so intense was the pleasure. My hands fisted in the pillow behind my head, and I groaned with pleasure, panting when he moved his mouth to the other breast and did the same. Moments later, my breasts were twin beacons of exquisite, intense pleasure, and Michael wasn't done with me yet. He slipped down my belly, pressed a brief kiss to my belly button, and then hovered at the apex of my thighs.

"Ready?" His low, sensual murmur rolled over my skin, increasing the intense pleasure. My nipples were so hard they ached, and I felt as if I'd come off the bed if he didn't put his mouth on me again. "Michael, please. Oh, please——"

When he put his mouth on my sex, the entire world upended itself, right then and there.

Everything began and ended with Michael.

A few hours later, after Michael had fed and we'd had sex again, we snuggled under the blankets. Neither of us had chatted much afterward, but we weren't ready to sleep, either. The sun would be up soon enough, and we'd sleep then. Until he closed his eyes, I'd kiss and caress every inch of him.

His fingers brushed circles on my skin, and I traced the contours of his chest, feeling every ridge of his six-pack. "So why is Mariah obsessed with you?" I finally asked.

He sighed heavily. "I think it's because I'm new to the community. She views me like an exotic toy, and I'm single and have no blood partner. She thinks that since she's a female vampire, I should be grateful that she wants me for a blood partner."

"And why don't you want her?" I asked, although I wasn't sure I wanted to know the answer.

"I don't want to be with Mariah. A blood partner is for life, and eternity is a long time to spend with someone who's just a convenient meal."

I continued to run my fingers over his chest. "You mentioned blood partner. Is that like marriage?"

"Somewhat. Vampire rules are pretty fluid, but one thing that is sacrosanct is a blood partner. If you're in a mated pair, you're off-limits to others. You wear the mark of the other's bite on your neck proudly, and you spend eternity together. I don't like Mariah enough for such a big commitment. She'd be much better off settling with Angelo, but as long as she has the hots for me, he's going to try to remove me from the playing field. He seems to think that if he gets rid of me, her attention will turn back to him."

"So there's your answer," I said, sitting up. "You need a blood partner."

He smiled up at me, brushing his fingers over my cheek. "I haven't found a vampire I want to spend eternity with yet."

Have you found a nonvampire? I didn't ask because I didn't want to know the answer. And how could I possibly hope for Michael to think about me that way? I was kidding myself. A were-jaguar and a vampire could date, but he needed a blood partner to save him from a bloodthirsty vampire. In the morning, I'd call the agency and see if they could set him up with a female vampire. Maybe their mutual need could serve them both.

I laid my head on his chest and forced myself not to think about those kinds of things. "You've been all over Europe, right? Tell me about it," I said, my throat aching. Distraction was what I needed. "What was Rome like?"

"Old."

I thumped him on the chest. "No, really."

"No, really. It was old. Everything smelled old. Everything looked old. That was the biggest thing I noticed. Everywhere I walked, I couldn't help but think that thousands of others had walked there for thousands of years. It's amazing and humbling all at once. And it's hot and crowded and noisy, and you just don't care, because you're standing in the middle of history."

I closed my eyes, trying to picture it for myself. "It sounds wonderful."

"It was." His hand idly stroked through my hair. "I saw the Pantheon, and the Colosseum, and the Trevi Fountain, and so many other things."

"The Sistine Chapel?" I asked, hopeful. I'd always wanted to see that.

"Nope. Couldn't find a night tour."

That was disappointing. I wondered how he'd felt about his vampirism when he found that out and stroked his chest consolingly. "I bet it's not that interesting anyhow. Tell me about the fountain instead." I wanted to picture him there, in the midst of the crowds in Rome, drinking in the sights, blending in with human tourists, surrounded by wonders. "Tell me about all of it."

As he thought for a moment, his hand stopped in my hair, then started again. "It's this enormous fountain. I thought it was a pool at first, because it's long and square like one, except there's people surrounding it and this beautiful, ornate Baroque building right behind it. The center of the fountain is full of statues, all beautifully carved out of all this rock, and you walk up and think that you've stumbled upon some grotto where the gods have come to play. And it's all lit up. I imagine it's lovely by day, but at night, all the marble is golden and shining, and the most incredible thing I've ever seen. There are thousands of coins in the water, and it's amazing to think that each one represents someone who stopped by the fountain and made a wish."

I smiled, my eyes closed. "It sounds lovely."

"It was."

"Now tell me about Paris."

"Paris . . . wasn't so great."

I thumped him again. "You're lying."

"Maybe."

I lifted my head and looked up at him. I raised one eyebrow. "Are you deliberately playing things down so I won't get jealous of your adventures?"

He gave me an enigmatic smile. "Maybe."

That was sweet of him. I laid my cheek back against his chest and gave his abdomen a hard pinch of warning. "Paris. Details. Now."

Michael chuckled and wrapped his hand in my hair again. "When I got to Paris the first time, it was raining . . ."

Chapter Six

My eyes flew open, and I stared across the small room, trying to figure out what had awakened me.

Michael was still curled up against my side, his breathing soft and even. I sat up, ears straining. Someone was in the front of the shop. I'd heard the soft murmur of the butcher's cheerful voice earlier as he'd helped customers, but it was six o'clock now, and the shop was closed.

The footsteps got closer. My ears pricked again. Maybe they were restocking the deli counter from the stuff in the freezer? As I listened to the footsteps, I noticed a pattern. Two steps and then a soft rap-rap. It happened again, and then again. My skin prickled with awareness.

Two steps, rap-rap. Two steps, rap-rap.

I slid from the bed and placed my ear against the door. Two steps, rap-rap.

Someone was knocking on the walls. I tensed, my predator instinct fully alert. Whoever was on the other side was testing the wall every few feet.

A pause, then another rap-rap. Then I heard the door to the antechamber slide open.

A growl formed low in my throat, and I swallowed it, but I allowed the claws forming at my fingertips to emerge.

The footsteps entered the small antechamber adjoining our safe room and paused again. I heard beeps as someone punched at the keypad. A pause, then a few more beeps. Then swearing and the punching of different buttons, phone buttons.

With my excellent hearing, I could hear the conversation through the phone.

"Angelo Gaston's office," said a cheerful voice.

"I found the place," the intruder said, and I caught a whiff of a dog scent. My fists clenched. The werewolf asshole had tracked us down.

"Excellent," the woman said. "Did you get him?"

"He's in a panic room. I need the pass code."

"I don't have it."

I nearly sighed with relief.

"Then get it for me," the werewolf said, surly.

"Mr. Gaston won't be awake for at least another hour or two," she said sweetly. "Shall I leave him a message?"

He swore softly under his breath. "No, no message. I'll call Taylor when his naptime is over."

"Very well, Mr. Anderson," she said, and the call terminated.

So the wolf was Anderson, the vampire hunting Michael was Taylor, and they were going to descend on us like vultures as soon as it was time for the vampires to wake up.

We had to get out of there. As the man paced on the other side of the door, I crept back to Michael's side and tugged his clothes out of the pile on the floor. I'd dress him, and as soon as he was awake, we'd get out of there. Maybe head to another one of his safe houses or go to my house, at least for some clothes. We just had to go somewhere else—I didn't care where.

I dressed him as he slept, edging first the underwear and then the pants up his legs. The button-up shirt was a bit more work, but I managed it, keeping my movements as quiet as I could. I kept glancing at the clock as I worked, waiting for the time to click over. What time did Michael wake up? Six? Six-thirty? Seven?

Outside the room, the man leaned against the door, whistling. He thought he was going to wait for the goddamn pass code and flush us out, but I wouldn't give him that chance.

I straddled Michael's chest and put my hand over his mouth, anticipating his awakening. I must have sat there for ten minutes, staring intently down at him, waiting for the flutter of his eyelids.

A few minutes later, his eyes flicked open and dilated, staring up at me. I leaned over him and pressed a finger to my lips, hoping he'd be awake enough to understand.

He paused for a moment, then nodded. I felt his teeth elongate against my hand at the same time that I felt his erection swell against my hips.

I leaned down to his ear, whispering low enough that the werewolf wouldn't be able to detect my voice. "There's a werewolf on the other side of the door. If he hears us, we'll lose the element of surprise."

I removed my hand, and he reached up to grasp the back of my neck, pulling my ear down to his mouth. "That's the only way out of here."

I nodded. I knew that. I leaned in again, unable to resist brushing my tongue against the shell of his ear. "I'll take care of him."

He grabbed my arm as I tried to slide off him, jerking his head in a quick, angry shake. He didn't like the idea of me taking out the werewolf? But I was the predator. I was the strong shifter. I flexed my hand, showing him the claws ready to pop out from my fingertips if I let the shift take over.

He shook his head violently again. "Ruby, no," he mouthed.

I turned away, heading for the door on tiptoe. I kept the finger to my lips, ensuring that Michael would remain silent, even if he didn't like my idea. Behind me, I heard his hand swish through the air, no doubt trying to get my attention and tell me what a bad idea this was.

But all of my attention was focused on the door. I could occasionally hear the wolf shifting his weight and the quiet clicking of keys on his phone. Texting? Web surfing? Getting the pass code even now?

My hand on the handle, I moved it down by silent millimeters until it had turned completely. Then I pushed the door open as hard as I could, using all of my weight to shove it backward with force.

The man leaning against it went sprawling on the other side. I heard the smack of his skull and his groan of pain as he was thrown against the opposite wall.

I leaped onto him. He'd fallen on his stomach, one hand cradling his head. I moved over his back, grabbed his hair, and slammed his head back onto the floor.

His head made a sick thud, and he went still.

"Damn," said Michael behind me. "When you said you were a predator, you weren't kidding."

His compliment pleased me, and I felt the absurd urge to purr. Instead, I brushed a finger under the nostrils of the wolf. Still breathing, just unconscious. "Save your flattery for later. Let's tie him up."

We used the bedsheets to hog-tie the werewolf on the bed, then locked him inside. Now no one would be able to get to him unless they had the pass code. Michael looked reluctant to abandon him, but I explained that as soon as he awoke, he'd start chewing through the bonds anyhow. Our goal was to get Michael to safety.

I changed to my jaguar form and led the way. Michael's other place and my house would probably be too vulnerable, so we'd head to my sister's apartment. It was on this side of town, and I hoped she wouldn't be too peeved when I showed up with a vampire and a bounty hunter on our tails.

Either way, she'd at least have clothing for me. I was getting rather tired of being naked.

I'd wanted to stick to the alleys and shadows, but Michael shook his head. "It'll take too long. Between that and the fact that they have a tracker, they could find our trail."

He had a point.

He put the pink bow collar on me, and while I hid in the nearby alley, he went into a nearby business to call a cab. When the cab driver saw us, I thought he was going to drive away, but Michael offered enough cash that the man let me into the backseat, although he kept the glass divider up and shot me nervous looks the entire time.

I did my best to appear as meek and house-cat-like as possible. Michael stroked and petted my head as we drove, his calm masking the nervousness we both felt.

As the car pulled up to a stop sign, Michael tensed, looking out the window. "Wait," he said to the cab driver. "Can we stop here?"

I lifted my head from his lap, confused.

The cab driver looked at the stop, then back at me hesitantly. "I'm not sure—"

Michael pulled out his wallet and extracted several bills, waving them at the cab driver.

"You got it," the driver said, pulling into a nearby parking lot. "I'll wait here."

The cab was put into park, and Michael opened his door and jumped out. He gave a tug to my leash, indicating that I should follow. "Come, Ruby. I've got something to show you."

As I slunk out of the cab, I heard the cab driver mutter the word "crazy" under his breath. I could see how Michael wasn't looking like the sanest person right about now. We'd stopped on a side street, with a chain-link fence dividing us from a nearby park. It looked familiar but not so much that I understood why we were there.

Michael leaped over the low chain-link fence and grinned at me from the other side. "Follow me."

As if I could protest while in jaguar form. I also couldn't stay out there, lest the rednecks bring out their guns. So I leaped over the fence, trying to figure out his plan.

He shoved his hands into his pockets, allowing me free rein, and began to stroll forward, whistling. Intrigued, I followed him, noting our surroundings. We were on a playground. I passed a soccer goal, the net gone. I could smell the chalk lining the field and hear the creak of a distant merry-go-round. Off to one side, a pair of swings swayed in the evening breeze, and Michael headed toward those. He sat on one of the swings and reached a hand out to me.

I moved forward, pushing my muzzle against his hand.

His fingers scratched just under my whiskers in a spot that was pure heaven. I began to purr, leaning heavily against him. I didn't know why we were there, but for a brief moment, I didn't care.

"This is where I first saw you," he mused in a low voice.

I looked up sharply. *Here?* I waited for an answer, and when he didn't go on, I pushed at his hand with my face. He scratched me again, so I bit him, lightly, just enough to get his attention.

Instead of being frightened, Michael chuckled. I guess teeth didn't scare a vampire. "Sorry. Yes, I saw you here first. I was here to pick up one of my cousins from school, and I think you were here to pick up Jayde."

I looked around. Sure enough, this was a school that Jayde had worked at a few years ago as a third-grade teacher. I'd forgotten all about it until he mentioned it. Had I met Michael here? I didn't remember.

"You were in the parking lot, and I noticed you leaning against your car door. I thought you were the most beautiful thing I'd ever seen," he said in an almost dreamy voice. "You had long, curly black hair and a small, curvy body. You looked so soft and sweet, but I couldn't take my eyes off you because you were so sure of yourself. Every bit of you seemed to sing with vitality and strength. I remembered thinking that I'd love to date a girl like that." He glanced over at me, skimming his fingers over the short hair on my muzzle. "You were reading a magazine. I kept trying to get your attention, but you never looked up. That was a week before classes. When I went into American History and you were sitting there with an empty chair next to you, I thought it was fate."

I'd had no idea. Such a small, chance meeting simply had not stuck in my memory, and Michael had never mentioned it to me, even back when we were dating. As far as I had remembered, my relationship with Michael had begun the first day of classes, when a handsome tall boy with wild hair had slid into the chair next to me in History and leaned over to borrow a pencil. His scent had been clean, just a hint of soap and cinnamon, as if he'd been chewing gum. I remembered being charmed by that and by the smile he cast in my direction. The first time he'd raked his hand through his hair and it stuck up in spikes, I was lost.

Michael scratched my whiskers again. "I suppose I'm just being sentimental," he said with a half smile at me. He stood up and brushed off his wrinkled pants. "Either way, I wanted to show this to you because . . ." He struggled for the right thing to say. "Well, I suppose because I'm glad you're back in my life, Ruby. It feels richer with you in it."

I couldn't smile, so I leaned in and gave his hand a gentle lick, as if to say, *I'm glad you're back, too.*

"Friends forever," he said quietly.

I resisted the urge to bite his damn hand.

Chapter Seven

After the cab dropped us off at Jayde's apartment complex, I led the way to her place. A small light was on in the window of her second-story apartment, and I sighed with relief. She was home.

Michael knocked on her door, and we waited. A moment later, Jayde opened the door and stared up at Michael in surprise. "Holy shit, Michael? I—" Her voice broke off as she spotted me in cat form, rubbing against his legs.

She opened the door wider, letting us in. "I'm hoping a kitty-cat fetish isn't why she's wearing that ugly-ass collar."

Michael laughed, but the sound was forced. "We needed a disguise for her. Might be too many questions otherwise."

I crouched on the floor, low, and began my transformation back to human.

"A disguise is one thing. A pink bow is just downright humiliating," Jayde said, then gestured toward the kitchen. "Coffee? She'll be a minute."

Michael looked at me changing, then back to Jayde. "No thanks."

She shrugged and crossed her arms, staring at him, then back at me. "And here I thought she might have finally found a guy to run off with when she turned up missing for the last three days." She sniffed the air, then frowned at Michael. "You smell like . . ."

"I am," he said, showing his fangs.

"Yuck," Jayde said with a wrinkle of her nose. She gave me a dismayed look. "Have we fallen so far?"

I shook off the last of my transformation and flexed, then stretched. "I'll explain it later, Jayde. Right now, I need to borrow your phone."

Michael immediately shrugged off his jacket and handed it to me.

"I'll get you the phone—and some panties," she said, tossing her long black hair. She reached into her purse and pulled out her cell phone, then gave it to me. "Call the agency first."

I frowned at her. "Why?"

"Because they put out an ATL on your vampire boyfriend."

I looked at Michael in alarm, then back at Jayde. "ATL?"

"Yeah. Attempt to Locate. The Alliance figured ol' 'Valjean' here went rogue and left your drained body in a ditch somewhere. There's a task force combing the area for him."

"You don't seem worried," Michael commented.

"I wasn't," Jayde said, and looked down her nose at him. "She's a were-jaguar. She could mop the floor with you if she wanted to. It's that high-strung blonde at the agency who's freaking out."

Oh, boy. "I'll call and explain everything."

Ryder sounded exhausted when she picked up the phone, but her exhaustion disappeared as soon as she heard it was me. I got an intense scolding, and I meekly apologized for scaring her. I hadn't intended to cause her days of sleepless worry, which it sounded as if I had. She'd truly thought that Michael had killed me and left me somewhere. She'd revoked his Alliance membership, canceled his record out of the Midnight Liaisons database, and said that she'd sent his profile to the Alliance security team, which was now search-ing for him.

That was bad news. Rogue vampires were to be killed on sight. I slipped on panties and a bra. "Valjean didn't do anything wrong, Ryder. I've spent the last few days protecting him."

"Protecting him from what?"

"Never mind," I said quickly, tugging a shirt over

my head. "How soon can you lift the ATL so it's safe for him to go out?"

She typed into the computer, and I heard paperwork shuffle. "I just sent the message to the late-night task force, but I don't know when they'll get it. And then I have to wait for the day shift to check their e-mails and text messages. You guys just lie low, and I'll call you when we have the all clear."

"Okay," I breathed. "Thanks. Sorry about all this."

"Just don't go to your house. It's one of the stake-out points. They might shoot garlic first and ask questions later."

"Got it."

"Or to his house. Just to be safe."

"Okay."

"Or to your sister's house."

I winced. *Too late.* "Thanks, Ryder. We'll hide out for another day or two."

I gave her my sister's cell number and ended the call, then pulled on some yoga pants, thinking hard. I needed to cancel my credit cards, check if they'd robbed my house, call my job and let them know I was alive—there were so many things I needed to do.

But I found myself drawn back to Michael. If he was leaving me soon, I wanted to spend every minute I could with him. I returned to the living room, my gaze devouring him. He paced as my sister watched from her perch on the arm of the couch, worried and uneasy.

He seemed to untense at the sight of me, although his gaze remained worried. "Ruby, I can't stay here."

"I know," I said with a glance at my sister. "It's not safe for Jayde. They have teams out looking for you—and me, in a sense. If they come here, I don't want the situation to escalate."

Jayde snorted and stood, arms crossing over her chest. "Don't be silly, little sis. Stay here."

I shook my head. "Michael's really unpopular right now. I'm going to stay with him."

"No." Michael's voice was quiet but resolute.

I turned to look at him in surprise. Dread curled in my stomach. "What do you mean, no?"

"I mean that it's too dangerous for you." He shook his head. "Worst blind date ever, remember? It's my fault that it's gone on two days too long. You're probably sick of watching over me, and I don't blame you."

Of course I wasn't sick of Michael. I loved him. Always had, always would. Being with him again made my world finally feel right once more. As if a missing piece had locked into place. I'd been okay without him, but I hadn't been happy. I missed being happy.

"But . . ." I said.

"It's okay, Ruby," he said, and took my hand in his.

Jayde said, "Looks like you two need a moment."

As she left the room, Michael placed his other hand over mine, staring down at our clasped hands.

"I really appreciate what you've done for me the past few days. You've been such a good friend to me."

There was that damn f-word again. "You can't go off on your own. That werewolf is working with the bounty hunter," I said, wondering if my voice sounded as desperate as I felt. "They can track you by scent. And there are even more people looking for you tonight. If you go out without me at your side, you might as well paint a big target on your back."

"Better on my back than yours," he said, and brushed his fingers over my cheek in a caress. "You've done enough. I know that you didn't want to see me again. I could tell the moment you took the blindfold off. It was obvious from the look on your face, and I'm sorry that you've been stuck with me. I need to let you get back to your regular life. I'm sorry I dragged you into this."

What life? Watching security cameras at the storage unit? Spending my nights off bored and looking for awkward first dates on the dating service? Spending my time regretting the choices I've made?

"I'm not sorry you dragged me in," I said softly.

He leaned in and kissed me. I felt the barest graze of teeth against my lip. "Good-bye, Ruby."

And before I could stop him, he walked past me and opened the front door, as I sat there and stared. He was leaving me. The nightmare of four years ago came crashing down over me once more.

Jayde came out of her room a few moments later,

no doubt scenting that Michael had left. "So you're just going to let him walk out again?"

I said nothing—the knot in my throat was as big as a bowling ball.

"I know you want him," Jayde prompted. "Normally, you have a miserable expression on your face, but tonight you're lit up like a firecracker. Doesn't take a genius to realize that it's him. And you're just going to let him leave? Again?" She gestured toward the front door. "Vampires aren't off-limits. What's the problem?"

"He thinks we're just friends," I said bitterly. "He's reminded me of that repeatedly."

She snorted. "I may not know what's going on between you two, but the way he looks at you? It's obvious you two were *never* just friends. Did you sleep with him?"

I felt my cheeks heat.

"Uh-huh," Jayde said knowingly. "And do you sleep with your other friends?"

"No."

"Do you think he sleeps with his other friends?"

Startled, I looked over at her. "I guess not."

She gave me a little push. "Then I *guess* you should go tell him that your girl parts keep having unfriend-like thoughts about him."

"But, Jayde, he thinks I cheated on him. He hasn't asked me about it, but he couldn't have forgotten."

I still remembered the look of utter anguish on

Michael's face, the sick clenching in my own stomach, the tears that wouldn't stop flowing after he slammed the door shut.

"You ever hear of second chances?" Jayde gave my shoulder a harder shove. "Go on. The worst he can say is no, and then you'll turn into the crazy cat lady that you're heading for anyhow."

She was right. I had to try. Even if he turned me away, I had to know how he truly felt. What did I have to lose? If he left, I lost everything.

I went outside and paused, sniffing the wind, looking for Michael's spicy scent. Maybe it *wasn't* too late. I could explain what he'd seen four years ago. Maybe we could go on another date, take it slow.

Maybe he'd stop calling me his friend.

The wind carried the scent of vampire on it, and I inhaled, wanting to fill my lungs with Michael's aroma. Maybe he'd give me a second chance—

But the vampire scent wasn't his. I gasped.

"Rube?" Jayde called from inside the apartment, hearing my gasp through the door.

I bolted through the parking lot, following the scent, scanning for Michael's familiar form. *There!*

He strode down the street in the shadows, hands shoved into his pockets, head bent. His spiky hair seemed flat and wilted, as if his entire being were dejected.

A shadow moved to his right, and I saw the other vampire raise the crossbow to his shoulder.

I dashed forward, screaming. "Michael! Duck!"

Michael dropped to the pavement, his jacket flaring out behind him as he rolled to the ground. I kept running to him, my legs swift even if my steps were short. I could reach him in time. I *could*.

I heard the thwack of the crossbow releasing, and something slammed me in the back, knocking me forward onto my stomach. I gasped, the wind knocked out of me for a moment.

"No!" Michael yelled, the sound rough and hoarse with outrage. He ran for the man in the bushes, and I heard his fist slam into the man's mouth. I heard them scuffle, yet I couldn't seem to focus in and see what was going on. Was Michael whaling on the guy? I heard the chuffing cry of a jaguar nearby, and the wind smelled like my sister . . .

And blood.

I couldn't seem to get off the ground. I pushed, but my hands weren't responding right. Something dug into my back, and it felt like a hot poker. Warm, wet liquid ran down my spine, and I realized I'd been shot by the crossbow. "Well, damn."

"Ruby?" Michael was at my side. I tried to get up again, but I was like a bug pinned to a board. Ridiculous that I was so strong and was felled by something so small. Michael's hands had bruises on the knuckles as he reached for me, and they were gentle as he helped me sit up. He cradled me in his lap.

"No, Ruby, no. Sweetheart, why did you come

after me?" I noticed blood smearing over his shirt—my blood. His eyes glittered with fury even as he tenderly pushed the hair away from my face. "I left to keep you safe."

"You were in danger," I said softly.

"You came after me because I was in danger?"

It was getting harder to breathe, my chest heavy. I wanted to cough but didn't have the strength in me. "Wanted to tell you," I said weakly. "I don't want to be your friend."

In the distance, I heard Jayde's snarl and the crunch of her teeth sinking into the vampire, ensuring that he wouldn't ever bother us again.

Michael stroked my face, his fingers shaking.

"I love you," I said softly. I was so tired, and it seemed important to say it now, while I could. "Always loved you. I didn't cheat on you . . . back then."

"I know," he said roughly, then kissed me. "I've always known. The whole blind-date thing was a setup. I just wanted to see you again. Everything I did—the blindfold, the stupid changes to my voice—all of it was to get you to stay just a few minutes longer."

"How . . ." I asked, but things were getting dark, and I was suddenly irritated at my body's failings. I wanted to hear the story. How had he always known?

"Ruby, I love you. I never stopped loving you."

I smiled weakly up at him, at his face growing fuzzy. "Your timing is shit."

He cradled me closer and pressed a kiss to my

mouth. "I don't want to lose you. Please, Ruby, don't let me lose you." His eyes flared black with emotion. "Do you want to stay with me? Do you trust me? Because I'm not ready to let you go."

"Me, either," I said softly, but I knew it didn't matter. Wouldn't soon.

"Then don't be mad when I do this," he said, and sank his fangs into my throat.

I stiffened at the flare of pain; he hadn't licked me to ease the bite. But only a little pain. The red-hot poker between my ribs had flared outward to encompass everything, and I was too far gone to feel much more. The world was growing dark and blurry.

I felt Michael's fangs slide out of my neck, felt him press a quick kiss there.

"Do it," I heard Jayde hiss faintly. "Just fucking do it!"

"What if she never forgives me?" Michael said, his tone anguished.

That's ridiculous, I thought faintly, the world growing black. *I'd always forgive Michael anything.*

Then a wrist was shoved between my teeth, bloody and dripping. Michael's face hovered over mine. "Drink, Ruby! Drink."

When I woke up, I felt . . . different. Not physically different but in my awareness. As if a door had been opened. As if something was suddenly flicked on like a switch. As if it was safe to come out and play again. Why I felt like that, I had no idea.

The world was deathly quiet around me. Too quiet. My eyes slid open, and I peered at my surroundings. A hand brushed over my cheek. "You're awake."

Michael's voice. I automatically turned toward him. He was smiling down at me, his expression incredibly tender as his fingers stroked my cheek.

"Why is it so quiet?" I murmured, my words sounding like anvils in the stillness.

"Don't worry about that. Everything's fine. How do you feel?"

"Different," I said slowly. "Not bad, just different. Did . . . did something happen?"

"You don't remember?"

I remembered bits and pieces, but there was a mental fog that I couldn't seem to shake. "I remember Jayde . . . and you leaving . . ." I thought hard for a moment and then gasped as the memories burst forth from a dam. "The bounty hunter! He . . . he shot me, didn't he?" My hand rose and slid over my chest, feeling for an arrow hole. I didn't feel that hot, stabbing poker of pain anymore. Someone had taken the arrow out? "And then it got dark, and you . . ." I vaguely remembered Michael shoving his wrist between my lips and the taste of blood flooding my mouth.

My teeth tingled, and something shot out of my mouth, the tip of it digging into my lower lip.

"Ow!" I put a hand to my lip, shocked. My two incisors had distended at the thought of blood. I felt along one tooth and realized it was long and wickedly curved. Like a fang. Like Michael's.

I looked over at him. He'd smelled spicy and uniquely vampire before, but now the scent of him was . . . intoxicating. Delicious. It made my mouth water just to get near him. He'd changed. And I had fangs.

I looked at him in surprise. "Fhoo fhturned me?"

Michael watched me, his eyes intense. "If you want to retract your fangs, focus on mentally pulling them inward. It's like learning to use a new muscle. You'll figure it out in time, just like you'll figure out how to speak around them."

"But—"

"Fangs first," he said softly. "Then we'll talk."

A thousand questions burned in my mind, but I wasn't going to be able to hold a conversation without sounding like Elmer Fudd. So I closed my eyes and concentrated on thinking about normal teeth, and my fangs retracted. I felt them slide back under my gums. Okay, that was freaky. My eyes flew open, and I gave Michael a meaningful look. "Answers now?"

"You were dying," he said, his voice low with anguish. His hand stroked my hair, then he tangled his fingers into it, holding me pinned against him. "You took an arrow for me—an arrow that would have staked me through the heart. Instead, when he heard you coming, he shot you."

"I couldn't let him kill you," I said, running my

hand over his chest, looking for wounds. Odd, but his skin felt warm to me now. Was my body temperature that much lower? Just running my fingers over him felt delicious, as if his wonderful smell was rubbing off on my own skin.

Michael groaned at my exploring fingertips, and his hand captured mine, keeping it pressed over his chest. "Ruby, you . . . I asked if I could save you. Surely you knew . . ."

Actually, it hadn't occurred to me. "I wasn't thinking clearly. Some goofball shot me through the chest, remember?" He looked . . . delicious. Both sexually and physically. Hunger had an entirely different edge when one was a vampire. "I didn't really know what I was agreeing to."

"I am so sorry, Ruby. I couldn't let you die, so I offered it." He closed his eyes and bowed his head, as if pained by the thought of turning me against my will. "I have a small fortune left to me by my vampire benefactress. Vampire courtesy states that I pass on the favor and give you half."

I looked up at him, at his beautiful, firm mouth. I wondered if he'd taste different when he kissed me now. My fangs nudged out again, and I willed them to slide back in. I was only half listening to what he said. "Half? Half of what?"

"My fortune. Ten million."

That registered in my mind. "Your fortune is ten million dollars?"

"Actually, my fortune is twenty million. Half of it is yours. It's the least I can do for turning you against your will." His gaze searched my face, desperate. "I'm not sorry you're alive, though."

I wasn't, either, really. I thought for a moment. "That weird sense of relief when I woke up?"

"The sun is down," he murmured. "You'll feel that every day. It's instinct telling you to keep away until it's gone."

Smart instincts. I licked my lips and looked over at him, noticing how decadent his pale skin was. This whole vampire thing was kind of . . . erotic. I rubbed my thumb against his bare chest, just now noticing that my legs were twined with his. We were both cuddled under the sheets in a large bed. I was in my borrowed bra and panties, and Michael wore nothing. That was so unfair. I dug my fingers into his chest, scratching at his skin and inhaling sharply at the delicious scent of him. "I—I think I'm hungry."

As if on cue, my teeth slid down again, although this time, they didn't stab my lip. As I looked over at Michael, I noticed his teeth flick out, also descending, and his erection grew hard against my leg.

"Then you must drink from me," Michael said softly. He leaned back in the bed next to me and bared his throat. "But go slow, and don't take too much for your first time."

My mouth watered at the sight of his pale neck.

God, he smelled good. "Will fhoo help me? Walk me fhroo it?"

His hand moved to my shoulder, and he nodded, pulling me in closer. I didn't need much encouraging. I leaned over him, my hair spilling over my shoulder. He brushed it aside, and I shivered at his fingers grazing my sensitive skin.

"Find the carotid," he said, his voice low and strong and thrumming through me. "There's no pulse on a vampire, but you can smell the blood concentration there."

I leaned in and sniffed his neck and nearly swooned at the heady scent of him. "But all of you fhmells fho good," I said, unable to resist brushing my breasts against his chest.

He groaned. "Then pick a spot. Remember to lick the skin first."

My tongue darted between my fangs, and I nuzzled the side of his neck, swiping at his skin with my tongue. My panties became instantly wet. Good Lord, this was a major turn-on.

"Lick . . . again," Michael said, his voice sounding strained.

"Did I not get enough?" I mumbled between my teeth.

"Just lick me again," he growled, and his hand went to the back of my head, pressing me against his neck. "Feels amazing."

An intense bolt of pleasure shot through me, and I licked him slowly, enjoying his groan. That was *hot*.

"Now," he said, breathing hard. "Bite down. Gently. When your teeth are in, you'll know what to do."

I licked his throat again and then gently pressed the tips of my fangs against his skin. They punched through, razor-sharp, and I felt my mouth fill with blood—thick, rich, and decadent. I heard Michael's groan of pleasure as I swallowed my first taste of blood . . . and latched on to drink more. It was better than anything I'd ever tasted—Michael's sweet, intoxicating scent made into pure, distilled ambrosia. I sucked hard, my tongue lapping against his skin as I drank, not wanting to miss a drop.

"Not too much," he cautioned, even as his mouth nuzzled my own neck. I felt him pull my hair aside and lick my throat. "God, Ruby, I want to drink from you, too. Can—"

I pushed his head against my neck in response, still drinking.

I felt his tongue flick against my throat once, then felt his fangs sink in, and intense pleasure washed over me. My body stiffened in orgasm even as I continued to drink, the two of us with necks entwined, teeth sunk into each other.

Chapter Eight

In the afterglow, Michael's fingers twined with mine, and I curled up against his chest.

"Did you mean what you said back there?" he said softly.

"Mean what?" I was still reeling from the most intense orgasm of my life, and not a single breast or cock was involved. Weird. Not bad, just weird.

"About always loving me?"

Oh. Suddenly shy, I tilted my head down, unable to look him in the eye. "I'm sure I was just saying things. Loss of blood and all that. We're cool. Don't worry about it."

"I'm not worried. I still love you, too." He kissed me lightly on the mouth, then the nose, as if he couldn't get enough of looking at me, tasting me. "I've always loved you. I never stopped loving you. Even when I went to Europe, all I could think about was how much you'd have loved being there with me."

I suddenly felt like the world's shittiest person. "Our breakup . . . with Thad . . ."

"You didn't sleep with him. I know."

I looked at him suspiciously. "How do you know?"

"Because I went to his dorm the next day and punched his lights out for touching you. He didn't protest in the slightest, just let me hit him. I guess it didn't hurt too much if he was a shifter." He grimaced. "At the time, I couldn't figure it out. I was just so angry. It took me a few weeks to calm down, and then I realized his actions didn't make sense—and yours didn't, either. I wanted to talk to you, confront you about it. But you were gone."

"I had to end it fast," I murmured, twining my fingers in his hair. The spikes were flattened, and I raked my hand through his hair, making it stand on end again. "It's against the rules for humans and supernaturals to have a relationship. One-night stand, yes. Relationship, no. Any number of things could have happened. I could have turned you by accident. Or if you found out my secret, it could have compromised my entire family and all the were-jaguars in the area. We'd get kicked out of the Alliance if you found out the truth, so I had to find a way to run you off for good." I pulled him close to me once more. "I cried for a month straight."

"I was miserable without you," he admitted. "Still angry but completely and totally miserable. I vowed that when I got back from my trip, we'd talk. Except . . . I was turned into a vampire. And I knew I couldn't have a normal life. After that, I felt like I couldn't approach you. We're not allowed to reveal ourselves to normal humans, just like you. It never occurred to me that you might be supernatural, too. Anyhow, when I came back, I still felt out of sorts. The local vampires all had blood mates, and the friend I'd been drinking from had left to spend time with friends in Australia. I met Mariah, and she offered to share blood duties for a while, but I hadn't realized that Angelo was interested in her. I told her I wasn't interested, but I didn't have anyone else to drink from, and Mariah started to follow me, showing up at the most inconvenient times. I blood-banked it for a while, but then Mariah got even more annoying. I needed to get rid of her and thought a date might solve both of my problems."

My heart felt a little twinge.

"Except no woman I've met compares to you. It wasn't until I joined the Alliance a few weeks ago that I found you. I was scrolling through the profiles at the agency and came across your picture. I thought it was a mistake until I saw your affiliation, and then, well, I had to set up a date."

I smiled even as tears spilled from my eyes. "Even after all this time, you wanted me?"

He leaned in to kiss away my tears. "Of course I wanted you."

"I hurt you."

"You didn't have a choice. And it enabled us to get here, to this place. I don't regret it."

I devoured him with my eyes, still finding it hard to believe that I could look my fill at him, touch him, taste him, without fear of someone or something tearing us apart. "I've thought of nothing but you. Did you think of me?"

"Every day. Every moment, every hour. I could think of nothing but you."

Dreamed of this, Michael had said when he'd touched my cheek.

I suddenly punched him in the shoulder.

"Ow! What was that for?"

"For constantly calling me your *friend*," I said in a heated tone. "If you called me that one more time, I was going to shove those fangs down your throat."

He chuckled and kissed me again, as if unable to help himself. "I was trying not to pressure you. Just because I was still desperately in love with you, it didn't mean you were still holding a torch for me."

"I was, and I still am," I said. "Does this mean we can be blood mates?"

If one taste of Michael's blood made me feel so dizzy with love for him, I wanted to do it over and over again. The thought of drinking from anyone else made me feel sick. Michael was the only one I wanted.

The only one I'd *ever* wanted.

He stilled against me. "You're not mad that I turned you?"

I flexed my fingers and was happy to see my claws pop. "I still have my jaguar. I'm alive and well. And now I have you. Of course I'm not mad."

"You're not doing this to save me from Angelo, I hope."

I shook my head. "I'm doing this because I love you."

I kissed him. I could kiss him for all of eternity now. I liked that. "Write him and tell him that you have a blood mate and she's going to Europe with you."

He grinned. "I would love to see Europe with you by my side. But I won't take you as my blood mate until you're absolutely certain that it's what you want. The first day after you've turned isn't the time to make that decision."

"You can still write him and tell him we're partners. It'll get him off your back, regardless." I wrapped my arms around him, feeling as if everything in the world had shifted back into place. "Whether we wait one year or twenty, my answer will be the same. I love you, and I want to spend the rest of my life with you. I don't want anyone to come between us ever again."

"We have eternity," he agreed. "And you might want to think about a new name. I wasn't joking when I said vampires picked new names to start over."

I ran my fingers down his back. "Let's pick something happier than *Les Miserables*."

"Something with a happy ending?"

"Exactly."

At first, we argued over names. I thought it would be fun to be Lizzy and Darcy. Michael flat-out disagreed. Too obvious. He'd suggested Edmond Dantes and Haidee, but I was the one who protested that. Edmond and Haidee? Seriously. And here he thought I was the obvious one. I'd suggested Edward and Elinor from *Sense and Sensibility*, but he'd hated the thought— no vampire should ever have the name Edward again, he'd claimed.

I could see his point.

We settled on Marianne and Christopher Brandon and traveled Europe in style. By the time five years had passed, I was more than ready for the mate mark. Michael stubbornly insisted on giving me more time, so I went ahead and marked him at the top of the Eiffel Tower. And at the Sydney Opera House. And at the Great Pyramid in Giza, and the Acropolis in Greece, and the Taj Mahal.

He eventually got the picture.